August 1, 1945
Dear Mernelle. Bet you are surprised you
know somebody in California! We just
moved here yesterday. My father is working
in the shipyards. My room is the fold-up
couch in the living room. I have to keep
my postcards under the couch. We
couldn't take our cat Curly. He was to
mad to ride in the car. My father
said if we sent Curly to Japan the
War would be over in three days.
My mother is trying to get a job
in the shipyard too. Oh well, a new
school
Your

Miss Mernelle Blood
RFD
Cream Hill
Vermont

Miss Mark Blood
RFD
Cream Hill
Vermont

Postcards

**Center Point
Large Print**

Don't
NO MORE
INSEMINATION RACKET
got rid the Holstins. Guess
we stick with god local
Jersey stock Do it the
OLD FASHION WAY WITH A
BULL.

Minkton M. Blood

County Agent
Office
Cream Hill

Mrs. Mernelle MacIdmy
Randall Court
Bethany, VT 05086

is working
fold-up
room. I have to keep
under the couch. We
to take our cat Curly. He was to
said if we sent Curly to Japan the
War would be over in three days.
My mother is trying to get a job
in the shipyard too. Oh well, a new
school tomorrow.
Your adventures penpal, Juniata.

Miss Mernelle Blood
RFD
Cream Hill
Vermont

**This Large Print Book carries the
Seal of Approval of N.A.V.H.**

ॐ श्री गणेशाय नमः

August 1, 1945
Dear Mernelle. Bet you are surprised you
know somebody in California! We just
moved here yesterday. My father is working
in the shipyards. My room is the fold-up
couch in the living room. I have to keep
my postcards under the couch. We
couldn't take our cat Curly. He was to
mad to ride in the car. My father
said if we sent Curly to Japan the
War would be over in three days.
My mother is trying to get a job
in the shipyard too. Oh well, a new
school tomorrow.

Miss Mernelle Blood
RFD
Cream Hill
Vermont

Postcards

a novel by

E. Annie Proulx

...... to keep
...... Curly. He was to
...... sent Curly to Japan. My father
...... be over in three days.
Mother is trying to get a job
in the shipyard too. Oh well, a new
school tomorrow.
Your adventuros penpal, Juniata.

Miss Mernelle Blood
RFD
Cream Hill
Vermont

....nelle. It's awful about
....g. He was a good man. Sorry
we couldn't make the funeral.
Things down here are bad. Withery
....nothy, damps, deadconpts, chines.
....mustiness. It used to be so
beautiful. The prairie continues.
Some achievement! Polks had
a new project. Be happy for
what you and Ray had. Justice
follows.
Love, Dub

Mrs. Mernelle McClintry
Randall Court
Bethany, VT 05086

Center Point Publishing • Thorndike, Maine

FOR ROBERTA

This Center Point Large Print edition
is published in the year 2001 by arrangement with
Scribner, a division of Simon & Schuster, Inc.

Copyright © 1992 by E. Annie Proulx.

The Maltese Falcon by Dashiell Hammett,
copyright © 1929, 1930 Alfred A. Knopf, Inc.,
and renewed 1957, 1958 by Dashiell Hammett,
is reprinted by permission of Alfred A. Knopf.

The text of this Large Print edition is unabridged.
In other aspects, this book may vary from the original
edition. Printed in Thailand. Set in 16-point
Times New Roman type by Bill Coskrey.

ISBN 1-58547-147-X

Library of Congress Cataloging-in-Publication Data

Proulx, Annie.
    Postcards / E. Annie Proulx.
        p. cm.
    ISBN 1-58547-147-X (lib. bdg. : alk. paper)
    1. Farm life--Fiction. 2. New England--Fiction. 3. Rural conditions--Fiction. 4. Large type
books. I. Title.

PS3566.R697 P6 2001
813'.54--dc21

2001028979

"But that's the part of it I always liked. He adjusted himself to beams falling, and then no more of them fell, and he adjusted himself to them not falling."
—Dashiell Hammet, *The Maltese Falcon*

ACKNOWLEDGMENTS

I am grateful for financial support during the writing of this book from The Vermont Council on the Arts and from The Ucross Foundation of Ucross, Wyoming.

I appreciate the help given me by librarians at Dartmouth College Libraries in Hanover, New Hampshire, and The Sheridan County Fulmer Public Library in Sheridan, Wyoming.

Many people eased the passage of this story with time, advice, money, lunch, garden help, encouragement, silence, barbecue, music. Thank you Roberta Roberts, Tom Watkin, Elizabeth Guheen, Laurent Gaudin, Lois Gill, Abigail Thomas, Bob Jones, Gordon Farr, John Glusman, Ernie Hebert. Special thanks to my editor, Barbara Grossman, and to my sons, Jonathan, Gillis and Morgan Lang.

PART ONE

1. Blood

October 1944

Dear Mr. Blood;
Our national agriculture program is the
biggest job we've ever tackled—and there is
no ''maybe'' about it—the job *must* be done.
It's our obligation to put up the best
electric stock fence money can buy. When you
call on us YOU KNOW YOU CAN DEPEND ON ELECTROLINE. In
response to your request a representative
will call on you.

Mr Loyal Blood
RFD
Cream Hill, Vermont

EVEN before he got up he knew he was on his way. Even in the midst of the involuntary orgasmic jerking he knew. Knew she was dead, knew he was on his way. Even standing there on shaking legs, trying to push the copper buttons through the stiff buttonholes he knew that everything he had done or thought in his life had to be started over again. Even if he got away.

He couldn't get any air, but stood on his knocked-out legs gasping and wheezing. It was like he'd taken a bad fall. Dazed. He could feel the blood hammering in his throat. But there was nothing else, only the gasping for breath and an abnormal acuity of vision. Mats of juniper flowed across the field like spilled water; doghair maple crowded the stone wall wavering through the trees.

He'd thought of the wall walking up the slope behind Billy, thought of it in a common way, of working on it sometime, setting back in place the stones that frost and thrusting roots had thrown out. Now he saw it as a scene drawn in powerful ink lines, the rock fissured with crumpled strings of quartz, humps of moss like shoulders shrugging out of the mold, black lignum beneath rotten bark, the aluminum sheen of deadwood.

A stone the size and shape of a car's backseat jutted out of the wall, and below it was a knob of soil that marked the entrance to an abandoned fox den. Oh Jesus, it wasn't his fault but they'd say it was. He grasped Billy's ankles and dragged her to the wall. He rolled her up under the stone, could not look at her face. There was already a waxiness to her body. The texture of her bunched stockings, the shape of her nails glowed with the luminous hardness that marks the newly dead in the moment before the flames consume or the sucking water pulls them under. The space beneath the rock was shallow. Her arm fell outward, the hand relaxed, the fingers curled as if she held a hand mirror or a Fourth of July flag.

Instinctively he translated the withering shock into work, his answer to what he did not want to understand, to persistent toothache, hard weather, the sense of loneliness. He rebuilt the wall over her, fitting the stones, copying the careless, tumbled fall of rock. A secretive reflex worked in him. When she was locked away in the wall he threw on dead leaves, tree limbs and brush, raked the drag marks and scuffed ground with a branch.

Down the back fields, keeping to the fence line, but

sometimes staggering onto open ground. No feeling in his legs. The sun was going down, the October afternoon collapsing into evening. The fence posts on the margins of the fields glinted like burnished pins, the thick light plated his face with a coppery mask.

Grass eddied around his knees, the purple awns burst, scattering a hail of seed. Far below he saw the house varnished with orange light, balanced against the grove of cottonwoods, like a scene etched on a metal plate. The sag of the roof curved into shadows as delicate as a bloom of mold, thickening the trees.

In the orchard he knelt and wiped his hands over and over in the coarse grass. The trees were half wild with watersprouts and deadwood. The mournful smell of rotted fruit came into his nose. "If I get away," he said, dragging breath into his constricted throat, and briefly seeing, not what had happened up beside the wall, but his grandfather spraying the tree with Bordeaux mixture, the long wand hissing in the leaves, the poisoned codling moths bursting up like flames, the women and children, himself, on the ladder picking apples, the strap of the bag cutting into his shoulder, the empty oak-splint baskets under the trees and the men loading the full baskets into a wagon, the frigid packing room, old Roseboy with his sloping, bare neck and his dirty hat, pointed like a cone, nothing but a trimmed-up old syrup filter, tapping on the barrel heads, serious, saying over and over, "Take it easy now, one rotten apple spoils the whole goddamn barrel."

Evening haze rose off the hardwood slopes and blurred a sky discolored like a stained silk skirt. He saw and heard everything with brutal clarity; yet the thing that had happened up beside the wall was confused. Coyotes singling along the edge of the duck marsh called in fluming howls. Wet hand ticking the skeletal bean poles, he walked through the withered garden. Moths like pinches of pale dust battered in his wake.

At the corner of the house he stopped and urinated on the blackened stalks of Jewell's Canterbury bells. The seed husks rattled and a faint steam rose in the trembling shadow of his legs. His clothes had no warmth. The grey work pants, knees stained with soil, were stippled with grass heads and bramble tips, his jacket spattered with shreds of bark. His neck stung from her raking scratches. A gleaming image of her fingernails swerved into his mind and he clamped it off. The cedar waxwings rustled stiff leaves with a sound of unfolding tissue paper. He could hear Mink's voice in the kitchen, lumps of sound like newly plowed soil, and the flat muffle of Jewell, his mother, answering. Nothing seemed changed. Billy was somehow up there under the wall, but nothing seemed changed except the uncanny sharpness of his vision and the tightness that gripped somewhere under his breastbone.

A length of binder twine hung with bean plants sagged between the two porch pillars, and he could see each hemp fiber, the shadows in the folds of each desiccated leaf, the swell of the seed inside the husks. A broken pumpkin, crusted on its underside with earth, parted like a mouth in a knowing crack. His foot crushed a leaf as he opened the screen door.

Wire egg baskets were stacked in the corner of the entry. Water had drained from a basket half full of pale eggs and pooled under Mink's barn boots. The reeking barn clothes,

Dub's jacket, his own denim coat with the pocket gaping open like a wound, dangled from nails. He scraped his shoes on the wad of burlap sacks and went in.

"About time. You, Loyal, you and Dub can't get to the table on time we re not waitin.' Been sayin' this since you was four years old." Jewell pushed the bowl of onions toward him. Her hazel eyes were lost behind the glinting spectacles. The ridge of muscle that supported her lower lip was as stiff as wood.

The white plates made a circle around the kitchen table, the shape echoed in the curve of grease around Mink's mouth. There was stubble on his face, his finely cut lips were loosened by missing teeth. The dull silver lay on the yolk-colored oilcloth. Mink clenched the carving knife, sawed at the ham. The ham smelled like blood. Cold air crawled along the floor, the ferret scurried in the wall. On a hill miles away an attic window caught the last ray of light, burned for a few minutes, dimmed.

"Pass the plates." Mink's voice, gone thin since his tractor accident a few years ago, seemed caught in some glottal anatomic trap. He tensed his neck, creased across the back with white lines, and cut at the ham. The label on his overall bib read TUF NUT. The red slices fell away from the knife onto the platter, the glaze crackled by heat in crazy hairlines. The knife was thin-bladed, the steel sharpened away. Mink felt its fragility against the ham bone. Such a worn blade could easily break. His pallid gaze, blue as winter milk, slid around the table.

"Where's Dub? Goddamn knockabout."

"Don't know," Jewell said, hands like clusters of carrots, shaking pepper out of the glass dog, straight in the chair, the flesh of her arms firm and solid. "But I'll tell you something. Anybody that's late to supper can go without. I cook supper to be eat hot. And nobody bothers to take the trouble to set down when it's ready. Don't care who it is, they're not here they can forget it. Don't care if it's Saint Peter. Don't care if Dub's gone off again. Thinks he can come and go as he pleases. He don't care for nobody's work. I don't care if it's Winston Churchill with his big greasy cigar wants to set down to dinner, we're not waitin' for nobody. If there's something left he can have it, but don't expect nothing to be saved."

"I don't expect it," said Mernelle, squinting her eyes. Her braids were doubled in loops bound with rubber bands that pulled painfully when they were worked loose at night, the teeth too big for the face. She had the family hands with crooked fingers and flat nails. She had Mink's diffident slouch.

"Nobody is talking to you, miss. You make some money on the milkweed pods and you've got to put your two cents in on every subject. How money does change a person. Glad I haven't got any to spoil me."

"I got more good stuff goin' on than milkweed pods," said Mernelle scornfully. "I got three big things this week. I got six dollars for the milkweed pods, I got a letter from Sergeant Frederick Hale Bottum in New Guinea because he read my note with the Sunday school cigarettes, and our class is goin' to see the rubber show in Barton. On Friday."

"How many milkweed pods you picked for that six dollars?" Mink pulled off his ham cap and hung it on the chair's ear. A lock of hair hung down and he continually jerked his head to the left to get it out of his way.

"Hundreds. Thousands. Thirty bags. And guess what, Da, some of the kids turned in milkweeds that was still green, and they only give 'em ten cents a bag. I let mine get all nice and dry up in the hayloft first. The only one picked more than me was a old man from Topunder. Seventy-two bags, but he didn't have to go to school. He could just fool around pickin' milkweed all day long."

"I wondered what in the hell all them milkweed pods was doin' spread out over the floor up there. First I thought it was some idea Loyal had for cheap cowfeed. Then I thought they was goin' to be some kind of a decoration."

"Da, they don't make decorations out of milkweed pods."

"Hell they don't. Milkweed pods, pinecones, spools, popcorn, apples, throw some paint on it, that's it. I seen women and girls make a goddamn hay rake into a decoration with crepe paper and poison ivy."

The door opened a few inches and Dub's florid big-cheeked face thrust into the kitchen. In the thicket of his curly hair a bald spot appeared like a clearing in the woods. He pretended to look around guiltily. When his eyes came to Jewell's he twisted up his mouth in mock fear, sidling into the room with his arm crooked across his face as if to ward off blows. His thighs were heavy and he had the short man's scissory walk. He knew he was the fool of the family.

"Don't hit me, Ma, I'll never be late again. Couldn't help it this time. Hey, I got talkin' with a fella, said his uncle was one of the ones that was up on Camel's Hump where that bomber went down, looking for the survivors of the crash?"

"For pity's sake," said Jewell.

Dub turned his chair around and straddled it, his good arm across the back, the empty left sleeve, usually tucked in his jacket pocket, hanging slack. A Camel cigarette balanced behind his right ear. For an instant Jewell remembered how shapely his forearms had been, the swelling flexors and the man's veins like tight fine branchwood. Mink cut a slice of ham into pieces and scraped them onto Dub's plate.

The kitchen seemed to Loyal to be falling outward like a perspective painting, showing the grain of the ham, the two shades of green of the wallpaper ivy, the ears of drying popcorn joined together in a twist of wire hanging over the stove, the word COMFORT on the oven door, Jewell's old purse nailed to the wall to hold bills and letters, the pencil stubs in the spice can hanging from a string looped over a nail, Mernelle's drawing of a flag tacked to the pantry door, the glass doorknob, the brass hook and eye, the sagging string and stained cretonne covering the cavity under the sink, the wet footprints on the linoleum, all flat and detailed, but receding from him like torn leaves in a flooding river. It seemed he had never before noticed his mother's floral print apron, the solid way she leaned forward, her beaky nose and round ears. They had those ears, he thought, every one of them, forcing his mind away from what was up under the wall, and Mink's black Irish hair, so fine you couldn't see the single hairs.

Dub heaped the mashed potato on his plate, poured the yellow gravy over it and worked it in with his fork. He stuck a lump of chewing gum on the edge of the plate.

"Plane was all over the mountain. One wing clipped a part of the lion, and then it just end-overed, wings broke off here, tail farther down, cockpit belly-bunted half a mile down. Tell you what, they don't see how that guy lived through it, guy from Florida, just layin' on the snow, guts and arms and legs from nine dead men all around him, and all he had was a couple cuts and scrapes, nothing even broke. Guy never even see snow before."

"What lion?" asked Mernelle, picturing the beast behind snowy rocks.

"Ah, the top of the mountain, looks like a lion gettin' ready to jump, other guys thinks it looks like a part of a camel. The lion party wanted to call it 'crouchin' lion' but the camel lovers got their way. Camel's Hump. It's just stone up there, grade A granite. Looks like a pile of rock. Hey, don't look like a camel or a lion or a porcupine. Don't they learn you nothin' in school?"

"Seems like it's been a terrible time the last year or so for terrible things. The War. The Chowder Girl stabbing that needle in her eye. That was terrible. That poor woman in the bathtub in the hotel." Jewell unleashed one of her gusty sighs and stared away into the sad things that happen, that she guiltily savored. Her eyes were half closed, her thick wrists resting on the edge of the table, fork lying across her plate.

"What about the *fool* things," said Mink, the words tangled in his mouth with potato and ham, the stubbled cheeks flexing as he chewed, "what about that fool that brought the can of blasting powder into the kitchen and put a match to it to see if it would bum. A fool thing, and half the town on fire on account of it and him and his brother's whole family dead or torn up."

"What the hell is this?" said Dub, pulling something from the mashed potato on his plate. "What the hell is this?" holding up a bloodied Band-Aid.

"Oh my lord," said Jewell, "Throw it out. Take some new potato. I cut my finger peelin' potatoes, then when I was settin' the table I see I lost the Band-Aid somewhere. Must of fell in the potatoes when I was mashin' 'em. Give it here," she said, getting up and scraping the potato in the pig's slop bucket. She moved with a quick step, her lace-up oxfords with the stacked heels showing off her small feet.

"Thought for a minute there," said Dub, "that the taters had the rag on."

"Dub," said Jewell.

"I don't get it," said Mernelle. "I don't get what a bomber was doin' near the Camel's Hump. Is there Germans on the Camel's Hump?"

Dub roared in his stupid way. Mernelle could see the thing at the back of his throat hanging down, the black parts of his teeth and the empty gums on the left where the train men had knocked his teeth out.

"Don't worry about the Germans. Even if they made it across the ocean what the hell would they do up on Camel's Hump? 'Ach, Heinz, I am seeink der Blood farm und der dangerous Mernelle collecting ze milkveed pods.'" Dub's grin hung in his face like an end of wet rope.

The food lay on Loyal's plate as Mink had sent it along, the ham hanging a little over the edge, the cone of potato rising, a single iceberg from a frozen sea.

Loyal stood up, the yellow kerosene light reaching as high as his breast, his face shadowed. His leaf-stained fingers bunched, braced against the table. "Got something to say. Billy and me has had enough of this place. We're pullin' out tonight. She's waitin' for me right now. We're pullin' out and going out west, someplace out there, buy a farm, make a new start. She got the right idea. She says 'I'm not even goin' to try to see my folks. Suit me good if I never have to see one of them again.' She's just goin'. I wanted to set it straight with you, give you some idea. I didn't come back for no goddamn dinner. Didn't come back to listen to horseshit about Germans and potatoes. I come back to get my money and my car. Ask you to tell her folks she's gone. She don't care to see them."

As he said it he knew that's what they should have done. It seemed so easy now he couldn't understand why he'd fought the idea.

There was a silence. A discordance spread around the table as though he had blindly hit piano keys with a length of pipe.

Mink half-stood, the hair hung down over his eyes. "What in hell are you sayin'! This your idea of a joke? All I ever hear from you for ten years is how you think this place oughta be run, now you say just like you was talkin' about changin' your shirt that you're pullin' out? For ten years I been hearin' about what you wanted to do with this place, how you wanted to switch off the Jerseys over to Holsteins, 'get a milkin' machine after the War as soon's we get electricity in, specialize in dairy.' Get the pastures and hayfields up, alfalfa, build a silo, grow more corn concentrate on commercial dairy farmin'. Profit. Put the time into dairyin', don't bother with no big garden, or pigs or turkeys, it's quicker and efficienter to buy your food. I can hear you sayin' it now. You said it until my ears turned blue. Now this. You expect me to swallow this like sweet cake?

"Hey, mister, tell you what else you said. You bitched and whined about the juniper movin' into the fields, talk half an hour about the orchard, suckers, deadwood, the bull spruce is chokin' out the spring in the pine tree corner you said, west hayfields ain't been cut in three year, full of cherry trash. That's what you said. Said you wished the day had forty hours of light so's you could get somethin' done."

Loyal hardly heard him, but saw the rubbery folds from the wings of his nostrils to the corners of his mouth, saw the cords in Mink's neck, thought of the glistening strings just under the skin, thought of the arteries swelled with ropes of blood the size of his finger, thought of the crackling sound of rib bones when he kicked in a fox's chest.

"You can't leave us run this farm alone," said Mink in his buzzing voice, the self-pity getting into his rage. "Jesus Christ, your brother's only got the one arm and my health is down since the damn tractor laid on my chest. I was up to my health I'd beat the shit out of you. You're not worth a pig's patootie. You tell me how in the hell Dub and me can hand-milk nineteen cow alone, two of them damn Holsteins of yours, the one holds her milk back, and kicks. Christ I hate that cow's eyes. You son of a bitch, we just can't do it."

"Goddamnit, the Holsteins are good-natured cows, better than them mean little Jerseys you got. They give damn near twice as much milk as any Jersey." He tumbled into the relief of the old argument.

"Yes, and look how much they eat. And half the butterfat of the Jerseys. The Jerseys is made for this country. They can make out on thin pasture and keep a farm going. They're rugged. Tell you another thing. You just try walkin' off the farm they'll have your ass in uniform so fast it'll take your breath away. There's a War on, in case you forget. Farm work is essential work. Forget out west. Don't you read no papers? Don't you hear no radio programs? Them out west farms dried up and blowed away in the Dust Bowl. You're stayin'."

Dub popped a wooden match with his thumbnail and lit his cigarette.

"I got to go," said Loyal. "I got to. Oregon or Montana—somewhere."

"Put the record on again, Charlie," said Dub, "everybody likes to dance to that one." The smoke streamed out of his nose.

Jewell put her hands to her cheeks and drew down on them, stretching her face and exposing the red inner lids of her eyes behind her glasses. "I don't know," she said. "What about the Army Dinner, we're puttin' on the Army Dinner Saturday night, the big beef stew dinner in the cafeteria style, Army style. I was expectin' you to take me down to the church on Saturday mornin'. You can stay for that. Billy's one of the ones that wears the chef's hats and ladles out the food. She has to stay for that."

"It's on Billy's account we got to go tonight. There's certain reasons. No good to talk about it. I'm goin'." He leaned wildly at them, the black hair curling at the opening of his shirt where the blue-white skin showed.

"Well Jesus Christ, I see the whole thing. You knocked

21

her up. She wants to clear out so nobody don't know. There's a word to describe a fella like you lets himself get backed into a rutty corner where he can't turn around," the voice squeezed along, "but I won't say it in front of your mother and sister."

"Hey, you leave, Loyal," said Dub, "you're finishin' off this farm."

"Well I knew this was goin' to be like takin' a bath in boiled shit, but I didn't know it was goin' to be this bad. Can't you understand nothin'? I'm goin'."

He ran up to the slant-ceilinged room he shared with Dub, leaving the ham on his plate, leaving his chair turned away from the table, leaving the fly-spotted mirror reflecting Mernelle's face. He hauled out the old valise, opened it and threw it onto the bed. And stood a long minute with the shirts bunched up in his hands, the valise gaping like a shout. Down there Mink was firing up, bellowing now, something smashing and rattling the door to the pantry. Loyal dropped the shirts into the valise, and afterwards believed that was the moment when everything shifted, when the route of his life veered away from the main line, not when Billy slumped beneath his blind rutting, but as the shirts collapsed in their cotton limpness.

He found Dub's bottle in a boot in the closet, tightened the cap and tossed it in, working the stiff strap through the valise buckle as he came down the stairs double-stride, hearing Mink hammering now, seeing the son of a bitch nailing the kitchen door shut. So he couldn't get out.

He was across the room in a few seconds. He kicked out the window and stepped over the raking glass onto the porch, leaving it all, the trapline, the rough little Jerseys, the two Holsteins with their heavy flesh-colored udders, Dub's oily rags, and the smell of old iron in the back of the barn, the wall up by the woods. That part of things was over. It was over in a rush.

Down on the town road he thought it was a sour joke how things had turned out. Billy, always yapping about moving away, getting out, making a new start, was staying on the farm. He, who'd never thought beyond the farm, never wanted anything but the farm, was on his way. Clenching the steering wheel.

Something was sticking in his backside, and he felt around, grasped Mernelle's ocarina, the swirled novelty pattern of the Bakelite scarred from kicking around the floor. On the sides were decals of donkeys carrying panniers of cactus. He started to crank down the window to throw it out, but the window slipped off the rail again when it was only a crack open, and he threw the ocarina into the backseat.

It was almost dusk, but at the low place where the meadows swept the trees off to the sides he pulled over to take a last look. But jammed the spurting flashes of what had happened. Had happened and was done.

The place was as fixed as a picture on a postcard, the house and barn like black ships in an ocean of fields, the sky a membrane holding the final light, and there were the blurred kitchen windows, and up behind the buildings the field, the rich twenty-acre field propped open toward the south like a Bible, the crease of the water vein almost exactly in the center of the ten-acre pages. He fished in the valise and got Dub's bottle, swallowed the cold whiskey.

Beautiful pasture, four or five years of his work to bring that field up, none of Mink's labor, his, draining the boggy place, liming and seeding to clover, plowing under the clover three years running to build up the soil, get the sourness out, then planting alfalfa and keeping it going, look at it, sweet good stuff, nutty, full of nourishment. That's what made those cows give the butterfat, nothing Mink did, but him, Loyal, the best pasture in the county. That was why he had wanted to go up above the junipers, even though Billy didn't care about the field and couldn't tell good fields from bad, not to do what she thought he wanted, but to look at his pasture from above.

'I heard it all, now," she said. "Looks like any stupid old field to me." She shook her head. "I don't know if I can make something out of you or not, Loyal."

The field looked like black-green fur in the dull light.

"That's your last look," he said, laid Dub's bottle in the glove compartment and threw the car into first. Out of the corner of his eye he half-marked a white dot up in the field. Too big for a fox, wrong shape for a deer. And no stumps in that field.

But he was fourteen miles away from home and half across the bridge, stepping gingerly on the brake to keep from hitting a burr-covered stray, before he figured it out. The dog. The dog was up in the field right where he'd told him to sit. Still waiting. Jesus Christ.

2. Mink's Revenge

Don't come out my FARM
NO MOre with your DAMN
iNSemNAtioN RACket. We
got Rid the HoLstiNS. Guess
we stick with good LocAl
JeRsey stock Do it The
olD FASHioN WAY with A
BuLL.

Minkton M. Blood

F. FuLLeR
CouNty AgeNt
OFFice
CReAM HiLL

MINK, panting in unsatisfied rage, limped through the house throwing down Loyal's things, a model airplane impaled on a nail in the front hall, school photos in warped folders edged with gold—Loyal the only one in his class with wavy hair, handsome—standing in a crowd of frames and button boxes on the piecrust cherry table in the front room. The 4-H ribbons, red, white and blue for calves, pasted on a piece of propped cardboard, the high school diploma with its black pointed letters proving Loyal had completed courses in Agriculture and Agronomy and Manual Training, the *Dairy Management* book from his single year at the agricultural school, dark blue and heavy, the certificate for pasture improvement, a newspaper clipping with a photo of Mr. Fuller, the County Agent, handing the certificate to Loyal, all these things he threw on the floor.

He crammed Loyal's barn coat into the kitchen stove, scraped the untouched food on his plate in after it. Smoke swelled out of a hundred stove cracks and eddied along the ceiling before curling into the stream of warm air pouring out through the smashed window. Dub fumbled behind the pantry door for cardboard to tack over the window and Jewell, her face red and her eyes narrowed to slits, juggled the stove damper. A roaring came from the stovepipe as the creosote in the bend of the elbow caught and heated the stinking metal to a dull red.

"Christ, Ma, you're workin' on a chimbley fire, damper the goddamn thing down," shouted Dub.

Here came Mink, cool now, but with vicious eyes, coming downstairs with Loyal's .30-.30, limping through the kitchen, leaving the door open. Dub guessed the old man would throw it in the pond. Later he could drag through the mud with a potato fork and maybe get lucky. Probably take a day of cleaning and oiling to get it back in shape, but it was a good rifle and worth the trouble. Laid across the windowsill of the hayloft he could shoot it, get his deer like anybody else. He pieced and tacked cardboard boxes, all slots and creases, to the window frame, holding the cardboard in place with his left knee while he hammered.

"I'll cut some glass, put it in tomorrow if somebody'll give me a hand puttin' in the points." But he was pale.

Jewell swept up the curving slivers, putty chunks and dust, stoutly bending over, her print dress riding up, exposing the ribbed cotton stockings, the flesh-pink slip from Montgomery Ward.

"There's glass in the food, Ma, there's glass all over the table," said Mernelle. "There's big pieces on the porch, too."

"You can start by scrapin' the plates, and don't put it in the pig pail. Have to take it out and heave it. I don't know about the hens, if they'd pick up the glass, but I suppose they would. Heave it out back of the garden."

There was the slamming sound of a shot from the barn, then another, and, after a long interval, a third. The cows were bawling like alligators, flat roars, stamping, rattling their stanchions. They could hear Father Abraham's bellow above all the others.

"That is a hell of a thing to do," said Dub. "That is a hell of a thing to do." Jewell shuddered, her fingers across her mouth, watched Dub go out to the entry, jerk his coat off the nail. Back through the kitchen to the woodshed door.

"Be careful," she said, hoping he knew what he should be careful about. Mernelle started to snivel, not over the cows, but because of Mink's rage that was spurting out of him like jets of water from a kinked hose. He could chop them all with the axe.

"Get hold of yourself and go up to bed," said Jewell gathering the plates from the table. "Go on now, I got enough trouble without you blubberin' around the place."

She was sitting at the table when Mink came in. She saw how a little burst of greyed hairs had grown on his cheek since morning. He threw the rifle up on top of the cupboard without cleaning it and sat across from her. His hands were steady. The streaked hair stuck out from under his cap, the bill like a menacing horn over his eyes.

"By god, that's two of them we don't have to milk." There were fine drops of blood across the front of his overalls.

Mist rose from the brook like a stage curtain. In midmorning the trees still bent wet and silent. Every surface was coated with beaded drops that paled bark, wood, paint, soil. The coming and going of Dub and Mink made dark paths across the porch, through the grass like stiff hairs with seed pearls at the tips. The top of the barn dissolved, the pigs rooted in the manure pile, heaving bubbles on the surface of a black swamp.

Mink was out before daylight. Jewell struggled from sleep to the sound of the tractor dragging the Holsteins down to the swamp where the dogs and foxes and crows would find them. The engine echoed and dotted through the fog.

"We could of at least took the meat," she thought, and Mink's anger seemed to her so wasteful he would have to burn for it in a hell as crimson as the landscape seen through the red cellophane strip on cigarette packs. Not a new thought.

He had done a hundred things. She could not forget all of them. The knock-down slaps, the whalings he gave the boys, same as he'd had himself. Loyal, maybe three years old, stumbling across the muddy barnyard in his little red boots, bellowing like a lost calf but still hanging onto his empty milk bucket. It was a quart cream can, really. The milk all spilled when he slid in fresh manure. Mink had slapped him halfway across the barn. "I'll learn you to watch your goddamn step! Don't spill the milk!" Loyal's broken nose had swelled up to the size of a hen's egg by the time he got to the porch steps, the cream can banging, and for two weeks the kid had slunk around dodging Mink, looking like a raccoon with his double black eyes. When she'd run out to the barn in her own fury Mink'd been astonished. "Listen here. We got to start him young. We got to. It's for his own good. I went through it. And guarantee you he won't spill no more milk." Nor had he.

And Dub, too, who'd got to eating under the table with the dog when he was what, five or six, until Mink hauled him up by his hair and held him screaming in the air, "Will you eat off'n your plate or not? Will you?"

But she couldn't hold it against him because he came off the fire as fast as he heated up. The Blood temper. Loyal had the same flash temper. And mild as milk afterwards.

Mink and Dub were late coming in from the barn. It was nine by the kitchen clock when Dub went for the speckled coffeepot on the back of the stove, relishing the hot chicory taste. He poured some into a chipped cup for Mink. Shifting weights and counterweights of regard shot back and forth between them like abacus beads on wires. Animosity and bridling softened. Mink tried to smother his contempt for Dub's wandering habits, hopeless taste for nigger music, those sly records by Raw Boy Harry he brought back from distant places. He went for the Kong Chow restaurant in Rutland, too, where he'd eat three dollars' worth of vegetables in a rat-brown sauce at one sitting and the Comet Roadhouse where he got drunk on Saturday and pawed the women with his grimy hand.

Dub, in his turn, swallowed the remarks under his breath about Mink's monotonous ideas and narrow corridors of toil, his pathetic belief that cattle auctions were the height of entertainment. Dub could even choke down the way the old man had shot the Holsteins.

Working in the dim lantern light, their calloused hands

touched like pieces of wood as Dub dipped for the handle of the full milk pail and passed a new one to Mink, as Dub went ahead, wiping down the flanks and udder of the next cow, soothing Myrna Loy who tossed her head, still nervy. They fell into the companionship of work. The weight of the work without Loyal pressed them close. Dub hustled; Mink milked on and on, fourteen, seventeen cows, his forearms aching, his back cracking, and Dub saw it was a prodigious job. For the first time he felt sorry on Mink's account that he'd lost his arm.

Now that Loyal was gone some kind of hunger for his father's affection came up in Dub, an appetite he hadn't known he had, that had lain quiet and flat under his joking and travels, and that could never be satisfied at this late date. It did not displace the ancient hatred and what he murmured like a charm against fate, "won't never be like he is."

They worked without speaking, listening to the farm report and egg prices and War news coming from the crackling, chaff-coated radio that ran off the big farm battery, on its shelf beside the milk room door. For a while, in those hours of carrying, of spurting milk, they passed from being father and youngest son, became two equals subordinate to the endless labor. "We'll get it tuned up, all right," Mink said, the muscles in his arms swelling, falling, as he milked.

"Three and a half hours of milkin'. I done the milkin', Dub lugged the goddamn milk, and it adds up to seven hours a day on milkin' alone, add in grainin' and hayin' 'em, clean out the barn, got to spread some of that manure before the snow comes, tomorrow we got to get the cream down to the road by seven, plus the rest of life's little chores like diggin' the potatoes we got to get dug, we ain't got the wood hauled down yet. The butcherin's got to be did this week if we stay up all night doin' it. If I was to make a list of the things that got to be did right now it would take every piece of paper in the house. I don't know if I could hold a pencil, don't know if I can get my hands around anything but cow teats. You and Mernelle will have to take care of them chickens and get in what apples you can, dig the potatoes. Mernelle will have to stay out of school for a week or so until we get on top of it. There ain't no way we can do it unless we give up sleepin'." What he said was true. But the set of his furious mouth got Jewell's back up.

"You'll put up with scratch suppers if we got to do outside work. I can't kill and pluck chickens and lug potatoes and apples and then come in and make a big dinner. Can't you get one of your brother's boys there, Ernest or Norman, to help?" She knew he could not.

"Be nice if I could slack off on the milkin' just because I got to haul wood. Goddamn it, I need a good dinner and I expect you to fix it for me." Now he was shouting. "And no, I can't get Ott's boys to help. First place, Norman's only eleven and got about as much strength as wet hay. Ernie's already helpin' Ott and Ott says he puts about as much into it as he would into takin' poison."

She'd like to see *him* take poison, he knew it.

There was the threshing sound of a car coming up the lane. Jewell went to the window.

"Might of known she'd be along; it's old Mrs. Nipple and Ronnie."

"Be out in the barn," said Mink, hitching at his overalls. The argument had brought up his color, and Jewell had a

31

flash of how he'd been when he was young, the milky skin under the shirt, the blue flashing eyes and the fine hair. The vigor of him, the swaggering way he walked and hitched at his overalls to free his private parts from the chafing cloth.

He and Dub went out the door to the woodshed, moving like a matched team. The porch door hissed. Mrs. Nipple's heavy fingers crooked around the door edge.

"Don't just stand there, Mrs. Nipple, come on in and Ronnie too," shouted Jewell, putting on water for tea. The old lady had burned her mouth with hot coffee as a baby and never touched it again, let her tea stand until it went tepid. "Thought we might be seein' you pretty soon." Mrs. Nipple had an instinct for discovering trouble as keen as the wild goose's need to take flight in the shortening days. She was sensitive to the faintest janglings of discord from miles away.

"After what she had been through," Jewell once told Mernelle in a dark tone, "she probably knows what ain't right in Cuba."

"What's she been through, then?" asked Mernelle.

"Nothin' I can tell you until you're a grown woman. You wouldn't understand it."

"I'll understand it," whined Mernelle, "so tell me."

"Not likely," said Jewell.

"Ronnie's gone out to the barn to talk to Loyal and them," said Mrs. Nipple sidling through the door, taking in the broken window, the potato peelings in the sink, the woodshed door half open, Jewell's twisted smile. She smelled the rage, the smoke, sensed some departure. In Mink's chair she felt the warmth of the seat even through her heavy brown skirt. Nobody had to tell her something had happened. She knew Mink had gone out to the barn when he saw her coming.

The old lady had the look of a hen who had laid a thousand eggs, from her frizzled white hair permed at Corinne Claunch's Home Beauty Parlor, to her bright moist eye, plump breast, thrusting rear end that no corset could ever bend in and the bowed legs set so far out on her pelvis that when she walked it was like a rocking chair rocking. Dub had snickered to Loyal once that the space between her thighs had to be three hands across, that she could sit on the back of a Clydesdale like a slotted clothespin on the line.

She sighed, touched a needle of glass on the oilcloth. "Seems like there's trouble everywhere," she said, building up a platform for the news Jewell must tell. "It's a nuisance you have to bring your own paper bags to the stores, and just last month Ronnie got a letter from the milk truck, said they are consolidating the route. Can't come up to the farm no more. If we want to sell them cream we got to lug it down to the roadside. He's been doing it, but it's pretty irksome work, takes a good deal of time. I suppose he'll lose heavy on it. Don't know how they expect us to manage. Then my niece Ida's sister-in-law, you remember Ida, she stayed with us when Toot was still alive, helped me in the garden all one summer, picked berries, apples, I don't know what, helped Toot and Ronnie with the hay. She was the one got stung by yellow jackets had a nest under a pumpkin. Well, now she's livin' over in Shoreham, I hear from her that her sister-in-law, Mrs. Charles Renfrew, runs the U-Auta lunchroom in Barton, her husband's at the War in the Air Force, and she been arrested. I have never ate there and I don't believe I ever will. She shot this feller, Jim somebody, worked for the electric light over there, with his own shotgun. Seems he come sneakin' around, peepin' in the windows to see what she was doin' and he saw plenty. She got this cook in to help her run the lunchroom, a colored fellow from South America, she didn't say what his name was, but Mrs. Charles Renfrew was seen by the electric company man kissin' the cook, and in he comes with the shotgun. See, he was sweet on her himself She's a good-lookin' woman, they say. She gets the shotgun away from him and shoots him. And he died. When they arrested her she admitted it all, but said everything was an accident. Got six children, the youngest one isn't but four. Them poor little children. It was all in the paper. Terrible, ain't it." She waited for Jewell to begin. Few things could be worse than Mrs. Charles Renfrew's multiple crimes laid out in public view, and she'd told the story to give Jewell a chance to whittle her own troubles down to size. She leaned forward.

Jewell slid the cup of tea over to her, the string dangling over the edge of the cup. "We had a little surprise here last night. Loyal comes in for supper, stands up in the middle of it and says that Billy and him is goin' out west. They left last night. Kind of took us by surprise, but that's the way the kids are these days."

"Is that right," said Mrs. Nipple. "Takes my breath away. Ronnie will be upset. Him and Loyal was tight as ticks." There was something awry, she thought, told straight out like that, no details of who had said what. She knew there was something deeper. Mink must have been crazy mad. The way Jewell told it now, it didn't seem like the kind of story that would gather with time, but instead would retract, condense, turn into one of those things that nobody talked about, and in a year or so it would all be forgotten. There were plenty of those stories. She knew one or two herself. It was all serious business. She never understood why Ronnie liked Loyal, no standout, even in the crowd of Bloods with their knack for doing the wrong thing, except for his strength and his sinewy hunger for work. But one man couldn't bring that farm up again. It had too much against it. Look how it had gone down since the grandfather's time when it was tight-fenced for the convenience of trotting horses and fine merinos, only three cows then for family butter and cheese on the place. She liked Jewell well enough, but the woman was a dirty housekeeper, letting the men in with their barn clothes on, letting the dust and spiders take over, and too proud for milk room work.

"Well, Billy was smarting to get out, and I can't say I blame her. But I'm surprised Loyal would go. He's a country boy from the word go. She'll find you can take the boy out of the country but you can't take the country out of the boy. It won't be easy to milk all them cows, just Mink and Dub. Dub's still here or is he off somewhere again?" Her voice so custard smooth now it would cure a sore throat.

"Been here pretty steady since his accident. But you know how he is. The two of them can't do it all. Not run this farm, just the two of them. We'll have to hire somebody to come in, I imagine."

"You won't find nobody. Ronnie tried all last winter, this spring and summer, and I guess he got to know everybody for twenty mild around that could hold a pitchfork, and I'll tell you, the best he could find was school kids and hundred-year-old grandpas with wooden legs and canes. Some places they're takin' on girls. How about Mernelle? She could milk, maybe. She's comin' on what, twelve or thirteen now? She get the curse yet? I used to milk when I was eight. Or you could milk while she takes over the house. Some say it makes the cows restless when a woman's got the curse milks 'em. I never noticed it myself." The old lady sucked at her tea.

"No ma'am. I don't work to the barn and my girl don't work to the barn. Barns is men's work. If they can't handle it they can hire. I give two boys to the barn, that's enough. Mink's already set me and Mernelle up to take on what seems like half his outside work."

"I've noticed that with the help so hard to get and the boys off to the War they's quite a few of the farms for sale. And the way the cream prices moves around. Course it's good now, with the War, but it could go down again. I notice that the Darter farm is been sold. The three boys is in the service, the other one's in the shipyards, the girl's gone into nurse's training, and Clyde says, 'I don't know why we're hangin' around here when we could be makin' good money instead of killin' ourself.' They say he went over to Bath, Maine where the other boy is, they learnt him how to weld and he's got a high-payin' job now. They say she got one, too, and between what they get from the wages and what they got from sellin' the farm to a teacher from Pennsylvania who's just comin' up for summers, they are fixed up good. Seems funny that Loyal and Billy would go off so sudden like that. He didn't say nothin' to Ronnie. Ronnie and him was plannin' to go goose huntin' one day this week. That's the main reason we come by, so's Ronnie and Loyal could set their time. I says they ought to try and get some of them hen hawks that have been takin' my hens and now there's a turkey gone. I don't know as a hen hawk could lift a turkey, but I suppose they could eat it where they brought it low. But maybe it was a fox took the turkey. I don't know how Ronnie'll get along without Loyal, they was that close. You'll find it quite a chore without Loyal. A worker."

"I suppose we'll figure somethin' out. But I don't know what. One thing, I'm not goin' in any barn and neither is Mernelle."

3. Down the Road

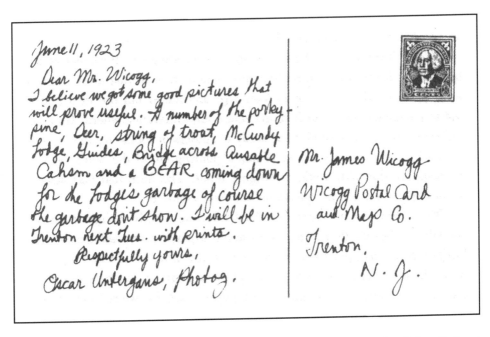

June 11, 1923

Dear Mr. Wicogg,
I believe we got some good pictures that will prove useful. A number of the porky-pine, Deer, string of trout, McCurdy Lodge, Guides, Bridge across Ausable Cahom and a BEAR coming down for the Lodge's garbage of course the garbage don't show. I will be in Trenton next Tues. with prints.
Respectfully yours,
Oscar Undergans, Photog.

Mr. James Wicogg
Wicogg Postal Card
and Map Co.
Trenton,
N. J.

HE made good time, heading north for the end of the lake. He had his little roll of money, country money, dollar bills oily and limp from passage through the hands of mechanics, farmhands, loggers. He had enough gas ration stamps to get him somewhere. It wasn't like anybody was after him. He didn't think they'd ever be after him. That wall was built good, he thought. If the foxes didn't dig in under. If nobody went up there. Who in hell would go up there? Nobody would go up there.

The roads had hardened in the autumn cold and there wasn't much traffic. Good hunting weather. A few cars, a log truck coming out of the dark woods, leaving a double-curve of cleated mud where it turned onto the hardtop. Must of gotten stuck in some soft spot. He had forty-seven dollars, enough to take him some distance. If the car would hold up. It was in pretty good shape, a '36 Chevy Coach, except for the back of the seat that had broke and had to be braced from behind with a wooden crosspiece. The heater only put out a trickle, less warmth than a bat's breath, but the defroster did well enough. The battery was old, and the Coach was a bitch to start on a cold morning, about as simple as getting port wine out of a cow's left hind teat. The tires still had tread. He'd nurse them along. If it broke down bad he could get work. Walk onto any farm and get work. What bothered him was the gas stamps. He only had enough for twenty gallons. That could just get him across New York state. He'd have to get it any way he could.

He didn't think where he was going, just heading out. It seemed to him there didn't have to be a direction, just a random traveling away from the farm. It wasn't the idea that he could go anywhere, but the idea that he had to go somewhere, and it didn't make any difference where. No spark had ever ignited his mind for the study of spiders or rocks, for the meshing of watch gears, or the shudder of paper pouring out of the black presses, for mapping the high arctic or singing tenor. The farm had had answers for any question, but no questions had ever come up.

West, that was the direction. That was where Billy thought there was something. Not another farm. She wanted a place with roadhouses, some kind of War work, good money in the factories if she could find a job that didn't bust her nails, save some dough for a start, go out Saturday night, hair curled, parted in the middle and pulled back by two red barrettes set with rhinestones. She wanted to sing. She sang pretty good when she got the chance. Go up to the Club 52 packed with guys from the base. Like Anita O'Day, cool, smart, standing there in front of the microphone, holding it with one hand, a red chiffon scarf dripping down from her hand, her voice running through the room like water over rock. Clear, but a little sarcastic.

He was supposed to get a job. The money was good, she said, dollar an hour and better. Guys were pulling down fifty, sixty bucks a week in the aircraft plants. He'd drive west, but keep to the border. Those cities she'd named, South Bend, Detroit, Gary, Chicago, those were the places. What Billy would have wanted, but his mind kept jumping away from whatever had happened. The gas would be a problem.

The road ran along the railroad tracks up near the lake. That was another way; he could ride the rails. He'd never done it, but plenty had. Dub had, even dumb Dub had bummed around, riding the boxcars in the times he went off his nut and drifted out and away. He'd come back a mess, stinking, lugging an old feed sack of trash, his hair stiff with dirt.

"Presents. Got you a present, Ma," he'd say, pulling out the junk. Once it was about thirty pie pans, the edges gummed with baked-on apple and cherry syrup. Once five little bales of cotton about six inches high, the tags saying "A Gift from New Orleans, Cotton Capital of the World." Another time the best he could do was half a BURMA SHAVE sign. All it said was BURMA. He tried to tell them it came from the real Burma. And the time he brought back about fifty pounds of red dirt from somewhere down south, he didn't even know where.

"It's all like this, all red dirt down there. Red as blood. Red roads, the wind blows red, bottom of the houses red, gardens, farms red. But the taters and turnips is the same color as ours. I don't get it. Because there is red taters in this world. But not in the land of the red dirt." He dumped the soil in one of Jewell's flower beds where he could look at it now and then and be reminded of the place it came from.

A light appeared and reappeared in the darkness behind him, gradually growing larger in the rearview. Loyal heard the whistle blow for a crossing, somewhere behind him, he thought, but when he steered around the long corner before the bridge, the train was there, its light sweeping along the rails, the iron shuddering past a few feet from him.

The worst was the time Dub had come back honed down to his bones, the scabs on his face like black islands and his left arm amputated except for a stub like a seal's flipper. Mink and Jewell, all stiff in their best clothes driving down to get him, first time Mink had ever been out of the state. Dub called it that, "my flipper," trying to make a joke but sounding loony and sick. "Could of been worse," he said, tipping a crazy wink at Loyal. He'd only gone off once since then, no farther than Providence, Rhode Island, and hitching on the road, not riding the rods. There was a kind of school in Rhode Island he said, a place to learn tricks of getting things done with half your parts missing. They could fix you up with artificial arms and hands and legs made out of pulleys and aluminum. A new kind of plastic fingers that worked so good you could play the one-man band with them. But when he came back he was the same. Didn't want to talk about it. Some VA place for servicemen, farmers had to get along the best they could. It was just a question anyway of how far you got before you were crippled up one way or another. A lot of people didn't make it past the time they were kids. Look at Mink, pitchfork tines through his thigh when he was five years old, two car wrecks, the tractor rollover, the time the brood sow got him down and half tore off his ear, but he was still there, gimping around, strong as a log chain, getting the work done. Tuf Nut. The old son of a bitch.

Miles into New York state he pulled the car into a field behind a row of chokecherry trees. The broken seat back could come in handy, he thought, pulling out the brace and letting it flop down into a kind of narrow bed. But as he twisted near sleep his chest seized up again, a blunt stake slammed into a place under his larynx, and with it a choking breathlessness. He sat up, dozing and waking in starts, the rest of the night.

No station came in clearly on the radio, not even the jabber of French and accordions, riding along the edges of the Adirondack conifer forests, spruce and miles of skeletal larch like grey woods static, sometimes a tangle of deer legs and phosphorescent eyes in the road ahead of him, far enough ahead that he had time to tap the brakes while he laid on the horn and watched them go, worrying about the brake lines, the worn drums. He passed houses not much bigger than toolsheds, threads of smoke floating out of the cobblestone chimneys, passed boarded-up, log cabins, signposts saying "Crow's Nest," "Camp Idle-Our," "The Retreat," "Skeeter Gulch," "Dun Roamin." Bridges, water racing away, the gravel road punched with potholes, all the roads nothing more than notches through the tight-packed trees, roads that took their curves and twists from the St. Lawrence River thirty miles to the north. The strangeness of the country, its emptiness, steadied his breathing. There was nothing here of him, no weight of event or duty or family. Somber land, wet as the inside of a bucket in the rain. The gas gauge needle tipped down and he kept his eye out for a gas pump. The farther away he got the better it seemed he could breathe.

Late in the morning he pulled up to a tourist trap, BIG PINETREE, lying in wait in the trees beyond a long bend. He was half sick with hunger. Four or five old cars and trucks, standing so long their tires had gone flat. A row of sheds covered with signs: "Little Indian Moccasins," "Peanut Britle," "Balsom Pilows," "Lether Work," "Groceries," "Sovenirs," "Tire Change Wihle U Wait," "Lunchroom," "Botomless Cup of Coffee 5c," "Rest Room," "Gifts & Noveltys," "Auto Repears," "Worm & Bait," "Torist Cabin." There was a half-closed look to the place but the light was on in the pump's round head, the glow shining through the red-painted Tydol Flying A gasoline. The parking lot as rough as a cob, full of mud sinks and wash-board ripples. There was a garage bay with a hinge-sprung door that left a scraped semicircle in the gravel. Somebody had dumped a load of cordwood near the main building.

He went in. A wood lunch counter with a few stools home upholstered in red oilcloth, three booths varnished the color of orange peel. He could smell cigarette smoke. The radio was going, somewhere. "What a dart you placed in my heart the day that we parted." Beyond the counter were islands and aisles of moccasins, pincushions, colored feather dusters with handles carved in the shape of a spruce tree, canvas water bags to sling over the car fender, felt pennants, wooden plaques burned with jokes and mottos, green bumper stickers stamped *This Car Has Been to the Adirondacks,* and on the wall the stuffed heads and mounted bodies of bass and pike, eight-pound trout with square tails, bear, moose and deer, a porcupine bigger than any of the bobcats arched on their birch half-logs, a king snake lumpily crawling over the door lintel and everywhere fly-specked photographs of men wearing knee-high hunting boots holding up carcasses and bodies.

"Help you," said an irritable woman's voice. She sat in one of the booths, comfortable in a space designed for three people, a fat girl with blond hair parted on the side and pinned back with a black grosgrain bow. She wore a man's grey sweater over a housedress printed with sea-horses. In front of her was a chicken salad sandwich cut square across the middle with strips of bacon hanging out the ends, and a pot of coffee beside a souvenir mug, a magazine folded open. He could see letters spelling out "The Telegram Came While I Was Two-Timing Joe."

"Like to get cup of coffee, sandwich, you got any more like that," pointing with his thumb.

"I s'pose we can manage it." She heaved to her feet and he saw the wrinkled dungaree legs under the dress, the oily work boots.

"Are you the Big Pinetree?"

"Close enough. Big enough. Mrs. Big Pinetree. Piney's in the Pacific and I'm here keepin' the bears out of the lunchroom and fixin' cars much as I can without no parts or no tires. Want it toasted?"

"Guess so."

She pulled the uncovered bowl of chicken salad out of a big Servel, the door around the handle discolored with garage grease, slapped three pieces of bacon on the grill and laid three slices of white bread to toast. She pressed down on the bacon with a spatula, forcing the oil out. She opened the Servel again, grasped a head of lettuce like a bowling ball, tore off an inch of leaves and dropped them on the cutting board. She turned the bacon, turned the slices of bread, pressed them with the spatula. She got the pot of coffee from the booth and poured it in a white mug marked "Souvenir of Big Pinetree in the Adirondacks." She slid the spatula under a slice of bread, toasted dark with a narrow rim of black around the crust, slid it onto a plate, plastered it with Silvernip mayonnaise, put half the lettuce on it, whacked a scoop of chicken salad dead center, then picked up the second slice of toast, laid it in place like a mason dropping a brick in line, hit it with the mayonnaise, the rest of the lettuce and the hot bacon. When the last slice of toast was on she looked up at Loyal, holding the knife.

"Kitty-corner or straight?"

"Straight."

She dipped her head in a single nod, laid the knife dead center, horizontal with the edge of the toast, raised the heel of the blade and cut it clean. She pulled a two-inch cream bottle out of the Servel and thumped it all on the counter in front of him.

"There you go. I don't trust guys like it cut kitty-corner. City style. Fifty-five." He dug out the change, then sat eating, trying not to cram and wolf. She went back to her magazine and he heard her strike a match, heard the rounded exhalation of her breath, smelled the smoke. She was big, but she wasn't bad.

"This is a hell of a good sandwich," he said. "Any chance of another cup of coffee?"

"Help yourself," she said, rattling the pot on the booth table. He brought his mug over and she poured the coffee, steadying his mug with one hand. Her fingers touched his.

God! He hadn't washed up since. He started to jerk away but thought of the gas. He drank a mouthful of coffee, trying to force down the nervous tightness. He sat down on the bench across from her and cocked his head a little.

"Hate to leave good company," he said, "but I got to be on my way."

"Where you headin'?"

"Out west. Thought I'd get off the farm, get in one of the War work factories, make some money."

"Wish I could do that. They're makin' real good wages. Women, too, payin' 'em the same as men on the production lines. Rosie the Riveter. I'm stuck right here until Piney gets back, and I don't see five cars a day. Sure wish

I could just stow away in your backseat."

"I can guess what Big Pine would do. I guess my head would be up on that wall next to the stuffed skunk." He got a whiff of a cold sourness from her like the gravelly soil under stones.

She laughed and gave him a look, but he slipped out from under it with a wink.

"Hey, Mrs. Sweetheart Pinetree." He made his voice soft. "Chance you could sell me a little extra gas? Awful short on coupons."

"Well, you stopped the right place, but it'll cost you double." Her voice hardened up, she seemed to turn into a kind of pot metal. He went out with her and leaned against the car while she filled the tank with gas. Out in the light he saw she wasn't much, just another penned-up woman who didn't know how to dig her way out, all grease and grits, but ready to give it away to anybody that came by. Her knuckles were skinned, her nails rimmed with black. She was surly now, too, feeling his intention to get going now that he had the gas.

"That will hold you." She shoved the yellow cat that had come twisting around her legs away with her foot, lofting it a few inches into the air. "Beat it, cat." She meant him, of course.

She didn't seem to know how good off she was, he thought. That she could be here, comfortable, running this place, eating big sandwiches, all the gas she could want, cheating on the gas, getting black market prices, cheating on Big Pinetree out there in the Pacific, touching his hand, she didn't know who the hell he was, and God, poor Billy, where was she? The woman didn't know how close she was coming.

"How about some kind of bonus for the one that's sellin' you the gas." She bunched up her mouth.

"Maybe we just ought to step back inside for that kind of bonus," he said, smiling like he was holding nails in his teeth, the oily metal taste of nails ran right to the back of his throat, and he could hardly wait to get the door slammed shut and locked.

His arms wrapped around the postcard rack for support and he fought for clear breath. He wasn't sure what was going on, but all of a sudden it was like digging a pit on the hottest day to pull a breath into his caved lungs. His pants were wadded around his boot tops. He could see the stained underwear and he wanted to haul them up, but he couldn't get a breath.

"That looks cute," she said from across the room, watching him retch for air. She walked toward him. "I said, that looks cute, you dirty chokin' bastard." She threw a sandwich plate in his direction. It hit the postcard rack and fell into his pants. He could see it between his ankles, see the hardened grease and a red tick of bacon, a white dirty plate. How had he got into this. How had he got into this. He didn't want her, he didn't want anything from her but the gas.

He dragged for a breath, kicked the plate onto the floor, got his pants up and wheezed in another breath. Something the hell wrong. A heart attack or something. He stumbled against the door. His hands were full of postcards. There was wind outside, and cold air, and if he was going to die he wanted to do it outside, not in here.

"Go ahead, get out," she said. "You're lucky. You're lucky I don't get down Piney's shotgun. If you're smart you'll be out of here and travelin' in about one minute or I'm going to get down Piney's shotgun." She was wading toward him. He twisted the lock and got the door open.

The parking lot was compressed by the black spruce across the road, stacked on itself as a scrap of paper folded smaller and smaller. His car waited pale against the trees, the chromed handle on the driver's door a silvery rod that, as he grasped it, connected him with the possibilities of distances. Wheezing and hauling for breath, he swung inside the car, it started, smooth as syrup, started and he backed across the gravel, out onto the lonely road past the waves of spruce and fir, the nicked driveways leading to dark, mosquito-stitched camps in the forest.

As he pulled out onto the road something moved near the woodpile. He thought it was a falling block, but it was the yellow cat, the same color as the fresh wood. They'd had a barn cat once, the same butterscotch fur. He remembered how it favored his mother, sat on the porch gazing up at her. She had called it Spotty and fed it cream. It made the mistake of rubbing against Mink's leg when his temper was up, shoveling manure out of the gutter and he'd broken its back with a swipe of the shovel.

In an hour he could breathe more easily. The front seat was strewn with postcards, seventy or eighty postcards all showing the same thick-bodied bear with a red snout coming out of the black trees. "Must be worth about eight dollars," he said aloud and took a cold pleasure in the minute gain.

4. What I See

The land levels as he comes down out of the trees and into miles of vineyards, the crooked branches crucified on wires. The Coach jars along a road knotted with tar patches, unraveled along the edges, the crumbling asphalt mixing with the gravel, weeds, rows of creosoted posts with winking reflectors, angled tops. But the land as monotonous as a lawn, and on he goes past the tourist cabins with their tiny porches and metal chairs, the gas pumps and whirligig ducks, the metal signs saying Nehi.

The sky grows. Yellow dirt roads cut away to the north and south. Plaster ducks on withered lawns, snapping flags in the wind coming down the flat rows. A dog races beside the car for a hundred feet.

In the steamy warmth of the Olympia Café he eats thick pancakes with Karo. The coffee is heavy with chicory. He leans his elbows on the counter watching the cook. A kid parks his Indian motorcycle and comes in. He pulls up his goggles, exposing white circles of skin.

"Dogs," he says to the cook. "Dogs gonna dump me yet. I hit one son of a bitch come out and went for my leg."

"That right." The cook presses the potato with his crusted spatula. "It better not a been my Irish setter, Rusty, just up the road here at my place."

"Might a been," says the kid. "No, no, I'm just kidding you. It was a black one about five mile back. Big son of a bitch. Size of a cow, damn near. It wasn't no

Irish setter."

In Pennsylvania the vineyards are spaced farther apart. The grapevines fade, cornfields swell up. The levelness of the land disturbs him with its easiness. The road is a slab seamed with asphalt ridges that strike the worn tires, jar his hands and shoulders, on and on. Cars turn off the highway onto side roads ahead of him, raise dusty billows. The radio is nothing but static and broken voices crying out a few words. "Jimmy Rodgers . . . pray to God . . . happy birthday . . . in the European theater . . . good-by folks . . . Pillsbury . . . organ inter . . . Duz does . . . the story of a . . . oh . . . hello folks . . . Jesus said . . . our listeners write in . . ."

He passes old trucks humping along on bald treads. He is worried about his own tires. He turns off onto a gravel road but the stones fly up, dust chokes him. Grit in his mouth. When he rubs his fingers against the ball of his thumb he feels hard grit. And turns back onto the concrete.

Miles of snow fence. A peregrine falcon balances on a forgotten hay bale. The flatness changes, the earth's color changes, darker, darker. Prayers and long silences out of the dusty radio. In the autumn rain the houses become trailers among the trees. Oaks come at him, flash, burst into thickets, into woods. H&C Café, EATS, AMOCO, GAS 3 MI. AHEAD. Fog. A little night fog. The soil in Indiana a deep brown-black. The cattle sink into its blackness. Southering geese spring up from the sloughs and ponds, scissor over him in the hundreds. The water is streaked with the fines of their angular necks, fractioned by dipping heads and beaks.

In the diner hunched over the cup of coffee he wonders how far he is going.

5. A Short, Sharp Shock

june 13, 1926

mister Sims, we have got the same problem agian with pole 18 on the ne-2o line, roce and me found another bear dead at the bottom of the pole, something is drawing them to this pole, can you put the engenero on it it, d. frye.

mr. albert sims
Wind Kink elec Cooprative
Wind Kink n.y.

THE bear, like many bears, had led a brief and vivid life. Born in the late winter of 1918 in a stump den, he was the oldest of two cubs. In personality he was quarrelsome and insensitive to the subtle implications of new things. He ate the remains of a poisoned eagle and nearly died. In his second autumn, from the height of a cliff, he saw his mother and sister backed against an angle in the rock by lean bear hounds. They went down in squalling that drew nothing but dry rifle fire. He was hunted himself the same year but escaped death and injury until 1922 when a coffin maker's charge of broken screws swept up from the shop floor smashed his upper left canine teeth, leaving him unbalanced in mind and with chronic abscesses.

The next summer McCurdy's Lodge, a massive structure of dovetailed spruce logs and carved cedar posts, opened on the eastern side of his range. The bear's sense of smell was sharpened by hunger. He came to the Lodge's garbage dump and its exotic peach peelings, buttered crusts and beef fat that melted in his hot throat. He began to lurk impatiently in the late afternoon trees for the cook's helper with his wheelbarrow of orange peel and moldy potatoes, celery stumps and chicken bones, trickles of sardine oil.

The helper was a lumber-camp cook learning the refinements of carriage trade cuisine. He saw the bear in the dusk and ran shouting up to the Lodge for a rifle. Hotelier McCurdy was in the kitchen talking *Tournedos forestière* with the cook and went to look at the bear for himself He saw something in the hulking shoulders, the doggy snout, and told the Lodge carpenters to build benches on the slope above the dump. They set the area off with a peeled sapling railing to mark the limits of approach. The bolder guests walked twittering through the birches to see the bear. They touched each other's shoulders and arms, their hands sprang protectively to their throats. The laughter was choked. The bear never looked up.

Through the summer the guests watched the bear flay the soft, fly-spangled garbage with his claws. The men wore walking suits or flannel bags and argyle pullovers, the women came in wrinkled linen tubes with sailor collars. They lifted their Kodaks, freezing the sheen of his fur, his polished claws. Oscar Untergans, a timber-lot surveyor who sold hundreds of nature shots to postcard printers photographed the bear at the summer dump.

Untergans came again and again, walking along the path behind the cook, picking up any fetid rinds or dull eggshells thrown from the jouncing wheelbarrow. Sometimes the bear was waiting. The cook pitched the garbage with a pointed spade. He hit the bear with rotted tomatoes, grapefruit halves like yellow skullcaps.

Two or three summers after Untergans snapped the bear's image they ran electric line to the Lodge. One evening the bear did not appear at the dump, nor was he seen in the following weeks and years. The Lodge burned on New Year's Eve of 1934. On a rainy May night in 1938 Oscar Untergans fell in his estranged wife's bathroom and died from a subdural haematoma. The postcard endured.

6. The Violet Shoe in the Ditch

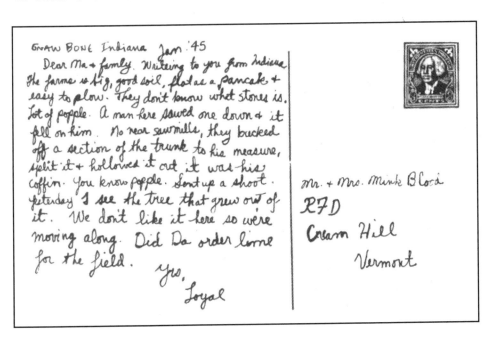

MERNELLE slogged down the steep road, the snow

53

packing into her boots. The dog plunged into her tracks, up and out, like a roller coaster. "You're knockin' yourself out for nothin'," she said. "Nobody's sendin' you no letters or postcards. No pen-pals for dumb dogs. I can guess what you'd write. Stuff like 'Dear Fido, Send me a cat. Wuf-wuf, Dog.' "

Later Mink would get out the snow roller that the town had sold him cheap when they went over to the snowplow and hitch it to the tractor. The roller was a slatted rolling pin of a thing that crushed the snow down into a smooth pack. After the roller went up and down the truck still couldn't make it, even with chains. In November, before the big snows came, Mink parked the truck at the bottom of the road. He hauled the forty-quart cream cans down every morning with the tractor.

"Leave the truck up here, we run the risk of bein' trapped for the winter. This way we got at least a chance if the place catches on fire or somebody gets hurt bad. Get down to the road, we got a ride." That was Jewell talking through Mink's mouth. Jewell was the one afraid of accidents and fire, had seen her father's barns burn down with the horses and cows inside. Had seen her oldest brother die after they pulled him out of the well, the rotten cover hidden by years of overgrown grass. She told the story in a certain way. Cleared her throat. Began with a silence. Her fingers interlaced, wrists balanced on her breasts and as she told her hands rocked a little.

"He was smashed up terrible. Every bone in him was broken. That well was forty foot down, and he pulled stone on top of hisself as he was falling, just hit a stone and it'd come right out. They had to move eighteen rocks off him, some of them weighed more than fifty pound, before they could get him out. Those stones come up one by one, real careful so they wouldn't jar no more loose. You could hear Marvin down there, 'unnnh, unnnh,' just didn't stop. Steever Batwine was the one went down in there to get him out. It was awful dangerous. The rest of the well could of caved in any minute. Steever liked Marvin. Marvin had did some work for him that summer, helped with the hayin', and Steever said he was a good hand. Well, he was a good hand, only twelve but already real strong. The rocks they were pulling up could of come loose from the sling and beaned Steever." Dub always laughed when she said "beaned."

"Marvin's the one you're named after," she said to Dub, "Marvin Sevins, so don't laugh.

"Then they put down a like little table with the legs pulled off it, put the table in the sling and lowered it down. The table only got halfway down when it stuck and they had to bring it back up and saw the end off before it could fit. Steever was down there expecting more rocks to come any minute. He picked up Marvin and laid him on the table. He screamed terrible when Steever gathered him up to put him on the table, then went back to moaning. Steever said the only thing holding him together was his skin, he was like a armful of kindling inside. When Marvin come out of the well on the little table all black and blue and covered with blood and dirt and his legs twisted like cornstalks my mother fainted. Just swooned right down and laid there in the dirt. The hens come pecking over by her and this one hen I always hated afterwords, just stepped in her hair and looked in her face like it was thinking about pecking her eye. I was only five or so, but

I knew that hen was a bad one and I got a little stick and took after it. So they brought Marvin into my mother and father's room and the hired man, he was just a young fellow from the Mason's place was the one that started to wash off the blood. He was real gentle about it, but he could hear this crackling like paper when he wiped off Marvin's forehead, and he seen it wasn't no use, so he put down the bloody washrag in the basin very soft and he went out. Took Marvin all night to die, but he never opened his eyes. He was unconscious. My mother never went into that room once. Just stayed out in the parlor fainting and crying by turns. I held that against her for years." And the mother's brutal selfishness of grief again thrown up like a billboard for everyone to see and shudder. Grandma Sevins.

Mernelle was sweating inside her woolen snowsuit when she reached the bottom of the hill. The town road was plowed and empty, the snow corrugated with patterns of tire treads and chains. The mailman's truck, an old Ford sedan with the back end sawed off and a plank bed and slatted sides added on, left a distinctive pattern. You could hear it coming a long way off, the loose links clacking and rattling. Mernelle could tell if the mailbox was empty, just the disappointing gnaw of hinges, when the tire tracks ran down the middle of the road without slewing in.

Usually she walked all the way down, anticipating something, maybe a mysterious buff envelope addressed to her father, and when he slit it open with his old caked penknife a green check for a million dollars would slide out onto the table.

There was mail. Loyal's *Farm Journal* that kept coming even though he was gone, a cattle auction flyer, a postcard for her mother that the Watkins man was coming the first week in February. At the bottom he'd scrawled "whether permiting." Another bear postcard for Jewell, written in Loyal's handwriting, so small it was a nuisance to read it. There was a postcard for her, the third piece of mail of her life. She counted them. The birthday card from Miss Sparks when Loyal was going out with her. The letter from Sergeant Frederick Hale Bottum. And this. She hadn't told her mother that Sergeant Frederick Hale Bottum wrote that she should send him a picture, a snapshot, he wrote, "in a cute two piece bathing suit if you got one but one piece is ok. I know your cute by your cute name. Write to me." She sent a bathing suit picture of her cousin Thelma rummaged from the tin box in the pantry where letters and photographs curled. Thelma was fourteen in the snapshot, her arms and legs like rakes. She squinted, looked Mongolian. The Atlantic Ocean was flat. It was a tan bathing suit, sewed at

Dear Mernelle, I saw your name and address on the penpal page and decided to write to you. I am a girl, 13, have red hair, blue eyes, 5ft. 3 in. tall weigh 105 lbs. My hobbies are collecting postcards of interesting places and writing poems. If we send each other postcards we will have a good collection. I will try to pick nice ones none with hotels or ha ha ballheaded men spanking fat ladies.
Your penpal (to be).

Juniata Calliota, Homa, Alabama

Mernelle Blood
RFD
Cream Hill, Vermont

home by Aunt Rose. When it was wet it sagged like old skin. In the photograph it was wet and sandy.

This postcard showed a white-columned building behind trees swathed in angry green moss. 'An Old Southern Mansion.'

Dog was running up and down the plowed road, digging his toenails in and racing for the bend, then turning on a dime, kicking up a spurt of snow in the tight circle and racing back to Mernelle again. His happiness matched up with her getting a postcard. His fur was yellow against the snow. The snowplow had cut the banks far back and leveled them off in two tiers, ready for February and March storms. The blade had pulled up thousands of sticks and leaves like pieces of bat wings. Dog raced off again, around the bend this time.

"You get back here. I'm goin' home. Milk truck'll run over you."

But she walked toward the bend herself for the pleasure of feeling the firm road underfoot after a mile and a half of wallowing. "Juniata Calliota Homa Alabama" she sang. Dog was rolling in the novelty of leaves, sweeping them with his gyrating tail. He looked at her.

"Come on," she said, slapping her thigh. "Let's go." When he ran willfully away from her in the direction of the village, she turned back without him, the mail in her coat pocket. She was almost to the culvert, the brook frozen inside, when he caught up with her. He had brought her something, but didn't want to give it up, like a child bringing a birthday present to a party. She wrestled it out of his wet jaws. It was a woman's shoe with a strap, a pale lilac color, stained and half full of leaves, the silk wet where Dog had mouthed it.

"Dog. Dog, look!" Mernelle made to throw the slipper, feinted. Dog's eyes got the deep hunting gleam. He stiffened, watched her hand with everything he had. She threw the slipper and he marked where it fell, then plunged into the snow for the prize. It took them all the way home and she threw it for the last time, up onto the milk house roof. And went in singing.

"How come he don't put no return address on these things," asked Jewell, turning the postcard over and frowning at the bear. "How does he expect us to answer him? How are we supposed to tell him anything that's went on?" Jewell asked Mink. This question could not be asked.

"Don't mention the son of a bitch's name to me. I don't want to hear from him." Mink jerked on his extra socks. His shoulders sloped in the stiff work shirt, the mark of the iron on the smooth sleeves. His hairy hands came out of the cuffs and grasped.

"You can send it to General Delivery of the place that's postmarked," said Dub.

"Chicago? Even I know that's too big a place to send General Delivery."

"You gonna gas all day or can we get on with the milkin'?" said Mink. His arms were in the barn coat, he slotted the buttons through the stretched holes. "I want to look over these cows, decide which ones we're goin' to sell to get down to where we can manage. If we can manage. Right now there's not enough money in the damn milk checks to do more than buy shoes and tractor gas." The feed cap, greasy bill tilted at the door.

Dub gave his foolish smile and thrust into barn boots. The laces trailed. He followed as close behind Mink as a dog.

In the barn sweet breath of cows, splattering shit, grass dust sifting down from the loft.

"Them cows has got to pay the taxes and the fire insurance. And your mother don't know it, but we are a long way behind in the mortgage department."

"What's new," said Dub, burying himself in the dark corner, wrenching the pump handle until the water shot out. Began to fill buckets. " 'Oh the farmer's life is a happy life.' " He sang the old Grange song with the usual cracked irony. Had anybody ever sung it another way?

7. When Your Hand Is Cut Off

February 7, 1945

Cosmi-Pro artificial upper limbs are the acme of quality. Specializing in cineplastic amputations.
• custom fit
• choice of natural-colored high impact plastic or lignum vitae wood
• available with articulated fingers or stainless hook
• comfortable figure-8 harness

Write for free color brochure today.

Miss Myrtle Higg
c/o Dr. J. Williams, M.D.
4 Bridge St.
Diamond, Vermont

DUB had his newspaper clipping, and for three years he'd kept it in a bureau drawer that would hardly open.

Marvin E. Blood of Vermont was injured after he jumped from a moving freight train entering Oakville, Ct. and slipped under a boxcar. He was taken to St. Mary's Hospital where his left arm was amputated above the elbow. Oakville Police Chief Percy Sledge said, "Men are bound to be injured if they ride the rods. This young man's strength should have gone to the War effort, but he has become a burden to his family and the community."

Mink and Jewell had to drive down to the hospital in Connecticut to get him. Mink stared at the empty sleeve of the donated corduroy jacket and said, "Twenty-four years old and look at you. Jesus Christ, you look like a hunderd miles of bad road. If you'd did your hellin' around up at home you wouldn't be in this mess."

Dub grinned. He'd grin at a funeral, Mink thought. "Gonna have somebody sew that onto my pajamas," Dub said. But it was no joke. And when Dub saw the package store on the street in Hartford he told Mink to pull over.

It was hard, opening the pint with just one hand. The cap seemed sweated on. He clenched the bottle between his knees, spit on his fingers and twisted until his fingers cramped. "Ma?" he said.

"I never opened a bottle of that poison for anybody in my life and I won't start now."

"Ma, I need you to do it. If you don't I'll prob'ly bite the top of the goddamn bottle off."

Jewell stared fixedly at the horizon, her hands folded hard into each other. They traveled another mile. Dub's breathing filled the car.

"God's sake!" shouted Mink, swerving over to the grassy verge. "God's sake, give me the damn thing." He bore down on the cap until it gave a crack and spun free. He passed it back to Dub. The smell of the whiskey flowed out, a heavy smell like roasted soil after a brush-fire. Jewell cranked her window partway open and for the two hundred miles north Dub said nothing about the air that chilled him until he shook and had to drink more whiskey to see straight.

They'd known he was a fool since he was a baby, but now they had the firsthand proof he was a cripple and a drunk, too.

It was a little easier, Dub thought, since they'd culled four of the cows, but they still didn't get done with the evening milking until six-thirty or later. Even if he skipped supper he still had to clean up and get the stink of the barn off him. No matter what he did, whether he took a bath, sliding under the grey water, or scrubbed his arms and neck with Fels Naptha until his skin burned, the rich mingle of manure, milk and animal came off him like heat when he danced with Myrt. But on Saturday night after the milking he cleaned up and took off for the Comet Roadhouse. Try and stop him.

It was cold. The truck wouldn't turn over until he set the hot teakettle on the battery for half an hour. He probably wouldn't be able to start it again at midnight when the Comet closed, but he didn't care now and a kind of impatient joy sent him skidding around the gravelly curves, running the intersection stop sign. He didn't see any lights coming. He rushed toward the Comet's warmth.

The parking strip was full by the time he got there. Over the roadhouse's roof the red neon comet and its hot letters glowed in the icy night. Ronnie Nipple's truck, with a load of wood in the back to give some traction on the hill, was parked at the far end of the row of cars and trucks. The snow squeaked as Dub cramped the tires and pulled up beside it. He could probably get a jump from Ronnie if he had to. Or Trimmer, if he was here. He looked down the row for Trimmer's woods truck but didn't see it. His breath gushed out, building up an edge of rime on the windshield where the heater air hadn't warmed it. He slammed the truck door, but the worn catch didn't hold and it bounced open again. "Fuck it, no time to fool around with that." He ran toward the door with its frosted glass and jingling bell, anxious to dive into the roar of sound he heard coming from inside.

The steamy, smoke-hot room sucked him in. The tables were jammed, the bar was a row of bent backs and shoulders. The jukebox glowed with colored bubbles, saxophones flaring, gurgling out of the bubbles. He threw himself toward the fire of wooden matches, the glint of beer bottles, the mean little half-moon smiles of emptying shot glasses. He stood on the bar rail and looked for Myrtle, looked for Trimmer.

"How the hell do you get it so hot in here," he shouted at Howard who was rushing back and forth behind. The bartender turned his long yellow face toward Dub. The sagging smoke-discolored skin seemed fastened in place by a pair of black metallic eyebrows. The mouth opened in a grimace of recognition. A wet tooth winked.

"Body heat!"

A man at the bar laughed. It was Jack Didion. His arm hugged the older woman next to him, wearing a long baggy dress printed with navy blue chevrons. She worked at Didion's, milked cows, wore men's overalls all week. Didion whispered something in the woman's ear and she threw back her head and roared. "Body heat! You said it!" Her broken fingernails were rimmed with black.

The colored bottles stood in a pyramid. After Howard's wife died he had taken the round mirror etched with blue-birds and apple blossoms from her dressing table and hung it on the wall behind the bottles so their number was doubled in richness and promise. Howard, too, was doubled as he passed back and forth, the back of his head reflected among the bottles.

The little stage at the end of the bar was dark, but the microphones were set up, there was the drum set. A cardboard sign on the easel—THE SUGAR TAPPERS in glitter-dust letters. Dub, gyring through the dancers, saw Myrtle at a table against the wall, leaning out into the throbbing light so she could watch the door. He came up behind her and put his cold hand on the back of her neck.

"My god! You could kill a person that way! What took you so long, as if I didn't know." Her brown hair was screwed into a chignon that had slipped its moorings and rode low on her neck. Her mouth was drawn with lipstick into a hard little crimson kiss. She wore her secretary suit with its ruffled blouse. Her small eyes were a clear teal blue fringed with sandy lashes. Her shallow face and flat chest made her look weak and vulnerable, and Dub enjoyed that illusion. He knew she was as tough as oak, a trim, tough little oak.

"What always takes me so long; milking, washing up, get the truck going, drive down here. We didn't get through the milking until late. Usually I don't care, but tonight I was goin' crazy tryin' to get out. He was just squeezin' slow, I guess. What a fuckin' hopeless mess."

"Did you tell him?"

"No, I didn't tell him. He'll go through the wall. Want to make sure the rifles are all locked up before I tell him. I thought he got a little mad when Loyal took off, but it'll really rattle his marbles when I drop the word we're getting hitched and moving out."

"It isn't going to get any easier the longer you put it off."

"There's a lot more to it than just telling him. I can't clear out until I know he's got a way to get out from under that farm. Sell it, is what I think he ought to do. Then *I* got to come up with some money. Some real money. It's o.k. for us to talk about moving off, about me taking the piano tuning course and all, but money is what makes it happen and I don't got any."

"It always comes down to money. That's what we always end up talking about. It never fails."

"It's the big problem. He don't say much, but I know damn well the mortgage and the taxes is way behind. He ought to sell but he's so damn stubborn he won't. I try to mention it he says 'I-was-born-on-this-farm,-I'll-die-on-this-farm,-farmin's-the-only-thing-I-know.' Hell, if I can learn piano tuning he could learn something different. Run a drill press or something. Want a beer? Fizzy drink? A martini?" His voice puffed, rich, comic.

"Oh, I might as well have a gin and ginger ale." She

pushed the chignon up and drove another hairpin into the slippery mass.

"The one I feel sorry for is Mernelle. She runs up there to her room cryin' because she don't have any decent clothes. She's grown out of everything. She had to wear one of Ma's dresses to school the other day. Come home bawlin'. I feel bad, but there's not a damn thing I can do about it. I know how she feels when the kids pick on you. Rotten little bastards."

"Poor kid. Listen, I got some dresses and a skirt and sweater she can have. A nice green cashmere sweater and a brown corduroy skirt."

"Honey, she's six inches taller than you and about twenty pounds skinnier. That's the problem. She's shot up wicked the last few months. Bean pole. Wish she could put the brakes on."

"We'll think of something. She can't wear Jewell's dresses to school, poor kid. By the way, I've got a surprise for you."

"Better be good."

"I think so." The inverted red prints of her lips mapped the rim of the glass. "Doctor Willy got a postcard from the Railway Express today. It's in."

"What's in?"

"You know. You know what I mean. What you were measured for." Her face washed red. She could not say it, not after two years as the doctor's secretary and appointment manager. Not after seven months of sitting with Dub in the farm truck that leaked mosquitoes, engine fumes, road water, and leg-paralyzing cold, kissing and planning a hundred escapes and futures and every one without a farm in it.

"Oh yeah, you must mean the fancy arm. The prosthesis. That what you mean?"

"Yes." She pushed the stained glass away from her. She could not stand to hear him breathe that way.

"Or is it a hook, big shiny, stainless steel hook? I forget. I only know my girlfriend Myrt says I gotta get one, but she can't say what it is I gotta get."

"Marvin. Don't do this to me," she said in a low voice.

"Don't do what? Say 'hook'? Say 'prosthesis'?" His voice rolled out across the dance floor. He saw Trimmer at the bar, saw Trimmer cross his eyes and draw his hand across his throat. All at once he felt better and began to laugh. He pulled the cigarette pack from his shirt pocket and shook out a cigarette. "Don't be embarrassed, honey, I hate to say it, too. 'Prosthesis.' Sounds like a nasty poison snake. *'He was bit by a prosthesis.'* That's how come I been so long without doing anything about it. Couldn't say it. Atta girl, big sweet smile for the mutt. I'll tell you, little girl, a couple months after it happened I hitched down to this place in Rhode Island where you can get fitted for something, the hook, I think, but I couldn't go in. I was too embarrassed to go in. I could see the girl sitting there at the desk, and I just couldn't go up to her and say—"

"Dub. How you doin'?" Big old Trimmer, beefy and wide, long johns sticking out of his filthy red-checkered shirt. He stank of gasoline and oil, of horse and BO and roll-yer-owns. He winked at Myrtle with his heavy eyelid and made a sound with his tongue, the same sound he made to his team of skid horses.

"Trimmer. How goes?"

"So goddamn good I can't stand it. Here I am lookin' for

some grief to tone down my joy and exuberance, and I look across the room and there the two of you sit, made to order, glarin' at each other. That's it, true love, I think, only a question of time before she throws him out the door on his ear. Dub, I wanna talk to you later, you got a minute."

A spot at each end of the stage went on, the beams pooling in the center, lighting up the dirty microphone cords, the blue drums. A man with receding hair and the devil's pointed teeth came out, dressed in a powder-blue jacket. He held a dented saxophone. Two other old men, the gimpy one with his Red Pearl accordion, the fat shuffler with a banjo, both in grimy powder-blue jackets, sidled onto the platform. They looked disgustedly toward the anteroom at the side of the stage. Smoke eddied. In a minute a teenaged boy wearing brown slacks and a yellow rayon shirt loped to the drum set, a cigarette still burning in the corner of his mouth. He rolled the snare for a hello and the saxophonist's hollow voice came out of the microphone. "Good evening, ladies and gents, welcome to the Comet Roadhouse. Gonna have some fun tonight. The Sugar Tappers for your dancing and listening enjoyment. Starting off now with 'The Too Late jump.' "

"Back in a couple of minutes, my boy. First Miss Myrt and I got to show the yokels how to do it."

Didion shouted as they walked onto the dance floor. "Watch out, sparks gonna fly now!" Howard came down to the end of the bar to watch. The drummer began with a barrage of hard, shattering sound, and one by one the men in the powder-blue jackets straggled after him, the saxophone hollow at first, but working up into a set of squeals and shrieks.

Myrtle and Dub stood hunched like herons, facing each other, only Dub's upheld hand moving, shaking, fluttering like a strip of cloth in a gale. With a Zulu leap he sprang at Myrtle, spun her under his arm until her skirt stood out like a dark cup, and began to snap her to and from him. Her patent leather shoes like ice. The other dancers stood away, giving them the floor. Dub kicked as hard as a horse. The bright sweat flew from his face. A rain of hairpins behind Myrt, the cascade of crimped hair tumbled loose, their feet thudded.

"Save yer peanut butter jars," screamed Trimmer.

"Deer meat! Deer meat!" Didion, with the highest accolade he knew.

When Dub came back to the table where Trimmer sat in a cloud of pipe smoke he carried the two-quart glass pitcher of beer. His sides heaved, runnels of sweat glistened in front of his ears, hung in bright drops under his chin. Myrtle leaned back in the chair, panting, her legs opened wide to let the cool air move up in under her skirt, her damp blouse unbuttoned as far as was decent. Dub first poured her a glass of the cold beer then drank thirstily from the pitcher. He set it down in the middle of the table and lit a cigarette for Myrtle, then for himself. Trimmer hauled his chair closer in to the table.

"That was some dancin'. I couldn't do that in a million years." He knocked the dottle out of his pipe into the ashtray. "Was gonna ask you if you thought you'd be up to runnin' Loyal's old trapline, or if you'd want some help. Fur prices are good. Specially fisher cat. Fox. Looks like you could run 'em down, reach over, turn 'em inside out while they're still movin'. Way you dance."

"It's just a different kind of thing. You lose your arm or something you feel good you can do something like that. Run Loyal's trapline? You don't know much about it, do you?"

"I know he made damn good money at it. I know he got some good fur and he didn't have to go up to the North Pole for it, neither. Fox. Awful nice fox he had last spring at the fur auction. Thick, fluffy. I mean nice. See him get up there in front of them all and spin around holdin' up them red furs, the tails'd all whirl out. Seems natural you'd want to keep it up."

"No," said Dub, drawling it out, "Trimmer, you don't begin to know about old Loyal's traps and trapline. I couldn't do what he done with the traps in a million years. I don't even know where the traps are."

"Shit, it couldn't be too tough to look for 'em, could it? Out in the hayloft, or up in the attic, the shed? I'll help you, smoke 'em, put out the sets. I'd give you a hand runnin' the line. You got to have a general idea where he set."

"What Loyal done with the trapping was not what you or me might do. He didn't hang 'em out in the shed and trust to a day in the smoke to get the human scent off like most of the guys around here. First, when he was a kid he learnt from that old critter used to live out in a bark shack in the swamp down below the place the ferns grows so big."

"Ostrich fern."

"Ostrich fern, yeah. Loyal'd hang around down there every chance he got after chores on Saturday, summer evenings when the milkin' was finished. Old Iris Penryn, half wild hisself. Loyal learnt all his trap-wise ways from old Iris, and he was sly about it, he was secret. You know how Loyal was—slip around, do things when nobody's looking. First, he has him a little shack on the brook where he keeps all his trap stuff, but not the traps. Just listen. You'll see what I mean.

"Loyal was real clever in layin' his sets. He was a god-damn genius with guide sticks, knew how to lay a stalk of hay or bend a goldenrod stem so the fox would step over it every time, right into the trap. Snow sets? He'd put 'em near a tuft of grass stickin' up out of the new ice along the river edge, see, the foxes go there to play on the new ice, or he'd make a trail set in the snow you couldn't tell anybody been walkin' there, or he'd lay a mound set near the edge of the woods where the ground's heaved up the way it does, a real smart crust set when the snow was hard, maybe two dozen more kinds of lays. You got to know your fox and you got to know your terrain. You got to have the trappin' instinct."

"O.k., I can see he was wicked smart about it, but it's not impossible you or me to do some of them things pretty good and get some fur."

"Nope. Tell you why. End of the season Loyal'd pick up his traps, bring them in to his shack. What he done, and I only remember part of it, he'd build up a fire in the yard, boil some water, scrape off and clean up all his traps, then scrub them down in the hot water with a brush he never used for nothin' else, and wearin' waxed gloves. Rubber's no good, even if you could get 'em. Then he takes a wire hook to pick up the traps and throws 'em in a big wash-boiler, never been used for anything else, dumps in lye and water and boils 'em for an hour. Takes the traps out'n the lye with his hook and throws 'em in the brook. Leaves 'em in the brook overnight." Dub held his hand up as Trimmer started to open his mouth. He drank from the pitcher, watching Myrtle twist and pin up her loosened hair.

"Next morning, here's old Loyal again, lookin' around over his shoulder, make sure nobody's spyin' on him. 'Course I did every chance I get. When I was little. Goes in the shack, builds a fire in the stove. Gets down this big bucket he never uses for nothin' else but this, fills it full of brook water upstream from where he's got the traps. Sets the bucket on the stove and puts in a pound of pure beeswax never been touched by hand, he takes the honeycake himself from out'n Ronnie Nipple's hives, puts it in the extractor, won't let Ronnie touch the wax, keeps the wax in a canvas bag been boiled and brook-soaked like the traps. When the wax is melted and foams up in the pail, he gets a trap outa the brook with his hook, brings it in and in she goes, into the bucket of wax and water for a couple of minutes, then out again with the hook and he carries it out to a birch tree at the edge of the woods and hangs it up there. He does the same thing with every damn trap. When them traps is dry and aired out good, he lays them up according to how he's goin' to use them next season. For his field traps, which is what most fox traps is, he lines a big hollow log he's got some-where with pulled-up grass. Never touches that grass or log with his hands, he's got another pair of special waxed gloves he keeps in a scent-free canvas roll, then he stuffs them traps up into the log on that grass and that's where they stay until he sets 'em out next season. He does the same thing with the traps he's gonna set in the woods, only he boils them in bark—and he's particular about what kind of bark he uses— and he keeps 'em under some ledge in the woods until the season. Then he's got all these scents and lures he makes himself, I don't know any of that. Trimmer, we are skunked right out of the barrel, even if I wanted to run his trapline, because I don't know where he hid his traps. And I don't want to go rustlin' through the woods jammin' my arms into empty logs lookin' for my brother's traps. He could do it, he liked it, he liked the careful part and the study of the set. I'd rather know how to tune pianos, do the job, get paid when you finish."

"Well, I'll be a son of a bitch," said Trimmer. "I still think I could get enough pelts to make some money. You tell me how else you gonna get enough set by to do what you and Myrt want to do?"

Dub swallowed the last of the beer. Myrtle was staring at him in a way he understood very well. She was asking the same question without saying a word. Dub had an answer for both of them.

"Way I see it, when a man don't know how to do anything else, he traps." He looked at Myrt. "You ready to jump on that floor again?"

An hour later Dana Swett, Myrtle's brother-in-law, came in, peering through the smoke until he saw her, then raising his right hand twice, fingers outstretched, showing ten minutes for him to have a beer, for Myrtle to finish up and get ready. She danced with Dub a last time, a slow one, sad, good-by War song, humming until the boy drummer began to pick up the beat, trying to jostle the old musicians into another hot flash, but they were cold, played out, ready to go out back and drink out of their flasks, smoke Luckies and yawn.

"Don't stay too late," she said. "Remember, you got to

milk in the morning. And come down Monday afternoon to the office. I'll put your name down so doctor knows you're coming."

"For you, O Flower of the Meadow, anything your little heart desires." He swept a low bow, danced her into the coat hall and pressed her deep into the wool-smelling coats, kissing, tasting the bitter tobacco on her tongue, the musky gin.

When Dub left the Comet the air was burning cold. The hard snow squealed. Even with his glow on he knew the truck was frozen solid. The door groaned on stiff hinges. Frost covered the windshield, the steering wheel. The seat was like a piece of bent sheet metal. He stepped on the clutch, shifted the lever toward neutral. It was like shifting a spoon in a pot of mush. He twisted the key and a short weak groan oozed from the starter.

"Son of a bitch, she won't even turn over." Ronnie'd gone an hour ago. He'd have to get a jump start from Trimmer. He turned back to the Comet, now hating the thought of the smoke and liquor stink, the collapsing jukebox music, and noticed that the red of the neon sign blurred into the red of the sky. Flutes of red light, the watery red of ripe watermelon, pulsated over his head. He could see the stars through the redness. Long green rods fanned out from the dome of the sky, the high cold air wavering, stuttering with the electric storm. Mink always claimed he could hear the northern lights crackle or make a sound like a distant wind. Dub opened the door.

"Hey, the northern lights is puttin' on a show."

"Shut the damn door. It's freezin'," Howard yelled.

He'd started drinking around eleven. Trimmer was lying across three chairs, spittle glinting at the side of his mouth.

Dub shut the door, looked at the quivering air, the snow in the parking lot stained red, the trees and river shining in the lurid night. If Loyal came walking into the parking lot now, he thought suddenly, he would beat him until the bloody water streamed from his ears and blackened the red snow. A pent rage at being stuck with it all rose in his throat like caustic vomit. What the hell. Might as well walk home, burn off the liquor, cool down. He could do it in two hours.

8. The Bat in the Wet Grass

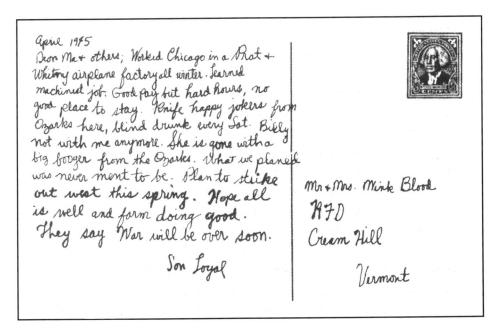

April 1945
Dear Ma + others; Worked Chicago in a Pratt + Whitney airplane factory all winter. Learned machinist job. Good pay but hard hours, no good place to stay. Knife happy jokers from Ozarks here, blind drunk every Sat. Billy not with me anymore. She is gone with a big booger from the Ozarks. What we planned was never ment to be. Plan to strike out west this spring. Hope all is well and farm doing good. They say War will be over soon.

Son Loyal

Mr + Mrs. Mink Blood
RFD
Cream Hill
Vermont

LOYAL crossed the Minnesota state line near Taylor's Falls, thinking he'd work his way up through the farm country toward the forests. He'd heard there was logging up in the Chippewa National Forest. The money might be poor but he had to get outdoors again. He couldn't bring himself down to hire onto a farm, but he had to get in the open air. Work his way across, maybe end up in Alaska in the fall, work the fish canneries, anything but the machine shops again, the men pulling down more money than they'd ever made in their lives, their women, too, but not ever getting enough of it after the depression years without work. That little weasel, Taggy Ledbetter from North Carolina, with his deep-kneed walk that made the cluster of keys on his belt bounce against his groin, socking money away. He lagged slyly at the job during the day so he could put in for overtime. He picked up other men in his car and drove them to the plant, collecting a dollar a week and gas ration coupons from each, stole tools and parts, paper clips, pencils, burrs, calipers, drill bits, slipping them into his pockets, inside his green work pants, under his belt, in his humpbacked lunch box. He made his wife and kids save everything that could be turned in for money, patched bicycle tire tubes, tinfoil, paper bags, nails, used oil, scrap metal, torn envelopes, old tires. Sold a little black market gasoline, pork from his backyard pigs. And kept it out of the banks. He bought house lots. Had a little after-hours repair shop in his backyard.

"Money's in the lots. Gonna be a lot of servicemen comin' back, lookin' to build. Lot of money changin' hands. I'm gittin' my share sure as dammit."

Tired of getting up in the stench of unwashed clothes and working through the day into darkness again in the stink of burned metal and rank oil, the work never slowing, churning around through three shifts like a bingo tumbler spinning the numbered wooden markers until it slows and a lucky number falls at random. On New Year's Eve he went to a bar. He went with Elton and Foote who worked the next stations on the line. The bar was jammed with drinkers. War workers with money burning holes, women in slippery rayon dresses, their rolled hair limp in invisible hairnets, powder between their breasts and the black-red lipstick that left soft prints of their lips on the beer glasses and the smell of cigarette smoke and dime-store "Evening in Paris" perfume from tiny blue bottles. When someone came in from the street a broadsword of frigid air cut the smoke.

Loyal pressed up to the bar with Elton and Foote, ordered beer. Elton, a lean hillbilly with crooked arms and a weak bladder was spit drunk in half an hour. Foote nursed a whiskey, staring straight ahead. Loyal found himself between Foote and a woman with a red patent leather belt cinching in her black dress. Her hair was a mass of black-purple curls heaped on her head. The neckline of the dress, shaped like the top of a knight's shield, presented the tops of her powdered breasts. She smoked Camels, one after another, gradually turning away from Loyal toward an unseen man on her left. Her back pressed against Loyal's arm. Gradually she shifted her hot taut buttocks until they came up against his thigh. He felt his prick hardening, bulging the front of his good trousers. It had been a long time. Slowly he began to maneuver his hand until it cupped her firm behind and she pressed it against his palm, wriggling until his index finger fitted the gully between her buttocks. Heat came off the sleek rayon. He slid his hand up and down and, with the suddenness of a falling beam, the choking spasm gripped him with terrible strength. He could not breathe. He threw himself backward into the wall of drinkers, bucking and tearing at his throat as if the hangman's rope cinched his neck. He smelled the char of a burning cigarette against cloth, the pressed tin ceiling with its remorseless design heaved, then fell on him.

When he came out of it he was on a table with a ring of faces staring down at him. The thinnest man pressed bony fingers on Loyal's wrist. The skeleton's hair, parted in the middle, was scraped back like a metallic cap. His teeth and eyes were rimmed with gold and there were gold rings on his fingers, a wedding ring and a signet ring on the little finger of the right hand. Loyal felt himself shaking and trembling with a thunderous heartbeat.

"You're lucky I was here. They'd have stacked you in the corner with the other drunks. Would have put your light out for good."

Loyal could not speak his jaw was trembling so hard. His arms shook, but he could breathe. He sat up, and the crowd, disappointed he was still alive, turned back to their glasses.

"It's Adrenalin that's making you shake. I gave you a shot of Adrenalin. You'll calm down in half an hour or so. You've had these attacks before, I take it."

"Not like this."

"Allergic reaction. Probably something you ate or drank. Tell you what. Make up a list of everything you've had to eat or drink in the last day and come see me the day after tomorrow."

But Loyal knew it wasn't anything he'd swallowed. It

was the touching. Touching the woman. If it wasn't Billy it wouldn't be anyone else. The price for getting away. No wife, no family, no children, no human comfort in the quotidian unfolding of his life; for him, restless shifting from one town to another, the narrow fences of solitary thought, the pitiful easement of masturbation, lopsided ideas and soliloquies so easily transmuted to crazy mouthings. Up there beside the wall some kind of black mucky channel that ran from his genitals to his soul had begun to erode.

A soft day, warm enough to grind down the window and get the smell of the country. The black fields stretched for miles, the furrows rising and falling like a calm sea. He thought about pulling into a place and asking if they needed a hand, but didn't think he could work on another man's farm, stand there with his hat in his hands asking to be a hired man. He passed a sawmill, tasting the spicy odor of new-sawn wood mixed with the musty smell of old sawdust piles. He smelled his own body on his clothes, even through the laundry soap and a day on the line, not rank, but familiar, the smell of tangled sheets on the bed at home, of his folded blue work shirts.

Corn and wheat farms spraddled out to the horizon, fields cut by white ruler roads edged with farms, everywhere the corners square, the partitioned earth hypnotic, the only relief in converging lines of perspective and distance and the angled flight of birds. Miles of cropland rolled between the rigid farmhouses. Far away he saw a tractor drawing multiple plows in black, contoured furrows as though the driver lay his pattern of curves and bends against the image of a sinuous river held in his mind.

The scale of the farms bothered him. The home place would be a joke to these birds, his twenty-acre field a turnaround space. As he drove he imagined the kind of place he half-planned to find and settle on, not like the home place with its steep rough fields and sour soil, its invading brush and trees, but not like these unrolled landscapes with their revolving skies. He hadn't known Minnesota was so level. But it was not a quiet landscape. The rise and fall of wind made the land seem to move in slow shudders.

His own place would be a small farm, maybe two hundred and fifty acres, gently swelling earth like the curve of hip and breast, good pasture. He saw his Holsteins grazing, up to their hocks in good grass. The soil would be crumbly and stoneless. There would be a stream with flat rich bottomland on each side for corn and hay crops, and a woodlot, say fifty acres of tall straight hardwood, a sugarbush, low-branched sweet trees on a south slope. On the height of his land he imagined a stand of evergreen, and in the dark spruce a spring welling up from the earth's pure underground water. Get a tractor, good machinery. He'd make it pay. His hands gripped the steering wheel, he looked in the rearview mirror seeing his steady eyes, the black springing hair. His strength pressured up in him, waiting to be used.

A few miles north of Rice he slowed down when he caught the hitchhiker's silhouette, flaring bell-bottom pants and jaunty cap. The sun baked the hood. He was feeling good moving out again after the greasy shop, in the mood for company. He pulled up. The echo of the engine's smooth beating sounded sweet to him. The sailor was a big, sandy-headed man, a potato face and needle eyes, his mood to talk entering the car before he did.

"You're a sight for sore eyes," said the man. "I been standin' here and shufflin' along and standin' some more for about two days. I Jesus Christ swear I got to look like trouble, must put the fear of the old Harry in drivers. Ain't this a nice spring day? Everybody picks up a serviceman, I get rides from Norfolk to here took me two days, three rides, but not in Minnesota! No sir, not here in my god-damn home state where Suspicious is everybody's middle name. Goddamn scandahoovians. One guy slowed down, come on the brake so's the gravel sprayed up a little, but the minute I put my hand on the door handle and he looked over at me he took off like there was a big prize for whoever got to Little Falls first, and he was in the back row."

"You headed for Little Falls?" asked Loyal.

"General direction, yes. Right on the spot, no. I'm goin' to pay a surprise visit to my better half, to my little missus up in Leaf River, north of Wadena. About four people live there, and when I'm around I'm one of 'em, milk cows, cut hay, fight with the neighbor. When I'm not around I want to know if anybody is takin' my place. Where I been I seen too many dear johns came slippin' in like the old knife and I got to thinkin', what about Kirsten, see I know about the scandahoovians 'cause I married one, I think, what about Kirsten and Jugo. Jugo lives the next farm down, we work together, hay, fence, help out, whatever you have to do, I got a broken harrow Jugo lends, he's got a hay rake the teeth fall out, he takes mine. So she writes to me, tells me Jugo's wife died around the end of March, nice woman, good-lookin', good full woman, I could of appreciated that. She was bit by a skunk, says the letter, tryin' to clean out behind the woodshed, died from rabies. Doctor couldn't do a thing for her. So I start thinkin', what's Jugo do when the axe handle breaks? He comes over and takes mine. What's Jugo do when he needs some twenty-penny nails? He comes over, sees if I got any. What's Jugo do when his wife passes on? Maybe he comes over and helps himself to mine since I'm not around. So I got a week's leave and only three days is left." He broke off the flood of words and pointed at a shambling figure on the shoulder of the road. "Hey, pick up that guy. He's o.k., I talked to him yesterday, and won't nobody pick him up until hell freezes sideways. He's a Indian, but he's o.k."

Loyal thought hitchhikers were coming out of the woodwork on the first warm day. He'd driven a thousand miles without seeing anybody thumbing, and here were two of them within a couple of miles.

"You know him?"

"Naw. He walked past me yesterday afternoon, stopped and talked for a while. He just got out of the Army. He's some kind of different, but he comes from right up the road here. He'll liven things up. That's the reason you pick up hitchers, right? Liven things up, tell a few stories, show you where they're tattooed sometimes." He winked at Loyal, the little left eye disappearing behind the fatty eyelid, the sticky lashes.

Loyal slowed as he came up to the man, looked at him in the rearview mirror. He saw black hair combed like Clark Gable's, a broad face with the skin tight over the cheekbones, a tweed jacket, dirty jeans and a pair of snakeskin boots.

"Looks more like a lawyer with that coat than a Indian to me," he said.

"Thanks." The Indian got into the backseat, nodded two or three times. His cheeks were smooth and he smelled of some spicy after-shave lotion. But there was an animal feeling in the car. The Indian's black eyes went to the sailor. "Heyo again," he said.

"Goes to show that you never know how things is goin' to turn out, Skies. This here good samaritan is anonymous so far."

"Loyal," he said. "Loyal Blood."

"Third Mate Donnie Weener," said the sailor, "and he's Blue Skies, no shit, that's his name."

"Skies for short," said the Indian. "Don't sing the song, please."

The thought occurred to Loyal for the first time that the pair might be in cahoots, close as a pair of nickels in a pocket, tight as two corks in a bottle, as single-purposed as a pencil sharpened at both ends. He didn't like the Indian sitting behind him in the backseat, didn't like the way sailor Weener had one arm over the back of the seat, and was half-turned toward him as if he was getting ready to grab the steering wheel. He pulled out onto the highway, steering north, but all the sweetness had gone out of the day from the minute the Indian got in.

The Indian said he was heading for the White Moon Reservation, fifty miles south of Cork Lake.

Weener said he would drive if Loyal wanted, but Loyal said no, he'd drive his own car. He kept the window open against the heat that began to shimmer up from the road.

"Damn nice farmland," said Loyal, looking over the richest soil in the world, a million years of decomposing grass layers, unrolled in earthy floors on each side of the road. The farms lay in great squares, each with its phalanx of windbreak trees sheltering the house.

"These fields is so level," said the Indian, "you can stand on your running board and see from one end to the other. But you oughta see it if the floods comes, if the river goes over the banks. Everything, it's like a mirage, houses, tractor sheds sticking out of the water, it's like the ocean, no place for the water to go but spread out. A little wind riffles it you see it move along for a mile."

"Must be some kind of mud," said Loyal.

"I known people fell in it and never get up."

"That's right," said Weener. "Drowned in mud, choked in mud, find you in the fall plowing like some old stick." He told jokes. The Indian sat quiet in the backseat, chain-smoking.

Late in the morning they could see thunderheads bunching up behind them in the southeast. Loyal pulled into a Texaco filling station in Little Falls around noon.

"Fill 'er up?" The attendant rubbed at the windshield with a dripping rag. His arms were too short to reach the center of the glass. His shirt pulled out of his pants, showing a hairy belly creased with grimy lines.

"Yeah. And check the oil and water."

Loyal paid him with a five but before he could pull back onto the highway the sailor told him to wait a minute, opened the door and got out.

"Tell you what," said Weener in a quick gabble, "I'm just gonna run over to that café and get some grub. We can save time, get some ham sandwiches and beer and eat it on the road. I'll get it. My contribution." He ran across the street and into a storefront café. Raised letters spelled out THE LONE EAGLE and below an eagle and an airplane were painted on the glass, flying toward a setting sun.

Loyal and the Indian waited for a few minutes at the pump. When a truck drove in behind them for gas Loyal parked on the street where Weener could see them when he came out. They sat in silence. After a while the Indian opened his suitcase and took out a notebook. His fingers flivelled the pages. He scribbled.

"What the hell is takin' him so long? He's been gettin' them sandwiches half an hour," muttered Loyal.

The Indian turned a page. "Gone. See him come out the side door right after he went in the front. Ducked up the street."

"You mean we're sittin' here and he's took off? Jesus Christ, why didn't you say something?"

"Thought you see him, too. Thought you had your reasons to sit here."

Loyal got out of the car and went across the street. He was inside the café before he thought about the keys in the ignition. He ran back outside, but the car was sitting there with the Indian in the backseat. He went into the café again. A thin man whose lips curved down on one side in an expression of distaste was slicing a cake behind the counter. His thick hair was parted low on the left, the rest of it heaped into a massive pompadour on top of his head. His great glassy eyes were of a blue so pale they seemed colorless. He gripped a serrated knife with a broken blade. There was a pyramid of sandwiches wrapped in cellophane under a glass dome, red stripes of ham, grey tuna.

"A sailor come in here fifteen, twenty minutes ago?" said Loyal, swiveling his head to look at the car and the Indian. "Big, heavyset fella. Named Weener."

"A sailor come in, don't know his goddamn name. Right out d'odder door. People takun a short cut. I put sign on door, NO EXIT, but it don't do no good. Still do it. Had enough. Like highway in here but nobody buy. Tonight I board a goddam t'ing up."

Loyal looked out the window. The Indian was sitting in the car. He decided to get rid of him as soon as he could.

"You give a guy a ride and he takes off. What the hell, give me two of them sandwiches. Give me one of the ham and a tuna."

"Ain't tuna. Chickun salad."

"Yeah. Give me one of each of them. Two pieces of cake. You got Dr. Pepper?" He'd feed the Indian, then get rid of him. No hard feelings that way.

The thin man wiped his hands on his apron and slowly laid the sandwiches in a white bag. He wrapped the slices of cake in waxed paper. He rang it up on an ornate old cash register that must have been in the café since Woodrow Wilson, Loyal thought.

"Come to one sevendy."

Loyal reached into his right pants pocket for his money and as he did he knew why sly sailor Weener had disappeared.

"The son of a bitch took my money. He fucking robbed me."

The thin man took the wrapped pieces of cake and the sandwiches out of the bag. He shrugged, not looking at

86

Loyal.

The Indian was still in the backseat, his head down, intent. Reading something.

On the sidewalk Loyal plunged his hands into all his pockets feeling again and again for the thick wad of money, most of the six hundred dollars he'd saved over the winter, the grubstake, the new start, his traveling money. It was gone. He got into the car, throwing himself back against the seat. The Indian looked up.

"You know what he done? The sailor? Picked my pocket. He got away with all my money. He must of got it right after I paid for the gas. I worked in a stinking factory all winter for that money."

After a minute the Indian said, "Never to keep more than a five spot in your pocket. Never keep all your money in one place."

"Oh, I ain't that dumb. He didn't get every penny. I got a hundred in my shoe, but he got all the rest. I could of lived a year on what he got away with." He looked up the street in the direction the Indian said Weener had taken. "Anyway, I know where to find him. He told me he's headed for his place in a little town up past Wadena, Leaf Falls. That's where his wife lives."

"Leaf River, you mean," said the Indian. "But he don't come from around here. Didn't you hear how he talked? Not from around here. He told me he's on his way to see his girlfriend in North Dakota. Said he had a letter she's been real sick, but he thinks she got knocked up so he's going to find out. He says."

"Thief and liar," said Loyal. "I bet you anything he's not in the Navy, either. Probably stole that sailor suit. Just a thieving, lying bum on the drift. Probably stole that sailor suit. If I find him he won't never tell another lie because I'll rip his tongue out. I'll take his brain out through his nose." He started the car and drove slowly up and down the streets of Little Falls, stopping and running into stores, the Black Hat Bar, the feed store, asking if anyone had seen the sailor. The Indian sat in the backseat, his index finger in the folded notebook. The heat was building up. The sidewalks slowly emptied, people drifting inside to cool shade, to sit on kitchen chairs and the old couches covered with pastel bedspreads.

The streets petered into empty dirt roads. At the end of a short lane they saw a sign LINDBERGH PARK. Loyal pulled in under the trees and shut the engine off. He leaned his head back and closed his eyes. His hands and feet were swollen. The sweat trickled down the sides of his face, from the hairline down in front of his ears. The wind stirred and stirred. In the aspen grove the trees swayed, hissing like heavy surf on sea stones. The Indian began to sing.

"You think this is funny?" shouted Loyal. "You think it's something to sing about to see a man robbed and trying to get his money back?"

"I'm singing The Friendly Song. It goes 'The sky loves to hear me.' I want, to be friendly with the sky. Look over there." He pointed to the southeast where the sky was a bruised blue with purple swellings like rotten spots in peaches. Loyal got out of the car. In a minute the Indian, singing under his breath, got out as well. The aspen leaves, green wet silk, tore loose from the trees. The Indian caught a cluster, rubbed the new leaves, as soft as the thinnest glove leather, between his thumb and forefinger.

The wind strengthened in logarithmic increments as they stood watching the sky. The clouds churned, their undersides studded with globes the color of melon flesh. A spatter of rain and branches hurled down, and something twisted in the wet grass with a doomed persistence. It was a bat, injured in some way, gnashing its needlelike teeth. Hail pelted the bat, stung their arms and rattled on the car roof like thrown gravel.

"See that," said the Indian, pointing. A monstrous snout dangled from the cloud. There was a howling roar. The yellow air choked them.

"Tornado," said the Indian. "The sky loves to hear me," he bawled. The snout swayed like a loose rope and came across the immense landscape toward them.

A setting moon as white as a new dime shone in Loyal's eyes. Enormous toasting forks loomed over him. He heard the cries of geese flying north. He thought he was on the farm, crushed under the stone wall and stretched out his hand to ask Billy to help him.

With the morning light people came. They lifted him in a blanket and laid him on a mattress in the back of a pickup truck. Someone put a paper bag on his chest. On the way to the hospital, the wind of passage beating coldly on his bare feet he began to move his right hand painfully. After a long time he brought it to his head and felt the wet pulpy mass. There was something in his left hand. Hard, smooth, like a blunt cow's horn. But he could not find the strength to bring it up where he could see it. The trees flared above like flames and the ocarina fell from his hand.

"A tornado can do freakish things," said the doctor. He leaned at Loyal. The close hair stubbled a head that resembled a truncated cone, ears like cupped hands. An ugly son of a bitch, yet the brown eyes behind cow's lashes were kind. "You hear about straws driven six inches into a burr oak and houses shifted two feet without breaking a teacup. In your case it seems to have taken your car and pulled off your shoes and stockings as neat as could be. You're lucky you weren't in that car. We'll probably never be sure exactly what injured you, but in a manner of speaking, you've been partially scalped."

There was no sign of the Indian.

9. What I See

Loyal, going along the roads, the shadows of white poplars like strips of silk in the wind; pale horses in the field drifting like leaves; a woman seen through a window, her apron slipping down over her head the hairnet emerging from the neckhole, the apron faded blue, legs purple mosquito bites no stockings runover shoes; the man in the yard nailing a sign onto a post; RABIT MEAT; a plank across Potato Creek; a swaybacked shed, the door held closed with a heavy chain, white crosses, windmills, silos, pigs, white poplars in the wind, the leaves streaming by as he drove. A fence. More fence. Miles and miles and miles of fence, barbwire fence. Three girls standing at the edge of the woods, their arms encircling masses of red trillium, the torn root bulbs dangling. Sigurd's Snakepit, OVER 100

LIVE SNAKE'S SEE THE GILA MONSTER 7 FT. ANACONDA COTTONMOUTH COACHWHIP BULL SNAKE'S RAT SNAKE, and old Sigurd in his long, long overalls and his leather coat standing, beckoning, calling, with a bull snake around his neck, his mouth flickering with promises. A Boston fern in the window. A sofa on the porch. A newspaper on the sofa. A man sleeping under a tractor in a black strip of shade. U.S. POST OFFICE. Take Home Kern's Bread. Black oak, shellbark hickory, shagbark hickory, black walnut, black maple, Kentucky coffee tree, highbush blackberry, Appalachian cherry, chinquapin oak, moss, winter grapes, creeping savin, white pine, a burial mound in the shape of a bird, white cedar, spruce, balsam, tamarack, prairie chickens. Seed clover. A cow lying in a sea of grass like a black Viking boat, a table with a white cloth under an apple tree and at the table a shirtless man with a mahogany face and soft white breasts.

In a diner the painted wooden tables, each place set with a paper napkin, the fork resting on the napkin, to the left a spoon and a knife and an empty water glass. The simple menu is held up by the salt and pepper shakers. Clouds shaped like anteater tongues, like hawk tails, like eraser bloom on a chalkboard, like vomited curds. The ray of the flashlight in the darkness. Wet boulders along a lakeshore.

10. The Lost Baby

August 1, 1945

Dear Mernelle. Bet you are surprised you know somebody in California! We just moved here yesterday. My father is working in the shipyards. My room is the fold-up couch in the living room. I have to keep my postcards under the couch. We couldn't take our cat Curly. He was too mad to ride in the car. My father said if we sent Curly to Japan the war would be over in three days. My mother is trying to get a job in the shipyard too. Oh well, a new school tomorrow.

Your adventuros penpal, Juniata.

Miss Mernelle Blood
RFD
Cream Hill
Vermont

MERNELLE had almost reached the blueberry swamp, had just come to the first bushes, smelling the sourness of the place, the sun drawing scent from the leathery leaves, from the blue dragonflies and her own mucky footprints, when she heard Jewell's voice calling, too faint to understand the words which sounded like "solo, solo," drawn out and mournful.

"What!" she shrieked, and listened. Only the faint "solo" floated back, in a long-drawn, hollow tone. It could not be her name. Her name, called from a distance, sounded like "burn now, burn now." She stepped into the blueberry bushes and picked a few. They were still tinged with purple and sour. She squinted at the sky remembering the dusky brass color it had taken in the eclipse a month ago, though the sun had stayed visible and white. She had been disappointed, had hoped for a black sky with a flaming corona burning a hole in the darkness of mid-morning. No such luck. The mournful call came again, and she stripped a handful of berries and leaves, chewed them as she climbed the hill back to the house and only spat them out at the fence.

She could see Jewell in the yard under the pin cherry tree, her white arms go up, hands raised to her mouth, calling, calling. When Mernelle came into her sight line she beckoned her to run.

"The War is over, President Truman's been on the radio and a baby is lost. Ronnie Nipple just come by for help. They want us to come help 'em look. It's his sister Doris's baby. And wouldn't you know Mink and Dub is down talking to Claunch about selling off some more of the cows. It makes me mad I can't drive. There sits the car and we have to walk right past it. Doris is visiting for a week, and this is the first day and look what happens. Seems they was all so tied up with listening to the radio tell about the Japs surrenderin' and people goin' hog-crazy wild, they're dancin' and screamin', so that nobody saw the little boy, he's just a toddler, little Rollo, you remember they brought him over one day last summer before he could walk, nobody saw him go outside. Ronnie, of course, blaming everybody, yelling at his sister, 'Why didn't you keep an eye on him.' They never did get along. So I told him we'd start walkin' when I got you out of the blueberries and he said if he saw us on his way back from Davis's he'd pick us up. Davis got a phone."

"Hooray, we don't have to collect fat any more, or tin cans and used clothes to take to church. But they probably won't need the milkweed pods any more, either."

"Guess so. And the gas rationin' ought to ease off right away, they say.

"It didn't sound like you were calling my name. It sounded like something else."

"I hollered 'Rollo.' Thought if he'd got this far he could be somewhere in the bushes. But I guess not."

"Ma, it's two miles." The strength of it took over the afternoon. Perhaps a baby had to be lost to end the War.

They walked through the August afternoon. The town truck had spread new gravel on the road a few days earlier and the loose stones and pebbles pressed painfully through their thin-soled shoes. Far away they could hear the hoots and blares of sirens, horns, bells, the booms of shotguns fired into the air from the farms along the ridge sounding like planks dropped on lumber piles.

"One thing they said on the radio was that sewing machines and buckets and scissors will be back in the stores pretty quick. Can't be quick enough for me. I'm sick of using those scissors with the broken blade, twists everything you try to cut." Bees mumbled through the goldenrod growing along the fence lines. With a rush of feet and rapid panting the dog caught up with them, trailing his rope.

"That miserable dog," said Jewell, "I thought I tied him up good." A sense of being too late hung in the dusty goldenrod. The steady grill of crickets burred in the gaping field. Grasses pointed like lances.

"He can help look for the baby. Like a bloodhound. I'll hold onto his rope." She thought about Rollo lost in the goldenrod, pushing at the stalks with weak baby hands, the air around him laced with bees, or deep in the gloomy woods the little face wet with hopeless tears, imagined the dog nosing along the leaf mold, then straining forward as he did when he picked up rabbit scent, pulling her after him, heroically finding the baby. She would carry him back to his mother through the snowstorm, the dog leaping up at her side to lick the baby's feet, and she would say "Well, you're lucky. Another hour and he'd be gone. The temperature's going down to zero," and Doris crying gratefully and Mrs. Nipple rummaging in her nest egg money and handing Mernelle ten dollars, saying, "My grandson's worth a million to me."

"I can't believe we are walking on these rocks when there is a perfectly good car sitting in our yard and I can't drive it. My lord it's hot. You better learn to drive a car Mernelle soon's you can so you don't get stuck on a farm. I wanted to learn years ago but your father said no, still won't have it, no, doesn't like the idea of his wife drivin' around. Besides, then we had that Ford that started with the crank, he said it was enough to break your arm to wind the starter up."

The lane to the Nipples' place was smooth and hard with a strip of thin grass up the middle. The maples threw a breathless shade. Old Toot Nipple had tapped the trees each March, but Ronnie didn't make syrup and said he'd cut them all down for firewood one of these days. In the winter when the ice storms broke big limbs down into the lane he swore he'd do it the next good day. And never did.

"Ma, say the counting thing, the way your grandfather used to count."

"Oh, that old thing. That was his way of counting sheep,

the old, old style of counting. He used to count the sheep out. See if I can remember it. Yan. Tyan. Tethera. Methera. Pimp. Sethera. Lethera. Hovera. Dovera. Dick. Yan-a-dick. Tyan-a-dick. Tethera-dick. Methera-dick. Bumfit. Yan-a-bumfit. Tyan-a-bumfit. Tethera-bumfit. Methera-bumfit. Giggot. There! That's as much as I ever knew. Up to twenty."

"Bumfit!" said Mernelle. "Bumfit." She started to laugh, as she always did. "Oh, bumfit!" She screamed with laughter.

"Wait," said Jewell, laughing herself, "wait. He said for ewes after the first shearing—'gimmer!' He called the runts 'pallies.' He said—"

"Gimmer! Bumfit!"

"And granny, that was his wife, mouth straight across like a nail, somebody give her a box of grapefruits once. She didn't know what they were. Never seen a grapefruit before. You know what she did with them?"

"Gave bumfit of 'em to the gimmers?"

"If you're going to be so smart, why, I won't say."

"Ma! Say it! What did she do with them?"

"She boiled 'em. Boiled 'em an hour, then brought them to the table on a platter, big pat of melted butter on top of each one. And don't you know they ate them grapefruit right up, all hot and buttery. Grandpa said, 'They'll never put the 'taties out of business.' "

The orchard and then the barn with its swaybacked and tilting front came in sight. Jewell panted on the rise. Out of the trees the road dust like flour, puffing up at each step. She stopped to catch her breath, looking up at the Nipples' fields. The chokecherries white with dust. The asters.

"Look how the juniper's come into that pasture," she said. "In only a couple of years. When I think how hard Loyal worked to keep it out of ours I just shudder. I suppose it'll move right in as fast as it can. Course now that the War's over, maybe we can find some help. Though it seems like the boys coming back don't want to work for another man. I guess they got enough of bossin' around. They all seem to want their own place. And I keep thinkin' Loyal won't take to it out west. I expect he'll come back pretty soon. Make the farm hum."

"I can hardly remember what he looks like. Tall. 'Use Wildroot Cream Oil Charlie' on his hair. Curly hair. He gave me piggyback rides when I was little. Remember when he gave me the blue doll dishes for my birthday?"

"Them doll dishes was from him and Dub both."

The west wall of Nipples' barn was dotted with thousands of flies and thousands more spun in circles and dipped down to the manure pile. The house stood to the southeast where it caught the winter sun in morning and stood in the barn's shadow in summer afternoons. As they came up the steps they could see through the screening Mrs. Nipple standing on the porch, rocking on her heels and crying into a dish towel. Her geranium collection, in empty lard tins and rusted-through enamel kettles, lined the edge of the porch. The radio, smashed on the ground, trailed its traitorous cord.

"We come to help you look," said Jewell, opening the screen door. The waxed linoleum gleamed like water. "Mernelle thought the dog might come in handy." The dog looked a fool, clawed at his fleas.

"Ronnie's gone up to Davis's to call up on their phone

for some help. Doris is lookin' in the barn again. First place we looked, but she says he loves the cows so much she thought that's where he'd be. He couldn't of got too far on them little legs of his. It was only a few minutes since we see him, and we was listenin' to the news about the War bein' over and everybody screamin' in New York, just standin' around the radio when Doris says all of a sudden, 'Where's Rollo?' " (Mrs. Nipple couldn't help telling it like a story.) "Well, her and me starts to lookin' upstairs, downstairs, in the pantry, down cellar, Ronnie still listenin' to the radio, then Doris sees the porch door is open and we look out there, then look in the barn. By this time Doris is real upset and she makes Ronnie go up to your place and the Davis's. It's been way over a hour now, and not a thread of that baby! I said to Ronnie, 'The time we're losin' because of not havin' no telephone. I want that telephone put in.' "

Mrs. Nipple found Rollo's sweater for the dog to smell. He took it in his mouth and shook it as though it were a game until Mernelle got it away and led him outside, holding the rope and saying "Where is he? Find the baby! Where is he? Fetch the baby!" The dog trotted around the corner of the house and lifted his leg to water down the stones edging Mrs. Nipple's flower beds.

"Get going," said Mernelle, but the dog sat down and stared at her with stupid eyes. "Find that baby or I'll grind you up," she hissed. The dog wagged his tail tentatively and looked in her face. "You dumb puke," she said and tied him to the porch steps rail. The dog thrust his nose under the steps and snuffled as though at rare perfume. Mernelle went down to the barn.

Doris was up in the hayloft saying, "Rollo, Mummie wants you sweetheart," though Mernelle didn't see how any baby could climb the slick, worn rungs of that steep ladder. She looked in all the dim cow stalls, seeing where Doris had scraped at the matted hay, under the table in the milk room, in the old harness room and the cobwebbed horse stalls with the names WAXY and PRINCE carved on the posts. Doris's footsteps overhead knocked from corners to shallow cupboards to the chute where the hay came down. Her black frenzy filled the barn. Mernelle went outside and looked in the manure pile. Rollo might have fallen into the mire and drowned in cow shit. She'd heard of it. Jewell knew of somebody it had happened to. She braced to see the blue, lolling head, the smeared arms. But there were only hens. From the manure pile she could see her mother and Mrs. Nipple in the uncut orchard, wading through the grass calling, "Rollo, Rollo," their voices heavy and sad.

When Ronnie's car, packed with men in work clothes, drove into the yard Doris ran out, crying, to tell them the baby was still lost. The men talked in low voices. After a while they spread out and began walking through the mown hayfield, heading up toward the spring in the woods, the spring just open water, ten feet across, white sand at the bottom bubbling with the icy water that pulsed up from underground. Doris, knowing suddenly about the water, ran after them.

Jewell and Mrs. Nipple came up from the trampled orchard, and Mernelle followed them into the summer kitchen with its screened windows and kerosene stove off the end of the porch. Their arms were streaked with welts from the saw-edged grass. Mrs. Nipple pumped them each a glass of water. A few drops fell in the iron sink, rubbed to a gloss with a few drops of kerosene on Mrs. Nipple's cleaning rag.

"I dunno," she said, looking out the window at Doris running behind the men, tripping and going down on her knee, scrabbling up on her feet again and floundering on. And Ronnie, turning to point angrily at her, shouting at her to keep away. As if knowledge was more dreadful. "How could he get that far away in just a few minutes?" A thin keening sound came from the water pump.

"Sometimes the little ones can surprise you," said Jewell. I can recall Dub gettin' down to the road while I was gathering eggs and he wasn't old enough to even walk. Crawled all the way, a whole mile. He's kept it up, too." The pump wailed with an eerie shriek.

"What in the world is that," said Mrs. Nipple, letting water tip out of her glass.

"Sounds like your pump, some kind of pump trouble."

"That pump's never made such a sound in its life," said Mrs. Nipple. "That's the baby, and he's down under the summer kitchen. Rollo, ROLLO," she bellowed into the pump mouth. And was answered by a gobbling howl.

Jewell sent Mernelle to run up and tell Doris and the men that they could hear the baby under the summer kitchen floor near the water pipe, but how should they get at him, tear up the floor? Mrs. Nipple was crouching under the sink calling encouragement and prying at the boards with a kitchen knife. She got up and stepped around to the pump end of the sink where the water pipe rose from below, where the boards under the curling linoleum were as soft as cheese. The pump handle's dull red curve was stamped LITTLE GIANT.

Jewell, watching Mernelle sprint up the hill toward the spring with a child's demonic strength, heard a thick crumpling sound and looked around. Mrs. Nipple was half gone, one leg sunk to the hip in the rotten floor, the other bent like a grasshopper's, the muscles folded tight. She hung onto the edge of the sink with one hand, the other clenching the knife. Frightful shrieks came from below.

"Pull me up, I'm standin' on him!" shouted Mrs. Nipple, but before Jewell could reach her, Mrs. Nipple, the pump and the sink descended on Rollo.

"The little son of a bitch is bruised up pretty bad but he'll make it," said Dub at the supper table. "You'd think he'd of been squashed flat with that load comin' down on him, but it seems like everything fell slow, settled, instead of fell, and the old lady sort of squatted as she landed, so he come out of it pretty good. The old lady's worse off than him. She got rusty nails in her like a pincushion. They tried to keep her in the hospital for a day or two, but she wouldn't have it."

"When I think how all that rot was layin' there under that proud housekeepin'," said Jewell. "There's a lesson in it." Her glasses, lenses spotted and dull, lay on the table. She rubbed at the bridge of her nose where the flesh-colored rests had pinched two red ovals.

"How'd he get under there, anyway?" asked Mernelle, remembering the crying and keening, Mrs. Nipple lying in the back of Ronnie's car with her bloody knees showing at the window, the baby howling in the front seat in Doris's lap and Ronnie shouting, "Get out of the way" as he skidded down the lane.

"Crawled under. They figure he went in under the porch steps, farther in under the porch to a narrow place where he couldn't get turned around, so, since nobody never learned him to crawl backwards, he had to keep goin' and the last stop on the line was the water pipe under the summer kitchen. Just remember Mernelle, always learn your babies to crawl backwards."

"Don't talk so smart about babies and crawlin'. I remember when you crawled all the way on down to the road through the mud, over a mile, and too dumb to come back," said Jewell.

"No," said Dub. "Too dumb to keep goin'."

11. Tickweed

Sept. 9, '45
Dear Neighbor, since the death of my mother I
have got out of farming and into Real Estate.
With our boys coming back from the war there
is a good market for farms. If you are
thinking about Selling your place why not
deal with a Neighbor who can get you the Best
Price? Call Nipple Real Estate at 4989 and
let's talk turkey.

Boxholder
RFD
Cream Hill, Vt.

RONNIE, red-eyed from the funeral, leaned over and put

the china dog in the center of the table as in a place of honor. The port-wine mark that stained his chin was deep in color, as though he'd rested it in a dish of crushed blackberries.

"When she see she was goin'," he said to Mernelle, mumbling through swollen lips, "she said she wanted you to have this. Said that your dog was on the right track sniffin' at the porch steps. It might of all turned out different if somebody had paid attention to that dog, she said." He pushed the dog again with his forefinger, then turned and went out to his car.

Loyal's alarm clock on the windowsill clacked. They all looked at the china dog. Its vapid face and impossible pink gloss accused. Mrs. Nipple, silently declaring, if only you had noticed what the dog was trying to show I'd be alive today and not buried in a closed casket because of blood poisoning that turned my face black.

"I doubt that dog was sniffin' anything but where some other dog pissed," said Mink. He patted Mernelle's hand twice, the first time she could remember an affectionate gesture from him since the time she was coming down with mumps and was too dizzy and feverish to walk and he carried her up the stairs to her bed. Jewell shoved the dog behind some empty jars in the pantry.

In the afternoon Mernelle walked over toward the Nipples' place. There was a field at the lower part of their farm where the old house had stood before it burned down. A few coreopsis had escaped from the flower garden and spread unchecked for thirty years until they covered three or four acres of poor land. Mrs. Nipple called it tickweed.

They were in bloom now, a billowing ocean of yellow panicles. Mernelle waded into the swashing field, a trail of bent stalks behind her. She stood nearly in the center, thinking of herself as a dot in the quivering yellow landscape, thinking of Mrs. Nipple who would never again ride past the tickweed, never again sit in the passenger seat next to Ronnie saying, "That's a harndsome sight."

Mernelle looked at the sky, a cloudless blue. She stared, and the blueness shook with purple dots. She could hear a vast, slow breathing. The sky.

"Mrs. Nipple is an angel," she said. She imagined a diaphanous sparkling angel rising from Mrs. Nipple's black underground corpse, but couldn't hold the image, and thought instead of the body dissolving into the earth, thought of the earth crawling with invisible hungry mites that devoured rotting bits, that cleaned the bones of dead animals, sucked the fire from consumed logs and the dew from the grass, all the effluvium of plants and animals, rock and rain. Where does it go, she thought, all those rivers of menstrual blood and the blood of wounds and injuries from the beginning of the world, imagining a deep, stiff lake of coagulated blood. To be killed by nail scratches! She ran at the coreopsis, tearing at their heads. She trampled the elusive, bending stems, broke and flung them, the roots sprayed soil. The maimed plants fell silently and merged again with the swaying mass.

12. Billy

> December 17, 1945
> Dear Wilma
> We have not heard a thing
> from Billy sence she left
> home. Not one word. Cant
> say we are too cut up. That
> blood wrote she went with
> somebody else. How sharper
> than a serpent's tooth.
> Hib is better. We are plan-
> ning to come down your way
> in about two weeks and
> will bring eggs. Bet you
> miss your chickens. Praying
> for you. Your sister in law
>   Irene

> Mrs. Wilma Handy
> 2 Court ST.
> Albany, New York

FROM a long way off Loyal thought of Billy, her stinging hail of kisses, her little shoes with the bows, her pointed fingernails and elbows, the knees coming up every time he tried to slide his hand down her belly to her fork, the way his cracked fingers snagged the rayon.

"No you don't. I'm not getting caught. I'm getting out of here and I'm going to be somebody. I'm not going to end up on your goddamn farm pouring slops to the pigs and looking a hundred years old before I'm forty with a big belly every year and kids all over the place. I'll go just so far with you, and then, if you want what I got, you come the rest of the way with me. Loyal, there's so much money out there you can't believe it. The money's just pouring down, all you have to do is stand in the right place with your hands out. And this ain't the right place, buster."

But for all the hard knees and elbows Billy gave off heat like a smoking griddle. The orange hair crackled with the warmth of her electricity when he smoothed it; her hands were always hot, even in winter, and when she wet her lips with her pointed tongue the slippery gleam shot straight down the chute of desire to his groin. She could have been the best in the world if she hadn't fought so hard against it.

Before Billy he had gone with the schoolteacher, May Sparks, big and arch-pelvised, almost the same color of orangey hair as Billy, but frizzed out over each ear in muffs. There was something about the ones with that reddish hair that got to him. Everybody thought he'd marry May. Thought of her flat drooping buttocks and the wide freckled breasts like saucers of cream scattered with droplets of honey. Easy to tumble as a rocking chair in the wind. Ready to rock, never a no from that generous mouth. They'd broken the front seat of the Coach with their bouncing. And like butter around Mink and Jewell, helping out with the dinner whenever she came over, showing how handy she'd be around the place, putting her arm around Mernelle and saying, "What's the capital of Nebraska?" and Mernelle with her head down, shy about the teacher transplanted from the blackboard to the Bloods' kitchen as if she were human with real thoughts and feelings, would say "Omaha," very softly, smelling the sweet powder on the teacher's skin.

He met Billy in front of Ott's house. Mink had told him to pick up Jewell after the card party. And never looked at May again, never answered the letters she sent, dodged the other way when he saw her in the village.

The wind had blown all week, sweeping the cold sunlight.

The yellow and purple leaves thrashed, though few fell. On the seventh day it calmed, and by noon of the Saturday card party the air was still, the sky scumbled over with clouds like folded cheesecloth through which a pallid light strained.

In the calm of dawn the leaves began to fall, and they fell on and on, all day. Leaves struck the branches of young saplings, slid and glided down the limbs and trunks. Leaves rattled leaves and knocked them loose, heavy stems pulling them down. They stuttered as they fell against branches, hit with light leathery smacks.

The first time he saw her. The clucking, sibilant leaves falling. Driving through the slow cascade toward his uncle's house.

"Go pick your mother up over to Ott's. Damn fool card party. And make it quick." Mink, shouting from the milk room. "Step on it."

Four cars empty under the trees, their wheels cramped in against the hill's slope. The downstairs house windows glowing, the barn still dark, but the sound of cowbells and Ott's boys' yoicking cries from a near pasture.

He coasted past the parked cars and drew up at the front of the line ahead of a blue Studebaker coupe. A woman leaned on the fender, smoking a cigarette, watching him come along. Even under the trees he saw everything, the pointed fox face, the smart georgette dress with the round white collar, the little jacket with puffed sleeves, a full mouth, lipstick almost black. He couldn't see her hair twined up under the gold lamé turban she wore. She had a strange glamour, like a magazine advertisement, strange and beautiful, standing there dressed all the hell up in front of Ott's tree with its dangling tire swing, the grass spattered with duck shit. He got out.

"I'll be darned," she said. "I'll be darned if it isn't Mr. Loyal Blood himself. I'll be darned."

He'd never seen her before.

"Bet you don't remember me. Bet you don't know who I am." The sharp little teeth flashed at him. She winked. "Think back to eighth grade picnic. At Bird in the Rock pond. The wild strawberries. A couple of us picked wild strawberries like they was goin' out of style. The one next to you picking strawberries—Beatrice Handy, that was me. From Bonnet Corners. I had a crush on you. But now I'm named Billy. Don't call me 'Bee-triss' if you want to stay healthy. I'd recognize you anywhere. There couldn't be two guys so good-lookin' around here."

He remembered the strawberries, Christ, he remembered the strawberries all right, the relief of getting away from the giggling screamers, strange kids from the other district schools, sneaking away from the picnic tables with their piles of paper plates held down by jars of mustard and piccalilli. He went into the birches just to get away, and found the field of red stars. He remembered he'd picked berries for a long time. Away from the others, thirteen years old, picking wild strawberries alone. Had he even eaten any hot dogs? He shook his head. In Ott's parlor window now there were the outstretched arms of women putting on their coats.

Billy dragged on her cigarette, her nails gleamed.

He shook a cigarette out of his own pack, lit it. "You didn't go to Cream Hill High School. I wouldn't have forgot you."

"Nope. We lived over in Albany near my aunt and uncle for two years. Albany, New York. Civilization. But we come back here when I was sixteen. I dropped out of school and went to work. Been earning my own keep ever since. I worked at Horace Pitts in Barre, at Meecham's in Montpelier, at Capitol Sundries, at Lacoste's Corsets, salesgirl at most of them, but assistant-assistant buyer at Lacoste's, then I worked at Bobby's Rare Steaks back in Barre, and La Fourchette, waitress. I worked for Mr. Stovel the lawyer in Montpelier doing secretarial stuff until last spring when Mr. Stovel tried doing some secretarial stuff himself and I quit. Last spring I started doing what I'm doing now, what I wanted to do since I was ten years old. Singing. I sing at a supper club. Where I'm going now after I pick up my mother and dump her back home. In case you think I go around dressed up like this all the time. Club 52. You ought to come over and hear me sing. Tell me what you think. I'll give you a hint. I'm pretty damn good and I'm going to get somewhere."

The lights went on in Ott's barn.

"You married yet Loyal? Probably got a half a dozen kids, huh?"

He wanted to make it a joke, say, "No, I been lucky so far," but he couldn't.

"No. You?"

"No. I almost was, but it didn't happen. I escaped in time."

And Jewell and Mrs. Nipple sailing down on them, waving to the knot of women on the porch, some still working their arms into coats, and calling good-by, good-by.

For some reason she had picked him.

Lying in the hospital bed he had to remember. At first he'd

looked through the Indian's book, and had not let himself think of home, but images of the farm like huge billboards along a nightmare highway came to him as he half-dozed, in and out of a painful sleep, and he could not turn off the road away from them.

He was hunting partridge and a snow squall came in. He'd been following up on a bird, flushing it far out again and again, and had gotten turned around. The spruce swallowed up the light. The snow obscured landmarks, whited out the hawk cliffs. He couldn't get his bearings, clutched the old gun with stiff hands.

At the edge of a strange swamp he made for the high ground, moving up through wild brambles, maples ten feet through and nearly dead but for the persistent top branches. The snow surged through the dead leaves. He got into a stream gully, then followed it upward toward the fading light and came against a barbwire fence, rusted and broken in places by deadfalls.

But it was Mink's fence work, the four strands, one more than anybody else used, the familiar flat-headed staples came from the barrel in the barn. A sense of his place, his home, flooded him. It was easy enough to follow the fence line. He recognized the far corner of the woodlot when he came to it, even in the half dark, and smelled the faint apple-wood smoke from the kitchen range half a mile away.

In the hospital bed he stood against the unseen landscape, the ozone smell of fresh snow on his wool jacket—the last light, and the smell of snow.

His blood, urine, feces and semen, the tears, strands of hair, vomit, flakes of skin, his infant and childhood teeth, the clippings of finger and toenails, all the effluvia of his body were in that soil, part of that place. The work of his hands had changed the shape of the land, the weirs in the steep ditch beside the lane, the ditch itself, the smooth fields were echoes of himself in the landscape, for the laborer's vision and strength persists after the labor is done. The air was charged with his exhalations. The deer he'd shot, the trapped fox, had died because of his intentions and commissions, and their absence in the landscape was his alteration.

And Billy.

The last time with Billy replayed like a cracked film jerking through a projector. An image vibrated, the trees in the woods above the field toppled endlessly in shivering light.

13. What I See

Jewell, in May, carrying the basket of wet laundry out through the kitchen, passes through the muddy entryway and into the yard. The clothesline is limp, knotted, there is the naked pole, the clothespin bag swinging like a wasps' nest.

She hangs the overalls and blue shirts, glances at her ruined hands, then at the worn scene, the same fields falling away, the fences, the scalloped mountains to the east, the same thing she has seen since she hung out her first wash here thirty years earlier. In the pin cherry tree birds crawl along the branches, washing themselves with the wet leaves. The rain has darkened the barn to a molasses color; some tools lean against the wall of the milk house. The window is filthy with cobwebs and chaff. Crows bray through the woods pulling fledgings from their nests. She thinks again of the elderly piano teacher in Bellows Falls who has drowned herself in a hotel bathtub after weighting her body with encyclopedias and jamming her arms into a belt around her chest.

Dub and Mink drive the cows, Dub, ragged clothes flapping, slides back the poles that fence the cowyard from the pastures, Mink switches at the dung-caked flanks with his brass curtain rod. He bends slowly, picks up the rod he has dropped in the mire, and turns back into the barn. His leg drags. Just pingling along, she thinks. A clothespin breaks as she forces it onto the black denim and the patches stand out like new-plowed fields.

PART TWO

14. Down in the Mary Mugg

SEPTEMBER , 1951

JACK, COUPLE INTERESTING CASES HERE TIE IN W. YR. IMMERSION FOOT STUDY. MARY MUGG MINE COLLAPSED. 3 MEN TRAPPED A WK. KNEEDEEP WATER. 2 SURVIVORS. BETTER COME TAKE A LOOK. WE CN. PUT YOU UP.

T. VEERY, M.D.

JAMES R. WEMP, M.D.
HYPOTHERMIA RESEARCH
JOHNS HOPKINS UNIVERSITY
BALTIMORE MARYLAND

CLIMBING the back trail in his automaton's stride, Loyal

rolled the mountain air through his mouth. The taste of it was a little like the ozone smell that came after a lightning strike. It flared in his lungs, started his morning cough, and he hawked up stone dust.

He heard the jingling sound of Berg's mule up at the mine entrance. To the west the summit ridge of Copper Peak fired with red light. The timbers of an old ore tram support reflected violet and rose. The rock blazed orange, splayed black, cut like a deck of cards.

Berg could drive up in his truck if he wanted but he rode the mule, had named it Pearlette after his oldest daughter. Every time he said "Pearlette" Loyal wondered about the little daughter, imagined her as thin and sad, her reddish hair in braids, staring from an attic window onto the road that rolled away to the Mary Mugg. Did the kid mind sharing her name with a mule?

Deveaux, the shift boss, was up at the mine entrance too, squatting off to the side, making a pannikin of coffee. He could get a paper cup of coffee from the canteen, but he liked to do it this way. Showing off his gritty uranium days after the War when he wandered around the Colorado Plateau with a Geiger counter strapped to his back. He let the grounds settle, then drank it black from the pan, soot smearing his mouth, and, as he wiped it away, griming into his pasty skin and yellow beard. With his short neck and hunched shoulders there was something of the vole in Deveaux.

"I come back to the Mary Mugg," he told them in his peculiar voice that was both sweet and grainy, like the meat of a pear, "as a relief from them red mudstone beds up on the Plateau, a relief from them headphones. I hear that click-click-click in my sleep." He'd returned an earth-colored man, not the miner's wormy white. He was an old hand, had worked the Mary Mugg through the dirty thirties. When Roosevelt closed down the gold mines during the War Deveaux had gone into the Army as an explosives specialist. The mine opened again in 1948 but by then he was strapped into his Geiger counter, sleeping out uneasily with the coyotes, dreaming of the cool silences underground and the way the bed squeaked when his wife rolled over.

As compact as a jackknife, he'd been dulled by his miner's life. "I spent so many years underground, Jesus Christ, off and on since I was seventeen, I felt like I was peeled down to the meat up on the Plateau. Mrs. Dawlwoody thinks I come back to do her a favor, but I swear to Christ I'd work for nothing, get out from under that sky. I seen red spots in front of my eyes all day long, squint, old eyes start to water and tear. Too bright, too hot, everything watching you. The wind never lets up, like a kid pullin' at your sleeve all day, 'Daddy, buy me some candy.' That's what I hated about farming. I tried that five years. You set out there all day on the tractor or stringing fence and the wind throws trash in your face, whips your hair in your eyes, knocks your hat into the next county and laughs to see you run for it." He put his head down, murmured at his knees, "It's not so bad in the mines. And I missed the old lady. Least I can go home on weekends, sleep comfortable instead of down in the dirt."

Mrs. Dawlwoody's maiden name had been Mary Mugg. Limp and elderly, with cold waves of white hair rolling over her ears, she came to the mine each Friday to sit in proprietorial stateliness behind the paymaster as he handed out the checks. Her husband, DeWitt Dawlwoody, was killed before the War in a car accident in Pough-keepsie, New York. He was on a money-raising visit to his cousin, the manufacturer of Kronos time-clocks. The mine needed new machinery. Mrs. Dawlwoody believed the hand of God would show the truth about new machinery. Just before an afternoon storm she had Deveaux set out two pumps on Copper Peak, one an ancient hand pump with tandem iron handles, the other a new electric C. J. Brully. Let God speak whether we get new machinery, she said. Yet lightning struck neither pump for a month. At last Deveaux nailed each pump to a post set in the rocks, and then blasted the old one with a little dynamite. Showing the need for new electric pumps. But by then Mrs. Dawlwoody knew it was a stupid game.

The Mary Mugg was a hard-rock mine. An ancient stamp mill broke the low-grade ore, and the conveyor belt dragged it into the sheds where they separated the gold from the glassy rock fragments. Much gold escaped the stamp mills. The big mines had all gone over to the new ball and rod mills. The Mary Mugg wasn't the kind of mine where high-paid Cousin Jacks worked; those stone-headed Cornishmen were all up in South Dakota at the Homestake, talking the gold out of the rock with their white sunless mouths, bending other miners to their will, making them thrash the metal out of the stone no matter if it drew blood, or they were up in Michigan at the Ana-conda, battering the copper loose with their flinty rutting. Coal for hearts, granite for fists, silver-tongued and liked to see blood. None worked at Mary Mugg. They were expensive labor.

The Mugg was a little operation that attracted outlaws and cripples; 30 percent waste, gold *and* men, Deveaux said. But you never could tell what they might hit, never could tell who'd end up a millionaire governor. That was the trouble, said Berg when Deveaux was out of hearing; they did know. The little Mary Mugg was a cripple herself.

Berg tied Pearlette to a pine and emptied the water bags into her pan. He looked past Loyal without speaking. There was something brutal about Berg though he treated the mule gently and hummed. He had a pale mustache, like two withered beech leaves hanging from his nostrils. The pan had done double service all summer. He used it to wash in before he went down the trail in the evening. Loyal was damned if he'd want to wash up in mule slobber, but Berg had to have his scrub-up. For a man who'd farmed he was fastidious. He claimed his freckled skin plagued him after a day in the stone. Once, on a clear February afternoon with the daylight getting longer, he'd come out at the end of the shift and built a fire on a pile of rocks, then, when the fire was down he raked the coals out and propped up his poles, covered them with a couple of canvas tarps from the mule's lean-to. The length of his naked legs and arms suggested locomotive drive shafts. They'd watched him burst out of his jury-rigged sauna into the dusk, a luminous pillar of mule-scented steam around him. He got down and rolled in the dry snow until he was as frosted as a sugar doughnut.

"That's the scandahoovian for you," said Deveaux.

Jugging engine sounds bounced back and forth between Copper Peak and the rock face under the Mary Mugg.

Trucks and cars jerked up the grade from Lemon. The turnaround and the parking lot were a hundred feet lower than the mine entrance. Boots clattered on the path, there was a laugh, the sound of coughing and spitting. First their hats showed, then their heads and shoulders, bobbing as they climbed. Loyal could see the shining track of blood already running from Cucumber's thick nostrils, see the hand holding the blood-stiff staunching rag rise and dab. Nobody could say his unpronounceable foreign name. Cucumber was close enough. Deveaux dropped his cigarette butt, stubbed it with his little shoe, but the smoke still rose upward.

"Think he'd find some other kind of work if he can't stand the altitude," said Deveaux. "Sick of looking at that red snot." He said it where Berg couldn't hear him, dumping his coffee grounds, and wiped the inside of the pot with a wad of grass. He pitched his voice up. "Guys on day's pay, up in the Red Suspenders. Contract guys know where they're working."

Berg and Cucumber had worked contract together for two years. Loyal was the new man, come to them from the hourly wage mucking crew. He'd talked to Deveaux.

"I need a chance to make more money than I'm makin'. Savin' up for a farm. Put me in with some contract guys, o.k.?" Could not keep the insolence out of his voice. Letting Deveaux know the Mary Mugg might be here today but gone tomorrow.

"I don't know. Those guys choose themselves up pretty much. Anyway, you oughta do all right on what you make—no kids or wife." But he'd said something and Berg had nodded.

Berg would talk weather and land and season from his wheat-farm days, telling it all to buffalo-shouldered Cucumber, and the crabbed Friesian would mumble and stumble on about boats and kids and home. He had a bifid thumb, a great wide thing with two dirty nails crowding each other. Silence for Loyal.

Cucumber's wife rarely gave him enough food to satisfy his incessant hunger. He ate slabs of pork, biscuits, wedges of cheese, then stared hungrily at their sandwiches in the humpbacked lunch boxes, swallowed and licked his mouth like a dog at a picnic. Loyal gave him one of the oatmeal cookies he bought from Dave at the boarding house, Old Dave the accordion and harmonica salesman, who'd done all right, until he got gold fever and took up prospecting. A drunk fall ended in a broken pelvis.

"What else to do on Sadday night but fall down and break your ass?" he demanded. The bones had welded back together stiff as metal so that he walked like a trick dog on its hind legs. He'd cook at the Lemon boarding house for the rest of his life. He put piñon nuts in the cookies. "An acquired taste like yer lah-di-dah stuffed olives and caviar."

A few days later Loyal found the cookie on a shelf of stone in the face of the stope. He told himself that Cucumber had laid it there and forgotten it, but remembered some mumbled laughter between Cucumber and Berg on the way out, and a bitter name swelled in his throat. Not good enough for him! The damn foreigner.

Cucumber had a sockful of strange ways. On the way down to Lemon at the end of the shift they'd pull in at Ullman's Post for beer to sluice the rock dust.

"Pick me a Red Fox," Cucumber mumbled in an off-hand voice to the backs climbing out of the car, keeping his money in his pockets with his hands. Somebody would bring one back. And Cucumber would take the beer, rest the cap on the edge of the window frame and knock it off with the heel of his thick hand, drink it in two swallows and sit, looking unfinished, holding the empty bottle between his thighs. Other times he'd charge out of the car and run in, pulling at both pockets, and come back lugging a case of bottles.

"Take it. Take it! Don't insult me, say no!"

And Loyal had seen him fight a man who wouldn't drink.

Down in the stope the mine floor was damp, the rucked dust tracked with footprints. The rock walls glistened. Their clothes, worn cotton denim, hung in weak folds. They listened to the faint creaking of the timber supports. The ventilator snored. Berg began to bar down, prying off loose ceiling rock that might hang overhead after yesterday's blasting. The muckers had hauled out the ore on the second shift. As he worked, small chunks of rock showered onto the rubble, then a big slab, two hundred pounds of rock, smashed down, thrashing dust.

"Jesus, that give you a godalmighty headache," Berg laughed and kept prying. The rock creaked.

"That, that damn rock's the main reason you want to work with a Cousin Jack," said Berg to Cucumber for the hundredth time. "They understand the ore, the rock, like it was talking to them. And when they say she's not right, you better listen, because they know. I worked with this guy, Powys, in the Two Birds up in Michigan. Copper mine. My first job after I lost the farm. 1936. Wet, dirty, didn't pay nothing, dangerous as hell. Powys was smart. I don't know what he was doing in the mines. He could of been anything. Come from Cornwall. He'd quote old Shakespeare, poems. Said he'd mined since he was old enough to put his pants on by himself. Funny about them guys, how smart some of 'em are, read Latin, talk philosophy and still they go down in the mines long as they last. Oh, we was in there, drilling, you know, and there come this little cricking sound like somebody was tearing cardboard, nothing you'd pay any attention to. Powys yells, he yells—"

"Berg, I hear this two, three hundred times. This the one he gets away by big farts? Or the one he holds up the roof with one hand and picks his nose with the other?"

"Yeah," said Berg. "Well, let's make some money. We got to push it today." Light from the yellow headlamp twiching over the rock. Loyal wore his respirator for a little while, but the awkward thing, like a rubber snout, got in his way and he let it dangle around his neck. What the hell, two guys working together, one would wear his mask every day and still get silicosis, the other never bothered and was fine. He'd seen it.

The familiar smell of wet rock, the metal taste of the charged air, the burr of the drill, the rows of deep holes extending along the rock face blurred into dim, chilled hours. Loyal looked over at Berg. Even in the mushroom-colored cone of the miner's light he could see Berg talking to himself again. Berg had quarter-turned ideas. He believed dead miners came back from hell to the mines where they'd died, and loitered just out of sight in their faded, mangled bodies, and that sometime, if he whirled, he would catch a glimpse of some old rock rat out of the flames on a day's excursion, posturing behind his back and pointing ironically in the direction of riches. He did that, sometimes, jump and whirl.

"Goin' pretty good?" Loyal asked. They'd answer if he spoke first.

"Well, lot of holes, anyhow. We'll see tomorrow after it comes down. They ought to regrade this rock pretty soon, next week, maybe. The stuff we been seeing, I'd say they ought to grade us up to high B."

"I was thinking of quitting this in a couple of months," said Loyal. "Maybe try what Deveaux was doing, the uranium stuff. I got to get back outside bad as he wanted to get into the mine again. I get a feeling down here in the everlasting Christly dark."

"Something to that. Guys used to spend time outdoors, trapping or in the woods, they never feel good in the mines. You're lucky you got no family. It's kids keep you in the mine. I always thought I'd hit it, tap some sweet vein, but everything pinched out on me and here I am for life, prob'ly, working in the mines. Hey, Cucumber, Deveaux ever tell you why he quit uranium prospecting?"

Berg gave in too easy, thought Loyal.

Cucumber gobbled in his lumpy accent. "Heard it two ways. Heard he didn't like country. New Mexico, Colorado, Monument Valley, Arizona, Utah. The stuff in the sandstones."

"Carnotite. Christ, there's guys made millions." Loyal loved thinking about it, the search, the lucky strike, do what you want with the rest of your life. "How about Vernon Pick a couple of years ago? Nine million."

Berg knew something. "Deveaux found a petrified log. It was almost pure carnotite. He made over thirteen thousand on just that one."

"Even if you don't hit a big one. The government says they'll guarantee a fixed price until 1962. There's ore-buying stations all the hell over the place. Christ, there's bonuses, they'll practically stake you, give you all the help in the world."

"I was to make that kind of money I'd go up the northwest coast, buy me a boat and fish. Big sea salmon." A flickering of longing, a much-kinked wire in his talk.

Cucumber gave his pumping laugh. "You in boat? Only one kind of boat for you, Berg. Rowboat. Rowboat in harbor."

"What the hell do you know about it?"

"Know boats good. Born on the boats. Born on Spiekeroog. You don't know this place. Fishing boats. I worked passenger liners. Before the War."

"Bet you worked the *Titanic*, didn't you? God, I'd ride a case of dynamite down the Yellowstone before I'd ride on a boat that you was steering, Cucumber."

"What'd Deveaux do with his money? The son of a bitch was rich," said Loyal. Furiously. The drill bucked and chewed on stone, spit dust.

"Different stories. One thing I heard, heard he give it to Mrs. Dawlwoody, bought into the Mary Mugg. I also heard he lost it all in one hour in a blackjack game in Las Vegas. Cucumber, you ever been to them casinos?"

"Hell, no. I got trouble makin' it, never mind lookin' for

ways to throw it out." He went into a long coughing spell. There was a light patter of rock flakes somewhere behind them.

"No good," said Cucumber. "Wasn't barred down good. She don't flake off when she's barred down good." He tapped very lightly on the roof with a bar.

"She's barred down," said Berg. "Hey, why the hell did you ever leave Squeaky-Gut or whatever the hell it is?"

"Island. Island in North Sea. I work on boats, o.k.? Do it for years. Happy. One day I go by fortune teller in Oslo, what they call a dukker. She say, 'You die by water.' She know those things. So I come America, work in the mines."

"You believe that shit?"

"Yeah, Berg, believe it. This dukker tell this guy worked on the ship, 'Watch out for wine.' He laugh. He don't drink only water, tea, coffee. In Palermo they loading, Jesus, falls on him a crate. This crate full of wine. You bet believe it." But did not tell deeper reasons.

"Dinner whistle," said Berg, imitating the hoarse shriek of a factory whistle. They sat together under Berg's wall. He could imitate the mule, horses, any model of car at any speed when he felt like it.

"Hey, what's the government pay for uranium, anyway?"

"Heard the guaranteed maximum is seven dollars twenty-five cents a pound. How many pounds per ton depends on the strike. There's an average of four pounds to the ton. There's a rich Canadian strike paid out eighty pounds. I got a article in a magazine, *Argosy*, you want to look at it." Loyal shined the light over the ranks of holes drilled twelve feet into the rock.

"Goin' pretty good. Guess Berg'll get his rowboat."

"Yeah, and you get your farm. If you're still crazy enough to want one."

"I just want a little place I can work myself."

"No such animal," said Berg, opening his lunch box and taking out the thermos. As he unscrewed the threaded cup they felt the floor heave beneath them, followed by a roar as the tunnel leapt into itself The floor bucked. There was the choking dust and the tinkle of Berg's thermos cup hitting the rock.

Cucumber's headlamp smashed against the wall and went out. Loyal lay on his back, dust and rock flake raining onto him. Berg was swearing, his light swinging from side to side as he looked around. An icy coldness seized Loyal and he wondered if his spine was snapped; he'd heard there wasn't much pain with a broken back; you went cold and numb. You couldn't move. He didn't want to try to move. Berg was splashing around, cursing, shining his light over the cave-in rubble. There was a terrible moaning. Loyal thought it was Cucumber, then knew it was coming from the ventilator as thousands of tons of rock settled on the pipe.

"Cucumber. You o.k.? Blood?"

"Dropped my porkchop," said Cucumber. "Porkchop down in water."

Loyal understood then that the cold numbness was an inch of icy water, that he was lying in it.

"Jesus Christ, where's the damn water coming from?" His voice sounded panicky. He got up, stood shuddering. Nothing was broken. The water was up to his ankles and his back was sopping wet. His knees stung.

The water came from everywhere. It limped and trickled from the ceiling and walls in thousands of tiny drops like sweat, fell in streams; it welled up underfoot.

"Jesus, Jesus, Jesus," moaned Cucumber. "Ah, Jesus, drown in dark. Water."

"We don't know how bad it is. They could be o.k. up there, be tryin' to get us out right now." Berg's voice was tense but controlled. They stifled their ragged breaths, listened for the chinking sound of hammers. The rock creaked. The heavy drops fell and fell, echoing in the flooding stope. Loyal felt a calm. Was it to be by drowning or crushing? Under the rock.

Berg had been in cave-ins before. He knew the drill. "We save our batteries. Don't turn on your lamp. They'll last us a few days."

"Days!" choked Cucumber.

"Ah, you old son of a bitch, you can live for weeks in a cave-in as long as you got water. And have we got water. Let's move up to the high end of the stope. Get out of the slop good as we can."

They waded up the floor of the stope in the dark until they reached a band of dry rock at the end where they'd drilled in the morning. By groping with their hands they felt the beach of dry floor was about three feet wide, barely enough to sit down on. Loyal fished string out of his pocket and knotted off the measurement. Berg felt for the tools. The water rose gradually. All around them the patter of falling water, the deadly tinking and tonking. The water crept up the dry strip.

"This stope is thirty foot high. It take one hell of a lot of water to fill this up," said Berg.

"Yeah, what you do, climb up walls like fly and stay up? What you do, swim around? Have water race? I tell you what you do, is Dead Man's Float. Nobody never open this up. Standing in grave, Berg. I told you, take third man, bad luck. Now you see!" Cucumber's voice was raw. He spit and gobbered in the dark as though Berg had tricked him into this deadly hole.

They stood with their backs to the wall, facing the water. Loyal tried not to lean against the wall. The rock sucked the warmth out of the body. When his legs knotted, he squatted down. By stretching out his hand he could feel the edge of water. The hours went along. Cucumber sucked and chewed at something. He must have found the porkchop.

"Better save your food. We don't know how long we'll be down here," said Berg. Sullen silence from Cucumber.

Loyal woke up in a swooning fright, legs numb with pins and needles, knees billets of wood with wedges driven deep. Cucumber was bellowing what, a song, in another language. Loyal put out his hand to steady himself and there was an inch of water. It was up to the wall.

"Berg. I'm going to put on my light. See if there's a dry place." He knew there was no dry place. The headlamp's wavering light reflected from the sea that stretched before them to where the rockfall choked the passage. Before he shut the light off again he turned it on Cucumber who leaned his forearms against the wall and pressed his head against his wet hands. The water seeped into his boots. The leather was black with wet, shone like patent leather.

"Save the fucking light," Berg shouted at him. "You'll

kill for a light in a couple of days. Sense of wasting it now?"

There was no way to tell how long it had been since the cave-in without switching on the light. The only one with a watch was Berg. The water came over the tops of their shoes. Loyal felt his feet swelling in the slimy leather, packing the boots tight with stinging flesh. Their calves knotted, the muscles twitched against the cold. There was a rattling sound and he thought it was rock flakes before he reasoned that rock flakes would slip into the water as silently as knives. A little later he knew what the rattling was; Berg's and Cucumber's teeth, and he knew because the chills were racking him too, until his whole body shuddered.

"It's the cold of the water drawing the heat out of our bodies. The cold will kill you before you drown," Berg said. "If we can find the tools, a hammer and a chisel, we got a chance to cut out some stone and stand on it, nick out some steps or something, get up out of the water." They groped under the water along the wall where they had been working. The useless drills were there. Then Loyal's lunch box, full of mushy waxed paper and bread pulp, but the slices of ham were still good and he ate one, put the other in his jacket pocket. The stone hammers, chisels and bits were in a wooden carpenter's box with an ash dowel for a handle. They all knew it intimately, but it could not be found, even when they waded out to their knees, kicking cautiously along the bottom.

"Even if I walked into it I couldn't feel it," said Loyal. "My feet hurt so Christly much I can't tell if I'm walking or standing still."

"Carry it in," said Cucumber. "Feel it on arm. Don't know where put it down. Back by the rail line, maybe. Remember almost trip on it."

Loyal felt the weight of settling rock above them, half a mile.

Cucumber mumbled. "Could be there. Maybe I think we don't need today."

In the darkness their eyes strained, unseeing, in the direction of the rail line and the tool box, buried now under the rock. The red motes and flashes that trace through total darkness skidded before them. The water rose slowly.

After a long time, surely eight or ten hours, he thought, Loyal noticed that the pain in his feet and legs had eased to a cold numbness that crept up toward his groin. He leaned, half-fainting, against the wall because he could hardly stand. Berg was retching in the darkness, and between spasms shook so violently his voice jerked out of him *"eh-eh-eh-eh-eh."* Cucumber, on the other side of Berg, in the wet blackness, breathed hard and slow. A steady drip fell near him.

"Berg. Switch on your light and tell us the time. It'll help to keep some track of the hours."

Berg fumbled with his crazy hands and got the switch on but couldn't read the time on his dancing, leaping watch.

"Christ," said Loyal, holding the jerking arm and seeing ten past two. Which two? Two in the morning after the cave-in or twenty-four hours later, the next afternoon?

"Cucumber, you think it's afternoon or 2 A.M.?" And looked at Cucumber spraddled, arms pressed against the rock to take the weight off his feet, head down. Cucumber turned his head toward the light and Loyal saw the blood tracking from black nostrils, the wet shirt shining with blood, the water around Cucumber's knees washed with blood. Cucumber opened his mouth and his pale tongue crept from between his bloody teeth.

"It's easier for you. You got no babies."

Loyal turned the light off and there was nothing to do but stand and wait in a half swoon, listening to Cucumber bleed out drop by drop.

And now he knows: in her last flaring seconds of consciousness, her back arched in what he'd believed was the frenzy of passion but was her convulsive effort to throw off his killing body, in those long, long seconds Billy had focused every one of her dying atoms into cursing him. She would rot him down, misery by misery, dog him through the worst kind of life. She had already driven him from his home place, had set him among strangers in a strange situation, extinguished his chance for wife and children, caused him poverty, had set the Indian's knife at him, and now rotted his legs away in the darkness. She would twist and wrench him to the limits of anatomy. "Billy, if you could come back it wouldn't happen," he whispered.

He came awake with a shout, slipping into the water. He could not stand. His clubbed feet could not feel the ground. He knew he had to get the bursting shoes off, the leather that clamped the flesh, the tightening strings, if he had to cut them off. He crouched, gasping, in the water and felt his right shoe. The puffed leg bulged over the top of the shoe. He pulled at the laces underwater, worrying the wet knots, racked with shudders. After a long time, hours, he thought, he pulled the lace free of the eyelets and began to lever at the shoe. The pain was violent. His foot filled the shoe as tight as a piling rammed into earth. Christ, if he could see!

"Berg. Berg, I got to put on my light. I got to get my shoes off, Berg. My feet's swole up wicked."

Berg said nothing. Loyal switched on his headlamp and saw Berg leaning against the wall, half-sagged into a tiny shelf where his knees rested, bearing some of his weight.

He could barely see his shoes under the cloudy water, eighteen inches deep now, and the shoe would have to be cut off. He stood up and switched the headlamp off while he fumbled for the knife in his pocket. It was hard to open it, and harder to sit back down in the water—fall down— and cut the tight leather open. He used the lamp as little as possible while he sawed and panted and moaned. At last the things were off and he threw them out into the black- ness, the soft splashes, Berg to his left groaning. His feet were numb. He could feel nothing.

"Berg. Cucumber. Get your shoes off. Had to cut mine off."

"*Eh-eh-eh-eh-eh*-too-*eh-eh-eh* cold," said Berg. "Fuck- ing *eh-eh-eh-eh* freezing. Can't."

"Cucumber. Shoes off." Cucumber didn't answer but they could hear the blood falling into the water.

blood bloodblood blood blood bloodblood

It became difficult to talk, to think. Loyal had long, sucking dreams that he struggled to leave. Several times he thought he was sitting in a rocking chair beside the kitchen stove, and that a child was leaning asleep against his heart, light hair stirring in the whistling wind from his nostrils. He ached with the sweetness of the child's weight until his mother stiffed the fire, and said in an offhand way that the child was not his, it was Berg's daughter, that these things had been torn from his life like calendar pages and were lost to him forever.

Then he would rouse Berg for the time, but the head-lamps were dim and it always seemed to be ten past two.

"Stopped." said Berg. "Watch *eh-eh-eh* stopped."

'How long we been in here do you think?" He only talked to Berg now. He stood close to Berg.

"Days. Five or *eh-eh-eh* four days. If you hear them we got to tap, let them guys know we're still alive down here. Pearlette. Hope they-*eh-eh-eh-eh*-ey taking care."

"Pearlette," said Loyal. "She your only kid?"

'Three. Pearlette. James. Abernethy. *Eh-eh* call Bernie for short. Baby. Sick every winter." Berg directed his feeble light at the wall. The water had gone down two inches. "We got a *eh-eh-eh* chance," said Berg. "Anyway we got a chance."

The dying headlamps pointed in Cucumber's direction showed nothing. They called, with clacking jaws, but he didn't answer. Cucumber was beyond the circle of light, silent.

When at last the sound of faraway tapping came they struck wet rocks against the wall and wept. Away in the darkness Cucumber rolled in eight inches of mine water, his mouth kissing the stone floor again and again as if thankful to be home.

15. The Indian's Book

12-3-51

Hello folks, It is deep snow out here now, been snowing 6 days strait. In the hospital for awhile, but am alright now and looking for work. It is a tough place. I keep moving along.

Loyal

Mr. + Mrs. Mink Blood
RFD
Cream Hill

Vermont

HE carried the Indian's book around with him for years before he started to write in it. It had a supple cover, narrow bands of snakeskin sewed with a long-armed featherstitch. The pages had rounded corners. The Indian's hand was impossible; pitching letters with open tops and long, dangling descenders, words jumbled into one another, omissions stacked on top of the sentences. There were strange lists. On one page Loyal read:

sacrifices

lamenting

hungering

jail

dream & vision

journeys

In another place the crooked sentences said: "The dead live. Power comes from sacrifices. Give me good thoughts, calm my rough desire, strengthen my body, do not let me eat any wrong food. The sun and the moon will be my eyes. Let me see white metal, yellow stalks, red fire, black north. Rotate my arms 36 times."

Would the sacrifices be scalps, Loyal wondered under his cowboy hat.

The part about the dead that kept on living made him think of Berg and his idea about miners' ghosts, about Berg's daughter the way he had imagined her, realer than anything Berg had said. Berg's children, he thought, with the taste of snow in their mouths. And Berg himself, hobbling around somewhere now on aluminum feet. He'd heard that at the little hospital in Uphrates where they'd taken Berg a nurse had cut the laces on his shoes. She began to work the left shoe off. With a wet sound the shoe came away, and with it, adhering to the inner sole, the turgid, spongy bottom of his foot, baring the glistening bone. Loyal couldn't remember if they had taken him to the same place. At least he could still walk well enough, at least he had not lost his feet or any of his toes, although the pain seemed locked permanently inside his leg bones.

There were drawings of birds in faded ink, a page much creased and dirtied as though the book had fallen open on the floor, trodden for days until someone picked it up. But most of the book was still empty, as if the Indian had recently started it to extend the paths of earlier volumes. Some of the page headings seemed useful enough.

Income

Expenses

Places I Been

Sights

Dreams

Birthdays & funerals

Tricks

Medicine Thoughts

Troubles

On the page for **Birthdays** the Indian had written: "My son Ralph born Aug 12 1938 died of diarrea Aug 11 1939." Under **Sights** he had noted only "bonfires beside the road" and "little shining ones."

Loyal crossed out the Indian's notations. On the **Birthday** page he wrote his own name and birth date, then those of his family. He was thirty-six years old. Tentatively, barely pressing the pencil against the paper, he wrote "Billy," but erased it a minute later. Sitting in his underwear on the edge of his bed he wanted to write something about the watch, but on an empty page could manage only a stiff, insufficient sentence, "The watch I gave her."

She had a junky little watch that would not keep time. He'd got her a beaut—half the winter's fur from his trapline for a Lady Longines with a tiny face no bigger than a dime set with diamond chips to mark the hours. Six fox furs to Mrs. Claunch who sewed her a fur jacket for a Christmas surprise—"a chubby," Billy called it. She'd come into a place wearing the jacket, letting the watch slip down her wrist to show it off. Looking like a million. So careful of her things, keeping them polished and fine.

Then helping Toot with his hay. The old cock still hung onto his horses, Rainy and Cloudy. The horses would draw the wagon along the windrows and he and Ronnie would pitch the hay up to Toot who built the load, the sweat pouring down, the field crackling with heat. Mernelle tailed along behind them, twisting her pitchfork to gather the lost wisps of hay. Toot had promised her fifty cents for a day's work. Toot and Ronnie unharnessing the horses while he pitched the last load into the hayloft, struggling with the wads of hay Toot had knitted into a puzzle. Only the man who builds a hay load knows where each forkful lies. The suffocating perfume of grass, the air shot with chaff and dust until his skin was on fire with itch. Mernelle running in to say that Billy was there with her car and they were all going swimming at Bobcat Pond.

He sees Billy, bending, the hairless legs taut, sees the flash of her nails as she rolls her watch in a stocking and tucks it in the toe of her shoe, the shoes side by side, and over them her folded rayon dress and the thin towel from the soap flake box. And Mernelle, sloshing up out of the water, "Please, Billy, can I wear your watch while you go swimmin'? Please, Billy!" The way she hesitated. But said yes. Mernelle cocking her arm at the sky while they swam out to the sunken rock shelf. The delicious water. He'd told her a pickerel almost five feet long hung around under the rock shelf. Her flesh, greenish under the water.

Later, Mernelle thrashing up to them and Billy's low, clear voice, "Did you put my watch back in my shoe exactly like I had it?" Mernelle like she'd been punched. Her arm coming up out of the water, the watch face already so fogged they couldn't see the diamond chips.

Billy holding the watch loosely in her hand for a few seconds, while Loyal said never mind, that they could take it to a good jeweler, then Billy, looking straight at Mernelle and hurling it out into the pond. Never said a word.

Many nights that winter he wrote, sometimes only a few lines, sometimes until the wind shaking the window frame chilled his hands. Things he planned to do, song lyrics, distances traveled, what he ate and what he drank. When he turned the light out he saw the blue night fitted into the rectangles of window glass, the crumpled earth glowing with phosphorescent metals, the blurring wind and stars.

The Indian's book. His book.

16. The Bigger They Are the Higher They Burn

1951 Fire Marshall's Report.
Investigations Conducted by Earl L. Frank, Deputy

Fire Marshall. Case 935 Minkton Blood, Cream Hill, Vt. fire occurred December 11, 1951. Property destroyed—Farm barn and nine cows. After considerable investigation Marvin E. Blood, the son of the owner, was arrested on the charge of first degree arson, a confession obtained, and he was sentenced to serve one to three years in the State's Prison at Windsor. In his confession, he implicated his father, Minkton Blood, as having counseled him to burn the barn in exchange for a share of the insurance. Minkton Blood was arrested, a confession obtained, and he was sentenced to State's Prison for not less than two years nor more than four years. At the time of the fire, insurance of $2,000 was collected on the property. Recovery of the money is being attempted.

THE inside of the barn had never been darker. They were down to dregs of kerosene and the murky light from the lantern illuminated little in the dark chill of the morning. Cow piss gushed. There was nervous stamping, an atmosphere in the barn, worse than it had been the night before. Mink felt his way into the milk room, bending for the pails, pouring the hot water from the kettle into the wash pail for Dub. A column of steam boiled up. He fumbled for the rag. The barn stank of ammonia, sour milk, cloying hay and wet iron. He heard the door swing open. Dub. The light of the second lantern spilled sullenly out of his hand.

"Colder'n a witch's patootie. Christ, why is it so cold so early? Feels like January. Five more months of this I'll be hangin' from my tail and givin' the monkey laugh.

WAHOOHAHHOOHOO!" Dub gave the monkey laugh.

"You do that fuckin' noise again I'll take a piece of stovewood to you. I'm pushed near as far as I can go this mornin'." There was a deadly silence while their separate rages churned and mingled.

"*You're* pushed? Did I hear right? You are PUSHED? You old son of a bee, you're the one doin' the pushin'. You raise a hand to me and I'll part your hair from ear to ear." The lantern shook in Dub's hand. He hung it on the nail near the dead radio. The battery had been flat for a long time. He took the bristle brush and the pail of hot water, cooled now to warm, and began to work down the row of impatient cows, sweeping at their dung-caked flanks with the brush, washing the udders stuck with bits of chaff and manure. The light gave a dim radiance to his balding head, his lips moved. He seized the cow's tail. She liked nothing better than to slap her stinking tail onto the side of his neck. This morning she kicked as he squeezed in beside her, then shifted her weight, pressing him over against the next cow. She'd been licking at her sides as far back as she could reach, and the hair was rubbed away down to the bleeding skin.

"What the hell is the matter with you this morning?" he muttered. He got the bag balm and smeared it on the sore. As he did every morning and evening he thought about the electricity, what they could have done with it. The cow on the end was blatting. Mink didn't bother with names now, but Dub gave them all movie star names, and this one, a table-topped hulk with rolling eyes, was Joan Bennett.

"You'll get your damn water in a minute." Now he moved into the tricky rhythm of lugging Mink's foaming pail into the milk room, pouring it through the strainer into the milk can, picking up the full pail of water from under the trickling faucet in the stone sink, and, with his hook, seizing the empty milk pail. In the barn again, he set the full water bucket in front of a cow, hooked up an empty from the next one and, on his way back to the milk room, swapped the empty milk bucket for Mink's full one. It almost never worked out. The faucet would run slow and he'd wait at the sink while Mink shouted for him to get a move on; or sometimes the cow would hold back her milk, probably at the feel of Mink's leathery old hands, and Dub'd lean against the wall, waiting, listening to the shallow firping sound of the milk rising in the pail.

He'd think about a radio that worked with a plug and a wall socket, a radio that put out a good beat, and a light bulb to cheer the damn old brown dump up, the easiness of a milking machine and a water pump and the pipe running right along the wall in front of the stanchions, like Phelps's place across the lake. The electricity was all around them. If only there'd been some little easy cheerfulness for him and Myrtle. He didn't blame her for leaving. None of it, not a thing, had gone right. The power lines came within twenty miles south of them, across the river on the east, up over the border, and west, well, thirty, thirty-five miles. He'd believed that crap Loyal used to give the old man, that stuff about the electricity coming in right after the War. "First priority to farms." He'd read it out of the paper. That was a laugh. First priority to towns, any town, to garages, stores, knickknack shops. Six years after the War and they still hadn't made it here. Now a new War coming along. Korea, whatever the hell that was. And if stinking MacArthur had his way, they'd be fighting China. It could be another hundred years. The herd had gone down because Mink wouldn't let the AI man on the place. Should have done what Uncle Ott did, getting rid of his farm right after the War, buying another one, a good one over in Wallings, a farm with power lines. He had electricity, he'd improved his herd, had got as bad as Loyal used to be talking bloodlines and production. But now he was milking fourteen cows that averaged out over a thousand pounds of 4 percent milk a month and he was making money. Sprayed the DDT, no flies in the barn. Had a new maroon Henry J. in addition to the pickup, a '47 Ford with less than fifteen thousand miles on it. Dub would not have bought the Henry J. himself. If he had Ott's kind of money he'd of gotten a Buick Roadmaster, the big 152-horsepower Fireball engine and Dynaflow Drive. The AI man and a little electricity could of saved him and Myrt.

O, Myrt, I tried, he thought. He heard himself persuading her, persuading himself, after the piano-tuning school director turned him down, "Mr. Blood, we're sure you understand that you need perfect pitch in this business, and that it's, it's a calling that requires considerable strength on the tuner's part, that he be *fully able*," telling her that it was just for a few months until the old man could see they had to get out on their own, a couple of months to look around, find something else he could do. Dammit, he was as strong as an ox, could lift pianos with one hand, and had showed the son of a bitch, raising one end of the grand up eight inches and letting it drop with a tingling sound and the crack of the cover slamming.

It took less than a year. He'd tried for every job he heard of, but the War vets were pushing in and grabbing the best stuff. The hiring guys didn't even look at a one-armed farmer. That good-sounding ad from over in New York state, even if it was a glorified hired man position: *Wanted. Married man, small family, work with purebred Holsteins. Ability to operate De Laval milking machine highly important. Working, living conditions better than average. Ten-hour day, six-day week. Potatoes, milk, coal, garden privileges. $150 month. Character and ability thoroughly investigated.* Myrtle wrote the letter for him, both of them pretending he could do what was wanted, not mentioning the prosthesis, and when the letter came back with a date for an interview, she went with him. It had been their only outing, riding the ferry across Lake Champlain, the bright wind swinging Myrtle's hair and blowing the empty waxed papers from their sandwiches into the dark water to toss in the ferry's wake. Donald Phelps. Black letters on a red mailbox. The smooth driveway, crushed stone on it. Fences taut as the lines on sheet music. Phelps in his model barn, showing him the layout, the fluorescent lighting, the four-cow milking parlor, the stainless steel milk room. He'd missed a beat when he saw the hook but he didn't say anything. Very courteous. Donald Phelps was the kind to let you hang yourself.

"Well, Mr. Blood, one thing we are doing with all applicants for this position, and we have had quite a few, is ask them to work through a milking with the De Laval so I can see how they manage. And I guess we're at that point now." Looking at his wristwatch, the first farmer Dub had ever seen with a wristwatch. The milking machine's gleaming parts lay in the stainless steel sterilizer. Dub stared at the coiling tubes and pneumatic parts.

"I can manage it." He laughed horribly. "It's just we ain't got the electric on the home place, so I ain't had the chance to learn the tricks of it. But I'm quick, oh I'm plenty smart enough, and I can maneuver with one hand better'n most guys with two. I want this job and I'll do my best at it." He gobbled, spit flew with the words. But it was no good. Phelps just shook his head slowly and opened the door into the sunny afternoon. Myrtle and Mrs. Phelps were standing in the yard, their arms folded against the wind. Myrtle was doing all the talking, telling her something, maybe about working in the doctor's office, or the ride across the lake, maybe about the kid. She looked happy until she saw him, coming across the yard. The way he walked, she said.

Two weeks later he took the bus down to Groton, Connecticut, an all-day ride. *The Electric Boat company has immediate openings for experienced inside machinists, outside machinists, inside electricians, outside electricians, sheet metal workers, draftsmen. Six-day work week.*

Twenty minutes to fill out the application form. The interview took less than twenty seconds. "Naw. Able-bodied AND experienced. PREFERENCE to veterans. You don't qualify for this work. What in hell made you think you did?"

But he didn't give up. The Elmore Grain company wanted a grain salesman, and he guessed he could do that, take the cash and throw the hundred-pound bags onto the back of the truck. He started the day after the big windstorm in November, people out sawing downed trees and working on washed-out roads, but Dub up at Elmore wrestling grain bags all day. He got back in time for milking. They let him go at the end of two days. The hook ripped three out of four bags, and the yellow grain trickled off the trucks and into the street, drawing flocks of birds and even a few barn rats.

Mink felt himself slow as a nailed board. The milk pulsed, empty seconds hung between the spurts. The cows shifted and bawled. It was worse, whatever it was, this morning, the way they fidgeted. There was a crack of memory of something from a long time ago, he and Ott climbing on a board fence with a ferret-faced boy, Gordon or Ormond, his father and some other neighbors leaning over the fence. A lot of men, a low twist of voices. There was a pig on a bed of straw. There was a .22. Or was it a .30-.30. The matter was serious, but there was a feeling of coming through whatever it was all right, that it was a bad, but fated, part of life. But he couldn't remember what it had been about. The night before he lay awake late into the night trying to remember what was wrong with that pig, and was deathly tired this morning. The automaton-like pulling on of clothes, the groaning of the winter stairs, the rattling of lime deposits in the kettle all seemed too heavy to endure. The kitchen seemed a rabbit cage, himself the rabbit subdued into crouching silence.

Now Dub's barn clatter, the scrape of the pail handle on his homemade wooden arm with the old gambrel hook screwed into the end, deliberately crude and heavy, the light stainless steel hook they'd paid so much for thrown into the river after the last fight with Myrt. He'd heard the wildness in Dub's voice, like the town idiot years ago, Brucie, Brucie Beezey, grey-haired and screeching for roasted apples like a baby for the tit. He could hear that note in Dub's voice now and then. What did he want, somebody to say it was all going to be o. k. ? He should know better by now, crippled, divorced, a father who'd never seen his son. He was always a fool. A goddamn periodical with the boozing.

He leaned his head against the cow, stripping, stripping. What he thought was that in some way he didn't understand yet, this cow was going to finish him off. And tired because he'd been awake most of the night trying to think of the trouble with that pig and come up with a way to break from his downward course. Poorer every year, the work harder, the prices higher, the chances of pulling out of it fewer and fewer. It was so different now. He couldn't get his bearings. There had been poor people when he was a kid. Hell, everybody had been poor. But things kept going, like a waterwheel turning under the weight of flowing water. Relatives and neighbors came without asking to fill in. Where the hell were they now when he was sinking under the black water? Ott moved, Ronnie out of farming, Clyde Darter sold out and disappeared into Maine. The bank had changed hands, bought out by some big outfit over in Burlington, mean sons. The Dovers were storing hay in the old Batchelder house, the bales filling the kitchen and front room, packed on the staircase, pushing the banister spindles out. He remembered Jim Batchelder as if he'd seen him last night, the chapped face and parsnip nose, could hear him talk to his horses in his spare voice. And the past swelled out at him with its smell of horses, oats and hot linseed poultices. When the horses went the people went.

But how to get out of this? Dub and his screechy voice a weight, Mernelle with the constant harping about going to the movies and a goddamn "Victoria" hair wave and Jewell, not saying much but showing what she thought by staring away when he was trying to tell her something, twitching her head as if a fly was at her.

And this. He couldn't believe that he was wearing out. His arms, his knotted thighs, the swelling shoulders looked the same, but every joint flamed. The artheritis. It had bent his mother like a hoop. She'd twisted in her chair for years, calling for hot water bottles, scalding hot, as hot as they could get them to relieve the inner twisting that bent and bent her spine like fingers at a length of basket osier. And with the image of his mother arched in a hoop of pain, at last came the memory of the pig on the straw, tearing convulsively at its side until the loops of gut fell out and dragged through the muck, the pig stepping on its own bowels before sinking to the straw and still it rolled its mad eyes and strove to bite through its flanks. And this cow, swaying and lifting her back leg to scrape and kick at her raw side—Mink stopped milking, got up and studied the staring eye, noted the stringy slobber.

There were only one or two tricks left in the bag now. The cunning tricks.

"You know what we got to do," he said to Dub.

"We got to finish the goddamn milking, I got to feed these goddamn cows," said Dub, his voice muffled in the milk room.

"No. I mean about the farm."

The water pail slopped as Dub raised it from the sink.

"Sell it, you mean? Be the smartest thing you could do. I been at you to sell it for God knows how long. Do what Ott did, get a place with electric. They're never gonna bring it in here."

"Not sell it. Don't you know nothing? Don't you know the kind of a mortgage we got on this thing even if we was to sell it even for the top prices they're getting for this size of a farm even if it had the electricity and all, we wouldn't clear enough over the mortgage payoff to buy a pair of earmuffs. And there isn't no electricity. Even if this farm was perfect it'd be no good. That's the God's honest truth and now you know. We can't make nothing on selling it. We can't break even. That is not the way out. Don't you think I thought of that the day after that son of a bitch left? We wouldn't get nothing. How do you think your mother and me is supposed to live? We got fucking nothing."

"The cows."

"The cows. The cows. That is why we got to do something else. And damn fast. Come over here and let me show you something. You'll see why the cows isn't no pot of gold. You'll maybe get it in your thick head that we are at the place now where we got to dodge."

He pointed at the cow, her head stretching out, the craning neck, the tongue rasping at the raw side. Her eye showed a ring of white. Mink gestured at the row of stanchioned beasts. Dub stood, back against the door, staring. The cow bellowed and strained to pull her head through the stanchion.

"What the hell is wrong with them?"

"I believe it's Mad Itch. They got the Mad Itch."

"You want me to go for the vet?"

"You are the stupidest son of a bitch I ever seen. No, I don't want you to go for no vet. I want you to go for the rifle and five gallon of kerosene."

17. The Weeping Water Farm Insurance Office

12-11-51

DeAr Sirs, AFter paying iNS. For 20 yrs. MY BArN BurNed DowN this A.M. FroM A LANterN tiPPed over iN the HAy ACCiDeNtAL. PleAse seND CHeCk As We NeeD it.

Yrs.

MiNkton M. Blood

WeePing WAter FArM iNS. Co.
MAiN St.
Weeping WAter Vt.

THE offices of the Weeping Water Farm Insurance Company took up three rooms above the Enigma Hardware. The wooden floorboards creaked with distinctive sounds. Steam radiators under the windows put out tremendous heat that made the employees drowsy and secure on stormy days.

In the first room Mrs. Edna Carter Cutter, secretary, receptionist, information bureau, guard dog, indoor gardener, coffee maker and caterer, bookkeeper, weather forecaster, supply clerk, bank messenger, mail distributor and comptroller, sat in a leatherette chair amid two hundred potted houseplants. They crowded every surface, velvet plants, wandering jew, a purple-leaved Ti plant from the South Pacific, African violets by the dozen, a great leaning Norfolk pine in a lard tub, a lipstick plant swinging over a file cabinet, a kangaroo vine over another, a fatsia in a jug behind the door, a thicket of dumb cane beside the umbrella stand, a Boston fern, the giant of the collection, stretching its fronds over the Gestetner copier. Most of the plants had come as condolence gifts on the death of her son Vernon, run down in New York City by a drunken Marine in a stolen taxicab.

The office of Mr. Plute, the manager, was in the back with a view of an old cattle pound. There was an oak desk and three chairs, two oak file cabinets and an oak coat rack with brass hooks. The upper half of the door was set with a sheet of frosted glass that showed only Plute's elongated shadow when he walked in front of the window. It was he who had given Mrs. Cutter the Boston fern.

The other room was divided by low cellotex panels into three cubicles where the field men and investigators sat when they were in the office. Each cubicle contained a desk, a chair, a file cabinet, a telephone. When the occupants stood up they could look into each other's eyes, but when they sat down they disappeared except for curling tendrils of cigarette smoke or the flash of tossed paper clips.

Perce Paypumps was the old man of the office, predating Mr. Plute. He had worn out three oak chairs since 1925 through his habit of tipping back on the hind legs, and had lived through the great flood of '27, the epidemic of farm fires in the thirties, had tramped miles through blowdowns after the hurricane of '38 investigating claims of ruin and wreckage. When Plute was away, Perce was in charge. As senior man he had the deep judgment to do claims settlement.

John Magool was easygoing and fat, an ex-paratrooper who had ballooned up within weeks after he got out of uniform, a good talker, a good listener and a good salesman. He was on the road three weeks out of four. When he came in to write up his policies he usually found houseplants on his desk and along his share of the partitioned windowsill. He carried them out to Mrs. Cutter's office and stood silently, vines trailing over his arms.

"Oh, those plants! Hope you don't mind. I was just letting them get a little sun in there and forgot you'd be in this week. You have nice sunlight in the morning, John."

The third desk belonged to investigator Vic Bake, twenty-two, eager and smart at his first job. He had a face like a scoop of mashed potato, a slack body, a genius for making connections. A congenital wry neck forced him to carry his face thrust forward and tilted a little. Still untouched by life, except for this deformity, he divided all acts of men into connivance or philanthrophy. Uncorruptible, a tattletale in youth, a teacher's pet, a winner of gold stars, he was now trying for a bigger role. Plute, who scented his ambition, thought him a little brute and gave him the "fires of suspicious origin" to weasel into, sent him off to stoop and stalk the state fire inspector, to devil the state's attorney with his suspicions and his evidence.

A hundred miles upstate, back home, Vic's teeming family jammed into a house that smelled of dirty laundry. The father left before full light to drive a mail route. Five of the brothers went to their work in the bobbin factory. In Weeping Water Vic had his own room and a bath at a small boarding house near the river. He thought it luxurious.

He walked to the office through the ground fog in the mild February morning. Rotten ice crunched beneath his feet. A rind of snow stretched away into the fog. On the path he saw a blue thread, a stamp, two pulpy cigarette butts, a nail in its ice coffin.

He lined up his black rubbers so the toes touched the office wall, hung his poplin raincoat on the coat rack. He rummaged then, not in Mr. Plute's office which was locked with two keys, but in Mrs. Cutter's desk, taking the file cabinet keys and two of her Smith Brothers' cough drops to suck on while he read the letters and studied the office accounts ledger, then into Perce's cubicle to go through the folder of outstanding claims and put red mental asterisks in the corners of two cases. The Hakey business where old man Hakey told his daughter's boyfriend to take a powder and then, lo and behold, at midnight Hakey's Farm Feeds & Seeds burst into flame. The volunteer fire department couldn't get the fire truck started. That one stank of arson. And what about this. Cattle auctioneer, Ruben Quilliam. House burned. Nothing really obvious, but Quilliam's wife had just divorced him, and maybe he'd been drunk and set the house on fire to show her. He'd look around, talk to Quilliam's neighbors. Perce was too soft; he had these claims ticketed for payment.

Vic pulled out the PAID CLAIMS folder for January, just to take another look. Sometimes you got a feeling for something wrong after the fact. They looked all right. But he didn't remember seeing this one, "Lantern accidentally fell in hay. No telephone. Nearest neighbor a mile away. Driveway closed by snow." Perce must have checked it out and not bothered to show it to him. Those lousy old farms with no electricity or phone, something happened and it was all over. Seemed funny they didn't manage to get even one cow out of the barn. He looked at the fire inspector's scrawled sketch of the barn. It showed the place where the fire started outside the milk room. About twenty feet from the door. About six feet from the water pump. Seemed like they could have gotten some of the cows out. Or thrown a bucket of water on the fire. And they hadn't wasted any time putting in their claim. The postcard from the farmer was dated the afternoon of the fire. A fairly big claim, $2000. He wrote the name in his notebook. Minkton Blood. Maybe worthwhile to take a run out there and take a look around. It was never too late.

18. What I See

The wide street open at both ends of town, dust blowing, telephone poles nailed against the blue. "Welcome to MOAB Utah the Uranium Capital of the World." He looks in store windows, cranes at the neon sign "URANIUM SALES TRADE LEASE."

In Buck's Sundries there are copies of *Uranium Digest, Uranium Prospector, Uranium Mining Directory Digest.* A poster taped to the glass door promises "Miss Atomic Energy Contest, First Prize 10 Tons of Uranium Ore." He guesses a value of about $280. If she's lucky. Another sign, "Thatcher Saw, Realtor, Uranium

Broker," and a smaller sign beside it, "Ranches for Sale."

In Grand Junction he follows a black railing down into a basement with the smell of sweaty men and rolled maps. Pickups park along the khaki street. Most have trailers with gas cylinders chained on behind. And everywhere are men in dusty, crumpled clothes putting nickels in the red Coca-Cola machines. Hard hats to the wind, cupped hands, the match flame and the loose ribbon of smoke. He sees a hundred government men with name tags, AEC vehicles, exploration division equipment. The sprawl of black rock in a store window. CAMPING SUPPLIES & URANIUM—LISTINGS—SALES.

Prospectors in from the white bluffs look over the latest anomaly maps, talk of trying their luck somewhere else. The towns shake with the passage of dusty, dented jeeps the exhaust systems torn out, bulldozers and backhoes roll through on the semibeds. Stake trucks loaded with burlap sacks of ore. Along the roads and in the countryside the discarded cores lie in heaps on the ground. Cigarette butts, wire, dust, dust. No goddamn women. The dusty airstrips, the little white planes flown by Air Force vets in rolled-up sleeves, happy to be flying again. Aerial maps, Rapid City, Cheyenne, Laramie, Burdock, Dewey, Pringle, Wind River, Grants, Slickrock, Green River, Chuska District, Austin, Black Hills, Big Horns, Big Indian Wash, Big Beaver.

Big bust, maybe.

19. The Lonely Hearts Prisoner

March 6, 1952

Dear Son Loyal, I pray this reaches you we don't have address except try to guess by Post Mark your last card. Son, your Father has left us. It is a terrible thing but Mernelle and me is bearing up Come home. Dub is still to Windsor. Your Father was there to get it for the fire. That's where it happened, as terrible as can be. Come home soon. Your loving mother and sister.

Jewell Sleyins Blood +
Mernelle Silvietta Blood

ADDRESSEE UNKNOWN

Mr. Loyal Blood
(works at mines)
General Delivery
Lemon, Colorado

BEEMAN Zick had the lower bunk and the upper hand. He came out on top every time, but he'd been unlucky in his cellmate, a damn, dull old farmer who didn't do much but sit on his bunk, cracking his knuckles and staring at the floor. Old bastard wouldn't talk about nothing. Who wanted that leathery old horse. Not Beeman Zick, who yearned for the taste of dill, pickerel fishing and love.

The son, oh, he was different. He wished they'd put him in with the son. Guy only had one arm (advantage) and was getting bald (too bad, but who can tell in the dark), but what a ass, as plump and sweet as Christmas cake. And there the son was, in with the Frenchy, and the Frenchy, despite his years in the lumber camps where all they did was chop down trees and stick it into each other, was an on-the-knees Catholic who'd almost rubbed his lips off kissing first the gold cross around his neck and second the photographs of his fat wife and daughters. Wives. Somebody noticed once he had two sets of pictures, and they didn't match. Then it came out. One set down in New Hampshire, in Littleton. One set up in Quebec, in Roberval. Total thirteen daughters and not a single fucking boy. And stole a peavey from one of the little operators up in the kingdom, went on a rampage after drinking half a pail of potato wine and used the peavey to pry the back wall off the house of absent timber baron Jean-Jean Poutre. They found Frenchy lying naked in the silk sheets, surrounded by silver-framed photographs, pepper mills, embroidered scarves, mahogany-backed military brushes, beeswax candies, engraved letter openers, empty champagne bottles, leather-bound books, bell pull tassels, crystal vases, stuffed birds, a pearl-handled nail file, walking sticks, perfume flagons, powder puffs, patent leather shoes, quires of creamy paper, imported fountain pens, sheet music, and a telephone directory for Oyster Bay, Long Island. "Call me up sometime," was all he'd say.

Couldn't tell any of this to the old farmer. Oh, you could say it and plenty more, but that's where it stopped. He didn't hear a thing except the devil shouting in his private ear if those rapid whispers were proof. Beeman Zick couldn't make out a word. They made the farmer take his exercise alone, alone except for the guard. They said the son wanted to kill him or he wanted to kill the son. Keep them apart. That's what they said and that's what he thought, and he was as surprised as anyone else when the old farmer hung himself.

Beeman Zick was wakened out of the sweetest last hour of sleep. He drowsed in the warm pillow, unwilling to come fully awake, and tried to identify the noise through a dream haze. It was like someone snoring or talking in his sleep, a choked voice sound, and a fleshy slapping like the unstoppable moment, then the pattering of liquid accompanied by thrashing whumps and the hollow clangor of the water pipes. Beeman Zick had heard the water pipe song before. He leaped out of bed and stared at the old farmer writhing in the noose of his shirt arm, shirt tied to the water pipes, bare feet scrabbling against the wall, legs wet with urine.

"Guard!" bellowed Beeman Zick. "We got a dancer here." But by the time they cut the old guy down the dance was over.

Leatherette briefcase bouncing against his leg, his upper body encased in a tight plaid jacket, head rocking left, right, left, Ronnie Nipple came up the May path. In the drive his dusty blue Fleetline Aerosedan cooled. The spring peepers bleated down in the swamp, and even in the closed kitchen the relentless trilling pummeled everything that was said.

"Jewell. Mernelle. This is a sad time but life goes on," his voice pitched in terrible softness. The stain on his chin glowed.

"Don't talk like a funeral director, Ronnie. I had enough of that. Life don't go on, not like it used to. What we need is some help in straightenin' out this mess. The insurance company and the bank fellows come up here every day. He left us in a terrible pickle. No money, nowhere to go, the boys gone. It used to be your boys would go into farmin' somewheres nearby. The young ones start out in farmin' the older men would give 'em a hand. But now. If you can't help us find a way out I don't know what I am goin' to do." She snuffled and wept a little against the urgent swamp trill. Her fingers laced through each other. The wedding ring was worn to the thinness of a wire. "Ah, I dunno. When I was a girl there were so many aunts and uncles, cousins, in-laws, second cousins. All of 'em livin' right around here. They'd be here now, that kind of big fam'ly if it was them times. The men would put the plank tables together. Every woman would bring something, I don't care, biscuits, fried chicken, pies, potato salad, berry pies, they'd bring these things if it was a get-together or a church picnic or times of trouble. The kids go runnin' around, laughin', I can remember the mothers tryin' to hush them up at my brother Marvin's funeral, but they'd just slow down for a little bit and then start up again. And here we sit, the three of us. And that's all."

Mernelle sat dreamily rocking, staring out the window at the scorched barn foundation. She was apart from this talk. Fireweed had already surged up out of the cavity. The trilling was maddening. The weeds spurted, mallow, peppergrass, dog strangle vine, stinking wall rocket. The barberry bush near the old dog's grave in sullen flower, the moths nipping and jittering.

"Jewell, you was always a good friend to my mother when she needed it. And you know what I'm talkin' about. I don't know the whole story of *that,* when Dad passed over, but she let on quite a bit. And I'm going to be a friend to you and Mernelle." His voice limped away. Sitting at the table, his papers spread across the worn oilcloth like boats adrift on the seas, the brown kitchen light sifting over his hands.

"I never dreamed in all those hours her and me sat talkin' at this table that we'd be in the same fix one day. Your mother was a decent woman and a good soul. Somebody got sick why she'd go right on over and help out. Fix supper, do the warsh. I've often thought in the last few weeks that if she was here she'd know what I am going through," thinking both Toot and Mink had killed themselves in shame. Although the shames were different. She felt again that new stir of curiosity about her own death that came to her in the early morning, a half-eager willingness to consider its possible form, a stir that came and went like a jumping muscle.

"Well, I been workin' on this thing of yours, and I guess we've got a way to pull you out of the mire. Of course, keepin' out is goin' to be the problem."

"Ronnie. I want you to know you're a decent neighbor."

Mernelle made a face at the window, batting her eyes, stretching her mouth in mock humility so her upper teeth hung over her lower lip. The peepers shrilled. Blue-eyed grass winking, the crushing scent of lilac.

"It's complicated and it won't be too easy for you. It means splitting the farm into three parcels. I got two buyers and I managed to save the house and a couple acres for you to live in, have room for a garden." He drew on the back of an envelope. The farm became a shape like a pair of trousers, each leg a division of the property. His ballpoint pen stabbed the lines of demarcation. "A piece of the orchard so you can keep up your pies and applesauce. Ott has offered a real good price for the cropland and pasture, that field of Loyal's, prob'ly more than it's worth right now. And I got a doctor from Boston wants to buy the woodlot and the sugarbush, build a hunting camp up in the woods. Between Ott and the doctor you'll be free and clear of the debts. I'll lay it right out for you, Jewell. You'll have to swallow the sight of other people on your place and you won't have much left over. A roof over your head. Garden space. Maybe eight hundred dollars cash. Somebody's gonna have to scout around for a job, maybe both of you, what with Dub where he is. But that's how it goes. I don't need to tell you Jewell, when trouble comes we just have to do the best we can."

"It's awful good of Ott to step forward, at least keep some of the farm in the family," said Jewell, mouth filling with the bitter words. Her voice shuddered, fell away. "This farm been in the Blood family since the Revolutionary War days. I'll never know why Mink didn't go to Ott, why he didn't think the farm could bring anything," she half-whispered, thinking that Ott could have helped Mink, should have seen the trouble and stepped in. Brothers turning their backs on brothers.

"Well, Jewell, you got to know the market. Mink didn't even know there was a market, a real estate market. You folks kept to yourselfs up here. Missed out on a few things. Changes. It's not just what a farm'll bring for a farm, now. There's people with good money want to have a summer place. The view. That's important. See the hills, some water. The places with the barn right across the road from the house don't move good, but if there's a pretty view, why . . ." The word "pretty" sounded awkward in his mouth.

He meant that he, Ronnie, had smoothed out, had learned something. Jewell thought of him years earlier, a dirty boy who loped in the woods with Loyal, a tagalong with no ambition that she could see. Look at him now, see his jacket and briefcase, shoes with crepe soles. She thought of Loyal, lost out in the world, of Dub, locked up.

He must have been thinking the same thing. His fingers limped among the papers, folded the corners.

"You get in touch with Loyal?"

"He wrote he was workin' in a mine about a year ago. I tried to write to him about Mink, but he don't think to send his address, or I guess he keeps on moving." Loyal always said that the reason he liked to hunt with Ronnie was because he could tell what you were thinking, that you never had to stop and talk or wave your hands in dumb signals. He knew.

"The Boston doctor, now. Is he a half-decent feller?"

"Doctor Franklin Saul Witkin. Seems nice enough. About forty, forty-five. Real neat. Quiet-spoken. Wears glasses. A little stout, high-colored. Skin doctor, specializes in skin ailments."

"Can't be much to that, wouldn't think it would make anybody a living, would you."

"Makes enough so Dr. Witkin can drive a big Buick and wear a gold wristwatch. And buy a hundred acres of your farm. Course he's got to have a right-of-way to the top of the hill."

"What kind of name is Witkin?"

"I believe it's a German name or Jewish name."

"I see," said Jewell. And she breathed in slowly. He could have said Chinese.

The kitchen had not changed, Ronnie thought. Mink's grimy barn cap still hung from a hook near the ell door. The linoleum, the ivy crawling over the walls were as they always had been. There was half a loaf of bread standing on a scarred board, the knife with the broken point beside it; the sink was full of chipped dishes. He'd pulled out all the old kitchen fixtures at his own place when he married, covered the pine boards with Armstrong floor tile, a clean floor for little Buddy to crawl on, a chrome and Formica dinette set, a combination oil and gas range. He'd converted the old summer kitchen to his real estate office. A desk, three chairs, telephone, a big mural photograph of autumn mountains on the wall that had cost plenty. He thought there was no telling what Loyal would do when he came back and found the farm sold. He wouldn't blame himself or Mink or Dub, not Jewell nor Mernelle; he'd blame Ronnie Nipple. Cross that bridge when he came to it.

Ronnie was back two days later, coming out of the tender rain with the papers for her signature, the deeds, the stiff contracts and lien release documents. An earthworm writhed on the edge of his shoe, embedded in the rippled sole. But his ballpoint wouldn't work no matter how hard they scribbled with it on the back of an envelope. Jewell had to get Mink's old nib fountain pen with the mottled green barrel and the nearly empty bottle of ink and scratch her name. The farm was gone. Only the house on its two-acre island held a line.

"I want to learn to drive, Ronnie," said Jewell. "How do I go about it? There's the car out there and it should run. I'm determined to learn."

"I'd as soon teach you, Jewell. No sense to pay somebody when you got neighbors. It's a good idea. Let you get out. I'll take the batt'ry along with me today and get it charged up. You know, they're talking about hiring at the cannery. I've heard they'll take on older women. I don't know as you'd care for that kind of work, but you could drive back and forth. Look into it, anyway." His relief warmed the room. An old woman neighbor could be a terrible burden. But if she had something coming in . . .

"You'll need the telephone, Jewell. I'll call them up, get them to send somebody out."

"If you knew how many times I wished I knew how to drive. It would have made some difference if I could of gone out and got some work years ago, but Mink wouldn't hear of it. Had a fit every time I wanted to go somewhere." Remembering Ott's wife's card party and how they argued about it for days. Mink had worn his outrage to bed like a nightshirt, but for once she'd spoken up to him.

"Well, I don't care how you bunch your mouth up and bite your words into specks, I'm goin' to that card party. Think you'd be glad about it, your own brother's wife gives a card party." Whispering fiercely in the dark. They'd had the habit of whispering in bed since Loyal was a baby.

Mink rolled his head on the flat pillow, whispered back. "Why the hell should I be glad? And what the hell's that got to do with the price of beans, who's givin' it? Must be nice, go traipsin' off to a party on Saturday afternoon, the hell with the work, just go have a good time. You don't even know how to play no card games. Expect me to drop everything and drive you over there, set around, bring you back. Wish I could just skip the chores and go off and have a good time—" He rummaged around for an example of a frivolous good time. " 'Go to hell off and go bowlin'.'"

She'd smothered her laugh at the idea of Mink, standing

grim in his manure-caked barn boots in a bowling alley, the ball like a bomb in his knotted hands. She'd choked on the idea. Her shoulders heaved, she buried her face in the pillow.

"Goddamn it, you feel that bad about it, go ahead and go! Christ sake, you don't have to bawl about it. Go on! Who's stoppin' you?" But she could not quit. That he mistook her laughter for sobs made it even richer. Mink bowling. Her blubbering, because she couldn't go to a stupid old card party.

"Oh, oh, oh," she moaned. "I haven't laughed like that."

He sighed, the bitter huff of a man whose patience is eroded. "I know where Dub gets his fool ways."

She was almost asleep when he whispered again. "How are you goin' to get over and back? I can't take time off the milkin' chores."

"Ride over with Mrs. Nipple. Ronnie's takin' her. Loyal could pick us up, save Ronnie a second trip. He's got cows, too, you know. At five o'clock. It's from one to five. I'm goin' to start the supper in the mornin', a good chicken stew or something, so it'll be quick to get up when I come back."

"I suppose we got to do it."

She was gone and snoring, only half conscious of the warmth of him, his hard arm around her waist, pulling her up tight to him, fitting his jackknifed knees in behind hers . . .

"What about Mernelle? Be good if Mernelle learned." Ronnie, still harping on about learning to drive brought her back.

"I doubt she'll be interested. Mernelle has got something up her sleeve. Not telling me a thing. I don't know what it is, but she spends half her time up in her room, half over to Darlene's, and the other half up at the mailbox waitin' for the Rural Free Delivery. She took what happened hard. Quit school when they come for Mink. Since he passed on she hardly says anything. She's not sharin' any secrets with me."

Eight days since she sent the letter, too soon for an answer, she knew, but she couldn't help thinking he would feel some special quality about her letter even while it was still in the envelope. Hundreds of girls would probably write to him, and it would take time to sort through all that mail, even if he had help. She knew he would do it alone. He was used to doing things alone.

It had been on the front page of two newspapers, maybe even more. The story was written in a jokey way that tried to make a fool out of him. But she saw around that stuff.

'Lonely Hearts Prisoner' Advertises for Wife.

Ray MacWay, a 19-year-old lumber grader at Fredette's Building Supplies in Burlington, walked into the Trumpet *editorial room and said he wanted to advertise for a wife. 'I want someone who's lonely like me. I've been an orphan since I was young and I live alone in a furnished room. It's hard for me to meet any girls because of my work hours. I call myself the lonely hearts prisoner. I went to work when I was around six years old peeling pulp in the woods. I ran off when I was 16, been all around, to Maine, up to Canada, to Mexico and Texas. But this is my home state. I'm a good worker. I feel there's a young lady out there lonely like me that we could be happy together. I hope she'll write me in care of the* Trumpet.'

The photograph next to the story showed a young man with ragged hair standing by a pile of lumber. The lake spread out in the background. There were holes in his trouser knees. He wore a checked jacket and Mernelle could see the raveled cuffs. His face looked plain, but calm. Even in the cramped ink dots of the newspaper photo he had the lonesome look. She saw enough of it in the mirror to know.

Dear Miss Blood
Your reply to my advertis seeing told me that you know about the difficultys of starting out in life. I know you know how it feels to struggle after all you have been throu. It will be a hard life for both of us until I get on my feet. But I am willing to make you happy. Would you like to go to the show I can get it for you wholesale. I and the newspaper woman that has a vechile will come and pick you up on Saturday afternoon we can talk this over and see if we could be happy.
I bet we will.
Yours truly.
Robert 'Ray' MacWay

Miss Mernelle Blood
RFD
Cream Hills, Vt.

The answer came on a Thursday morning. It was still raining, a steady sluice that gullied the driveway. She walked down, her black oilcloth raincoat cracked open from breast to shin like the wings of a beetle readying itself to fly. Her boot heels threw specks of muddy gravel onto her calves. The postcard showed a view of Red Rocks Point jutting out into Lake Champlain. The message space was filled with small printing, very legible despite the spelling errors. As serious as her own letter had been. The alders behind the mailbox were blackly wet, cracking the sky.

At nine o'clock on Saturday morning Mernelle was drying the cereal bowls and thinking what to say to Jewell. The sink gave off its odor. She might say "I am getting away from the sink." Or, "What am I supposed to do, rot here in this place?" Her clothes were ready. The blue skirt, a deep violet blue that had hardly faded from hanging on the line, and the white blouse with the buttons shaped like tiny pearl hearts. She had a lemon put aside; when she washed her hair, lemon juice in the rinse water would give it a red tone. " 'Little spitfire,' " she whispered to herself, thinking of some movie. She could say "You and Da lived like pigs. I want a nice place like Mrs. Weedmeyer's that fixed up the Batchelder dump. A shower with a glass door. Carpets. Silverware with roses on the handles and matching plates with blue rims and a golden stripe."

It was already too complicated to explain to Jewell, to say it so Jewell would see she had to get away no matter how. It all boiled down to two stupid sentences, that she was going off with somebody she didn't know, and it was somebody who'd advertised in the paper for a wife. She could hear Jewell's dust mop on the stairs, and hear a truck straining up the hill. Uncle Ott bringing more machinery or equipment for his new property. He'd brought over a bulldozer two days earlier, a hulking mud-covered thing that made a noise like turkeys when it started up. It rolled down off the truck bed and stood huffing in the field of dandelions of the same matching yellow, in the coarse new grass.

"I'd like to know what he thinks he's going to do with that," said Jewell. "He says he wants to plant corn. I never see a farmer use a bulldozer for a plow or a seeder. Loyal would have a fit to see that thing in his field."

The heavy idling echoed from the dooryard, there were steps on the porch and a knock. Not Ott, after all, who'd opened the door all his life.

"Hello. I'm looking for Mernelle Blood." A steady voice, wired with doggedness.

She could hear Jewell's dust mop pause on the stairs. The heat of the May morning struck through the screen door, the smell of grass and white blossom pressing in past the figure on the other side of the screen. She recognized his stance from the newspaper photograph. A flow of air drifted into the kitchen, filled it with the scent of mock orange, the sour exhaust of the stuttering car in the yard. Through the screen she could see knots of flies hovering at the tips of the pin cherry branches, the curve of blue metal.

"Oh God, I'm not ready. I haven't washed my hair."

"I couldn't wait until the afternoon," he said. "I couldn't wait." The screen door rattled faintly under his trembling hand.

Jewell, listening on the stairs, guessed at most of it.

20. The Bottle-Shaped Tombstone

dear joE
ALVINA KILLS MAN say te tell
you she find most of what
you want the elk medsin the
werlwind medsin for bad
dream the little bufalo
medsin she say more but
No room she say tell you
somboy find plase wagdin
medsin grow she say
are you ok for dig it she
say hury up.
your fren ELMER IN THE GRASS

JOE BLUE SKIES
white moon res
south dakota

HE held open the car door for her and she slid in behind the driver, a heavyset woman with cascades of curly grey hair sweeping down her back and wet eyes the color of tea.

"This is Mrs. Greenslit. She's the reporter for the Trumpet that wrote the story."

"Just call me Arlene. Yep, this is my story and I'm sticking with it. You two kids are the guests of the Trumpet—within reason. That includes dinner and a movie tonight and Miss Blood, you don't mind if I call you Mernelle, do you, you can stay over at my place free of charge until you kids see how this thing is gonna go. The only people there are me and my husband Pearl and Pearl's brother Ruby. They don't care if I bring home the bald-headed sword swallower. It's all in the day's work for a reporter. Oh, the stories I covered Mernelle you wouldn't believe. I was telling Ray here while we were waiting for you about last year when this amazing truck driver with no arms, drove with his feet, rolled into town and I rode with him all the way up to Montreal. Caught the train back. He was just wonderful how he could manage, steer and everything. He stayed over, too. Slept in the same bed you're gonna sleep in. I did a big Human Interest story on him. That's my specialty, Human Interest. So this story, the story of you two kiddies, is a natural for me. Oh yes, I seen it all. This is nothing. From my own life and everything else. I just naturally run into these stories. I was born in New York state, but came across the lake with my family when I was three. Grew up in Rouses Point. My father was a heavy drinker. You know, when he died my mother had his tombstone made over in Barre in the shape of a whiskey bottle. Six feet high. I went back to show it to some people I know a couple of years ago and somebody had stolen it. So I did a feature story on it, 'The Stolen Tombstone' and the paper got a tip that a certain gentleman down in Amherst, Massachusetts, a college professor, was using it for a coffee table. The police got it back for us. The Massachusetts police. Of course we had to go down there with a flatbed truck and pick it up. My husband had a few choice words for the college professor. I wouldn't repeat them. You can't push Pearl around. The thing that surprised me was it had been gone a couple of years and my mother didn't even know it. And how did he get it down there? He would not say, but denied it was a truck. I did a story on a bat-shoot. Know what that is? Well, I guess you don't read the *Trumpet,* because it was one of the most popular stories they ever ran. I don't know how many letters they got on that story. It was about this hunting and fishing club and how they wanted to shoot clay pigeons on the weekend, but they couldn't get 'em, just couldn't get 'em here, so this one guy has bats in his attic, see, and he goes and gets them in the daytime when they're sleeping, puts them in this box, pokes holes in it so they can breathe, and then brings it to the club. They let the bats go and that's what they shot since they couldn't get the clay pigeons. They stopped though when there was a man wounded. The bats flew low. You know Mr. File, Fred File, that's the editor of the *Trumpet* thought you kids might want to go out dancing after the movie-dinner at Bove's, Italian, all you can eat, the lasagna is great, then the movie, I forgot what's playing, oh no, I remember, it's *I Can Get It For You Wholesale* with Irene Dunne or somebody. A comedy, supposed to be hilarious. But the dancing, there isn't any tonight so you might just have to walk around. Stroll. The important thing is to get to know each other. I was telling Ray here on the way over, that's the most important thing in the world, getting to know another person, and probably the hardest thing, too. One of the best stories I ever did was about this guy who fell in love with a friend of his mother's, she was, I don't know, maybe twenty-five years older than him, had white hair and all, but he was crazy about her. Of course the only thing he knew about her was what he saw when she came to visit his mother. She was always very nice and I guess that's what he liked. His mother drank, I think, and wasn't too kind to him. So one day this friend of his mother comes in and he gets down on his knees in front of her and says 'I love you,' and she thinks he's flipped his wig, she gets up and starts to go into the kitchen to get his mother, and he grabs her and she shoves him so he goes in his bedroom and gets a gun and comes out and says 'If I can't have you nobody can' and shoots her. Shoots her dead. And the mother's in the kitchen through all this stirring up iced tea. So the point is to get to know somebody as well as you can before you drag them off. Right, Ray?"

Mernelle and Ray MacWay sat in the backseat like pillars, each conscious of the heat of the other's body and hearing, not Mrs. Greenslit's waves of talk, but the sound of breathing. Over the mildewed upholstery Mernelle could smell soap, shampoo, pinewood, warm skin, Dentyne chewing gum. Her stomach growled and she hated it, willed it to shrivel.

In the kitchen a bumblebee that had mistaken the gap between the screen door and its casing for nirvana flew at the windows, seeking to enter again the familiar world, visible and near, but walled off by a malignant force.

Mernelle was back again in a week, banging the screen door against the house as she backed into the kitchen. She carried a cardboard circle with a store cake covered with coconut as thick as fur. The rumble of the exhaust in the dooryard stopped, car doors slammed.

"Happy Mother's Day, Ma. It's me and Ray. Mrs. Greenslit's here too." She hugged Jewell around the waist.

"Well, fill me in on the news," said Jewell, startled at the way Mernelle had changed, guilty at how little she had worried about her. Mernelle wore a long-skirted blue suit and a pink rayon blouse. She had on high heels and her face was made up. Her black hair cut and crimped in a permanent wave like a helmet of sheep's wool. She looked taller, even more gawky, but there was a sureness in her that estranged her from the old child's life.

"Tell you quick before Ray and Mrs. Greenslit comes in, Mr. Trueblood wouldn't marry us." Murmuring, half-whispering. "He said it was a publicity stunt and he wouldn't marry us until we'd known each other for a year. He said 'quick courtship, quick divorce.' Ray gave him a swat and he called the sheriff. So we all had to go down to the sheriff's office in Billytown, and Mrs. Greenslit busy writing it all up. Well, another story come out in the *Trumpet* and we got all these letters from other ministers who will marry us, including one up at Rouses Point that done the funeral service for Mrs. Greenslit's father when he died. So I guess we will go up there. Ray wants to see her father's tombstone anyway. So we're going up there today and want you to come. Mrs. Greenslit will bring you back. Ray and me is going on a honeymoon to Montreal. The *Trumpet is* paying for some of it. Ray don't like them to pay for it all. He's got some money saved up.

Jewell put on the kettle for coffee. The commotion in the kitchen seemed immense. Mrs. Greenslit, arranging paper plates, putting out plastic forks and knives. "Hello, hello, hello! Here we are," she cried. Mernelle shuffled through the chipped dishes, picking out the four nicest. "There's ice cream, too. Strawberry. Butter pecan. That's the new flavor. You'll love it."

Ray came in carrying a waxed tissue twist and held it out to Jewell. "The *Trumpet* didn't buy them," he said, and smiled. His stiff face broke in half, showed bad teeth. There were a dozen tea roses the color of boiled shrimp. She unwrapped the paper, as green as new popple leaves, filled a cream jug with water. "Been a good many years since anybody gave me flowers. Flowers from the florist, that is," remembering Mernelle's hot bunches of daisies and vetch, violets with half-inch stems, wilting lilacs.

"I'm happy I can do it," said Ray and sat down beside Mernelle. Mernelle handed Jewell a package in flowered paper. She made a fuss over the prettiness of the paper, smoothing and setting it aside. There were two pairs of nylons, 60 gauge, 15 denier, "Piquant Beige" on the label. Eating the cake Jewell looked at Ray from under her eyelids, looked at his forgettable face, his thin arms, his hungry eyes. She thought with melancholy of roguish Dub, of handsome Loyal, lost or stunted in their lives while this one got ahead. Ray cut more cake, Mernelle doting on the sawing motion of his hand. The frosting hung off their forks. Mrs. Greenslit jabbered. Jewell felt how fierce she had grown in her solitude. But she smiled and said, in her kindest voice, the cake was a treat, said she would ride with them up to Rouses Point for the wedding. And went to the attic with Mernelle to find a certain silk handkerchief edged in handmade lace.

"It was your father's mother's when she was married, and she had it down from someone else. I believe it came from Ireland. It's very old." They sat in the dusty attic chairs in front of the trunk with its freight of old schoolbooks, awkward clothing, a ruined buffalo robe, family papers and photographs, a parasol in tatters.

"I don't suppose there's anything I can tell you that you don't already know," she said. "There's things you'll learn that nobody can tell you."

"Well," said Mernelle. "It's not that I know so much but that I trust Ray. I know he'll never hurt me. I've never seen *him* lose his temper." Her voice vibrated. It was pitched lower as if she had been singing for hours every day. "So, I mean, I guess I didn't grow up on a farm for nothing. But there's something I wanted to know for a long time." Her voice wheedled. "About Mrs. Nipple. What it was about Mrs. Nipple and Toot you never would tell me?"

"My Lord, that's not anything to talk about now. Supposed to be a happy occasion and that morbid story's enough to depress an angel. It would spoil your day and poor Mrs. Nipple would roll over in her grave. Spoil my day, too, digging that up. Let's go on down and have a happy time of it."

"It must be something pretty awful," said Mernelle, half sulky. She'd been up to plenty, thought Jewell.

"You know, I'd say it was. Now I'm going to go put on my new nylons and see if I can't show up the bride. And there's something else I want to give you. The money from the farm that was left after the bank and all was paid out, I divided it up equal so's me, you and Dub and Loyal all get a share. It's not much, comes to two hundred each, but it's something. If I was you, I'd just put it aside in the bank or something, don't say nothing to Ray, not that he's not a nice fellow, just put it aside for your own little nest egg. You can't tell, you might want it someday."

"Ma, that money's to keep you. Ray and me'll make out o.k."

"Don't worry about me. I may have grey hair, but there's life in the old girl yet. Ronnie been teaching me to drive so I can get a job. You ought to know how to drive soon's you can, Mernelle. It'll make an awful difference in your life."

"Ma, we don't even have a car. We been going around with that reporter woman, Mrs. Greenslit, and if we ever get rid of her I'll be so thankful I won't mind crawling on my hands and knees. But Ray's saving up. I got to get a job too. What are you going to try for?"

"In fact, I already got two jobs. It's funny. Ronnie's been taking me over and picking me up as part of the driving lessons. If you'd come yesterday you wouldn't of found me here. I was working down to the cannery. It's just cutting up vegetables that come in on the trucks, carrots all week. They say they get everything, broccoli, celery, beans. In the evening I been knitting stockings for the Ski Shop or whatever they call it, Downhill Shop. Long stockings with a fancy design knit in the leg and contrast color cuffs. I made a pair with red valentine hearts all over like that hat I made you when you were in the eighth grade, and they went crazy over them. The two women that run the place, Jo-Jo, the young one, says she is taking the valentine stockings down to New York. Thinks they'll be good sellers. It seems funny to be knitting wool stockings in summer, but that's how you get the stock built up, they said. Anyway, it's enough for me to make out on pretty good. Where are you going to live?"

"We found an apartment. Can't afford our own house for a long time. Big old place down by the lake, this old house that's divided up into eight apartments. There's real big windows. It'll take just yards and yards to make curtains, but I don't want to leave them bare."

"Just dye some sheets the color you want and hem them up. Cover the biggest windows in the state. Listen, Mernelle, you keep this money to yourself. In case you ever have an emergency. Or it can be a start toward education money. For your kids."

But Mernelle told Ray MacWay on the way up to Rouses Point, whispering in his ear, while up front Mrs. Greenslit talked about her father's tombstone and the armless trucker. Jewell saw the woman was a miserable driver, treading on the brake for every curve, forgetting to shift down on hills until the car bucked.

21. The Driver

June 17, '52
Dear Wilma, Well, me and Gib is settled in. Our trailer is in Happy Park here in Kissimee. I hope you are alright. It is the first time I been out in over a week. We both had the flue. Gib won a pair of binaclors on the Sportmen showcase. He won't say it but got a ticket for speeting. Pray ing for you. Your sister in law Irene. P.s. as usual nothing from Billy this yr. So far,

Mrs Wilma Handy
2 Court Street
Albany, New York

ONCE Ronnie got her through the tricks of the clutch and gear shifting, it seemed she'd been driving for years. She had a feel for it, and by August her license was in her new brown purse and she ventured onto roads she'd never traveled. Her fear was that the car would stall on a hill in traffic and she'd hold up the parade while she tried to start it again, would flood the engine, forget the brake and roll down backwards into an ambulance.

At first she stayed on valley highways, but after a few weeks began to pick mountain roads where she could lean into the corners or nurse the old heap up the slope to a pull-off at the top and take in the panorama through her new eyeglasses. Continuity broke: when she drove, her stifled youth unfurled like ribbon pulled from a spool.

There was the idea of what outsiders saw in "views"—when you went somewhere you wanted to see something, when you'd been driving with your eyes on the road for hours, you wanted to let them stretch out to the boundaries of the earth, the farther the better. All her life she had taken the tufted line of the hills against the sky as fixed, but saw now that the landscape changed, rolled out as far as the roads went, never repeating itself in its arrangement of cliffs and water and trees. View was something more than the bulk of hills and opening valleys, more than sheets of riffled light.

When she turned the ignition key and steered the car out of the drive, the gravel crunching deliciously under the tires, she went dizzy with power for the first time in her adult life. The radio played "Cherry Pink and Apple Blossom White," and she was glad. She felt she was young and in a movie when she drove. She had never guessed at the pleasure of choosing which turns and roads to take, where to stop. Nor the rushing air buffeting her face and whipping her iron hair as though it were child's hair. As though they had given her the whole country for her own. Did men, she wondered, have this feeling of lightness, of wiping out all troubles when they got into their cars or trucks? Their faces did not show any special pleasure when they drove. Men understood nothing of the profound sameness, week after week, after month of the same narrow rooms, treading the same worn footpaths to the clothesline, the garden. You soon knew it all by heart. Your mind closed in to the problems of cracked glass, feeling for pennies in linty coat pockets, sour milk. You couldn't get away from troubles. They came dragging into the mirror with you, fanning over the snow, filled the dirty sink. Men couldn't imagine women's lives, they seemed to believe, as in a religion, that women were numbed by an instinctive craving to fill the wet mouths of babies, pre-destined to choose always the petty points of life on which to hang their attention until at last, all ended and began with the orifices of the body. She had believed this herself. And wondered in the blue nights if what she truly felt now was not the pleasure of driving but being cast free of Mink's furious anger. He had crushed her into a corner of life.

Coming back from her journeys, from seeing houses set in a hundred positions, some beside the road, some back in a knot of trees like a brooch on a hill's breast, her own house showed up as a slatternly lean of paintless clap-boards, the porch slipping away like melting butterscotch.

She saw the landscape changing. Ronnie was right. Everything was changing. Brush growing up. She was critical when the road crews cut overhanging limbs from the maples. Tears streamed when they cut the trees them-selves to widen the highway, hardtop now all the way to the Post Road. The village grew unaccountably, men sawed down the yellowing elms, tore up stumps with great corkscrew machines. The street spread like unpenned water to the edges of the buildings. Metal roofs glittered.

At the dump, heaps of broken slates invited potshots from rat shooters, then sent the bullets ricocheting back. The town sold off the timber in the watershed above the valley and for two years endured the nasal moaning of chain saws. The clear-cut left the hills as bare as the side of a scraped hog. The old common became a park with walks and concrete benches already crumbling in their second spring. A War monument, an awkward artillery gun plugged with more concrete, pointed at the Methodist Church. It peeled to rusted metal in a year. She hated the way boys spun their bikes on a bare dirt patch where the old bandstand had teetered, its fretwork a tease to look at.

New people. New people owned the general store, started new stores, turned barns into inns and woodwork shops. They moved into farmhouses hoping to fit their lives into the rooms, to fit their shoes to the stair treads. She thought they were like insects casting off tight husks, vulnerable for a little while until the new chitin hardened.

The local people who used to be good at something worked out now. Robby Gordy, who made a maple chair of simple but satisfying shape, strong as iron, worked in the new tennis ball factory. Yet this young fellow, Hubbardkindle, moved up from Rhode Island and began sawing out clumpy pine chairs. Charged an arm and a leg for them and got it. He had a clever sign in the shape of a chair that hung out front, put ads in the paper. You had to know Robby Gordy to know he made anything at all.

She was alone for the first time in her adult life, alone in a solitude that tasted like a strange but sweet tropical fruit. The big meals three times a day, the twice-weekly baking, were the first to go. She ate scratch meals, cold potatoes, leftover soup, sandwiches that Mink had hated as "city food." The huge loads of Monday wash no longer sloshed around in the wringer machine. She slept until six in the mornings.

Nor did the silent rooms bother her. She closed the doors, one by one, keeping just the kitchen and the spare room for sleeping. The night of the day they told her about Mink she got her pillow from their bed and took it into the spare room with its iron bed painted white, its flowery coverlet, the braided rug in all colors. The bed was hard, but its strangeness seemed correct. Silence deep as coal. When she woke in the morning to the pattern of light on the faded wall, the scent of sachet from the little embroidered bag under the pillow, she was already in her different life.

22. The Dermatologist in the Wild Wood

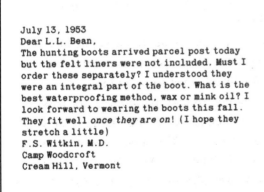

July 13, 1953
Dear L.L. Bean,
The hunting boots arrived parcel post today but the felt liners were not included. Must I order these separately? I understood they were an integral part of the boot. What is the best waterproofing method, wax or mink oil? I look forward to wearing the boots this fall. They fit well *once they are on*! (I hope they stretch a little)
F.S. Witkin, M.D.
Camp Woodcroft
Cream Hill, Vermont

L. L. Bean
Freeport, Maine

DR. Franklin Saul Witkin, forty-seven, stoop-shouldered,

urban in habitat but haunted from childhood by fantasies of wilderness, sat on the stone wall staring into the chaos of his purchased landscape. There was too much to look at. Knotted branches. The urgent but senseless angular pointing of tree limbs. Grass the color of wafers. Trees lifting soundless explosions of chrome and saffron. Mountains scribbled maroon, riven by mica-shot cliffs. The yelling light. He looked up and the sky filled with swarming points. If he walked into the woods, land tilted, trees thronged like gnats, the air turned sallow and he was lost. He always came back to the wall for his bearings, finding in its linear perseverance, its lichened stones, a rope in the wilderness.

Soon after he bought the property he drove up to plan the hunting camp. The idea of a hunting camp had come to him when he was fourteen, studying photographs of Teddy Roosevelt in some log room decorated with the heads and skins of animals. He called his dream camp "Woodcroft," believing a croft was a kind of lair.

"It won't be just a hunting camp. It's a weekend camp for all of us," he told Matitia. She came up with the twins twice or three times. But his half brother, Larry J., a New York gallery owner, a man with a hundred interests and a thousand friends, was excited. Larry was seven years older, the son of his father's first wife, Jolana. They did not know each other, had met only at their father's funeral. Who had told Larry about the property? His New York voice on the phone talked of shooting weekends in the autumn, deer season, about lovely dogs who might range and cast before them. Neither had ever hunted.

"It's curious, really. Neither of us knows anything about

the woods. Neither of us knows anything about the other. Yet we both love this place. We both dreamed about huts in the forest when we were kids." Larry stood among the trees, fallen leaves washing around his ankles, not looking at Witkin. "It's a different thing than coming up for the skiing or staying at a Woodstock inn, or even visiting friends or taking a house for the summer. That someone in the family owns this land—" They were awkward, describing their feelings. The property was like an ear trumpet through which they could understand each other.

The first time Witkin came up to take possession of the property he came with his wife and children, past the swaybacked farmhouse halfway up the hill, the tumbled heap of beams and stone that marked the old barn, through the fields and into the leafy maples.

He'd had an idea they could fix up the old sugarhouse on the property, but it was far gone. Spotted light dappled the caving walls. The door was buried in the earth. The sills, gnawed by porcupines, rotted, and shingles lay across the floor like a hand of cards. The only sound wood was in the two-by-six wall studs.

They pitched the new tent on a level under the maples and made a ring of stones. Slowly the light faded under the trees, the darkness settled around them. The tent glimmered. Kevin and Kim kept flicking their flashlight beam through the woods, the circle of light bouncing through the trees like a living thing.

"You two. Quit it or you'll wear out the batteries and have to sleep in the dark." They sat late around the fire. When twigs snapped in the woods Witkin told them not to worry, there were no dangerous animals, but he thought of bears with fear. None of them had slept outdoors before. Kim wet her sleeping bag because she was frightened in the night.

"I heard something big breathing right outside."

"It was just us, our breathing."

"No. no. Your breathing is quiet, see? This was a big, terrible breathing. Like this."

Witkin could not bear to hear the imitation of his sexual huffing coming from the innocent throat of his daughter. For after the twins slept Witkin had made struggling, excited love to Matitia, the sleeping-bag zipper gnawing at their arms. The new smell of the tent, the whimpering dreams of his children thickened his blood. He braced against the hard ground. The wind stirred the trees, he grasped his wife's living hair and panted at its phosphorescence.

He woke many times during the night to sounds outside the tent but, kneeling in his underwear at the zippered screen door and shining the light into the darkness, he could see nothing. When he switched off the flashlight the darkness seemed immense and ageless.

In the morning Matitia wanted to go back.

"Because of Kim's sleeping bag. Because I need a bath. Because I hardly slept. I'm wrecked. Later on," she said. "Later on, when the camp is done and we can sleep indoors. The tent is creepy and the kids aren't old enough yet. And I smell like a smoked herring."

"I am old enough," shouted Kevin.

"Not yet, Sweetheart," said Matitia.

"We'll come back," said Witkin. "Don't worry, Babbety babbety baby-bye."

"Don't call me that! I hate that baby name!"

But they did not come again and so he went with the half brother. In the drizzling rain they tore the sugarhouse down and burned the punky boards. Larry opened the champagne and they staggered around the stinking fire.

"Woo-woo-woo," said Larry. Mud smeared his stiff jeans. His Camp Mocs slipped on the wet leaves. Witkin saw something of his father in Larry's black hair with its reddish tint, the small fat lips like two pink capsules. But nothing of himself. They might have been acquaintances.

All week Witkin talked with patients about flaking skin, moles that winked in creases of the flesh, the highway worker's reddened cancerous ears, rashes and itches, hives and shingles, port-wine stains, and while he talked, he sketched at his desk behind the shelter of the photograph of Matitia and Kevin and Kim in the hinged three-part frame. He was drawing a rustic log cabin with small-paned windows. He wanted a porch the length of the place, the porch on the east side away from the heat of the setting sun in summer afternoons, but cheerful in the mornings, a place to drink coffee. Here a boot scraper. He already had the boot-scraper in the garage, unused for years, waiting for a wooden porch. Carefully he drew the butt ends of the logs with dovetail notches. Two steps leading up to the porch. A plank door with a wrought iron latch. He drew in two spruce trees, one on each side of the cabin, even though the site was in the maple woods. The spruce were on the other side of the ridge where there was no road.

Drawing the inside was wonderful. He sketched beams, a fireplace with flames, a coffee table made from thick wood. Over the fireplace he hung a 10-point rack, a rifle, and to the side he put a painting of two hunters in a canoe drawing a bead on a moose.

Larry smiled when he showed him the sketches. But his face was not unkind.

"Where's the kitchen? No sink, no refrigerator, no cupboards. This is a little impractical, Frank. I love the fireplace, but you can't cook in a fireplace unless you put everything on a spit. Did you ever try pancakes on a spit? What we need here is a stove. You're not going to believe this, but I've got a stove. It's a beautiful thing, square, a dark green enamel cube. It's an art piece. Came from Darmstadt. A dealer in Darmstadt sent it to me. I asked him to send a piece by this very strange guy, Joseph Beuys. I have—had, I should say—a client, collects German postwar art, heard of Beuys, wanted a piece by Beuys, anything at all, ship it straight over. But didn't know anything about the man's work. The stove, this is what the dealer sent. It's packed with big cakes of suet. The man works in suet, fat. So I had it delivered to the client's apartment. She's in Boca Raton. The next week the phone rings. She's back and she's furious. What is this smelly thing full of fat doing in her foyer? I explain that's her art piece. She says it's repulsive. She had her cleaning lady take all the suet out and throw it away, I should come get the stove. So I did. And there the damn stove sits, in the gallery, a ruined work of art. It's a very expensive stove and we might as well use it."

On Friday mornings in Boston Witkin got up before light, thinking of the drive north, the feeling of climbing up some great slope as though the north was higher in altitude. It was higher, he knew it. He loaded the station wagon before Matitia was awake and was at his office at eight. The last patient came at noon and then he was on his way. But once at the camp he felt uncertain. It was as if the road between his two lives was the realest thing of all, as if the journey counted more than arriving at the end.

23. Ott's Lots

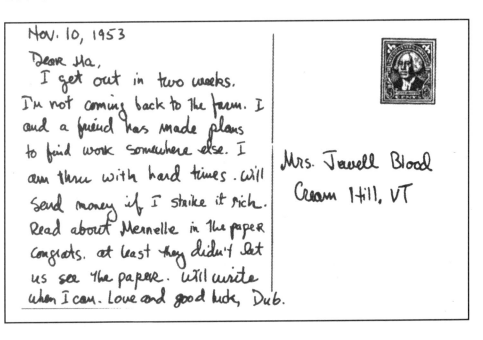

Nov. 10, 1953

Dear Ma,
    I get out in two weeks. I'm not coming back to the farm. I and a friend has made plans to find work somewhere else. I am thru with hard times. Will send money if I strike it rich. Read about Mernelle in the paper Congrats. at least they didn't let us see the paper. Will write when I can. Love and good luck, Dub.

Mrs. Jewell Blood
Cream Hill, VT

BUT, pulling onto the home road on a November payday afternoon, a paper carton of chop suey on the floorboards, the radio trilling with Organ Interlude, Jewell looked up at Loyal's—now Ott's—field and caught her breath.

The evening shadow moved up the field, caught low sloughs and extended the darkness of rocks beyond their corporeal forms, closed like a pincers from the low ground and from the wood at the top until only a fan of sunlight lay open. The cold light streamed across the raw bull-dozed roads that had not been there in the morning. Back and forth, up and down, roads divided the field into forty half-acre lots, too small for anything but cemetery plots thought Jewell.

As she drove past the field toward the house, trembling with anger, the fan of light blackened and disintegrated like burned paper except for the ridges of earth thrown up at the edges of the fresh roads. The metal gate to the field was gone, and in its place was the raw, open mouth of the entrance and a sign made from a single sheet of plywood. OTT'S LOTS & MOBILE HOME PARK. A painted phone number in big red numerals. Not Ott's number. Ronnie Nipple's.

24. The Indian's Book Again

June 17, 1957

Hello folks, I guess you could call me an old desert rat now. It is hotter than the hinges of hell out here this time of year. Hope all are well.

Loyal

Mr. & Mrs. Mink Blood
Cream Hill

Vermont

HE had written a question in the Indian's book, a warped, spiral-bound notebook with stippled orange covers. Was everything all right with him before Billy? And knew the dirty answer.

PART THREE

25. Garden of Eden

March, 1960

Dear Mernelle and Ma, Try this for size. I am living in Miami and going to real estate school. I work Mon-Wed and week ends at a kind of tourist attraction and school at night. Picking up some Spanish you got to know it. This a garden of Eden even with all the Cubans coming in to get away from Castro. Rt. now living in kind of a dump, but you wait. After all that happened, after bumping around for the last six years this is my opportunity. Like Mr. Bart says in class, I refuse to accept the fate life handed me. I will make my own fate. Pls. write, esp. any news. Myrtle and the Boys. Dub. 2131 Los Gatos. Miami Fla.

MRS. Jewell Blood
RFD
Cream Hill, Vt.

YARRA was excited. "He sent it. I know he sent it. Goddamn, there's a check in there, I didn't think he'd send it. But he did. That was a good list of names. Wasn't that the list where the woman sent a hundred? Sure it was. A good list." His tan porkpie hat was tilted aggressively down over his nose so he had to tilt up his chin when he looked at Dub. The jaws worked on the everlasting invisible piece of gristle.

"You open it?"

"No, course I didn't open it. Got your name on the front,

187

think I open somebody else's letter?" He flapped the envelope virtuously in front of Dub's face.

"So how do you know there's money in it?" Dub felt like he was underwater. The motel walls were the blue of swimming pools. On the rickety desk his bottle of whiskey, roll of stamps, the ballpoint pen, the packet of envelopes, the tablet of crinkly letter paper, lists of addresses and replies. He could whip those letters off.

Dear Mr. Randall,
Your name has been given to me as the name of a man who can be trusted and who would be interested in an excellent money making opportunity. I will come right to the point as I know you are a busy man, and tell you that due to no fault of my own, I am at this time a political prisoner in a Mexican jail. Things are done very different here than in the U.S.A. and it has been made known to me that if I can raise the sum of $300 I will be released from this prison. Liberty! The sweetest words on earth! Naturally I am not asking you to contribute $300 to me as a risk, but I can tell you in all confidence that I have a Large sum of money, close to $350,000 buried in the U. S. A. in a spot known only to me, and if I can get released from this place, I will split that sum with the man who befriends me, half and half. The money is of no use to me here in this terrible prison. The rats are very bad. If I could get at it I would be free in a minute. But I know you are a fellow American who can be trusted, and if you remit the $300 to insure my release I will contact you at once on my release and we will go

*together to where I have hidden the Large sum. You
as the good samaritan will get back five hundred
times your investment. Because it is risky to try and
send a letter across the border I have arranged a special hand delivery arrangement. Send the money in a
plain brown envelope or a money order addressed to
Mr. Marvin E. Blood #1408 Lily Garden Ave., Miami,
Florida. He will pass it on to a trusted friend who will
soon be in Mexico on business.
Yours sincerely,
Joseph W. MacArthur (a distant relation of Gen.
Douglas MacArthur)*

Some job. But this was the place, Florida, this was for
him, the lush brightness, the spiciness and fast-thinking
people. He felt alive here. He'd never go back north.

"I held it up to the window. I could see a money order
form."

Dub slit the envelope with his jacknife. A money order
for five hundred dollars slid out of a folded letter.

"Jesus! We hit the jackpot. This guy sent two hundred
more than I even asked for. Listen to this. Listen.

*'Dear Mr. MacArthur. Maybe I am crazy to take a
chance on you but I'm going to risk it. I think you will
pay me back. I have been down myself. Enclosed
please find the $300 to get you out of the "Mexican
prison" and another $200 to help you get started in
some legitimate calling. I hear men can make for-
tunes in Florida real estate and callings associated
with the tourist industry. Perhaps this will start you*

out. Sincerely, J. J. Randall.' "

"Hey, he knows it's a con."

"Yeah. And he sent it just the same. That's a hell of a nice guy." Dub floated in a sea of good luck.

"He probably done time himself, knows what it's like. Probably just pulled off a supermarket robbery or something. Could of whacked a old lady on the head, snatched her cat food money."

"Yeah. But maybe just a guy wants to give somebody a hand. Or some rich guy never even notice five hundred. There's people like that. Over at Palm Beach they're like that. That's the address we got on Randall, Palm Beach. You can't even go on the streets at night unless you got a pass. Those are rich, rich people."

"They hold on to it, too. Palm Beach. Where the rich families dump their retards. Pick a warm climate so the dummies don't freeze to death they don't know how to make a fire."

"Hey, don't be so sour. Let's go. Cash this thing."

"I want to buy the best dinner in town, steaks with onion and mushroom, get the hell out of this dump. How about Los Angeles? Get out of this dump." A little life comes into Yarra's lumpy face, complexion like an unbandaged foot.

"I'm thinking."

"Think on the way. Let's go."

"Anyway, I rather have one of them Cuban sandwiches, I love them things."

Dub read the letter again while he ate, cramming in the spicy pork. The crust sawed the roof of his mouth. The letter. What the hell, real estate. He hadn't thought about doing anything since the piano tuning. Just swindle letters. Dumb!

"Yarra, you know I started to be a piano tuner once?"

"Yeah? What happened?"

"Nothing. Nothing." He was thinking. It didn't have to be real estate. He could be anything. He tried to think of occupations, but all he could come up with was waiter, restaurant manager, post office worker, motel keeper, ideas he got by reviewing the day. He didn't want to do any of that. Where the hell did you find out about "callings"?

Late that night the idea came to him: look in the phone book. See what people did. He got up, ignoring Yarra's strangled question from the other bed, and took the phone book into the bathroom to sit on the cool throne among the cockroaches, flipping the yellow pages and considering how far he'd get as an adoption agent, private investigator, septic tank cleaner, diamond merchant, sign painter, marina manager, nurseryman, towel supplier, tennis court maintenance man, smoke odor remover, rope maker, bookseller, traffic analyst, or tattoo artist. He looked under Real Estate. Son of a bitch, there were pages and pages of appraisers, developers, estate managers. He was all reared up. There were a couple of real estate schools. In Miami. He'd call one up in the morning. Just for the hell of it. But God, he was all reared up and could not sleep.

Yarra drove him crazy. The guy wanted to take off for LA right away. He wanted cornflakes and bacon and pancakes for breakfast. He didn't like Miami. He hated the sound of Spanish he said, there were too many niggers, it was too hot, he had a sunburn just from walking around, the car was crusted with bugs, the windshield all gummed up, he hated fruit, the shrines had the wrong saints, let's get the hell out of here.

Dub left Yarra at a diner pouring cane syrup on corn bread and went up the street for Cuban coffee and a couple of sugared *churros*. The quiet phone booth at the back of the marina a block from the diner. He talked to people at two of the real estate schools. The phone didn't answer at the third. He liked the girl at the Southern Florida Real Estate Institute and called her back.

"I sure do remember talking with you ten minutes ago. And I'm glad you called back?" She made every statement into a question. "Because I thought of something else. We are a six-month school leading to the real estate license, just sellin' the real estate, you know. But. There's the real estate college, Miami Realty Junior College. Real good courses on every phase of the business if you're real serious about advancing in the field? Not just selling. But. Investment, development, stocks? You can work in the daytime and take courses at night? I'm not suppose to tell you this, but you sounded like you wanted to know it all?"

"I do want to know it all. I just decided that. And I want to know your name and what time you get done work. I'd like to buy you a drink for your help. And meet you."

"Mr. Blood, I have a surprise for you? You have been allured by a woman's voice. I am a sixty-two-year-old grandmother and my husband wouldn't like for me to run off to a gin mill with a stranger? But. I know about the college because my daughter graduated there seven years ago. She went to Houston? She's with a top development firm? So it can be done. But thank you for asking.

Bye-bye, now and you have good luck?"

Yarra was ugly. He was standing on the sidewalk in front of the diner looking up and down the street. He was snapping one fist into the palm of the other hand, showing his muscled forearms. Ropy arms, Levis creased like metal. His fishing hat was pushed back. He looked at his watch. Figured I run out on him, thought Dub. For a minute he was tempted, he had the money, but walked up behind him and tapped Yarra on the shoulder.

"Where the hell you been?"

"Making phone calls. Making plans."

"Yeah? Well, the only plan I want to make is get out of here. There was a fuckin' cockroach in the corn bread. I almost puked on the table. I just want to get out of here."

"Let's talk about it. I like it here."

"Like it! What are you, spic-lover or something?"

"I don't know, I just feel good here. There's something going on, there's this feeling of taking a chance. It's like going to the races every day."

"Miami stinks. It's better in LA. The climate's nice and even, not sweaty like here. I got contacts in LA. We'll clean up. Get some fancy stationery for the letters. We'll live good. Hey, Hollywood! A few more nice letters like yesterday we'll be all set."

"I don't want to go to LA. I don't want to write any more letters. I'll split the five hundred with you but I'm staying here. Gonna try to get in this real estate college. I got an appointment with the admissions this afternoon."

Yarra stopped chewing on the piece of gristle. "Oh oh oh I got a prince with me." He put the back of his right hand on his hip and fluffed his wiry hair with the other.

"Why, pardon my bad manner, sir, I thought we was on the same fuckin' trip but I see different. I didn't know I was goin' around with a prince. What the hell. You not much fun, anyway. Just a goddamn farm boy, dazzled by the bright lights. Give my two-fifty and I'm gone."

"Two-twenty-five—I gave you twenty-five yesterday after we cashed it."

"Oh yeah. Wouldn't want to forget that now, would we? But I want to ask you, who was it give you the idea of the letters? Me. Who was it showed you the scam? Me. Who was it got you that list of addresses? Me. Who was it picks the letter up when it comes? Me. And NOW, who is it gets kicked in the balls and dumped? Me. And I'll tell you something, you won't ever make it. You're not the type that makes it."

"Your ass. But if it makes you feel better I'll give you the two-fifty." He only wanted to get rid of Yarra. Minute by minute he was getting into Florida, feeling the charged-up rhythm.

"And what about the VW? Who gets the VW?" The stream of people parted on both sides, a woman, red toe-nails jutting out of peek-a-boo shoes, a black woman in a dress printed with violet orchids, a black woman in a uni-form carrying a Woolworth's bag. A pair of short Cubans, bellies swelling their guayaberas, hair springing up at their throats, the rich cigar smoke trailing after them, ran into him as they stared at two blondies in pedal pushers and ballet slippers. A tourist hauled a child holding a rabbit balloon by the ears. The dwarf with a red vest, three hard hats without shirts, belly hair rising out of blue jeans, a man with red glass rings on every finger, a hard-eyed

Mikasuki wearing saddle oxfords and a yellow shirt rolled past, the traffic, buses drowned their voices, left them spitting into each other's faces.

"O.k., let's take it around to a couple of used-car dealers, see what they offer. Strike an average. You want the car? You pay me for my half. We went halfsies on the car. We can sell it, split the dough. Both be better off that way, I think. You could take a bus to LA."

They got two hundred for the black VW and Yarra left on the noon bus for Mobile, New Orleans and west.

"Good riddance, meatball!" he shouted, leaning out the bus window, giving Dub the finger.

Mr. Bent came through the classroom door like a tiger. He stood in front of the class, stared at them for a long minute. His face was tanned a deep red-orange. A ridge of muscle around his mouth whitened the rim of his upper lip and gave him the look of a shrewd simian. The bags under his eyes were dusky blues. His hair, parted on the left, leaped up in a great quiff over his left eye. He wore a white linen suit with a nylon knit shirt of pale yellow. The collar flared over the suit lapels, and when he leaned out, Dub, sitting in the front row, could see the crown emblem stitched over his left nipple. He bent toward them and, in a coaxing voice, said, "I am a millionaire. How many of you want to be millionaires?"

The Cuban-looking woman beside Dub shot her hand into the air and held it there. Other hands went up. Dub hesitated, then thought why the hell shouldn't I be a millionaire and raised his hand. Only a heavyset man with a sad expression let his hands lie on the desk top.

"What is your name sir?"

"John Corcoris."

"Well, John, if you don't want to be a millionaire why are you in this class?" In the laughter the hands slid down again.

"Well, I was in sponge diving, my family done this for generations, Key West, Tarpon Springs, but the sponges is thin out, there's the synthetics. I thought maybe a good idea get into real estate. Never thought about being a millionaire. I just want enough to raise my family, live comfortable."

"Mr. Corcoris. I will invite you to step out into the hall and reflect a moment. If, at the end of five minutes you do not want to be a millionaire, kindly point yourself in another direction. This class WILL be animated by each student's desire to make a million dollars. And I will personally be insulted if every person in this room does not go for that goal with everything he or she has got. You CAN DO IT. You come from all walks of life, from every background, you are different ages—how old are you?" pointing at an acned boy, then at an older woman whose hair was streaked with yellow white—"there you are, twenty-two and sixty-three. Some of you may have had sorry pasts, others may have fallen from earlier glory or riches. Yet you are all here in this room, united by a single motive—the motive to be a success, to make a fortune, to make a million dollars. And I am here to show you how. The motto of this class is 'I refuse to accept the fate life handed me. I will MAKE my OWN fate.' In other classes you'll learn about deeds and conveyances, contracts, title searches, brokerage and mortgages, but with Maurice

Sheridan Bent you will learn how to be a millionaire."
Corcoris's hand was up.

26. Bullet Wulff

MAR '63 Dear Dr. Horsley. Got Angy digging with me now good at finding tRACKS. There's a lot of them. Remember you said not much market for footprints. Want to change your mind? See you in June at Medicine Bow.
Bullet Wulff

PRof. FAntee N. Horsley
DePT. Anthropology
BRown University
Providence, Rhode Island

ROAMING over the dusty Colorado Plateau, following the Morrison formation to Utah's Uinta range, to Wyoming into the Great Divide basin and up to the Gas Hills, across the Rattlesnake Range and into the Powder River basin, Shirley Basin, Crook's Gap, scanning the uplifts, the salt washes below the slickrock marker beds, rim walking the Shinarump levels, watching for the brilliant orange and yellow. He'd sorted out the subtleties of the Geiger counter's endless chipping, chipping, knocked around in the gritty bars and saloons. The electric feeling of quick money was everywhere. Christ. It excited him.

Crowded beside stinking desert rats to study the latest

government anomaly maps. But wouldn't you know, he was just in time for the federal cutback. The buying station shut down, the price guarantees dissolved. The smart guys were using helicopters and planes, skimming along the mesas with fifteen-hundred-dollar scintillometers. The scratch-dirt prospector had a hard time. What the hell, he kept moving.

The prices picked up again, high enough so that this time the big outfits moved in on the low-grade ore. Yellowcake speculation. Talk was of production levels. The rock rats disappeared. It was all big business now, deep mines, acid leaching, chemical extraction, company prospectors, poison wastes and tailings, sand slurry choking the streams, big fish kills and mountains of dead and reeking tailings.

He was finding a hell of a lot of bones, knowing you found what you looked for.

The bones and seashells, stone trees drew him more than the idea of a big strike. Once he found three enormous weathered-out vertebrae at the bottom of a ravine. He'd thought they were stones. The Geiger counter threw up a storm of clicks. As he dug the first out he saw what it was. It was heavy, uranium rich. He drove around for weeks with the bones wrapped in newspaper in a box in the back, thinking about it before he went to bone-buying Donald at his South Dakota ranch-supply-bar-grocery store.

Donald the Bone Man, gink with a ragged mustache hanging over his puffed mouth, chin sliding away into neck, hair over the ears, escorted Loyal into the back room with a sweep of his pearl-button cuff. Scar like a socket in his right cheek, the ten-gallon hat, brim curled and crown dented just right, the long, long torso in its western shirt disappearing into faded jeans cinched with a tooled leather belt and a buckle ornamented with the setting sun behind a sawtooth range, but he would pay decent money for bones and better money if you drew a map of where you found them. What Donald got nobody was sure, but he drove a mint pickup traded in every six months. Donald would not change the oil. He wore handmade western shirts. Donald's back room was stacked with boxes of bones where the archeologists and paleontologists from museums and universities back east pawed through them in the summer, asking Donald in wheedling voices for guides to the places where the choice specimens had been found. Donald was a checkpoint, a starting place for beginners.

Loyal saw the look come over Donald's face; knew what he was planning; he'd sell these specimens for the uranium.

"I want them to go to a expert at some kind of fossil museum. If I wanted to sell them for the uranium I could of done that myself."

"You could get more for them for the uranium."

"I want them to go one of the guys that studies the fossils—so he can tell what wore these."

"Hell, I can tell you that. These here is from a duckbill dinosaur and I bet you found 'em over near Lance Creek. Plenty of duckbill skeletons over there. There and up in Canada in the Red Deer country, up in Alberta. Want to see what they looked like?" Donald rummaged in a bookcase and found a grimy *Life* magazine with pink-faded color plates.

"Look at this. There's your goddamn duckbills." The illustration showed mud-brown beasts submerged to their chests. Dripping weeds hung from their muzzles. "That's what you found. Crawled around in the swamps. Too heavy to walk around on the dry land so it had to float in water. Suckers were more than thirty feet long. Not real rare. You'd get more for the uranium in your samples. You bet."

"Mister, I come across a lot of bones out there. I don't want these to go for fucking uranium. If that's what I wanted to do, I'd do it. It's the bones I'm interested in. I'm interested in these duckbill things."

The splinter was a freak thing. There'd been an old wooden box in the back of the pickup for years. He'd tossed ore samples and rock hammers into it until the sides broke and the ends fell out. Collapsed on the truck bed it was only the echo of a box. The rocks, bones, tools and pipe rolling around in the truck could be heard a mile out on the plains.

"Damn noise drive you nuts." He swerved up into a setback shaded by cottonwoods. He'd make camp early, straighten out the mess in the back of the truck. He laid into the mangled box with the heel of the trail axe.

"Good enough to make coffee even if you ain't good for much else." As if stung, the box shot out a two-inch splinter that pierced his right eyelid at the outer corner, pinning the lid to the eye itself. The pain was extraordinary, a rod of agony. He stumbled to the driver's seat and looked in the rearview mirror with his good eye. He didn't think it was in too deep. There was a pair of vise grips on the dashboard. He would have to pull it out. He would have to drive the sixty-something miles to Tongue Bolt where there was some kind of a clinic.

He didn't let himself think about it, but set the vise grips, held the lid with the trembling fingers of his left hand and clamped onto the protruding splinter in awkward pain. He smelled the metal of the vise grips, felt the fast beat of his blood. He gauged the angle of the splinter's entrance flight, then jerked. The hot tears streamed down his face. He hoped it was tears. He'd seen a dog hit in the eye once and the fluid drain from the collapsed ball. The pain was bad but bearable. He leaned his head back and waited. He couldn't see a damn thing from that eye. Maybe never would.

In a while he opened the glove compartment and got out the box of gauze. The box was dog-cornered and dirty from kicking around for years with spark plugs and matchboxes, but inside the bandage was still coiled in the blue paper. He covered his eye, wrapped the bandage around his head, looping behind his right ear to hold it in place. He started the truck and drove out toward the highway. Through blurred, monocular vision he was conscious of driving through a reddish haze. The dust the truck had raised on the way in had not yet settled.

At the clinic, glass door, stick-on letters. The waiting room was full of old men with hands folded over sticks, looking him over expectantly. A girl behind a glass wall with a sliding panel. She opened the panel. Curly hair, eyes shaped like squash seeds.

"Nature of your problem?"

"Got a splinter in my eye. Pulled it out. Hurts like a bastard."

"You just sit down. Dr. Goleman will get to you pretty quick. 'Nother emergency in there right now. Every time on Men's Clinic day it goes haywire. You're our third emergency today. First we had a woman opened the door of her station wagon and broke off both her front teeth and broke her nose, young woman, we had to get the dental surgeon over, now we got a man that one of his workers cut his fingers off with a shovel digging dinosaur bones, and you, and we've still got the afternoon. This is a doozy of a day. And some of the regulars for the Men's Clinic been sitting here for over two hours. Can you fill out this form, or do you want me to read it to you and you give me the answers?"

"I'll manage."

But he wrote only his name, then sat with his head back counting the hard painful beats of his heart behind his closed eyes until the old man next to him shook his wrist.

"I was raised in this country," he whispered. "My old dad was a surveyor. Come out in the old days. Twelve children and I was the third. I'm the only one left. Want to hear something funny? Tell you something very funny, and that was the way my old dad died. We was walking home in the dark to the cabin, me and my old dad and my sister Rosalee. I don't know where the rest of them was. Rosalee she says to him, 'Dad, how come we don't see no lions or tigers around here?' Dad says, 'There ain't none around here. Lions and tigers they all lives in Africa,' and we goes in the cabin. Well, the next day my old dad goes out to survey a line somewheres way up in the mountains and he don't come home when he's supposed to. After a few days his wife, that's his second wife who I never liked, says, 'He ought to be back by now but he ain't. I got a feeling something's got him.' Well, she didn't know how true she spoke. They found him up there with his transit and his flags and all layin' on the ground. There was claw marks on his chest and the prints of a big cat all around. And Rosalee said, 'It was tigers,' and you couldn't never persuade her otherwise. What do you think of that?"

But Loyal did not speak until the old man shook his arm again.

"They want you to go in now, buddy. Can you make it?"

"You bet." But the floor dipped like a ship's deck.

And in the other room saw a monster, left hand in a cocoon of bandage, feet in flapping basketball sneakers, a matted beard wet with the saliva of a swearing rage.

"What the hell happened to you?" It was the patient who barked the question, not the doctor, a faded man with the widest wedding ring Loyal had ever seen. Loyal told the splinter story in one sentence.

"What a fuckup," said Bullet Wulff, "what a pair of fuckups," while Goleman sluiced the injured eye with a saline solution.

"You can take off, Bullet," said Goleman, "instead of giving my other patients a hard time. But I'd like it if you hung around town for a few days so I can look at you again. The King Kong Hotel is comfortable enough."

"You bet it is," said Wulff clawing at his bloodstained shirt pocket with his good hand. He pulled out a bent cigarette and lit it. Most of the tobacco had fallen out and the paper flared up like a torch. He stayed on the table, watching Goleman lave the eye.

"You're lucky, Mr.—" Loyal could feel the heat of the

lamp, smell the doctor's stale breath.

"Blood. Loyal Blood."

"You're lucky, I think."

"That's good. I never been this lucky, run a splinter into my eye."

Wulff laughed. "That's telling him. Hey, do you like crab legs?"

"Don't know. Never had any."

"Son of a bitch! Never had no crab legs?"

"Please don't talk," murmured Goleman, pressing close to Loyal and peering. Finally he put a plastic flesh-colored patch over the eye, the patch secured by an elastic cord that pulled viciously at his hair.

"Crab legs are Alaska's gift to the human race. The King Hotel gets king crab legs—think that's why they call it the King Hotel—flown in frozen twice a week and they fix those suckers up would make your granny whistle Dixie. You will think you died and went to heaven. I hereby invite you to come to supper at the King with me. For the crab legs. Croix de Guerre. We'll talk about our war wounds. We'll compare trades. You can tell me about uranium and I'll talk dinosaur bones. I'd ask you too, doc, but you always want to talk about bowels and fistulas."

"You know something about dinosaurs?"

"I know something about dinosaurs? Tell you a little secret—nobody knows nothing about dinosaurs. Crazy ideas, wild theories, hot-shot guys oughta think up movie ideas. I heard 'em stand in front of a sandstone cut, put their fingers up their ass and scream. They guess, they fight, they get snakebit, they haul heavy stones by hand for miles. They run the other guys down," throwing his eyebrows up and down like Groucho Marx. "That's what I do. I hire out to the guys from the universities and the musuems. I find fossils, I dig 'em, I ship 'em to the paleontologists back east and let them figure out who ate who and how many teeth they needed to do it and what Latin name to slap on 'em. They write me letters all winter, great hands for writing letters. Then they come out in the summer with their assistants and graduate students. I'm the one makes the coffee. I'm the one that plasters the blocks and gets 'em loaded on the truck. I'm the one that crawls into the caves. You want a job? Make a nice change for you. The guy that was diggin' with me better be crossin' the California state line by now or he is goin' to be dead meat tomorrow. Had about as much idea of what he was doin' as a cog railway conductor at the ballet. We oughta be a good team, One-Eye and One-Paw. Maybe get up some kind of a sideshow act and not have to work no more."

Over the crab legs, swallowing the sweet meat, Loyal talked about uranium rambling, geologists and pitchblende, the way the mining investors were all over.

"Like stink on shit," said Loyal. "When I started out on the Plateau it was rim walking. You'd find the right beds, you'd know your background count and get out on there and walk along, old Geiger counter nipping along. Another good way was to get down below the cliffs and check out the rocks that had fallen off. That's how Vernon Pick found the Hidden Splendor deposit. He didn't know nothing about prospecting, he was sick, just about broke, worn-out. Stopped to rest at the bottom of a cliff and seen his counter licking off the scale. Turned it down to a lower setting, she's still off the scale. Knocked her down to the cellar notch and it's still right up there. For a minute he thought the counter was broken. Then he figured out the rock had probably fallen off the cliff face, so up he climbs up with his counter and he finds it. Today Vernon Pick is uraniumaire. Sold it for nine million dollars.

"Another thing I used to do, look at the maps real careful, look for names like Poison Spring and Badwater Canyon. You know why? Because a lot of times you find your uranium where selenium or arsenic shows up." He copied Bullet, squeezing the lemon juice on the crabmeat.

"And Charlie Steen, found the Mi Vida in the Big Indian Wash area up at Moab. They say he got sixty million on that one. Then there was this truck driver started working an old abandoned copper claim with his brother-in-law, The Happy Jack, and damned if they didn't get into uranium ore worth millions. Another guy was on his way to fix somebody's stock tank and got a flat tire. While he was fixing it, he just turned on his Geiger counter. You guessed it. There's a string of stories like that. It's out there. Some get rich. Me, I found something looked pretty good once. Staked my claim, but I didn't get it measured out right, it's got to be six hundred foot by fifteen hundred, and I got that messed up somehow. This guy been watching me all along. I go off to town with bags full of ore, get the claim registered, and he moves in, stakes right over me, jumps my claim and it holds up because I didn't measure right. I had it in my mind it was five hundred by five hundred. Live and learn. Another time I found a place seemed like low-grade ore, sold it to Uratex for ten thousand. Made something that time. Got myself fitted up good, nice new Willys Jeep, new sleeping bag, provisions, bought and mounted a thousand-dollar scintillator on the jeep and started out driving. Looking for more. I was sure I had the touch at last. Christ, I covered fifty thousand miles of the Plateau in that jeep. After a while it got tiresome. I don't know why. I couldn't keep my interest up. There's thousands of guys still out there, pimply kids and bus drivers wearing snakeproof boots." He stirred at his salad.

"What I seem to enjoy is the bones. I'll turn up this old stone tree trunk, or I'll find bones. Uranium, all right, but I hate to take 'em in to the AEC ore stations. I been taking the bones I find over to Donald in Spotted Dick."

"Donald! In the first place he undoubtedly robbed you blind, in the second place he was just a tourist trap no matter what he said, and in the third place where Mr. Donald B. Plenty Hoops is now he won't buy any more bones for a long time. Donald is in jail." Wulff sucked at the end of a leg section until the meat shot into his mouth. He drank a little from the pitcher of melted butter. His mouth and chin were glossy with it.

"How come?"

"Aggravated vehicular homicide. Couple of weeks ago. He got tanked at his own bar real good and drove home for something—what, six hundred feet down the road?—on the wrong side of the highway. Broad daylight. Hit a horse broadside and half tore off the kid's leg that was riding it. Kept going. Said later he thought it was a tumbleweed. Bled to death. Not a scratch on Donald. Little girl was the daughter of the new owner at the IR and S. I've heard there's a bunch would just as soon set the jail where Donald is awaiting his trial on fire and save some court costs. How about a steak? Surf and turf. I could do some damage to a steak, then I'm going to drink half a bottle of whiskey and lay down. This hand is starting to hurt like a son of a bitch. How's your eye?"

"Hurts like a son of a bitch."

"Hey! Two double whiskeys and two medium sirloins."

He dug with Wulff off and on for three summers. Wulff showed him what he claimed were the tricks of the trade.

"Two rules, Blood. Get the fossil out of the ground and back home in the best shape you can. And write every fuckin' piece of information about its location and bed and position that you can think of and include that information with the specimen. That's about all there is to it."

With Bullet he learned a kind of patience, the slow search by eye and feel through obelisks of cream and oxblood mudstone, the crumbling peach bluffs, the white ravines, the eroding streams of milky water, violet mounds and domes in a burning heat that left him choked for something to drink besides the rubbery water in the canteen.

"Goddamn it, Blood, if you can't see a rabbit jaw from fifteen feet you are in the wrong business."

The lime dust, the fine sand scoured their skin, inflamed their sore eyes. The heat sprang up from the white earth like an electric charge. Often they would go out after a rain hoping the freshets dashing down the coulees and draws would have torn away fresh layers of sandstone, exposing new fossils. He learned to walk bent toward the ground, casting his eyes for ridges and bumps of bone working up to the surface. He winnowed anthills for tiny rodent teeth and bones, screened small seashells out of sand, shellacked shells of crumbly bone protruding from weathered slopes, and later, at camp, sat with Bullet picking at encrusted bones, cleaning surfaces with a dentist's scratch brush, or packing the plastered specimens for shipping back east.

The front of the truck was a mare's nest of bundles of geological maps printed in turquoise and salmon. Beer bottles rolled on the floor. His hats were stuffed behind the seat, under the sun visor. Broken sunglasses all over the dash, pretzel bags. The back of the truck filled up as well with the fossil-hunter's gear, plaster, burlap sacks, chisels, rolls of toilet paper, newspaper, gallon cans of glue, shellac and alcohol, whisk brooms and paintbrushes, tape, picks and dental tools and a box of notebooks. The Indian's book, a cheap spiral notebook, lined pages stained with grease, lay buried in the pile. He wrote in it once in a while.

Every September, a few days before elk season, they would pack up the fossil gear and head north. Bullet had a camp in the Black Hills, and they went up into the pines to hunt until elk fever was satisfied or the first heavy snows forced them down. Bullet, who had a built-in compass when he was working fossil grounds, got lost in timber country.

"I don't know what it is, the trees throw me off, I get down in one of them damn gullies and I get turned around. The trees make it all look the same. You can't see far. It's not like you can get a bearing on some butte and tell where you are, just climb up high." Part of the disorientation,

Loyal thought, was because the old fossil hound slept like the dead in the higher altitude. In the mornings he would crawl out and nod over a cup of black coffee for an hour before he tottered into life. He dribbled evaporated milk into the cold coffee.

" 'Carnation milk, best in the lan', comes to you in a little red can. No tits to pull, no hay to pitch, just punch a hole in the son of a bitch.' "

He would head off into the hills late in the morning and be lost by noon. Once, after he'd been out all day and the next night, Loyal found him by the sound of a shot from Bullet's scarred old 30.06. He answered the shot and hiked until he met him toiling up a dry wash with flapping shoe soles, cradling a broken wrist in an improvised sling.

"Well, I learned something," said Bullet. His mouth was so dry and swollen the words blurred. "I learned never to shoot a fucking 30.06 like you would a pistol. Goddamn, I was being casual, just pointed the sucker up in the air like you would a pistol and pulled the trigger. Dammit, the Indians do that in paintings of Custer's Last Stand. See it in the movies, too. Like to broke my hand clear off my arm."

One season two or three inches of good tracking snow fell the day after the trucks wheezed up the wash to the cabin. Loyal was out early, easing the plank door closed on Bullet's breathing. The grey air was resinous, stinging his nostrils after the stink of the closed cabin. He felt violent with life, and cast out to the north. Less than a mile from the cabin he picked up elk tracks, five or six moving in a long trot. He followed the straight line for a few hundred yards before he came on pellets. He imagined they were faintly warm to his touch, and settled in for a long tracking walk. In the late morning he came up with a young bull standing in the timber and facing back along his trail as though waiting for death. Loyal put up the rifle, and the elk fell with grace as though acting a brief but much-rehearsed part in a play. It was that easy.

The overclouded sky was as dull as old wire when he reached the cabin. There was a light inside. His shoulders felt cut through by the hauling straps, the weight of the hindquarter. He hoped Bullet was in shape to help drag the rest of the elk out, then saw the black shape of a smaller elk hanging from the branch. Inside, Wulff hunched at the table gobbling canned spaghetti. Flecks of sauce shone in his beard. There was a smell of red wine.

"Get one?"

"Yeah. How'd you get it out, Bullet? That elk?"

"It was a miracle. I went straight up through the trees behind the camp, jumped a helluva big elk about ten minutes after I started. I was so goddamn surprised I hadn't even loaded the gun. He's just standing there, broadside. He don't see me. So I reach in my pocket and get a cartridge, slip it into the rifle, bring it up and son of a bitch she don't fire. Just click. The elk snorts and takes off. I open it up and you know what I done? I put a goddamn tube of Chapstick in the damn rifle." He laughed, a rough gurgle like a throat-cut hog, thought Loyal, who had heard the Chapstick story twenty times, not just from Bullet.

"But I see you got one, just the same. What I want to know is how you got it back here by yourself."

"Oh, that. Yes, well, that was a funny thing. I was so goddamn discouraged I come back down here, and on the way I crossed over your track, but I wasn't the only one that did and damned if there wasn't an elk that had seen your moccasin print and keeled over with a heart attack at the knowledge you was out there. Right outside the door. All I had to do was string him up. Whyn't you open a can of spaghetti and pull up a chair?" He was a good-natured old bastard.

After the elk hunt they went separate ways for the winter. Loyal picked up short-term jobs with a sheep or cattle outfit, good enough until the snow went off the hills. Wulff headed for Las Vegas.

"And I come back in the spring with a hell of a lot more money than I had the last fall, too," he said smugly. "I lead a wonderful, clean life. I got a laundry there in Vegas. My town partner, George Washut, how's that for a name for a guy works in a laundry, runs it the summers whilst I'm out poking around the rocks, then I come in in the fall with a big elk up on the top of the truck, not that I like to eat it that much, but it looks good, and then George takes off for Palm Springs where he has got some kind of a deal going and I run the laundry, keep regular hours, yes ma'am, no ma'am, don't waste my good money on gambling, take care of my two apartment houses, catch up on my book-keeping, see my kids, Barbara and Josie, see my ex-wife, see my girlfriends. Them two little girls is thirteen and fifteen now, but I got enough socked away so they can go to the best college in the country. Them girls are smart. They are gonna amount to something. Josie wants to be a scientist, but what kind she don't know. Biologist she thinks. She's gonna come out next summer and dig bones with me. Barbara plays the piano as good as Liberace. I'm not kiddin', either, she's real good."

Each spring it took them a month to get used to each other. At first they worked side by side, but nobody could work close to Wulff for long without feeling roughed up. Wulff said he got sick of Loyal's silences.

"Christ sake, it's restful to have a hardworking, quiet partner, but I feel like I got to do the talking for both of us. I ask a question and you just grunt. I gotta think of the answer myself."

Loyal sickened of hearing Wulff say the same two things whenever they came into different country. He'd say "I got a feeling there's fossils in that rock," or "My onmidirectional seat of the pants dinosaur locater says there's nothing around this place."

Gradually they worked farther and farther apart until they had to shout to tell where the other was.

His own feeling for where to look he couldn't explain. It was like trapping, part instinct for the way animals might move through a country, part feeling for the millennial landscape, an interior knowledge that suggested where lakes and mud wallows, where sinkholes and fissures had been in that vanished world.

"Damn it, you can smell fossils," said Bullet.

"That's right," said Loyal. "Smell like burned flour."

But what he liked were the tracks. How many times had he stopped cold, and dragged Wulff away from his own work?

"What the hell, it's just tracks." Wulff's plaster-coated hands stiffened into claws as he stood looking at the tracks. "We can't dig up tracks, for God's sake. It's a sequence, know what I mean? What do you want to do, dig up two hundred footprints? Each one as big as a warshing machine."

"I want to see where they go. It's not like the bones. The bones are dead, just remains, but the tracks—look, something alive, a living animal made the tracks. It's like hunting. We're on the trail of this animal and I get this feeling of it moving along on its own business before the first humans came out of the glue." He was startled at his own intensity. "See here, how the toes dig in deep but you don't see the back of the foot? Whatever made these tracks was running. Look at the size of the print. It's a foot long. Some big red-eyed bastard with big claws. How'd you like to have that coming down on you, charging out of the bushes? Or maybe something bigger was after it and it was going hell-bent-for-leather to get away. Think of it, Bullet, think of it."

"Whatever turns your burner on." But Wulff passed the word to Fantee Horsley at the Beinecke American Geological Museum that he was digging with a maverick interested in tracks and did anybody want, say, a mile-long footprint sequence?

They'd made camp after a long favorite argument, relishing the lack of proof for either side. It boiled down to a shouting match with Bullet, who had grown up in South Dakota, and imagined himself an authority on prairie grasses, slamming on the brakes and rushing at the roadside where he tore up tufts of grass to make his point.

"Look here, Blood, *this* is needle-and-thread grass, it's a cool season bunchgrass and I seen it all my life, and *this* is porcupine grass. See them long, long awns look like porcupine quills?"

"I don't know, Bullet, those're the ones look like needles with a little thread in the eye to me. This other one here looks like the porcupine quill."

"I like you, Blood, but you are ignorant. And stubborn. I'm not going to forget in a hurry what you said about the prairie chicken, either. It is practically the national bird here and you come along and dispute the way it sounds. I can find you hundreds of people that know it sounds just like blowing across the neck of a bottle, but you come out here from wherever the hell you come out from and bull your way in and won't listen to reason. 'Sounds like a ocarina.' Who the hell even knows what a ocarina is?"

"Anybody wasn't raised in a South Dakota hen coop and sent to the Badlands for finishing school knows that the ocarina started out as a prairie chicken call. Roy Orbison invented it with the prairie chicken in mind. Why'nt you ask your smart little girl that plays the piano there, little Barbara, what she thinks about it? That'll settle it once and for all."

"By God, I will, don't you think I won't."

But Barbara had never heard the prairie chickens boom, had never seen the cock run forward on his bit of ground, frown, puff up his orange air bladders and throw out a call like a stroked balloon. When Bullet dragged her, protesting, out onto the March prairie to look for booming chickens she was glad he didn't live with them all year. He felt her resentment, and for five or six minutes they sat silently in the cold jeep, the wind gliding over the shining grasses spiked through the snow. Bullet cleared his throat.

"You know, I'm not made to get along comfortable with most people." He scratched at the back of his neck. "I seem to comb their hair the wrong way."

Barbara said nothing and they drove back to town. As they pulled up in front of the blue ranch house Bullet said sadly, "Just the same, you ought to manage one of these days to hear the prairie chickens."

"Yeah, Daddy. 'Bye."

27. Crazy Eyes

An unmailed postcard

Dec. 25, 1964

Dear Pearlette, You don't know me but I knew your dad some yrs. ago, was in the mine accident with him, he talked about you alot. I have a kid sister about the same age as you. Pearlette is a good name I think of a little pearl handle revolver. Well, thats all I can think of to write except Merry Christmas

Yours truly,
Loyal Blood

miss Pearlette Berg
Invincible
Colorado

HORSLEY and his wife Emma met them in Medicine Bow. Emma drove the Land Rover. Three students slumped like dogs in the backseat. Horsley lay in the passenger seat, one foot, in a dusty engineer boot, thrust out the window. He straightened, opened his peppercorn eyes as the Rover slewed to a gravel-spattering stop. Emma, tanned almost black from two months of digging in Arizona, was decorated to her knobby elbows with silver and turquoise. Finger rings rayed, eyes glittered in the cocoa-colored face. Horsley and the students were the academic color of wet rice.

"You old son of a bitch!" Horsley jumped out, came close enough to caress Bullet's arm. His plastic spectacles reflected like paper discs. "O.k., everybody, this guy here's got the answers to everything you want to know. And he makes good coffee." Horsley brayed, jumped around like a goddamn fool, thought Loyal. Look at him. Dust flew from his sleeves. Bullet seemed glad, but Loyal couldn't stand any of them.

They ate chili in the Corner Cookhouse. Loyal cracked down on a small red stone. A tooth throbbed. Bullet would take Horsley, Emma and two of the students to Lance Creek. Loyal got the other student, the one interested in the fossil footprint sequences. Emma smiled when Bullet talked about the footprints. Her fingers slid over the enameled red cigarette lighter. A mechanical pencil drew the pocket of her silk shirt to a point over her left breast.

Loyal knew the one he was going to get, the fat kid with ringlets and cold, crazy eyes behind wire glasses. A shaft of light fell through the window and across the back of his neck like a bandage. The eyes were like bone buttons.

He didn't have to do this baby-sitting shit.

Crazy Eyes looked away from the landscape as they bumped along the white roads. An eagle pivoted over the creek bottom. They climbed into the Basque sheep country under the violet sky. Loyal pointed to the shuddering mass of sheep far out, the racing dot that was the dog. They could see the shepherd's sheep wagon high in the boulders. The student said nothing, but jerked through his notes. Sand gritted in the heat-curled paper.

The truck skidded around washboard corners. Crazy Eyes braced his hand on the dash. Pronghorns raced inside the fence, unable to get over or under.

"Damn sheep ranchers," shouted Loyal over the grind of the engine. The parching air pulled the moisture from his mouth.

In the afternoon they pulled up at the mouth of a wash. Bullet's pile of beer cans marked the place. Heat ricocheted off the colorless rocks. Nothing moved. The sky leaned on them, the earth pressed upward. The tooth was a wolf in Loyal's jaw. He walked up the wash, pointing at the tracks. Fifty feet of tracks suddenly plunged under the rock as though the ancient beast had thundered into the hollow earth.

Crazy Eyes came along. He stooped. Sweat streaked his yellow checks. The carpenter's rule rattled on the stone as he measured the footprints, the longitudinal distance between the imprints, the width of the track. He mixed the plaster, poured casts, his camera whined and reeled. He knelt, set his fingers in the tracks as if to gauge their freshness. But did not speak or look at Loyal.

"All right, what's next?"

They moved from site to site, Crazy Eyes shoving at his wire glasses, Loyal's tooth a drum now in concert with his pulsing blood.

"All right, what's next?" The student balanced his notebooks on his stained knee, swiping at his neck with a wad of toilet paper.

"Too far to get to what's next today. Drive for a couple of hours, make camp, start early tomorrow. It's about a five-mile hike in. Duckbill tracks."

"How do you know what they are?" Crazy Eye's arm braced in the window, his fingers hung onto the burning rain gutter over the door. The truck jounced southwest over the floury roads.

"I'm not entirely dumb about what I been doing the last three years." He was fed up. "Bullet says they're duckbill tracks. Couple of other people say they're duckbill tracks. I seen a few books on the subject now, including Howell, Swinnerton and Clemens. Clemens was out here in the Lance formation with us two years ago. Most of your so-called experts been out here with us. They all know Bullet."

"What do you mean, 'so-called'? Those are the major guys in the field."

"There's something that don't match up between the experts, the books and the tracks. And they don't see the problem." He had the punk's attention now. Crazy Eyes swiveled in his seat, the light turning his dust-coated face to a gargoyle's grimace.

"Like what? Like what's the problem? In your opinion."

"Like the duckbill. All the pictures show the sucker with his legs hung out at his side like a lizard. All the experts say the animal just waddled along, dragging himself from one mudhole to another. But I look at those tracks and I can see the width between the track lines doesn't match up with that idea. Looks to me like the animal's weight was under it, that the legs wasn't hung out at the sides at all. Christ, measure the lateral distance between the tracks. If the suckers'd had lizard legs the tracks would be two feet farther out on each side. And there's no tail drag marks. And there's a kind of feeling of quickness that you get from the pace of the tracks that don't match up with a sowbelly swamp-dragger."

Crazy Eyes ripped through his notebooks. Papers flew, slid to the floor.

"Stop! For Chrissakes, stop the truck." Crazy Eyes pounded Loyal's shoulder. "That's my theory. That's what I'm trying to show." He pounded on the seat. "That's what I came out here to look for. That's exactly my idea. That's why I'm taking these measurements. O.k., you want to see something, look at this!"

He rattled a drawing done in ballpoint pen on lined paper. The animal, drawn in nervous strokes, looked vigorous. A duckbill, and sprinting over a dry plain. The powerful legs worked beneath it like the legs of a horse. Its muscular tail stretched out level.

"What do you think of that?" The hot wind came through the window. The throb of Loyal's tooth shook the truck. Another abscess for sure. He wrenched two beers from the cooler in the back, passed one to Crazy Eyes. Would have to dig out the whiskey to make it through the night.

"It's better sense than Old Mudhole Charley. I think it's right on the money. Tell you, I thought you were a little lame when I seen you back in Medicine Bow, but I take it back. You must've done some hunting or trapping."

"Duck hunting. Geese. I grew up in Iowa and my daddy was a puddle shooter."

"That's the thing. Most of these guys, these experts

come out here, are experts on bone identification, they know the literature, they got minds like Einstein, but they never hunted or trapped and they don't have the feel for the way animals think and move. It's something you got to be brought up with."

"Hey," said Crazy Eyes. A sparkle of spit flew out of his teeth. "I got a hundred other farfetched ideas."

"I'll drive. You talk. Got to cover some ground before we lose the light." It would be all right if it wasn't for the tooth. Crazy Eyes had ideas. But was he any good with a pair of pliers?

"You ever pull a tooth?"

The student wrenched around in his seat and glared. "Horsley told you, didn't he. The son of a bitch."

"Told me what?"

"About dental school. That I was in dental school until I switched to paleontology. It was the teeth that got me interested in this."

"He didn't tell me, but it's the best news I heard today. I got a son of a bitch thumpin' in my jaw."

"How tough are you?"

"Oh, I had 'em pulled before with pliers. That what you mean?"

"Nah. They showed us this movie in dental school. Some tribe that knocks out boys' teeth with a big stick as the highlight of a puberty rite. I always wanted to try it."

28. The Kernel of Life

"I couldn't live without this place." Larry, the half brother, Larry, sitting on a stump in the twilight, drinking a tumbler of black wine like an Italian. Impossible the place could mean that much to Larry. He exaggerated. He was emotional. Everyone in the art world was emotional. The western cone of zodiacal light faded. The dog lay in front of them, waiting for a bowl of water. Too stupid, thought Witkin, to walk to the spring and lap up water from the overflow. There was a feather in his chop whiskers.

November 18, 1965
Dear Mrs. Scomps,
Dr. Witkin's summer office hours are Tuesday,
Wednesday and Thursday, 8 A.M. to 2 P.M.
Please call 606-3883 to reschedule your
appointments.

Mrs. Vergil Scomps
12 Badger Lane
Newton, Mass. 02158

Witkin, sitting on the porch boards, picked the birds. He grimaced as he worked, his curved teeth exposed, face bent over the half-naked bird, never able to release himself from the knowledge that he was handling flesh. It was as if some part of him believed in a confused way that the birds were tiny patients. The feathers clumped in his reeking fingers. Today there were woodcock as well. The autumn flights moving through. They had not expected them, little birds with long bills and great eyes flitting through the leaves, there, then gone, one, another, two more, the rest. But they had killed three, Larry had killed three. The first woodcock either of them had ever shot. He held the fragile bodies, looked into the chilled eyes. Robins too, there had been, moving through, thousands of birds in the air like gnats, like specks of pepper in a bowl of milk.

"They ate robins once," Larry had said after the dog sent a flock wheepling into the softwoods. "They ate them in the best restaurants at the turn of the century. Delmonico's. Served them on toast. Thrush. All the thrushes are supposed to be delicious. Delicious, delicious morsels."

The moon slipped up, showing a scorched edge like a dime in fireplace ashes. Its light coated Larry's hand, his glasses, the dog's enamel eye.

"Do you like shooting them? The birds, hunting for birds, I mean, do you like it?" Witkin could not imagine why he had asked the question. He did not like to hear people say how they felt. Tedium.

The half brother answered ambiguously. "This is a hunting camp. We bought the shotguns, the brush pants and game vests for bird hunting. We wanted to be bird hunters. The dog. Expensive training, the dog expensive. You walk through, the dog runs out in front. He points, he holds, you get ready. You are ready, you take a step. Keyed up. They startle you when they go up."

"But when you shoot and hit them, when they thrash their bloody wings and try to get up. Then what?" Their intimacy had advanced to such a point. Yet he was bored by the reply before he heard it.

"Several things almost simultaneously. Exultant, exultancy because I hit a bird, because I have killed this elusive—thing—that I hunted. I am glad, you see, triumphant, in a small way. And of course I feel sorrow, too, that this fine being, with its private life and pleasures is dead. I feel guilt that it is I who has terrified it, who has killed it. And I feel anger, anger against a possible someone who might say to me, 'That was a despicable act. Couldn't you let the bird live? Couldn't you sublimate your blood lust with a camera or a sketch pad?' No one has said this to me yet, but I am preparing my response, you see. Then too, I feet anticipation for the dinner and the praise of the dinner guests, 'Oh, you have shot this wily bird all by yourself? How intense!' And let me ask you, how do you feel about shooting birds?"

"Nothing. I feel nothing." His sense was for the place, and the birds meant as much to him as wild mushrooms, nothing in their singularity, everything as a part of the whole. A cold confusion was invading him against his will. A coldness toward his life.

He no longer cared for his family. Here, here at the hunting camp was the kernel of things. Here was Larry who knew of the violated cities, the packed trains, those other kinds of hunting camps as well as he. The places for killing. It was Larry who found the way through miles of brush, who kept his senses while cutting obliquely across the stone-mangled ridges. Witkin was off-balance with every step.

He caught his breath at the raw brown of fungus, the radiant bark, at shattered quartz, leathery flap of leaves, split husks. 0 gone, he thought, gone the constricted world of metal table and desk and human integument, the breath foul with fear, the nose swelling with cancer, Mrs. MacReady's toes humped inside her white shoes, treading the carpet. He shuddered at himself, at his cold self, his dulled tone, his hands in the sink like two hairless animals crawling over one another, the antiseptic soap jetting out, the sleek pages of medical texts, the photographs of deliquescing flesh, the dinner table, the vacuity of Matitia and the children like the children of someone else, their features and habits drawn from some other source than himself.

Only the half brother understood the atavistic yearning that swept him when he stood beneath the trees, when a branch in the wind made the sound of an oboe. He had only to walk into the woods far enough to lose the camp, and he was in an ancient time that lured him but which he could not understand in any way. No explanation for his sense of belonging here. He stared, numb with loss, into bark crevices, scrabbled in the curling leaves for a sign, turned and turned until the saplings heaved their branches and the trunks tilted away from him. He could hear a little drum, a chant. But what could it mean? The kernel of life, tiny, heavy, deep red in color, was secreted in these gabbling woods. How could he understand it?

29. Dazed and Confused

BULLET said that the student with the wire-rimmed glasses had choked to death on his own vomit. Horsley had written a letter about it.

"Yessir. Wind blew his pilot light out, that's for sure. He

got running with a rock-and-roll dope crowd, dress up in dirty tablecloths and beat on tambourines all night. Got drugged out, layin' on his back, throwed up and choked to death, says Horsley. Dirty hippies, ought to shoot 'em, every one. But you know what, Professor Alton Cruller wants to come out and dig swamps for duckbills this summer. Cruller is big. He's very, very big. Got an idea about a death star that could have wiped 'em out at the end of the Cretaceous."

mArch 17 '66
howdy, PARdner how About you
meet me rApid city Sd on
April fool Noon At hAmmer
Cafee get A eArly stArt
try the bAdlAnds remember
thAt plAce we see the
tyrAnosAr skull see
you sooN
your old PARdner
Bullet

Mr. loyal blood checkmate
rAnch
wineton, Wyoming

Why the hell, thought Loyal, did it always turn into a mess? His tongue went to the place where the abscessed tooth had been. He'd liked Crazy Eyes, liked his intensity and his peculiar humor. The plan to work together on the big projects, mapping all the known track sequences, taking casts and photographs that would prove dinosaur agility and speed—the hell, it was down the drain now.

The closest he'd ever come to doing something of value. He didn't give a shit about Cruller.

And after two weeks out with Bullet it seemed he'd had enough of the bones. It had gone flat. Bullet wanted skulls and femurs. It was the tracks that excited Loyal and without Crazy Eyes the search didn't have a focus. He was restless, as if the news of the student's death had triggered some migratory urge.

"I guess it's time, Bullet. I was thinking about it last year. I'm going to move on, do something else for a while."

"What the hell for? We're just getting good. What the hell you gonna do that can beat this? Your own hours, good money, most interesting work there is. You love it, I always knew you loved it. We're a good team, you bastard."

"I know it." But he wouldn't miss Bullet the same way he missed Crazy Eyes. He had hardly known him, but he still had the drawing of the duckbill running over the creased paper. Not a swamp in sight.

30. The Troubles of Celestial Bodies

THE cabin, eighteen miles north of the ranch they'd bought in the fifties, was where he came, Ben said, to drink. So Vernita would be spared the sight of the crawling sot she had married.

The sot was short with broad shoulders and a chest like a kettledrum. On his head a springy mass of white hair. The dulled eyes in their heavy hammocks of flesh were as incurious as those of a street musician, yet Ben's face still held a young man's freshness, perhaps because of the red smiling mouth. There were the pointed arches of the upper lip, the curving nostril with its thready veins. Anyone could tell. His voice was hypnotic, Russian in its darkness.

Oct 5, 1966

Dear B. Rainwater. Saw your ad for observatory helper Western Times. Never built one before, but handy + interested. Done some machining plus prospector, fossil digger, farming. Will be in New Mexico middle next month. Like to talk w. you about job. Let me know Santa Fe Gen'l delivery. Yours,

Loyal Blood

Mr. Ben Rainwater

Vengeance

New Mex.

"How I came to get the cabin dates back to the time when I was seeking a place suitable for a little observatory. You've heard me talk about that before, Loyal. I was looking for good darkness, smooth air. Vernita wanted room—some lab space, a study where she could write, a big kitchen. Had to have a good view of course." His words marched out in the amused basso, his fingers twisted an absent cork. "We found the ranch and it worked quite well at first. Vernita was gone all summer studying jellyfish in the Sea of Cortez. Came back in the fall to write and I was damn glad to see her. While she was gone I'd put a hole in the roof of the equipment shed for a temporary observatory and mapped out a couple of places where the main observatory could go. But Loyal, my friend, then I'd start to drink. After a week of it I'd sober up and work for a month and then it would all fall apart again. I had a pattern. I don't know what you know about astronomy, but I'll tell you something, you can't make accurate observations and you can't keep good records if you're drunk. Record-keeping is the heart and soul of astronomy. If the records are broken, what good are they?" The finger wagging, ticking off the reasonable points. Loyal had to agree.

"But I worked it out in my cunning wet brain that if I was consistently haywire and did meticulous work in the sober periods the records would still have some value because there'd be regularity to them. That's my rationalization. That's how I work. My work is flawed, but it's a consistent flaw." The smile slyer now. "When Vernita is around now I work it another way. I go to the cabin. As you know. Or I go down to Mexico City. As you know." The voice dropping, whispering, confiding. "Bought the cabin before the war. Been coming up here ever since when the sailor's home from the sea. Periodically. Consistently. With a pattern." That boiling smile.

He started as soon as the cabin was in sight, as though he had crossed a boundary into a more permissive country. The bottle came out of his shirt pocket, the pocket over his heart, his heart's desire. He tipped it back and let the whiskey flower in his throat. The long exhalation was mostly relief, a little pleasure.

"Leave the door open," he said to Loyal. From inside the dark log cabin the golden landscape filled the doorway. The wind was the color of fire.

"Have a drink. You come this far with me you might as well go the whole distance. Some kind of landmark. I never needed anybody to pick me up before this year. The clock is ticking out." The knotted hand, pouring, was steadier than Loyal had seen it in weeks, the blue hammer mark across the fingers showing purple. Drinks to keep his balance, Loyal thought. The wind swayed the plank door.

A wooden floor, log walls, the table, a bench, a single chair, a few chipped jelly glasses and tea mugs. No beds. Just roll up in your sleeping bag on the floor, or fall down and pass out where you dropped.

Ben stared through the open door at the writhing grass, the rocks and dust-ghosts; perhaps he was memorizing the horizon, the knotted mountains or the clouds like white flames from a celestial burner. A wedge of weather was moving toward them. He sat on the bench and leaned on the table. Still looking out the door he poured and poured again, he drank, smiling into the glass, he remarked that the wind was coming up, talked to Loyal, then to himself, and still he drank, slowly now, sipping careful mouthfuls of an amount he knew was right. The onerous bands loosened. The wind moaned.

"You know," he said, "you can get so used to silence that it's painful when you hear music again." Through the wind Loyal could not remember any music he had ever heard. The wind became all the music since the beginning. It disallowed musical memories. He tried to think of the tune of "Home on the Range," but the wind took everything. It whined in three different voices at once, between-the-teeth screaming at the corners of the cabin, around the woodpile, and away into the night and back again on a great moaning circle.

Ben sloshed whiskey into the cracked glasses.

And the skies are not cloudy all day, hummed Loyal to himself, following the wind's bleak tune.

"I'm one of the remnants of a dying species, the amateur astronomer." The voice roared. "I am not owned by a university. I do not depend on the publication of articles packed with incomprehensible mathematical formulas for my advancement through life. I go to no National Association of Astronomers meetings. But I pay! I pay a price for my ability to think freely! I do not get time at a big telescope! My amateur status bars me from the big ones! (The academics stand in line for years to use them.) I make myself content with what I can have and they cannot. And I've had a modest success. But the day is coming if not already here when there will be no place for the amateur astronomer except pointing out the moon at backyard barbecues or enviously applauding the coups of the technologically aided. It sounds like sour grapes? No. Nothing stopped me from the academic route. Except, perhaps, the depression, the war and my little hobby. That was a long time ago. I've had this little hobby for a long time. I was actually in graduate school and on my way, but the clubby gangism ate me out like acid. Do you know what I mean? The ones who play golf. And of course I was already a drunk. I hated the slap on the back, the favors for friends, the internecine feuds and fumed oak skulduggery. I spent five years in the Navy where, of course, none of these evil situations exist. The saintly Navy! When I got out I was ready for something new and married Vernita, quite ready to play the husband and father. I have not had a starring role in either part. What saved me—or ruined me—was an inheritance. It allows me to be what I really am, a cantankerous alcoholic who has occasional moments of lucidity when he can see far and deep into the way things work, the clocks of the heavens, the petty straw-tuggings of men and women." The red mouth moved around the words, the brain shuddered in its skull.

"Loyal, my friend. We get along, you and me. We make a damn good observatory." The hand poured, the face cracked in the egg-yolk light. The shadow of the door pointed into the room, the room fell into a pit.

"We are losing the sky, we have lost it. Most of the world sees nothing above but the sun, conveniently situated to give them cancerous tans and good golf days. The stinking clods are ignorant of the Magellanic cloud. They know not the horsehead nebula, the collars of Saturn like metal coils around the neck of a Benin princess, the vast black sinks of imploded matter like drain holes in outer space, the throbbing light of pulsars, atomizing suns, dwarf stars heavy beyond belief, red giants, the uncoiling galaxies. I am not talking about the jingoistic bus ride to the moon or the doggies woofing in weightless capsules among the planetary detritus, the petty and costly face slaps of the pudding powers. Think about it, Loyal, nations as puddings. No, the study of space unwraps the strangest and most exotic realities the human mind can ever encounter. Nothing seems impossible in space. Nothing is impossible. All is strange and wondrous in that nonhuman void. This is why astronomers do not seek the company of any but their fellows, for no one else has seen the mysteries as they have. Theirs is a ghastly joy felt in exploding stars, in galactic death. They know the dim light of a star filtering through our filthy, polluted sky has been on its way to that moment for a thousand years."

Often at night, when the heavens are bright, thought Loyal, but he was hearing.

"Look into the sky and you are looking into time and nothing that you see is now—it is all so remote and ancient that the human mind quails and shrinks as it approaches. Listen, extinction is the fate of all species, including ours. But before we go maybe we'll get a quick look at a blinding light. I have felt—I have felt—" and he stopped. The thrilling voice closed in on itself, became a whisper.

"And tell you something else. There's something haywire about you. There's something truly fucked up about you. I don't know what it is, but I can smell it. You're accident-prone. You suffer losses. You're tilted way far off center. You run hard but don't get anywhere. And I don't think it's easy for you." He looked at Loyal. The old black eyes looked at Loyal. Tiny yellow rectangles, reflections of the open door, invited him to step through. Loyal took a breath, exhaled. Started to speak, stopped. Began.

"I can stand it," he mumbled. "I'm not doin' so bad. I got some money saved up. What the hell do you expect?"

They sat in darkness, the thick apricot light firing strewn distant rocks.

"Some other time," said Ben. "Here, have another shot of the misery water."

The wind blew itself out. The morning sky was blue glass,

the lodgepole points touched the hard surface. If he threw a rock it would smash, if he breathed his whiskey-fumed breath at it, it would melt. An eagle turned a great circle under the dome. A strip of meadowlark's call. He urinated on a prickly pear cactus. The sky reeled. He saw the bright points of his water, the sparkle of bottle-glass, Ben weaving beside him, face caved in as from a blow. His dental plate on the table.

"No women," said Loyal. "I can't be around women."

Ben said nothing, one foot crushing a tuft of fleabane. The poisonous water jerked from his scarred bladder. His blind, drunk eyes saw through the glass sky, saw the black chaos behind the mocking brightness.

"There's something. I choke—like a kind of bad asthma—if I get around them too close. If I get interested in them. You know. Because of something that happened long ago. Something I did." The broken glass was everywhere. He saw blades and leaves of glass, the round brittle stems of red glass, insects as flying drops of molten glass hardening in the solid air, the gravel under his feet rough glass. He was barefoot. He could see the crust between his toes, the slackening skin on his forearms, toenails distorted by cheap boots.

"I see the way you throw yourself at trouble. Punish yourself with work. How you don't get anywhere except to a different place. I recognize a member of the club. I don't imagine you'd try a head doctor."

Talking crap. He should have guessed Ben's larynx had been shredded by the glass he'd eaten the night before. He could feel it sawing in his own throat and lungs. Christ, his throat felt full of blood. "No. Don't believe in it. Life cripples us up in different ways but it gets everybody. It gets everybody is how I look at it. Gets you again and again and one day it wins."

"Oh yes? And the way you see it you just have to keep getting up until you can't get up? Question of how long you can last?"

"Something like that."

Ben laughed until he retched.

31. Toot Nipple

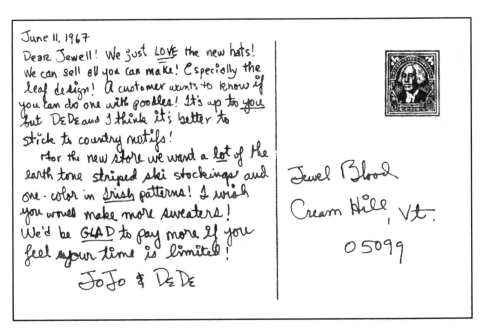

June 11, 1967

Dear Jewell! We just LOVE the new hats! We can sell all you can make! Especially the leaf design! A customer wants to know if you can do one with poodles! It's up to you but DeDe and I think it's better to stick to country motifs!

For the new store we want a lot of the earth tone striped ski stockings and one-color in Irish patterns! I wish you would make more sweaters! We'd be GLAD to pay more if you feel your time is limited!

JoJo & DeDe

Jewel Blood
Cream Hill, Vt.
05099

FROM the picture window in front of the table in her trailer Jewell looked out over the mobile home park below. If she pulled back the blue-flowered curtain in the bathroom window she could see the old house, down on its knees now. The roof had broken under a freight of snow the winter before. Ott wanted to bum it up, called it an eyesore that made the trailer park look bad, hanging over the pastel tubes like a wooden cliff, but she couldn't let go of the place, still limped in back of it every day in the summer to keep the old garden patches going, though the woodchucks and deer moved in with the weeds and did a lot of damage. Her ankles swelled so. It wants to go wild again, she thought.

"I worked on getting them gardens up the way I like for most of my grown-up life and I am not about to turn them over to the wildlife. What it needs is some boy to set a few traps around the fence. I asked that big fat woman, Marla Swett, down at the trailer park if she knew any boys that was trapping, but she said no. I guess they don't trap now. Loyal and Ronnie always used to run traps, even when they was little. Loyal made quite a bit of money with the furs. Another thing I could use up there is a couple loads of good rotted chicken or cow manure. Gardens need some manure, but try to get Ott to remember to bring any over. Nobody around here keeps cows or chickens any more."

Her gardens were smaller. She still grew tomatoes and beets, and other garden truck, but not potatoes or corn.

"Too easy to buy it. I get all I need of corn if I buy a bushel, put up some succotash, creamed corn for corn chowder. If Ray and Mernelle come over they'll bring a dozen fresh ears from some roadside stand. There's some kids from New Jersey moved into the old Perish place and they been growing Silver Queen the last few years. If they don't split up, like I heard could happen, and if we don't get a cool summer, I can keep on buying it from them."

She hauled some vegetables down to the canning factory where they let her put them up with the commercial loads. Ray and one of the men at the lumberyard brought her a freezer and set it in the extra room, the second bedroom, that she never used but kept in case Loyal came home. She tried it for two years, but didn't like the taste of the vegetables along in March when they were full of ice crystals. She went back to canning then, and because there was no cellar or pantry, she stored the jars in the unplugged freezer. But bought her beef and chicken at the IGA and complained they had no flavor.

"Mernelle, you remember the hens we raised were so good. I can just taste one of those big roasters, go seven or eight pounds, sitting on the platter all crispy and roasted with a good bread stuffing. Make your mouth water just to smell it. I always liked my food and I guess I miss the stuff we grew on the farm. Take the beef. Your dad used to keep out two steers each year for beef. We'd have two big butchering days, one in October, one in early December, right through the depression when a lot of people went hungry, and I'd put up beef. Can it. Make stewed beef sometimes and can it. There's nothing so tender and good as home-canned beef. You can't buy it for love nor money. There's nothing else tastes like it. Deer meat, too. That's the way we always used to do the deer meat. Loyal and Dub and dad used to keep us in deer. Now people, flatlanders, they get a deer, what do they do with it? They cut it up into 'venison' roasts and steaks and complain because it's tough or too much tallow. They put it in the freezer. Toughens it up, I'd say. The way we used to do, it was always as tender as custard and you could skim off the tallow just by letting it set in a cool place before you put it up."

The trailer, with its cunning spaces and cupboards pleased her. But sometimes she thought of the old kitchen, seven steps from the sink to the table, back and forth all day. It was Ray's idea, that she ought to have a trailer with a little oil heater and plumbing and electric instead of trying to heat the old house with the wind sifting through, struggling to carry in wood. It was like being on a visit to wake up in the morning in the narrow bed with the flowery sheets and see the sunlight like a handful of yellow rulers coming through the venetian blinds instead of the torn shade with its crooked mends and pinpoint stars. The plaid sofa had shiny arms and a matching chair on a swivel, a comfortable thing to lean back in. The chair faced the television set Ray and Mernelle had bought her and she turned it on while she cooked in the kitchen or knitted, just for the company, though the tinned quality of the voices never let you forget they were not real people. She enjoyed the little stainless steel sink in the kitchen, the smart refrigerator with its ice cube trays that she never pulled out unless Mernelle and Ray were visiting, "not being in the habit of ice," she said. Loyal's postcards with the bears were in a cigar box in the cupboard. Once in a while one still came. The smell of the trailer was the only drawback. In the old house she had never noticed smells unless something were burning or Mernelle brought in a big bouquet of lilacs, but here there was a headachey smell like the stuff they used to stick down floor tiles. Ray said he thought it was the insulation.

"Whatever it is, it'll wear off one of these days. What can't be cured must be endured." She could always go outside and get a breath of air.

Three days a week she drove over to the canning factory and worked in the cutting-up room. Extra days if there was a rush order. They'd gone over to automatic slicers with adjustable settings and blades, and she'd learned the new machines faster than anyone else. The forelady, Janet Cumple, had marveled.

"Look how good Jewell's caught on," she said in front of the others. Jewell couldn't think how long it had been since someone said a word of praise to her. She'd gone red and trembly when they all looked at her, thought of Marvin, the dead brother, telling her she was a smart little kid because she'd found his homemade baseball, hide stitched over a knob of rubber bands, in the long grass after he'd given up. She couldn't have been older than four.

The rest of the time she put into the garden, into knitting hats and sweaters for the ski shop, into driving around.

"Problem is, they want me to use that plain old wool, it's not even spun smooth, you'll find burrs and hayseed in it, instead of the pretty colors you can get down at the Ben Franklin. I'll go along with using the wool instead of the acrylic, the acrylic don't have the bounce and it sags, but I don't see a thing wrong with a little color. All that grey and brown and black it gets dull to work on a piece. So I let off steam with Ray's sweaters." Dub down in Miami didn't want to see wool. He sent photographs of himself playing golf in shorts and a flowery shirt. His artificial arm seemed very real, except the color was a pinker color than his tanned right arm. But every year for Christmas she gave Ray a patterned sweater in staggering colors and designs, jagged yellow bolts encircling his torso, red airplanes swooping across a cobalt-blue breast, endless green reindeer marching over maroon and orange sleeves. He tried them on, praising them and exclaiming over the fine details while Mernelle covered her eyes and moaned, "No, oh no, I can't stand it."

The duck sweater. She had been driving along the lake, eighty miles west of home on one of her excursions, and on a windy October day chanced on a church sale in an ugly strung-out village. Two women wrestled with a school easel, one tying posters to it with string, the other piling stones around the easel legs to keep it upright in the wind. "BAKE & RUMMAGE & WHITE ELEPHANT SALE. Benefit Mottford Congregational Church." There was a good place to park just beyond the sign.

The baked goods were not the same as they used to be. Instead of brownies, square chocolate cake still in the pan, apple pies, oatmeal cookies and home-baked bread, there were cake-mix things with three times as much frosting as anybody needed, cocktail snacks made out of cereal and nuts. The rummage tables had the same worn kitchen tools, statues of slave girls with glitter on them, wooden boxes and peg racks. The needlework seemed to be all tea cloths with embroidered windmills, never used, laid away in some mothball trunk since the twenties, pale yellow crocheted bedspreads with the texture of barbwire and baby bibs stained with ancient applesauce. The babies had to be grown men and women now.

A big square wicker basket with a lid. That caught her attention. The basket came up to her waist, and she lifted the lid and looked in. It was packed with yams, hundreds of colors and weights, fine hand-spun linen thread, hand-dyed skeins of wools, the dark green of cocklebur, red madder root, indigo blue, the cloudy gray of walnut, gold knotweed. Richer, more subtle colors than she'd ever used. The deeper she rummaged the more treasures she found, a tender color that made her think of teal-wing ducks, and in that minute she saw the sweater, saw it entire with the ducks in many colors swimming against a dark background, and every few stitches she'd work in cattails behind the ducks.

"That was old Mrs. Twiss's yarns, she died in July and the fam'ly wants to clear all the stuff out of the house," the woman blurted. She was lantern-jawed and with an anxious voice like prayers. "Half the reason we're havin' this sale is to sell off her stuff. They kept the sheep until Mr. Twiss died, and then she still had a lot of wool on hand. She made rugs on a loom. I never cared for them myself—I like a nice nylon carpet in a solid color—but I guess a lot of people, the summer people, bought them. She knitted, too. This basket was her knitting yarns."

"What are you asking?" Jewell wanted that basket as bad as she'd ever wanted anything.

"Five dollars sound about right? It's mostly a lot of leftovers. Prob'ly be all right for socks or something."

It took four of them to carry the basket out to her car, and then the lid of the trunk wouldn't close and she had to tie it down with string borrowed from the poster-tying woman. She took her name and address and mailed the string back the next day with thanks.

Jewell walked out to the strawberry bed behind the collapsing house early in the June morning and pulled the nets off the dark rows. She would get a head start on Mernelle. Quack grass choked the rows and something had gotten under the net and eaten the berries on the end plants. She remembered worse: the hailstorm that made strawberry jam in five minutes, the loose cows trampling the plants. She spread her piece of carpeting on the cool soil and began to pick, setting the full baskets under the shady rhubarb leaves as she went. The sun heated up quickly, the baking soil shimmered with heat waves. By the time Ray dropped Mernelle off she had stripped the plot of ripe berries and replaced the nets for another picking in a few days. The black soil was in her cracked fingers.

She sat in the rectangle of shade behind the trailer in an aluminum-framed lawn chair, Mernelle sat a few feet farther out for the sake of the sun. The marigolds blazed. Mernelle's arms and legs were the color of pecan shells. The black, long hair was teased up and twisted into a puff. She wore an orange playsuit. Her voice flung high words. But she was good-tempered.

"I'll make that strawberry-rhubarb pie for Ray if you can give me some of your rhubarb. Ray can eat a whole pie at one sitting."

"Well, I don't blame him. You make wonderful pie. Sure, take all you want of the rhubarb. There's plenty. And strawberries. Ought to do another picking next week. There's so many this year I can't begin to deal with 'em. And it seems like I lost my taste for strawberries. There was a time I could eat anybody under the table with strawberry shortcake. Jam. Just strawberries and cream." Jewell's fingers were red to the knuckles with hulling the heavy berries.

"Did you wash these, Ma?"

"I rinsed 'em under the spigot out back. You can see they're wet."

"I can see they're wet but they feel gritty."

"You must be workin' on the ones at the bottom of the basket. Dub. Dub was the only one of you kids could never eat strawberries. He'd break out in a rash—strawberry hives your grandmother called 'em. Old Ida. Any kind of a rash she called some different kind of hives. Mosquito bites? That was 'skeeter hives.' Get in the nettles you got a case of 'nettle hives.' Your father'd come in from pitching hay up into the haymow, all that chaff down the back of his neck and he'd itch just wicked and you know what that was, it was 'hay hives.' First time I heard that I bust out laughing. 'Hey-ho, Mink has got the hay-hives!' She didn't talk to me again for some time. This is before we was married. Quite the old hen, I thought. She'd say all hoity-toity, 'I don't b'leeve a person ought to be held up as a figger of amusement for what they say.' But she had to put up with plenty. Old Matthew, he was a miserable old cuss. Temper! That's where your father got his temper, and Loyal, too, I daresay. I see him one time, old Matthew, ask your grandmother something, wasn't very important, just something about where something was, if she'd seen it. She was rattlin' some pot lids at the time and didn't hear him. She got a little deaf as she got older. Lost most of her hair, too. Used to wear a switch up in the front that was a different color than the rest. Sort of a rusty brown color. Well, he took it the wrong way, that she didn't answer him and he flared up. Snatched up a jar of tomatoes she had standing on the shelf to put in something, and he held it out over the floor and just let go. The first thing she knew anything was wrong was this terrible smash right behind her, felt the wet on her legs, and looked around to see the tomatoes and glass all over her clean kitchen floor and old Matthew like a turkey cock with his face gobbled up so red. Yes, those old girls, they put up with a lot. It was considered pretty terrible to get divorced, so they put up with a lot, things no woman today would put up with."

"What about old Mrs. Nipple. You never would tell me what happened to her. You know."

"I have to say, though, old Ida was wonderful with the desserts. Made Queen of Puddings for Sunday dinner with raspberries—your mouth would almost faint it was so good. Apple puffets, plate cake. And the ice cream if she could get the boys to turn the crank. She made rhubarb ice cream. I know it don't sound good, but it was. Same with the Concord grape. Ice cream if the grapes made it. If we didn't loose them to a late spring frost."

"Quit stalling, Ma. I heard all that. What about Mrs. Nipple?"

"She had a hard life, but kept her humor, I don't know how." The dark cone of strawberries rose higher in the bowl. The white dotted undersides of the caps strewed the grass where they had thrown them. "I wouldn't of cared to have been her. I used to say that to myself, 'Thank god I'm not so bad off as Mrs. Nipple.' But in the end maybe I wasn't no better off. The way things fall out is funny. Life twists around like a dog with a sore on his rear end that he bites at to make it stop plaguin' him."

"That's a nice picture, Ma." Mernelle itched to plunge

her hands into the berries, lift handfuls high and squeeze until the juice ran down her arms. Unaccountable and strange wish, like her longing for children. They had the dog, she thought derisively.

"Well."

"Mrs. Nipple."

"You probably don't remember her husband, Toot, he died when you weren't more than five or six, but he was a big, good-lookin' man when he was young. Brown straight hair that fell over his eyes in a certain way, real nice eyes with dark lashes, sort of aquamarine color."

"It's funny but I remember his eyes. He was a fat old slob and I was just a little kid but I remember his eyes. They made an impression on me. A strange color." And remembers the old man rubbing his hand over her heinie when she was on the ladder in the barn. I'll give you a boost up, he'd said, and then the hot fingers.

"When he was young he was a big fellow, quick and clever, a terror on the dance floor. He wasn't a fat slob then. Good-lookin'. He'd joke, had an easy laugh and got along good with everybody. Girls was crazy about him. Called him Toot because after he'd been tomcattin' around he used to say, "Guess I been on a toot." He married Mrs. Nipple, of course she was Opaline Hatch, then. But soon became Mrs. Nipple and nobody could figure that one out because he kept right on like he wasn't married at all, dated girls, went out every night. Mrs. Hatch, that was Opaline's mother, had a big smile for everybody at the wedding. But Ronnie was born about three months afterwards so we had a good idea of what the attraction had been. It was a funny thing, she never got mad at him for all his hellin' around. He'd come draggin' home drunk and smelling like he'd been dipped in throw-up and perfume, both, and she'd fix him something for his stomach and make excuses for him the next day to whoever he was workin' for, that's before they moved onto the farm. That farm passed to her from her family. Toot's folks didn't have a pot to piss in. It got so he depended on her for an awful lot. She got to thinkin' she'd tamed him down, that life was finally evened out for her. Maybe he thought so, too. And that's when it turned on 'em and started to bite."

The naked, bleeding strawberries lay in the smeared bowl. Jewell reached for another basket and set it in her lap. Her fingers darted at the strawberries, plucking their crowns with cruel pinches.

"What happened was when he was around forty-five, forty-six he got cancer of the prostrate. The doctor told him, 'We can take the cancer out but you'll be impotent. Or we can leave it alone and you'll only have another six months or a year to live. You'll have to decide.' Well, he decided to have the surgery done. And he *was* impotent. He was that kind of a man, you know, where that was the most important part of life. He went cold, then. He wouldn't even put his arm around Mrs. Nipple any more, wouldn't joke with the ladies like he always done. Wouldn't touch any of them in tenderness or affection. It was as if he'd turned impotent all over. See, the touching was all connected with sex for him. Then he started in on suicide. He'd talk to her about it at supper. He wanted to kill her, then himself. Wanted to take her with him. 'Tonight,' he'd say while they was eating the string beans and the hamburger patties. 'We'll do it tonight.' Always at suppertime. He done this for six years. She stood by him, I'll say that for her. Short of giving in and letting him shoot her, she stood by him. He finally hung himself. It was after that Ronnie moved back to the farm. He never got along with Toot and lived over at his aurnt's place from the time he was about fourteen. And I pitied her so bad, that her life had taken this terrible turn. And when it came at me in the same way I felt like . . . I still can't say what I felt like. But I know one thing. You're never ready for when it turns on you and goes for the throat."

Mernelle held a strawberry in her hand. Her fingers folded, she squeezed. She threw the clot in the grass, glanced at her red palm.

32. Pala

June 18, '67
Dear Ma, In a couple of weeks you and Mernelle and Ray will get an invitation to a wedding. You guessed it! Mine! Her name is Pala Suarez. She is beautiful and smart. (I'm learning a lot!) Comes from Cuba originally. In real estate too, but with different connections. She is younger than me but has a wise head. I want you all to come down. Be my guests at The Biscayne. I'm sending airfare for you, Ma. Details in letter to come. Your son, Marvin E Blood.

Mrs. Jewell Blood
RFD
Cream Hill, Vt.
05099

SHE was clear about what she wanted. Looking at her

ivory face, her black oval eyes, he felt himself the fool again. She had the thick little Cuban arms and a crooked nose, but there was a cool glaze he loved. The quick hands moving while she talked, the hurrying voice drew him to her.

I want this secretary job to learn more about real estate. I want to understand the fine points, get familiar with the names and the ideas of the big investors from New York, see how you make things work." He nodded. She wanted his secrets.

"But a year from now I will be ready for a bigger position. I am very ambitious."

I can see that, Miss Suarez. What type of real estate interests you—residential properties?" The women in real estate all worked with houses.

"I am more interested. in the special commercial properties—centrally designed, landscaped projects that balance hotels, shopping malls, marinas and services in a beautiful and coherent way. Spaces with water elements, plants, esplanades, open-air restaurants. That is why I applied here. I have studied urban architecture and I admire many of your projects. Spice Islands Park. Enchanting, those ziggurat offices and shops built around pocket parks of fragrant trees. The lovely rooftop gardens, the flower balconies. All soft colors. And everybody wanted to work there right away. I know the architect you worked with well. He is my cousin. No other 'American' real estate developer would think of using a Cuban architect."

She was so serious, he thought, leaning a little forward in her grey silk suit, her stubby hands folded on her knees.

The hair was plaited and the plaits wound sleekly around her head. Her ivory skin was a little rough with old acne scars—it gave her a tough and interesting flavor that he associated with the name "Mercedes" for some reason.

"I can be useful to you, too," she said. He knew that.

"There are many invisible Cuban millionaires in this city. There are banks and bankers, a whole society that the American establishment in Miami ignores. In that world we have our own ideals and thoughts, our own television and radio, a certain style, a way of thinking and walking and talking, holidays, celebrations and balls, charities and school curricula utterly unfamiliar to your world. I can be your bridge to that society. If you are interested, of course." She was so serious.

"No," he said. "You cannot have the secretarial job. But I just realize that I am looking for someone to fill the position of Director of Intercultural Marketing and Development. Perhaps you would care to apply?"

When she smiled, he saw, in the white dazzle of pointed teeth, in the gold glint of a back tooth, that he had a pirate.

33. Obregón's Arm

IN the studio a mirror hung over the sink. He looked in it only to shave, and over the months soap spatters, dust and flyspecks dulled his image until after the trip with Ben to Mexico City, a trip made not for any reasons of his own, but to haul Ben up out of the street swill when he fell. It was the worst he'd ever been.

They got back, after two weeks. He helped Ben, trembling and voiceless, into the big house through the kitchen door, guided him past the dishwasher, the chopping block, past the swaying strings of chile and garlic, the bouquets of herbs hanging upside down, the Spanish ham in verdigris mold dangling like a punching bag from the heavy wrought iron hook.

Dear Mrs. Rainwater, you maybe don't know what your husband is getting up to when he go out of town with that bum that hangs around him. People of your wealth ouht to set a standard for the community, not do ugly things in public like we seeing. There is many around here that thinks what is going on is disgrace. IF your smart you will clean house.

A well wisher

mrs. Vernita Rainwater
LAST STAnd Ranch
VengeAnce,
    New Mexico

The cook stood in front of the refrigerator. She held the door wide, showing the meat, the jars of West Indian pepper sauce, French mustard, Niçoise olives, capers, piñon nuts, walnut oil, quarts of milk and cream, half-empty bottles of white wine, waxy cheeses, endive and chicons, brown peppers, the great black grapes, the breasts of chicken.

"Piano," Ben seemed to say. His voice shook deep and ruined. "Piano." Loyal could see past him into the living room to the painting like blood on the wall.

"He says for you to go away now too," said the cook to

Loyal. "The missus wants you to go. Wants you to leave. They both wants you to get out."

"Piano."

In the studio Loyal saw that Vernita, the biologist of jelly-fish, had ordered sea changes. All was drenched, swept away as by equinoctial tides. The walls were freshly cal-cimined a bitter white, the floor tiles scraped and washed and waxed until they reflected like red water. He read the message in the sheen of the aluminum kettle, spout tip like a cherub's mouth. Books and magazines squared on dust-less shelves, the bed stripped, window glass so clear it erased distance. He turned slowly. The curtains swelled, the empty sink gaped for a sweet gush of water, its faucets burning with light.

The mirror drew his eyes like a tunnel opening into another world. He had not looked in so long, still thought of himself as a young man, strong arms, the black fine hair and hot blue eyes. His face, he saw, had gaunted out. The blue mirror frame enclosed his fixed features. The ruddy liveliness, the quick rage of the eyes had faded. Here was the skin of the ascetic whose neck is never marred with sucking kisses, the rigid facial planes of someone who spends time alone, untwisted by the squinting disguises of social life. His eyes did not change when women walked past. It could be, he thought, that spark was finally dead. But did not believe it.

In an hour he was packed up and heading north in the truck. Age seemed at his throat.

But the old urge for the farm was like the heat of a banked fire, the time was slipping down. Fifty-one years old. The prospecting, the barroom nights, the summers digging with Bullet, the climbs up to the passes in the mountains, moving through the breast-high rabbitbrush, his way had been that of an exile for a long time. He had tried to keep the tremulous balance of his life, walking a beam between short friendships and abrupt departures. He thought of the nights on the sand, the squalls of desert foxes, the stars screeling points of light cutting paths and orbits, the gaping core. And the shuddering hours with Ben in the observatory tracing sidereal arcs with the still camera, trying to follow Ben's vaulting talk of distant energy and collapsing matter. Yet, reeling through corridors of galactic ice, chill remote starlight, could not completely forget the warmth of barn, kitchen, the spark-furred heaps of peltry. Never was the mood of farm work closer than when Ben was ruined with drink, slobbering in the black swillbowls.

In Mexico City swaying before the statue of General Alvara Obregón with Ben slouched against him, the old longing swamped Loyal. On a granite pedestal below the statue the general's arm floated in a lighted jar of formaldehyde. The yellow bone protruded from the flesh, and Loyal saw in the angle of the bone himself lying on his back in the bed, his hands behind his head, his elbows jutting up.

One of these days he would wake up dead. He had not yet made a start on the farm, on curing his trouble with earth, clacking hens and a dog springing up with muddied feet. He imagined a family of silvery children and warmth in the bed, a voice in the dark instead of the forceful stars and the Indian's silent book.

The limb swam in ichorous fluid and as he studied the naked ulna he knew it was late in the day to get out, late to buy a farm, never mind the rest of it, but he knew that he had to do something or burn his money in the stove. Maybe it would work for him. Maybe Vernita did him a favor. Why had he stayed so long?

Kiss the little adobe studio good-by, kiss good-by to the freezing nights. And the stupid hours leaning on Criddle's zinc-covered bar until Ben was ready to be hauled away.

34. Tumbleweed

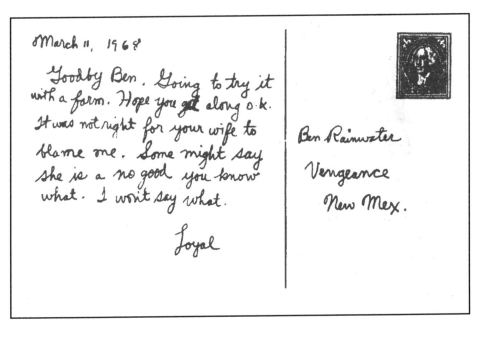

March 11, 1968

Goodby Ben. Going to try it with a farm. Hope you get along o.k. It was not right for your wife to blame me. Some might say she is a no good you know what. I won't say what.

Loyal

Ben Rainwater

Vengeance

New Mex.

SO there he was, fifty-one years old and in North Dakota. The farm a curve of earth, a slat-sided house leaning into the wind, starved fields among the ranches and sugar beet farms. Why the hell was he buying this, he wondered, even as he pushed the bank check at the vulture-wattled man in the sheepskin coat. Imprisoned in his mind, like an iridescent beetle in a matchbox, was the image of his slanting field crowned by scribbled maples, not this bony square of dirt. He didn't even know what he wanted to do with it.

Half an hour later on the street he saw the wattled man in his truck, leaning his head on the steering wheel as though resting a little before he drove off.

He couldn't think of it as his farm, and called it "the place." That's what it was, a place. He didn't know what he wanted to do, grow sugar beets, soybeans, wheat—the County Agent had mentioned the new kinds of Durum, Carleton and Stewart, good grain quality and resistant to stem rust. The machinery was expensive. He could run cattle or raise hogs. There was money in cattle, but you had to be born to it he thought. He only knew dairy farming, pasture, hay, woodlot, some crop management. It wasn't that kind of place. Things were different in farming now. He bought fifty barred rocks while he thought about it. He could go into poultry. Or dry beans or peas.

It was not a good place to sleep at night, that metal bed, paint chipped iron, sheets trailing on the floor. An uneasy house. There was always a fine grit on the linoleum, soil blown from across the world, brown roils that rose from the steppes of central Asia and ended lying on his windowsills. The plate on the table made a grating sound. He'd picked up a persistent cough; the dust was irritating his throat.

In the back of his mind he had believed and not believed that the work of a farm would set him right. His trouble seemed to shift rather than repair. He woke up one night after a dream of Ben, but a far younger Ben, melting under his hands, rounding into a woman, the gaping stitchery where his sex had been, the face of the whore in Criddle's showing her smeared eyes and coyote teeth. Thrashing awake he felt burning weals the size of pancakes on his neck and buttocks, his forearms. In the mirror his black fine hair, threaded with white, was shrinking back from his forehead. He still had his anger, hot as new blood. And hated it in himself.

It was three miles west to the next place, Shears's hog farm, a huddle of buildings scraped together by a careless stick. He ran into old man Shears with his feed cap matching his white hair and the mustache fringing a juicy mouth, at the feed depot. From a distance somebody pointed out the two wheat-colored oldest sons, Orson and Pego, farmers whose land butted onto the father's at the west. The hired hand, Oyvind Ruscha and his family of boys, swung in and out of a mobile home set beside the road.

Old Shears was full faced, tobacco chewing, violently progressive about new farm machinery. He urged Orson and Pego to go in together on an air-conditioned, self-propelled combine.

"Get it with the eighteen-foot cutter bar. Get the safety-glass windows and air condition. Tell him you want the lubricating bearings and the new V-belt and pulley drives. Get it as big and strong as you can. That's the way it's all going, big, quick machinery. You don't have that stuff you don't got a chance in hell of makin' it in farmin'." They added a windrow pickup attachment. When it was delivered the old man tried it first, praising the smooth gear and speed shifts.

"That son of a bitch can harvest anything you grow, wheat, oats, barley, flax, peas, rice, clover, alfalfa, soybean, hay, lupine, sunflower, sorghum or weeds, and them two can grow anything it can harvest."

"Yeah, especially the weeds," said Orson, the family joker. Loyal liked him. Reminded him of Dub. He'd write to them at home one of these days, let them know he had a farm.

The woman at the drugstore where he got his cough medicine told Loyal stories about the other Shears son, the youngest, who came back from the Vietnam War so misanthropic in spirit that he'd moved into a shed and took his meals from plates of bark, eating with a pointed stick or an old bayonet, she said, still stained with blood.

The drugstore was a crackling metal building hunched beside the Farmers' Cooperative Bank. The woman's shape was as formless as poured sugar. Two strange front teeth like the points of knitting needles clashed at her lip. "He don't help out on the farm. He's just holed up back there. Shears said he was gonna starve him out. So, they didn't put any food out for him for a week. But Mrs. Shears couldn't hold out and she was slippin' a plate out there every night when she went to feed the hens. Now they got him goin' regular over to the VA hospital in Fountain. Say it could take years and years to straighten him out."

Every time Loyal drove past Shears's farm he glanced at the shed and hoped for a sight of this specimen.

He thought he might grow sugar beet. The County Agent leaned hard on sugar beet. There was good high-yield hybrid seed now, resistant to curly top and downy mildew. When old Shears heard he was thinking beets he warmed up.

"O.k., here you got a real choice which way you want to go on your beet harvest equipment. You can go two routes. Your first route is your harvester that does in-place topping. It comes along, see, and cuts the tops off while the beets are in the ground. Then she's got two wheels that point in toward one another, dig into the soil, loosen and lift out the beets in one operation. The kicker wheels clean 'em off and your rod-chain elevator carries 'em back to the beet wagon. That's one way to do it. The other way, and the way I'd go, if I was you, is the harvester with a wheel, a spiked wheel, that lifts the beets out of the ground—the tops are still on. There's a pair of stripper bars that raise the beets off the spikes and your pair of rotating disks cuts the tops off at the height of the lift. Then they go back to the trailer. It's simpler. Man, I raised sugar beets back in the old days when the goddamn leafhoppers would wipe you out and what was left you had to get in with hand labor. Wouldn't do it again. No way, José."

Loyal saw the sign FREE PUPS propped against Shears's mailbox. He had not had a dog in all the years since leaving home. Did he want to start now? It seemed he did.

He pulled into the yard, watched it fill with dogs, the plumy-tailed mixed-breed bitch, part English sheepdog, part German shepherd with a dash of collie, showing her teeth and growling, four half-grown puppies racing from the side door to his truck. Shears's truck was not there.

He sat a minute studying the dogs. The door of the back shed opened and there was Jase, strange from his journey through the mountains of Vietnam. Talking to himself. Looking away from Loyal, away from the dogs, his blue-circled eyes skirting the edges of the buildings, slipping along the edges of clouds to motion on the ground, a bird, a car on the highway. Tall. Thin and stiff as a music stand, hardly twenty-one, with hair so light it looked silver. Now his flickering glance shot from one puppy to another, his mouth hung open with the effort to keep them all in sight. He pressed his chin down to his breast, wrenched his mouth to one side. Loyal hung on the truck door, marking out the pups he liked. There was only one after all, a quick-witted bitch who slipped through the snapping feints of her littermates, squatted near the truck tire to piss, and got behind Jase, out of his sight until he whirled.

"Guess that's the one I like," said Loyal. "Can I offer you something for her?"

Jase threw his head back until his Adam's apple strained white, tried to speak and failed, the words jerking at his mouth, tautening the cords in his straining neck.

"All—all—all—the rest of them," and, in a rush of jammed syllables, "overatthesitefortheMcDonald's. Neeeeee—ar thecrossroads. Building it. McDonald's."

Loyal crouched and made kissing noises at the pups. They rushed at him, laughing in his face, their hot paw pads and sharp nails paddling at his knees. He picked up the smart girl and put her in the truck on the floor.

"Obliged to you," he said to Jase. "Stop over some time. Have a beer."

"Ah—ah—ah."

The pup was on the seat, scratching at the glass.

"Down. Down Little Girl, down Girly." He knew dog names should be short and crack in the mouth like "Whip" and "Tack" and "Spike" but this was better. Little Girl. They drove away, the puppy lunging at the steering wheel as Loyal turned it, biting at the wheel and growling small growls until the jouncing stunned her into sleep, curled in a knot of sunlight.

At night on the ploughed prairie the darkness was darker than the Mary Mugg which at least had been illuminated by those blue and orange tracers of light that appear even behind closed eyelids. This darkness was thrown into deeper ink by the sprays of stars, asteroids, comets and planets trembling above him as though in a sidereal wind. As far as he stared across the fields there was no yellow window, nor crawling headlights pitching across the waste. The stars flooded him with longing for Ben, the great lover of cold points. Probably dead by now. The stars were not steady; they shuddered as though in a black jelly. That was the wind, the laminated streams of air flowing above the earth like distorting fluids, the silt-stippled wind wrinkling the distant astronomy.

The wind moved back and forth like a saw endlessly sawing. If he lay on his back, his ears free of the pillow, he could hear grains of sand strike the windows. On full moon nights the wind roared against the house, mooing and rumbling in the dark, rolling a bucket across the yard, dragging weeds along the clapboards until the squeaking and banging sent him up out of the grey sheets, shouting at the ceiling. When you lived alone you could shout at the ceiling. But it got the dog up, made her pace the kitchen linoleum, her toenails clicking, worrying if the menacing clouds that raced the daylight sky had at last attacked under cover of darkness.

He thought he'd go in for dry navy beans. The hell with sugar beets. Beans he understood. He fitted himself out with a used tractor, cultivating and planting attachments and made an arrangement to lease the Shears boys' famous combine at bean harvest, after their grain was in.

"If it goes good in a year or two you might want to get a blade-type bean harvester," old Shears advised. "It's got your vine turners, your row dividers and your windrowing rods. But you can probably do pretty good with the boys' combine, just so's you run it at about one-third speed. You still gonna lose quite a bit to shatter. When you're ready I wouldn't mind comin' over, take a look at how it goes."

The beans came along well the second year. Before he harvested them Loyal wanted to fence off the yard and set out a triple row of Scotch pines for a new windbreak. The old poplars were shredded and broken with age. Jase came skulking in unbidden one noon to help him build fence. Loyal was startled to see him, thought the poor bugger must have pulled himself together at last after months of therapy at the VA hospital. They worked in silence through the day, the scrape and chunk of the posthole auger, Little Girl's gallop stirring up beetles. Loyal looked over at Jase again and again. He knew how to set posts. There was a fluidity in the shift of muscle that drew his eyes. He must have come out enough to work for old

Shears lately; face and torso were a sore red. The silvery hair was knotted up in a club under the ranch hat. In the late blaze of afternoon Loyal called it quits.

"Five-thirty. That's enough for me," said Loyal. "Let's have a beer out on the porch, cool off a little."

The beer was sweet in their hot throats. They drank in silence. Loyal brought out a pound of rat cheese and some bread. The sun boiled away at the end of the plains and in the limpid sky the first stars came out. Jase slapped at his neck.

"Got 'im!" The bottle hooted when Loyal blew across its mouth. Jase stood up. There was something about the way he moved that brought the image of a trout hanging still in the current, then slipping away.

"Well, I'll be goin'. Just as soon come by again if you can use me."

" 'Preciate it," said Loyal, understanding he was hiring. He felt an absurd rush of pleasure and played the radio until late.

The pure darkness of the nights was broken by the spill of light from the McDonald's at the crossroads. Farm families drove distances as though to a son's wedding to eat meat in buns, lick at the slippery sauce, suck from waxed paper cups. The lights of the parking lot swelled like blisters on the droughty night.

Loyal and Jase sat out on the porch in their stiff clothes at the end of the day, the cold bottles in their hands, Jase, naked to the waist, his chairback leaning against the wall, hair wadded up off his neck, the twists of wet hair in his armpit visible every time he raised the bottle. Little Girl lay on her back exposing her belly to the stir of air, jaws smiling in sleep.

"Want some of this?" Jase, shaking the homegrown into a Zigzag paper and twisting it up, sucking in the hay-smelling weed smoke and passing it to Loyal.

The talk began slowly, Jase warily dragging out a few jagged words, warily, Loyal sorting through his mind for subjects. They could work in comfortable silence all day, just the words to pass the fence pliers. On the porch there was a difference. Loyal did not look at Jase now except from the corner of his eye. He felt his own withering skin hang on him like rotting wallpaper. The antiphonal conversation began with weather, drought, thunderstorms, ahh the goddamn wind and tornado weather. How much meat was left in the freezer. Was the gardens burning up or not. Sick animals. Water and wells. What the dogs been up to. An engine running sweet as you'd want but no brakes to speak of. Elvis.

"Yooooooo—u want Elvis? Look!" Jase, as perfect to look at as a river stone, flapping his arms began to howl, to thrust his pelvis at the yard. "Ah—oooo, ah—oooo!" until the dog sat up and tipped her muzzle back for a good yodel. Out in the darkness a coyote answered derisively and Loyal, heart beating, boot heels beating time on the step.

Coyotes then, and wheat, dry beans, soybeans, corn, pig litters and weight gains, Mormons, poison baits, and back to coyotes. Trapping, no not trapping, at the word "trap" Jase shook, his mind veered dangerously to booby traps, humping up the red mountains, probing the soil with a Kbar for a safe place to sit down, digging in, the pick

262

barely denting the root-shot soil. His panicked memory leaped from Bouncing Bettys, punji sticks, the old C-ration cans soured with spring-detonated bombs, the children who exploded when you clasped them. The random bits of metal, feet and tissue and splinters of bone raining around you. How few understood the frightening and devious intelligence of hunting humans. He would choke off the talk, stare at the dog's dream-twitched hind leg and rush away, be gone for days, leaving the work to collapse around Loyal.

"You dooooon't know. How smaaaaart. A huuuuman-beingis."

So, milder subjects, how small farms were doomed, was that son of a bitch Butz doing any good at all in the world or selling them out to the big corporations, bee stings, people with big feet, Mormons, the best wood for fence posts, what the dogs were doing, if beer was better ice-cold or just chilled a little, Frank Zappa, women, miniskirts. No, not women. Loyal would crackle his beer can in his scabbed hands, spit at the dirt.

Together they built hog pens, a new machinery shed, fenced in a square yard around the house, planted the Scotch pines, put up a garage for Loyal's truck. Why not, thought Jase, there was good money paid and not everyone would hire a crazy son of a bitch who smoked weed and howled. Why not, thought Loyal, it didn't hurt anybody to talk.

After the stifling August days of the third season a dry summer persisted, the wind never stopped. Loyal could not get used to the way it leaned over with him as he bent to loosen a wheel, crowded him around the corner of the hen coop. The dog, the hens, Jase. He was as isolated in his life as an exhibit. The farmhouse was barely furnished. The filmed windows reflected back his own face, his grizzled jowl, arms akimbo or hands half opened like someone moving toward a dancing partner.

He turned the kitchen radio up loud in the morning and only shut it off when he went to bed. On the dresser the old black and white television boomed tin laughter, and the other radio on the chair that served as his bedside table chattered along comforting with rosaries of songs repeated again and again, and again and again the excited voice crying, "National shoes ring the bell!" until he fell asleep, and in his sleep half-heard, under the wind, voices laughing between the music like a distant family, the crackling of galaxies in static.

Through that autumn the drought did not break. Jase took a back turn and again went to the VA hospital every day. The equinoctial dry storms came, wind and soil and locked knots of tumbleweed bouncing across the fields, gathering fellow weeds as they rolled, spraying the earth with seed. He'd hear them at night working up against the house with muffled scratches.

The last week in October, beans still in the row, the wind was a tidal wave from the west tearing over the earth. The house shuddered. Loyal sat on the edge of his bed writing in the Indian's book, now a green-paged book-keeper's ledger with vertical columns for income and debits. The farm was blowing away. The sky choked with dust, the stars smothered. The house nearly lifted on its foundations, the windows nearly cracked. The dog was tormented by the wind in the chimney. Only Loyal's pen, moving blackly, fluidly, was calm.

"Stung by a yellow jacket on thumb. Beans almost ready. Few more days. Wind strong all day. How is Jase doing."

In the morning his bedroom was muffled. He sat up, looked at the watch on the bedside chair and saw half past seven, full day and yet the room was dim. He could barely hear the wind, but he could feel it in the tremor of the bed. The window was covered with something, something like a choke of willow in spring runoff. He went to it and stared, drawn face reflecting in the glass, recognized tumbleweed, tumbleweed massed up against the second-story window.

All across the open land the wind had driven the balls of weeds, herding them until they hung up on barbwire or jammed against buildings and corrals, extending out into barrier reefs. He went downstairs. Pitch dark. He could not get the kitchen door open. He threw his weight against it. It gave an inch or two, then bounced back like a rubber door. He turned on the radio but the power was out.

Back upstairs a clearer light came from under the door of the spare room. This window, on the lee side of the house, was empty. He looked out. The wind was still streaming across the prairie, tumbleweed vaulting through dust. Tumbleweed was packed up ten feet and more below him, forced around the corner of the house from the weed-flooded yard at the front. He didn't want to shinny down a rope of sheets into the tangle below, then fight to where the front door had been the night before and wrestle tumbleweeds as big as trucks, but he couldn't think of another way. Take down part of the fence, maybe, so the weed could pass through.

Coming down the sheets he heard the sirens off to the west. Somebody hit one of those things at speed on the road and it would turn you over he thought. The sheet twisted on its knots. Never get them knots undone, he mumbled under his breath, and felt the hump of tumbleweed quiver beneath his feet.

The yard was filled with tumbleweed balls as big as chairs, as big as cars. The fence was down. The fence was the problem. It had funneled the weed to the house. His truck was in the weed. He could see the glint of glass, but couldn't work through the wiry Turk's head knots of twisted stems. The wind still rolled them along. He saw the great balls bound on the highway. He heaved at a cluster on the edge of the yard but they were knit together, springy and resilient. And dry as a bone. The brown stems cracked in his hand, powder spilled from the pith.

"I'll need a goddamn backhoe to get out of this." The dog was barking inside the house. "Unless you're smart enough to climb down a knotted sheet that's where you're going to stay for a while," he called. The sirens wailed again and he looked west in the direction of the sound. There was a pillar of smoke. Was Shears on fire? Was Jase gone wild? He started to run along the road, looking back over his shoulder to flag a ride when someone came along.

It was a stake truck from Wallace Doffin's dude ranch, the Walldoff Astoria. Wally himself, seventy years old, clenched the steering wheel, peered at Loyal from under his ruined Stetson.

"Well, where's your truck, Mr. Blood? She break down on you?" His jocular voice boomed.

"Damn tumbleweed's jammed all around it, jammed the front door, jammed the yard out to the fence."

"I've always favored a door that opens in, Mr. Blood. It seems best in heavy snowfall country or when you're under attack by the tumbleweed. I take it you are offering succor?"

"I'm offering to find out if that smoke is coming from Shears." The pale smoke writhed in the wind.

"Oh, it's not Shears's place, Mr. Blood, not yet, anyway. In about half an hour perhaps it will be. It's the McDonald's." The milky eyes peered forward at the shifting haze. "If I was you, I'd be worried, Mr. Blood. Your place is due east of Shears's. But then, you have no stock."

"Three miles east. Like to hope it's not coming that far. And I got fifty leghorns."

"Oh, leghorns. Prime stock, I imagine. Hope and pray, Mr. Blood. She could be at your place in an hour." He slowed as they neared Shears's turn-in. A cacophony of squeals swelled from the hogs. Old Shears and his two wheat-farmer sons were goading the animals into a truck as fast as they could work. Orson ran over.

"Jesus Christ I'm glad to see you Wally, you too, Blood. We got to get 'em out as fast as we can. The goddamn fire's all over the place."

Jase and old Shears prodded the panicky hogs up the ramp. Loyal looked at Jase. He glanced up, nodded.

"Hurry up, hurry up, hurry up!"

"Dad, might have to let the rest go, let them take their chances." The walleyed Pego, his face transformed by the seriousness of the danger into a red mask glazed with sweat.

"Chances? Unless there's a pig here can run sevendy mile an hour, his chances is fuck-all he roast while he run. I ruther get 'em down to the pond. I seen pigs come through a fire by going in a pond. You go open that pond gate, we'll see if we can't get them down there by the truck. They can make it in the pond. If they can make it anywhere."

"Mr. Shears, I sent word down the line that you needed trucks here. We will see reinforcements soon." Doffin's courtly voice.

Loyal was puzzled by the Shears's mad haste, the hogs ricocheting off the walls of the pens. He looked west again toward the smoke, saw a brown wall and at its base dots of sparking fire.

"There's one!" shouted Shears, pointing. One of the dots rolled obliquely across the highway and hit the fence. A string of smoke rose from it. Loyal saw that the tumbleweed was on fire, globes of flame running before the wind.

Under the sound of wind and crackling they hardly heard the two stock trucks come in from the east, the biggest one driven by Pearly-Lee, Dirty David's cigar-smoking wife.

"Hey, I heard you got some hogs you might want moved?" she screeched at old Shears, laughed. As soon as Jase moved the filled truck out she began maneuvering the truck into place. Dirty David slid out of the cab while the truck was still moving.

"We'n carry most of them hogs. Dunno about your buildings. Fire department's spread kind of thin this morning. Son of a bitsie manager over to the McDonalds found the weed all bunched up in his parkin' lot, throwed some gasoline on, tried to blowtorch the suckers. Blew his clothes off. They hauled him over to the hospital, more dead than alive, goddamn easterner."

A third truck pulled in, a pickup with flanks scarred like those of an ancient bison, windshield pocked with stellate bullet holes, shotgun and rifle in the window rack. It dribbled oil, curved across the yard with a drag of blue smoke. The back rattled like the traps of hell, two empty pails knocking against the snarl of chain, crowbar, toolbox, spare tire worn down to the fabric, empty wheel rims, broken bottles, come-along, posthole digger, oil cans, dented gas tank, loose hay, wads of feed sacks, rope, all on a bed of caked manure. Loyal recognized two of Jase's crazy VA hospital cronies, Wee Willy, the size and shape of a refrigerator with a matted beard like a floor mop and Albert Cugg who seemed fashioned from bleached mud. They were drunk and enflamed with the excitement of peril, absent too long from their lives. Wee Willy steered the truck through Shears's gates and out onto the prairie, northwest toward the point of the fire's advance. The line of fire slanted like the edge of a guillotine blade from the McDonald's lot out onto the open ground to the northeast.

"See what them bastards are doin'?" shouted Dirty Dave without stilling his jerking wrist, the limber rod urging the hogs up the ramp. Half a mile out the pickup bounced north across the ruts, lingered, turned and cut southwest, turned and wobbled north, working closer to the fire with every run.

"Them nuts is havin' a roundup!" bellowed Dirty Dave, pushing the gate closed on the last hogs. "They gonna get that one!"

In the distance a burning tumbleweed rolled out ahead of the fire. The pickup swerved and ran alongside the fiery mass. Albert Cugg hung out of the window, something in his hands. A plume of vapor blasted the tumbleweed. The weed poured out sullen smoke then flared again as the wind breathed through it. The pickup turned and came for another pass. They could hear Wee Willy booming "Olé!" and pounding on the door with the heel of his leathery hand. Cugg screamed victoriously.

More fireballs leaped out of the wall of flame. The pickup wheeled. They saw Cugg toss the extinguisher away and come up with another from inside the cab. Wee Willy drove daringly, swooping between tumbleweeds, forcing them apart, then herding each to a good position for Cugg to drown its fire.

"Hell good is that gonna do," said old Shears, turning his back on the pickup and flapping his hand at Dirty Dave to haul the hogs. He missed the sight of Wee Willy's too-tight turn that failed to butt a tumbleweed the size of a baby's playpen off the port fender and instead brought the truck squarely over the burning mass. It hung up underneath, and for a few seconds they saw the underside of the truck transfigured with pointed flames like the spinal plates of a stegosaur, saw Albert Cugg's door open and his leg extend, before the gas tank exploded.

"Ju-HEE-sus!" Dirty Dave saw the black and orange chrysanthemum in his rearview mirror. Loyal jumped in Wally Doffin's stake truck and turned it around. The old man slid in beside him. Jase leaped onto the running board on Loyal's side, his right arm behind Loyal's shoulders, gripping the metal rim of the seat back, his chest filling the side window. If Loyal wanted, he could bite the buttons off Jase's shirt.

"Now take it easy, Mr. Blood. If they're dead, they're dead, and if they're alive we'll get there. This truck is old so take it e-e-easy."

Cugg was not dead. The clothes on his left side smoldered and stank, his hair was charred and he said he was deaf, but in a few minutes he was able to stand up and wet his pants.

"Somehow I knew the day was gonna go like this," he said, staring at them with eyes full of tears and fumbling for a cigarette where his shirt pocket had been a few minutes earlier.

Wee Willy, on the far side of the truck, had shoved the door open, jumped and rolled the second he knew he'd cut it too close. The blast set the soles of his boots on fire and rained metal fragments onto him. A hot valve spring burned into his cheek and branded him with a scar that gave him the new nickname "Springs."

"I been needin' a new truck anyway," he said hoarsely. Jase began to laugh, then Loyal and finally Wally Doffin, crazy, uncontrolled laughing. They loaded Cugg and Willy into the back of the stake truck and bumped back to Shears. Jase rode in back with Cugg and Willy, his head down against the wind, passing a joint to the wounded. The fire turned with the shifting wind and pointed now like a long arrow almost due north where tractors were plowing a firebreak.

"I'd almost be tempted to unload them pigs again," said old man Shears. "That fire won't come down here now unless the wind shifts all the way around full circle. I don't know what we was in such an all-fired goddamn rush for, anyhow. On the other hand, you can't never be sure, so maybe I ought to just ship them out now. I was goin' to do in a few weeks anyway. But I'm sure to lose some of them hogs. They ain't been fed up and watered the way I want, and of course their weight is not what it should be."

"Mr. Blood." Old Doffin tipping his frazzled hat with the snakeskin band, watching the hogs surge in the stock truck compartments, "I suppose, on the way to dropping these boys off we could go and haul your truck out of the weed now, rescue the leghorns."

"Obliged to you," answered Loyal. "There's a dog as well. Stuck in the house unless she's learned to fly."

"Many dream, few manage it," said Doffin.

They dragged tumbleweed away from Loyal's truck for twenty minutes until the back bumper of the truck was in reach. The dog was barking hysterically inside the house. As he looped the hook of the chain around the bumper and shouted at old Wally to ease it away, Loyal caught the smell of smoke, stronger. The wind had been hitting obliquely at his left side as he worked, but now it was coming against his face; he had not noticed the shift.

He looked north. The tractors plowing a firebreak were turning back. The fire had jumped the line and was sending advance scouts of tumbleweed curving past them to the southeast, cutting around Shears's place in a great arc, but sailing toward Loyal's bean fields like great fiery bees. The closest were half a mile away.

"Wally! It's comin' this way again."

The old man got out of his truck and stared.

"I hope you got insurance, Mr. Blood. I believe it's going to get into your beans. Let's give a yank on that truck and see if we can get it free. Then you better skedaddle out of here and pray. You can stay over with us if you want. Plenty of room." He dragged the pickup out of its weed nest.

"The keys are in the house. I got to get the dog out." The first flames were in the bean fields, crackling strips of fire starting to run down the rows, rows of white smoke puffing up behind the flames. Tumbleweed still jammed the door. The old man was impatient.

"We don't have time. Put your pickup in neutral and get in here with me. I'll pull it." The crackling of the bean field was a roar. Loyal could feel the heat a quarter of a mile away. He threw the pickup in neutral.

"I got to try for my dog. If you have to go, then go, but I got to try."

The old man pulled onto the highway, ready to step on it. Loyal was at the back of the house staring up at the open window with its dangling sheets. A veil of smoke enveloped the house.

"Little Girl! Come on! Little Girl." She barked crazily, but the barking was muffled. He thought she was down in the kitchen at the front door.

He picked up stones and threw them into the open upstairs window. If she heard them that might bring her up the stairs and to the window.

"Come on! Come on!" He whistled. She stopped barking. Wally lay on the horn and raced the stake truck's motor. He shouted something Loyal could not hear. The dog was at the window.

"Come on, Little Girl. Jump! Jump. Come on!" She would not come. He saw her black front paws on the sill, heard her whine, then she dropped back to the floor and disappeared. The stake truck was creeping along the highway now, fading and reappearing in the smoke, Wally pounding on the horn with the side of his fist. A fiery bean stem and leaf floated past and touched down on the far side of the house. Loyal went for the truck, calling Little Girl as he ran.

He had the passenger door open and was up on the running board when Wally hit the brakes.

"Sweetness and Light! After all that be a shame if I was to run over her, wouldn't it."

The dog was in the cab, trembling, working her tail like a windshield wiper.

"She sailed outa the smoke like she was shot out of a slingshot." The old man put his foot to the floor and the stake truck picked up speed. Loyal craned around, looking out the rear window, but they were two miles east before he saw the flame of the house shoot up in the smoke. He kept his hand on the dog's neck, quieting her tremors. Down to a truck and a dog. Not even a change of clothes.

"Yes, a man works from can see to can't see and this is what he gets," intoned Wally. "I guess you had some kind of insurance, didn't you, Mr. Blood?"

There wasn't much to say.

35. What I See

The gopher shell yuk-chop-a-lund-kies hissing, the shrill whistles, the needles, blood, blood, O Chief Billy Bowlegs, still undefeated, the Seminoles, decked in the crimson vests and spangled capes, still dance the Green Corn Dance. But cowboy it up, too, blat through the saw grass with airboats, lure tourists with colored beads from Taiwan and alligator wrestles. Flat black eyes watch back.

Poling through the Green Swamp on a day's outing, Pala's unbraided hair shimmering in front of him, her brother Guillermo—Bill—the man of action, behind him, Dub feels the canoe slip through the tea-colored water, sees the water ruptured by iridescent gas bubbles, patterned by the checkerboard backs and wood-knot eyes of alligators, clouds of egrets slanting out of the choked trees. He breathes this stench of decay and the green light, the hanging moss, the spiderwebs stretched across the channels. Orchids. He shivers still at the sight of the fleshy blossoms in the end of his binoculars. The plangent call of rain crows under the long layers of clouds like pressed black linen. Bill slaps at mosquitoes.

"Pala, you like this?" He has to hear it.

"Yes. It's beautiful, and very strange." She turns and smiles at him, mosquitoes are enmeshed in her hair.

"I must of come here a hundred times."

This swamp is still itself in the red wilderness of development. Once he has heard a panther cough. Here, no men in mango beach pants, women with gasping mouths, nor bulldozers, drop-jaw technology nor the plastic fantasies. He's been in on the years of secret negotiations, the meetings in motels with purchasers disguised as traveling salesmen or graduate students in environmental studies. The Reedy Creek Improvement District. Disney World they will call it when it's done. Expensive plastic shit, he thinks. But winks and says to himself, thanks a million.

Later they slide back into the dangerous city, dodging along the highways, back to the smell of coffee and sweet cigars, the yellow sign "BARRA ABIERTA," the colored lights, rich smell of *palomilla* steak. Along the streets Dub sees the parade of bright dresses, gold chains and sequins. Above the city a fan of clouds like crimson knife blades, below, marble sidewalk. He passes a window, and in it an antique gramophone horn with painted morning glories surging out of its throat. I love this, he thinks, the shriek of jets, statues with flowery garlands, the front yard layaway saints lit with pink neon and the flashbulbs of tourists, windows heaped with conch shells, the raw bars and imitation shrunken heads, fish baskets and painted textiles and the funky music, the wild toughs, the deals and dirt, the eroding beaches, the sense of being in a foreign and lethal place. Home.

This dark urb, the hot slums of Liberty City and Overtown and the Black Grove. Yet he loves even the demonic riots that erupt like boils, does not shrink from the photographs of bloody corpses. All of it, the stinking money jammed into orifices, the street music and street food fading, fading into creamy women,

dark hair, hands weighed with opal cuffs, and men wearing handmade shoes, delight or rage twisting their burnished faces; if he looked until his eyes crossed he could hardly take in all that was there.

36. Shotguns

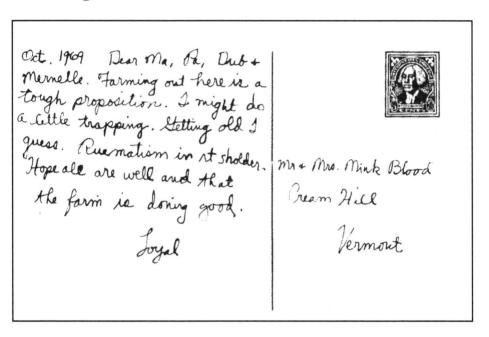

Oct. 1969 Dear Ma, Pa, Dub + Mernelle. Farming out here is a tough proposition. I might do a little trapping. Getting old I guess. Ruematism in rt sholder. Hope all are well and that the farm is doing good.

Loyal

Mr + Mrs. Mink Blood
Cream Hill
Vermont

"THEY'VE turned it back on itself, now," said Doffin. "It's the wind. The wind is as shifty as a greased pig." The dog would not let Loyal out of her sight. She lay under the table pressing against his foot. After supper Doffin, with the crooked walk of an old horseman, led them into the living room to watch the fire on television. Loyal saw how small the burning was from the air, a few thousand acres on the immense plains. The telephone wires dipped across the landscape. On the ground it had been like the world was on fire, a streaming fire that could ride the wind to

Canada or Mexico. The announcer said sixteen farms were gone. One of the corn farmers, a year's income gone in an hour, showed up at the hospital with a shotgun, calling for the burned McDonald's manager. There was a murky shot of the handcuffed farmer hunching into the sheriff's car.

Doffin poured trembling drinks for Loyal and himself The desiccated face, burned black-red, the eyes glimmering.

"You're welcome to stay here Mr. Blood until you get back on your feet again." The squat glass in the circle of the old man's hand. "Shotguns. I could tell you about shotguns around here until the clock's hands fell off." The big couch was framed in peeled cedar logs, cushions covered in cowhide. The lampshade made a light the color of a campfire when the stories begin. Mrs. Doffin sat apart, thin legs coming out of the skirt, crossed at the ankle like a pirate's flag of bones, hands calm after the ritual of pouring coffee, nodding at whatever was said.

Loyal nodded too. There was still the land. He could sell the acreage and take off. Get a new truck. Maybe one of those VW vans, fix it up inside, be like a little house on wheels. Hell, he could go anywhere. Alaska. California.

"I could tell you about shotguns, make it sound bad, describe you the grief they've caused, but I come to see it's more like a habit kind of a thing you know, like it's just a pretty good way to clean up a life that's gone dirty. They used to call it temporary derangement, but I always thought the act showed considerable lucidity considering the circumstances. Not all the time, of course, but most of the time. My wife's family picked that way quite a few times." Mrs. Doffin nodded. Her bony hands lay idle on the blue tapestry arms of the chair.

"Her father. Grandfather. One of her uncles. And I can think of others. All farmers, or at least most of them."

"That's right." The index finger of the right hand tapped a little. "I was the one to find my father. I was only seventeen years old. The shock made me blind for a week my mother said. I don't remember it."

"Your rancher or farmer now, Mr. Blood, will almost always choose a shotgun. They'll get a forked stick, you see, that lets them reach the trigger. They don't go in around here for that business with the big toe. Don't like to take their boots off. Die with your boots on, you know. They'll set the muzzle up to the forehead. That's where you aim when you kill a cow. Weakest part of the head. See, they know. Just around these parts I could name you a dozen. Alvin Compass, good-looking young fellow used to drive over to Wolfwing. He was courting some girl over there, we never did know who it was. He was a nice kid, come from a decent ranch family. His father has a nice ranch in the Whitewater valley. Many a time I've stopped and watched that herd. I watched one of his bulls in the spring grass. Paw the ground, red dirt spraying up under his foot, then get down and grind his shoulder like he had a bad one down.

"Alvin'd drive more than fifty mile to see that girl. One time he was going pretty fast and clipped a car coming through an intersection. Sent them into the ditch. The car rolled over on its side. Alvin, he stopped and ran over to the car. Looked inside saw five or six people, some of them kids, nobody moving, saw blood all over the driver's face. He went back to his truck, took his shotgun out of the rack and blew his brains out. Right there on the side of the road. The thing was that the people in the other car weren't dead. They weren't even hurt except the driver who got knocked unconscious and had a little cut on his forehead. You know how head cuts bleed. He come to after a few minutes. He was the one found Alvin. Don't that make you sick?

"C. C. Pope was another one. Lived way out in a big house with his sisters Dorothy and Brittania. None of them ever got married. Strange bunch, I tell you. They had flukey luck about four, five years in a row. Rain all around them, but not on their fields, or flood them out and leave the rest refreshed, or a tornado would light on the farm a week before harvest and tear up everything or all the machinery would break down at once and they'd find out the parts they needed to fix them up were all discontinued. Obsolete. You'd see sun dogs in their sky and nowhere else. Indians wouldn't come on the place. Called old C. C. 'Backward Speaking.' Who knew what that meant. He talked as good as you or me.

"Then old C. C. got lamed up with a pulled shoulder and the doctor told him to get it massaged two, three times a week. Doctor gives him the name of the wife of Earl Doffin, no relation of mine that I know of, she was good at massages and reasonable enough, so he went over there and scrapes his foot for fifteen minutes before he gets up enough courage to ask her if she'd give him a massage. 'Ya, ya, I do it.' She was a Swede. He'd go over there every week for his massage. I guess it was just the shoulder, but who knows? Poor old bugger, seventy-four years old, didn't know any women except the two old prune sisters, he fell in love with Earl Doffin's wife. Big fat woman, a grandmother six times, and about as romantic as a cow flop. Course he knew it was hopeless. He never said a word to her. Took his shotgun into his bedroom and shot himself while he looked in the mirror. Afterwards they found his bureau drawer just crammed with love letters he never sent her.

"Charles V. Sunday. He was a taxidermist. My goodness, he'd do a big cat that looked so real you'd go cold looking at it, isn't that right, Molly?"

The dog slept, her head on Loyal's foot. The weight was giving his foot pins and needles. He tried to inch it out from under her jaw but the slightest movement and she groveled closer. She'd have to get over that.

"He could stuff anything, tan deer or elk hide so nice it was like butter. He wrote away when he was a boy for one of those mail correspondence courses, Learn Taxidermy in Your Spare Time, but my stars he did well at it. He did mounting for some of the big museums, worked two years on a pack of coyotes they got in New Paltz, New York at the Municipal Museum they got there. They ran a magazine article of that exhibit that we saw somewhere."

"Western World," said Molly Doffin. "It's in one of the boxes up over the tack room. Plus there was one of the local papers did a big write-up. Pictures and everything."

"Show it to you tomorrow. Well there he is, Mr. Sunday, making a good living, esteemed for his skill, articles in the magazines and papers about him and all, nice family with a couple of kids, and he shoots himself. Right at the end of the winter. Finished up all his work, tacked newspapers on the ceiling, spread more paper out on the floor to spare whoever had to clean up, and blam! But they never knew why he did it. Affairs was in good order. He didn't give any sign and he didn't leave a note. After all that trouble of putting up the newspaper on the ceiling it was sort of ironic that all the mess, the brains and gore and blood, ended up on a pile of dominos on the table behind him. He'd been playing dominos with his youngest son about an hour before he shot himself. That was a good many years ago, but what's even stranger is that that son who'd been playing dominos with him shot himself on his eighteenth birthday. This was just two years ago. I don't recollect where he did it, do you Molly?"

"Way out in the field."

"That's right. It comes back to me now. The funny thing was he used an eight-gauge gun. His father had left his collection, you see, and this was in it."

"Christ," said Loyal. "There couldn't have been much left of him."

"That's right. Head was completely blowed away. But at least they know why he did it. He left a three-hundred-twelve-page suicide note behind. Started it seven months before he did the dirty deed. He'd been writing on it for months. He didn't think he had any kind of a future—said he was homely, girls laughed at him, he had bad habits, guess we know what that means, he was lazy, poor memory, didn't do well in school and suffered a variety of allergies, one leg shorter than the other and so forth. Every ill known to man."

"I never thought he was bad-looking," said Mrs. Doffin. "He seemed perfectly normal every time I saw him. But you never can tell."

"And there's a whole stew of them, lost crops, couldn't keep up their mortgages, financial problems. Of course we've had our troubles here, too, but somehow we always came out without having to resort to the pipe. Isn't that right, Mother?"

"So far," said Mrs. Doffin and laughed.

"So, Mr. Blood, you've had serious losses today, your bean crop and your leghorns and your house and out-buildings, but I hope you can still look on the bright side. You were spared and your truck and dog was too. I hope you're not thinking about taking the pipe like those we've been talking about. There's still a lot to live for."

"No, no," said Loyal. "The idea never crossed my mind. I been knocked lower than this in my life and never considered it. I wouldn't blow my head off with a shotgun if you paid me." But it seemed his life was like a weak chain, the links breaking one by one.

"Ha-ha. You know, if you want some kind of a job while you think about the next step, why we can manage to give you something here. There's always work on a dude ranch, even a small one like ours. Yes, and we've had two of those shotgun incidents right here, isn't that right, Mother?"

"Two? There was only Miss Bridal and I still believe that was an accident."

"What about Parger? You haven't forgotten him."

I have not forgotten him, but it was not a shotgun and it may have been murder. That deer rifle with a string that pulled the trigger when he opened the door. I will always believe it was a killing, and I hate to think of the motive.

Mr. Blood, we had some unsavory fellows if you take my meaning out in the bunkhouse at that time and one of them, a friend of this Parger, was as jealous as a woman. The sheriff talked to him for hours and they never arrested him, but I always thought there was more to it than meets the eye. He left before we asked him to go on his way. Probably still out there, roaming around."

The dog had wormed her way in between Loyal's right heel and the couch, twining through his legs and over one foot like a living rope.

"Your dog is a desperate lover, Mr. Blood."

"Hmm," agreed Mrs. Doffin, as though to affirm that a mention of love balanced the accounts of strewed brains.

37. The Indian's Book

Dear Deb, The box of grapefruit was an awful nice surprise. I never had such sweet grapefruit before and, such a pretty pink color. I took a couple over to Mernelle and Ray and they said you sent them oranges. So we swapped. It was awful good of you and Pala to think of us. love, Ma (Jewell Blood)

Marvin S. Blood
Sungate
4444 Collins Ave.
Miami, Fla.
33144

HE'D tried to write down the thing that happened in

Criddle's bar in the Indian's book. But it melted into nothing under the pen.

He'd sat at a table making scallops with the wet circles of his beer bottle, half-listening to the argument going on at the end of the bar. Marta, a husky woman with a tower of lacquered hair was arguing with a man. She was dressed like an Icecapades cowgirl, suede vest studded with nailheads, buckskin miniskirt showing linebacker legs with hairy collars up high where the razor had stopped. The man slouched over his beer, oil-limp clothes giving off a greasy vapor.

"So it don't run no better, that's what the problem is. You gotta fix it. I took care of you, but far's I can see you didn't do nothin' with my Chevy except maybe set on the front seat. Or maybe just lean on the hood. Did you do anything to it? That's right, don't answer, because I know you didn't."

The man scratched at his chest and half-turned away from her. She picked up her chair and moved it to the other side of the table so she was facing him again. Her voice rose.

"You think I just got to take it, huh? Ain't that what you think? I can't go to the cops about it, can't complain to nobody? Well, you are wrong. You have tangled with the wrong girl."

The man gave an exaggerated sigh and half-winked at Loyal. He signaled Mrs. Criddle for another.

"You want another beer walk over here and get it," said Mrs. Criddle through her white lips, wiping the bar. Her hard eyes accepted nothing until it was part of the past. She made no effort to draw a beer. The man twirled his empty glass on the scarred table.

"Didn't you hear the lady? She asked you to go over to the bar and get your beer," Marta's voice, sweet with a gagging edge. She got up. "I bet you think *I* ought to go get your beer, don't you? Yessir, you are just a man that likes to be waited on, hand and foot, ain't you, you cross-eyed, double-dealin', hang-nailed no-good TWERP!" On the last word she yanked his chair out from under him. The man sprawled back from the table and when he yanked at her leg, she stood fast and kicked him in the head and kept on kicking.

"How you like them dance steps, you like that you greasy old monkey? You want more?" The voice sneered like a comb dragged across the edge of a table. Every time the man tried to get up she kicked him with her scuffed boots, the rhinestones in a wave design around the upper rims.

"Hey, quit that!" shouted Mrs. Criddle, coming around the corner of the bar. Criddle came out of the back room, wiping his vinegared hands on a towel. The man scuttled under the table of a booth where Marta could not swing her foot. She tossed her head like a bull. The tower of hair swayed.

"Gimme a broom! Stick, baseball bat, something." Her eyes rolled over the room, skidded across Loyal to Criddles. They came back to Loyal again.

"What are you starin' at, you dirty turkey? Men! Look at you, you dirty turkey, settin' there like you are at a show. Well, how you like to be in the show?" She picked up the man's empty beer glass and hurled it at Loyal. It struck him on the shoulder, bounced onto the table and broke. She rushed across the room, knocking his chair over, carrying both of them with it. Her knees ground into the floor, stiff points of hair leapt up like flares from the surface of the sun and she whacked at him.

In the moment of falling he wanted to chop her throat, split the humped black hair to the brain. He came up from the floor like a hammer. He thought he would have killed her except for Criddle and Ben Rainwater, finally, coming in, felt hat tilted over his eyes. The three men staggered around in a surging dance. Mrs. Criddle shoved Marta out through the kitchen and into the alley.

"I don't care if you don't got your coat, you go on home if you got one."

And through the rage Loyal tasted an evil satisfaction that adrenaline had stalled his fit. Although no secret was unfolded. And wrote that night at the top of the page in the Indian's book, *Only one way*, then scored the words out until the pen tore the paper, shut those thoughts down. Who knew how many ways there were to love? Those who could not find any way knew the difficulties.

38. Looks Like Rain

JEWELL woke up with the feeling she had to make haste. There were things to be done, set aright. She drank her cup of tea standing up, looking out at the dark morning. Her hands rattled the cup. Unsteady on her pins, too, she thought, but felt restless. Must be a weather change coming in.

She washed the cup and saucer and ate a few slices of apple. No appetite these days. Stout since Dub was born, her flesh had fallen away in the past year. Her reflection startled her—old Grandma Sevins, beaky nose and wrinkles, peering at her. She was seventy-two and looked it, but felt like a young woman except for the shakes.

Dear Former Customer! Even though Its' Fall Instead of ᴍᴀʏ it ᴍᴀʏ Be That We ᴍᴀʏ Have Just the Car You Want! ᴇ–ᴢ Terms for Qualified Customers. Isn't it Time You Stop by ʀᴜᴅʏ'ꜱ ᴄᴀʀ ᴄɪᴛʏ? You'll be *Glad You Did*!

Jewell Blood
RFD
Cream Hill
05099

It was too bad, she thought. She'd missed the leaves turning color again. It had been at its height in October when the new car's brakes were being replaced, and then the whole idea had slipped her mind while Indian summer skidded past. She'd always intended to go up in the mountains over in New Hampshire at leaf time when she got done at the cannery. They said it was a treat, the colors and the views. She longed to drive up Mount Washington, up the toll road. And then, when she had time on her hands, she'd forgotten about it. She thought the Beetle would make it; they said the road was hard on cars and not a few had to turn back. The ones that boiled over. But at the summit you could see to the end of the world, could buy a sticker for your car bumper that said THIS CAR CLIMBED MT. WASHINGTON. Silly thing to want, a bumper sticker, but she did want it. Mount Washington. Now there was something for an old girl to do!

Ray had persuaded her to trade in Mink's ancient pre-War heap for a 1966 VW Beetle. "It's only got twenty-two thousand miles on it. It'll last as long as the old Ford did, it'll get good mileage and you can take it places most cars won't go. Rudy's got one in pretty good shape. The color's kind of funny but he says you can have it at a good price."

"I don't care about the color!" she said. Then, "What color is it?"

"It's orange, Jewell. With lime-green upholstery. It was a custom order but the people couldn't keep up the payments. It runs very good and it's got a good heater. No body rot at all. Rudy says he'll replace the brakes for free if you're interested in the car. I think he's having trouble selling it because of the color and that's a fact."

She liked the little car once she got past the way it looked. The vehicle's humped shape and eagerness seemed familiar; it reminded her of Mernelle's old dog.

She straightened up the trailer, ran the vacuum cleaner over the braided rug, spread a clean tablecloth and put fresh shelf paper in the kitchen cupboards. That was a little job. In the old days she would have stuffed the dirty paper in the stove and burned it. The electric stove was clean but it couldn't dry socks, burn paper, raise bread or provide comfort. Cost money to run it. They called it progress.

By nine there was nothing to do but knit. She was restless. The wool caught on her rough fingers. The trailer cramped in. She felt like a good drive, wanted to get out on the road and see something. The trailer was cozy enough, but it cramped her up. The truth was, she missed working at the cannery.

She studied the dull morning. The sky was like an old horse blanket. The gaunt weeks before the snow started. Well, she would just drive east, even though it looked like rain. See how far she got. Let the Beetle do what it could.

She was in Littleton at noon, tired and thirsty. She spent fifteen minutes looking for a luncheonette. She had the beginning of a headache. It was a longer trip than it looked on the map. The heavy sky loured. A glass of ginger ale would do good. Maybe a chicken sandwich while she studied her map. It was still a treat to go into a place and order what she liked, then pay for it with her own money.

She parked in front of The Cowbell Diner. Inside she sat in a varnished booth, pulled out the menu stuck behind the napkin dispenser. Crumbs and ketchup smears on the table. One waitress leaned on the counter; the other sat on a stool in front of her, smoking and drinking coffee. There were a few other customers. A man in a ragged jacket seemed at home; he helped himself to coffee from the murky pot behind the counter.

"Takin' their sweet time," Jewell muttered to herself.

The girl came over and swiped a rag over the table.

"Help you."

"I believe I'll have a glass of ginger ale without any ice and a plain chicken sandwich, just chicken and lettuce and a little mayonnaise."

"White or whole?"

"What?"

"You want the chicken on white bread or whole wheat bread?" She jiggled her thigh, looked back at the other waitress. Jewell recognized the type. There was a kind of salesclerk, waiter, waitress, cashier, barely civil to older people. They took their time, spoke contemptuously, slapped down the goods. Jewell bet this one would slop the ginger ale all over the place. Sure enough.

The bread curled up like a pagoda to disclose wilted lettuce and a wad of grey chicken. The ginger ale was mostly ice and slosh. She mopped up the spilled liquid with paper napkins and bent over her road map. Dismayed to see the auto road was on the far side of the mountain. She would have to drive north and all the way around, another sixty miles, it looked like. When the waitress brought her check—$1.75—she asked her if there was a faster way to get to the auto road.

"Auto road? I don't even know where it is. Melanie, you know where the auto road is?"

"For Mount Washington," said Jewell. "The auto road that goes up Mount Washington."

"I been up it," said Melanie. "It was cloudy."

"What's the best route?"

"Just take one-sixteen, then get on two, then get on sixteen, that's all I know. A couple hours from here, anyway."

"Aren't there any shortcuts, any back roads?"

The first waitress answered. "Not that I ever heard of. So, where'd you go last night, Melanie?"

The man in the plaid jacket swiveled around on his stool. "You got a good car?" Unshaven jowls, eyes like pickled onions. Old coot.

"Yes, I do," said Jewell, thinking of the earnest Beetle. "I drive it anywhere."

"Well, you got a good car and don't mind gettin' off the main road, they's a shortcut, save you eight or ten mild." He hitched across the floor and hovered over the map. "It's a loggin' road. Forget one-sixteen. See, you go down here, see, take one-fifteen, go down past Carrol, about three mild past Carrol, then you start watchin' on the right. Row of equipment sheds, I dunno, six, eight sheds, and after the sheds there's a right-hand turn. You don't take that one, but about half a mild farther there's another right-hand turn and that's the one you want. It cuts along over here, comes out somewhere there." His finger skidded across the map. "Save you some mild, 'bout ten mild. If you don't mind a dirt road."

"That's mostly what I drive on," she said. "Appreciate the information."

"I wouldn't take his advice if you paid me," said Melanie.

It was quarter of two when she came to the rickety pole sheds. She passed a right-hand turn, and watched the odometer to know when she reached half a mile. Nothing. At one and six-tenths miles a ragged gravel road cut southeast. She turned onto it. Not a breath of wind. The dark sky, the chewed spruce of the idiot strip and behind it rough hills choked with brambles and popple trash depressed her. She was tired. Cold seeped into the Beetle. Probably be close to four and starting to get dark when she reached the top of Mount Washington. What time did they close the shop where you got the bumper stickers? But she was so close it would be a shame not to try. An adventure, going up Mount Washington in the near dark. And coming down again. Don't let it rain, she thought, glad she had the new brakes.

The road roughened, narrowed, pale gravel through the dark woods. A mile or two in, the road formed a Y. There were no signs, no way to tell which went where. The right branch seemed the best bet and she turned onto it. The nameless road crossed a bridge, then twisted uphill in loops and curls; innumerable side roads branched to the left, the right. Mile after mile the road bored into the forest. She passed log landings, an ancient green trailer with a caved-in roof and a pair of antlers dangling over the gaping doorway. The road went black and mucky in the low spots. Mud sprayed up onto the windshield. The gravel had played out. She fought up a grade of shelf rock and onto a corduroy trail of rotting logs through a swamp. There was no place to turn around. She was frightened now and wanted to turn back, but could only go forward. The first ticks of freezing rain. A moose splashed into a stand of spruce stubs. The little car wallowed through holes and the muffler tore loose on one of the logs before she was out of the swamp. The track—it was no longer a road—steepened, a gullied out nightmare of stones. She could not turn around, could barely go forward.

The fine sleet built up on the windshield. The wipers rasped ineffectually at the mud and ice. Finally, a lurch to the side, a grinding. The Volkswagen was hung up. She switched off the ignition, got out and looked underneath, saw the rock pressing against the undercarriage. The sleet rattled on the little car, hissed in the spruce. It would take a helicopter to get the beetle off that rock, she thought. There had been a come-along in the old car's trunk, but it had disappeared when she got the Volkswagen. But if she could find a stout pole or two and get them under the Beetle maybe there was a chance to lever it off. If she had the strength. She was bound to try. But wished for Mink. Saw how he used his rage to pull him through difficult work, through a difficult life. Her heart was pounding. She stumbled into the slash, looking for a good, sound stub. She wasn't dressed good for this, she thought, the knit pants cuff catching on snags.

Branch slash, decaying trunks, green saplings—nothing that would do. It was the hardest kind of work getting through the tangle of deadwood. Panting, she came to a gully crisscrossed with dead trees, boiling with brambles. There was a stub that looked sound and of a size she could manage. She tried for a good position to haul at it. She could lift the near end free, but the far end seemed to be moored by another trunk. She was shaking. Would have to get to the other side of the gully and pry it loose somehow. Knew she could not balance her way over on the fallen trunks like a tightrope walker, like Mink would have done. She struggled, clawed down into the gully, began to force her way through choked brambles and rot. The sleet pattered. It was dark and stinking down in the close stems. Branch stubs jabbed. She fought her way forward, seven, eight feet, her heart hammering, so intent on reaching the other side of the gully she felt only astonishment when the fatal aneurism halted her journey. Her hand clenched wild raspberry canes, relaxed.

39. The Logging Road

November 17, 1969
Dear Mr. Blood;
There's been two complaints to the selectmen
about the septic system on your trailer park
property in Cream Hill. Could you come to
meeting next Thursday night. Joanne Buddle,
Cream Hill Town Clerk

Mr. Otter Blood
RFD
Wallings, VT, 05030

DRUMMING November rain streamed over the windshield. Gusts rocked the car, slapped wet leaves into the street. Ray's milky breath condensed on the side windows softening the glare of stoplights, the neon sign chin garden (the a in China had never worked) into colored lozenges. The heater whirred its warmth onto his legs. He turned onto Henry Street, the headlights throwing off sparkles from wet trees, the flecked sidewalk. Water charged with leaves raced in the gutters, wet boots flashed like flints. The windows of his house shone in the darkness like squares of melting butter.

He pulled into the driveway, aligning the wheels with the sloping strips of concrete on each side of the tufted ridge of grass that brushed the underside of the car. He could see the red of the kitchen curtain through the window, see Mernelle moving around the table, probably smoothing out the place mats or laying the silver out in short rows like children lined up for a photograph.

The door had swelled in the dampness and he had to push it twice before it would open. Mernelle, her rump to him in the tight black pants as she bent and reached into the cupboard under the sink for a fresh sponge said "Nasty out?"

"Pretty bad. Getting colder already. They're calling for it to go to snow before morning."

"The deer hunters will be glad." The wind smashed rain against the back door. The gas tank cover rattled against the house.

"Yeah, they'll like it. How long to supper? Smells incredible good. What is it?"

"Roast pork with baked squash. Seemed like a good idea with this bad weather. And I made apple pie. That's what you smell, the cinnamon."

"You want a drink?" Hung his damp coat on the wall hook where it could dry. From him came the bitter fragrance of raw wood. His slippers were in the hall.

"Maybe one. Make it light." She peered into the hot oven, jabbing at the pork with the meat fork. Ray turned on the little radio over the sink. Trumpet music, something Latin American with a clicking sound. He took the bottle of bourbon out of the sugar cupboard with its smell of dry pine and spices, the green ginger ale bottle from the refrigerator. Mernelle pulled the ice cube tray out of the freezer.

"I just filled it this morning," she said, "so the ice cubes don't have that old taste." She held the tray under running water until the lever cracked the cubes loose with a brief icy groan. Ray stood behind her, leaning against her, pressing her belly against the edge of the sink. He breathed into her hair. She felt the heat of his breath on her scalp, in her ear, felt his mouth at the nape of her neck, his tongue licking the stray hairs.

"Ah. Ah," he said. "Home. I love it."

Her blighted longing for kids flickered. "Want to give that roast another fifteen minutes. It's five pounds so we'll have enough leftovers to make shepherd's pie tomorrow." She took her drink from him. The glass was cold in her hand. The ice knocked glassily.

In the living room Ray sat in his leatherette recliner, Mernelle on the sofa rich in its gold tweed upholstery, tapered legs stabbing into the shag carpet. The coffee table, of sleek caramel wood, bore a lustrous dish of mints, stacked copies of *Lumberyard Review*, *Motorboat* and *Reader's Digest*. The plywood paneling shone with lemon oil. Photographs of autumn scenes in stamped brass frames hung around the room. On a table at the end of the room the television set faced them.

At the end of the sofa a cabinet with glass doors, and inside, Mernelle's bear collection: glass bears, ceramic, wooden, Bakelite, plastic, papier mâché, a varnished dough bear from Italy, a straw bear from Poland, stuffed cloth bears, twig and stone bears and a metal music box bear with a crank in his back who played "Home on the Range." She did not know why she collected them. "Oh, it's something to do, a hobby, like. I don't know, I just like them." Ray brought back bears for her from every place he went, from the lumber conventions in Spokane, Denver, Boise, from other countries, from Sweden, even

Puerto Rico and Brazil. In a way he collected them; she arranged them on glass shelves. She had to like them. She did like them.

Ray switched on the television set. The blue rectangle swelled out at them and the crooked figures shimmied through desperate snowfall. The images held their attention like flames in a fireplace. At eight-thirty Mernelle went into the kitchen to make Ovaltine and cut the pie, still as warm as sleeping flesh. She arranged the dessert plates, white with blue rims and gold leaves, on the tray, poured the pink-tinged Ovaltine into the cups that matched the plates. Against the sound of the storm she made a chinking of china, played the silver sound of spoons. In the living room Ray set up the little table, spread the yellow cloth on it. She set the tray down gently. They watched the flickering story, their forks muffled in crust and cream. The sight of his empty knees rent her. If there'd been kids they would be putting them to bed about now. Ray would tell the bedtime story. "Once upon a time there was a little girl who lived on a farm at the top of a tall, tall hill. Her name was Ivy Sunbeam Mac Way, better known as Sunny to all and sundry. Even on Sunday."

Late in the program the phone rang. Ray stretched. His sharp elbows pointed the plaid shirtsleeves.

"If that's someone at the mill—"

"I'll get it, Ray. You shouldn't have to go out on a night like this." The black streaming night. She answered the phone, but he was up, standing in the doorway and listening. The hollow voices of the television sank into grim music and the tough voice ". . . I'm a cop . . . on the day beat out of . . ."

"Yes, yes." In the nervous questioning voice reserved for strange authorities. Someone was telling her an address. She listened, gestured for a pencil and paper. He stood beside her watching her write a number, directions to a town a hundred miles away in the mountains. "She is seventy two years of age, she was heavyset, but thinner now, maybe five-foot-five in height, I'm not sure. She is shorter than me. She wears glasses." She listened to the young voice. "I tried to call her yesterday afternoon a couple of times but didn't get any answer. What time? Well, I'm not sure, but the rain had just started. Maybe about three. Tried again this morning. She is out quite a lot so I didn't think anything of it. Yes. Yes, I can bring a picture took of her last spring. Me and Ray'll start right away." After she hung up the phone she wondered why her hands didn't shake, she pressed them against her eyes, then dropped her arms limp to her sides, sucked air in past her teeth.

"That was the New Hampshire state police. Some deer hunters found Ma's car way up on a logging road. Looks to have been there a day or two they think—there's snow on it and no tracks around it. No answer at her phone the police said. It just rings and rings. They had Mr. Colerain drive by the trailer and check, Sheriff Colerain, and she's not there. They tracked us down through Ott." She was dialing, her fingers knowing the familiar number and stood listening to the burr-burr, burr-burr, imagined the ringing in the empty trailer.

"They said they don't know how the car could ever have drove up there. It is hung up on a rock. They said it is all just rocks and stumps and swamp, that a bulldozer would of had trouble making it up there."

"Is she hurt?"

"They don't know, Ray. There wasn't nobody in the car. Her pocketbook is on the seat. There's money in it. Thirteen dollars. They needed a description so they can call the motels and hospitals. They said it is snowing to beat the band up there. Ray, what in the hell was she doing on a log road up past Riddle Gap, New Hampshire? You know some burglar or worse could of broke in, kidnapped her, stole her car."

"Get your warm duds on. This will be a bad trip through them damn New Hampshire mountains."

The land steepened on the east side of the Connecticut River. Mernelle sat on the edge of the seat, braced her hand against the dash. The road gleamed black in the headlights, the windshield wipers nodded.

"She's been funny the last few months, Ray. Remember in August when she came home with somebody's mailbox dragging off the back bumper? It must have made a terrible noise going down the road and she said she never even heard it. And Ray, the time she tried to cross the brook when the bridge was out and got the car in a hole? She's been a terror in that damn car. She's too old to drive, Ray. I'm going to tell her, too, right to her face."

The rain clicked, grain of ice in each drop. As the temperature fell ice ridges built up at the extremities of each sweep of the wipers, leaving fans of clear glass outlined in ice. The wipers scraped and clawed. Ray pulled over gingerly and picked the ice off the wipers by hand. Black ice coated the windshield as he worked on the wipers. He scraped the windshield clear, but in less than a mile had to pull over again and clear the ice buildup. The defroster roared but only produced a saucer-sized rising moon of clear glass, forcing him to drive with his head craning up over the steering wheel.

The steep roads had not been sanded and the DeSoto slewed, the rear end throwing out on even the gentlest curves. On hills they slid and skidded sideways. No headlights came from the other direction but far behind them Ray saw the slow crawl of another vehicle in the rearview mirror.

"I bet that's the sand truck behind us," said Ray. They wavered along at twenty miles an hour, the sleet pouring down like salt. In Jarvis it changed to snow.

"Small favors," said Ray. But the tires held on snow, the wipers swept the flakes away. He increased the speed to a steady thirty.

She woke in the hot motel sheets and knew by the sound of his breathing that Ray's eyes were open. The cramped room, a plastic chair crowding the double bed, the television set, was stifling. Her head ached. The heat was on full blast, and from the gushing air she knew it was bitter outside.

"How long you been awake?" she whispered.

"Haven't been to sleep yet. I just keep thinking she might be out there. Getting awful cold out." He got up and pulled at the venetian blind, his wedding ring a glint. The slats rose at a crooked angle. A crystalline haze blurred the motel yard light. The fine, fine snow that fell when it was bitter cold. There was the wind, he thought. Even if someone was dressed warm and hunkered down in a hollow tree, in a sheltered corner, how long could they last? Did old farm women burn with fires of endurance or did they let go quick and easy?

"What do you think, Ray?"

"I don't know. I don't know. It don't look too good, honey. But we got to keep our fingers crossed. She might be in somebody's spare room right now. Don't borrow a worry."

"Ray. She's not in somebody's spare room." He said nothing but folded his long hard arms around her, pulled her up close so her ear pressed against his bare chest. His heartbeat thudded, his chest rose and fell with his warm breathing, a sleepy, vanilla smell came from him.

"Ah, Ray, don't know what I'd do . . . " But, folded in the sweet circle, she imagined Jewell in the drifts, one arm stretched out rigid before her, the other folded across her breast as if to pull an arrow from her throat. Snow crackled in her hair and drifted into the cold shell of her ear.

"Ray, poor Ma," she sobbed. And he stroked and stroked the fine hair until it rose in the darkness to meet his descending hand.

By midmorning the temperature was fifteen below. The snow drifted in hissing knife edges. A fresh search party had started out at seven with the first slow light. Mernelle talked to Dub in his Florida office. The connection was bad as though ice were forming in the lines.

They sat on plastic chairs in the dispatcher's office in maddening idleness. They strained to understand the coded, crackling messages. Men came in and went out.

The room smoked with cold. Smoke rankened the air. Ray began to think about the pipes under the sink at home, the heat of the house dying away.

"It's no good both of us waiting here. They could freeze up. What about if I go back and take care of the pipes and you stay here. I'll come back as soon as I can. And if they find a trace, you call me and I'll come right along."

On the next day, glittering cold, Ray came back but they had not found her, and on the third day the snow began again. The search was finished. Mernelle and Ray sat in their car in the play of heated air staring at the gas station where Jewell's orange bug, dented along the bottom panel, muffler gone, spattered with congealed mud and oil, stood off to the side. As the new snow filmed the dirty metal Mernelle said she'd never see it run again.

"This family," she said. "This family has got a habit of disappearing. Every one of this family is gone except me. And I'm the end of it."

"Don't say that, honey. We might still get lucky."

"The luck was used up long ago, Ray. Bloods been running on empty since Loyal lit out. Damn him, sends his damn postcards every year or so but never lets us know where to write. You realize he don't even know Pa's dead? He don't know about the barn or what happened to Pa, he don't know Ma moved into the trailer or that you and me been married almost ten years or that Dub is rich in Miami. Don't know that Ma is lost. Sends his dumb bear postcards. How many of those bears have we got to see? What makes him think I want to hear from him? I don't care about his damn postcards. What now? Put some kind of notice in every paper in the country, 'To Whom It May

Concern. Jewell Blood lost in the snow on Riddle Mountain in New Hampshire, will her oldest son who hasn't been heard from for twenty years call home'? Is that what I should do? At least I know where to get hold of Dub. At least I can call him up. I got an address. I don't need to wait for a postcard."

PART FOUR

40. The Gallbladders of Black Bears

Dear Brother Jensen, I'm now a true beliver after what happened to us. Things here been awful tight, but last Wed. Mrs. Cains a neabor asked me to go over Womens Pray Circle mtg. I went for the fellowship much as anything. During the prayers I just thot well I'll pray for some finance relief. Brother Jensen, beleive me 3 days later Trav decide to plow a little strip front of the windbrake for a Sparo gas bed. He turn up a mans shoe inside there was a $100 bill in there, real dirty but good. We both praying now. We watch your program "Come to Jesus" every nite. Yours in the Lord,
Mrs. Travis Butts

Brother Jens Jensen
T.V. Gospel Hour
WCKY-TV
Spineweed, Arkansas
72666

HE had it straight now; there were special roads and paths across the country that he could travel, but many more roads were closed to him. Permanently closed. He'd trained himself by now to need and want little. The unsecured scaffolding of his life rested on forgetting. Spare in eating habits, thin, alone, restless. His hair had gone mostly white. Damn near sixty years old.

Cowboy bars were his living rooms and he had a thousand from Arizona to Montana—Two Silver Bullets, The Red Spur, Cal's Corral, Little Wrangler, Spotted Horse Café, The Moose Rack, Rustlers' Roost, White Pony & His Friends, Sundance, Bronco Billy's Hangout, The Yellow Steer, Boot Hill, The Sage Brush Inn. He was quick to find his corner in each, the uneven table near the kitchen swing door, the booth with the cracked back, the bar stool that wouldn't crank up because the screw was stripped.

They were all the same and all different, the smell a blend of ugly coffee, frying meat, beer, cigarette smoke, skunky bodies, spilled whiskey, musk, candy bars, manure, bad plumbing, fresh-baked bread. The same stale light in each, whether dim or glaring, neon or, in the lonesome two-table Walrus Club at the top of Ounce Pass, yellow kerosene. These sounds were home sounds for him: jukebox, click of cues, cooler door slamming, chair leg scrape, talk, spinning coins, squeaking bar stools, hiss of beer, wandering door keening on its hinges. And around him, like the faces of relatives, men's faces—lean, prematurely old. A few girls with pocked faces and hair the color of skin, but mostly slat-built men who came from all points to this convergence like deer from the woods to a salt lick. Some were dirty. You had to watch out who you sat next to or risk picking up pants rats and seam squirrels.

He made himself a trapping wagon that he could haul around with his pickup, based on the Basque sheepherders' double-axled, fat-bellied, canvas-topped rigs. Inside, a built-in bed, a plank table that folded up against the wall when he didn't want it, a tight little stove. He sat on a lidded bench packed with gear.

Liked getting up in the morning and opening the door onto the back places. Bad Route Road. Whoopup Creek Road. Cracker Box Road. He could drag the wagon into almost any country, unhitch it from the truck and peg down. Wherever he stood the rest of it was far away. There, in the taut distances, he could go months alone, immunized from going "Basatia" or "sheeped" like the crazy Bascos he'd see now and then stumbling through the streets, insane from isolation.

He stayed on the slow move. In the spring, coming down from the fur auction he'd look over the country. Beehives on every ranch, use the honey on the morning biscuits. At night the skunks would come and scratch delicately on the hives until the sleepy bees crawled out, then eat them.

Loyal would pull into a little town in Montana or Wyoming or on his way southwest to the desert, get some of them at the bar started talking fur and game, strike up a conversation with some likely sheepman. He liked the ranchers better, but the sheepmen, with their land-killing dumb woolies were the ones that screamed coyote. Sometimes he hit on a young guy with a family, got to see the children on their horses or running around, as bright and beautiful as ornaments. Christ, he said, he liked to see little kids. He'd look the country over, listen before he knocked on somebody's door. There were plenty of sheepmen around, too many boiled-out alkies, but he liked what he heard about Jack Sagine, drove out one evening and knocked on the door.

Starr asked him in, gave him a cup of coffee and plate of cinnamon toast. He had not had cinnamon toast since he was on the farm. Trying to eat with decent manners he choked on a mouthful of toast and coffee.

"I hope I don't hear you complaining that the coffee's muddy," she said. "We only started boiling it last week."

It took him a minute to get it. He wasn't used to a joking woman. He laughed too hard and too long. He told them he was looking for a place to do a season's trapping.

"Coyote. Fox. Bobcat."

Jack tipped his pearl Stetson back a little with his thumb. Black hair on his arms, shirtsleeves buttoned at the cuff, the first two fingers of the left hand clubby, trimmed by a boyhood axe and healed in two stubs.

"Government trapper?"

"Christ, no. I'm no exterminator, just do seasonal trapping, move on so I don't make a big dent in the furbearer population. I take my share and move on. Make a living at it, such as it is. Leave the place clean, traps up, collect all my stakes, run the line with the guy that owns the land when I'm done so he can see for himself how I left things. No complaints yet."

"I done a little trapping. Tough way to make a living."

"Once you get the hang of it, it's decent enough. You get used to it."

"Yeah. Well, I won't say I haven't let fellers trap here before, but I had trouble with a couple of so-called trappers couple of seasons ago. Sons a bitches ate fresh meat all winter and I come up missing cows in the spring. Something the coyotes never done to me. These fellers baited. Guess I'd like to hear how you go about it."

"Generally park the wagon in a good camp, settle in, walk the land good in early fall after the coyotes moved onto their winter range. Take note of sign until I feel like I know what's there and how much, lay out the lines in my mind, get my traps and stretchers ready. Come your cold trapping weather and prime fur time and I'm out there—November until January. Used to be rabbit, skunk, chunk bait, dead stock were all useful to me, but I didn't go shooting cows for bait. But the coyotes in this country is different now. They're smarter than what they was. You got a dead animal, I can't use it. They're wise to bait, so I use blind sets and that's all. I run my line every day. I'm all done in February—coyote'll start hip rubbing and shedding, you can start to see hair singe in late January. Come February I'm gone. Bring them up to Soudack auction in Winnipeg or sell 'em through the Fur Combine."

"Well, I'll tell you what. You don't often have coyote trouble with Brahmas. I been raising Brahmas for seventeen years—they think I'm crazy around here in this whiteface country—and I haven't never lost a animal to coyotes. And I hate poison and I hate the government slobs come on the public lands that been sheeped out by and poison everything—we lost a beautiful dog, little border collie, to poison. Best dog we ever had, smart, good-natured. But I'm not opposed to hunting or trapping. It's hard to do what your neighbors ain't. You want to trap here, you'll do all right. I don't know how many coyotes there is on this place, but I'll tell you, though, I'm not one of those thinks the wild animals ought to be cleared right off the land. That's the sheepmen, because they don't bother to herd no more. Just shove two hundred thousand sheep out there and scream bloody murder if they don't all come home. Most of your cattlemen know damn well the coyote controls the rodents eat the grass—a couple of coyotes'll eat hundreds of mice and prairie dogs in a week. We got twenty-four thousand acres here. There's a place for everything. It's just there's too much coyotes, they say, and not enough place."

Sometimes the rancher would be a son of a bitch with sweet land. Frank Cloves.

But Jack and Starr Sagine were a pair of good ones, and their lean-looking range butted up against the Black Cloud National Forest. Remember the ice storm, Loyal thought, him and Little Girl, when he still had her, sleeping in Jack and Starr's kitchen. Couldn't remember why—was that the time he had to have the engine in the truck replaced? Jack's grandfather had scorned a low-slung ranch house and built a three-story building with towers and dormers and festoons of fretwork along the eaves like something from Victorian Ohio. The wind was hard on a house that stuck up that high. After the storm great twenty-foot peels of ice slid down the tin roof, curled in and crashed against the house with their falling. Glass broke. The wind bent trees, swung their bifurcated branches until they threw rinds of ice off the limbs. The pines, matted with ice, hunkered like dogs. Traps were all iced under. He saw a coyote slipping on the shining stuff, the blunt claws no use, and the animal sensing his amusement, humiliated.

The light, silvery-flecked coyotes of the high plains and dry mountain ranges, and the roan coyotes of the desert land were what he liked. Smartest animal on the face of the earth, he'd say in the bars. No one denied it.

"You can fool him once, but you won't fool him twice."

"Hell, a coyote can smell the exhaust from your vehicle a hundred yards downwind three days after you come through. They can see like a goddamn eagle and they're smart enough to write you a sarcastic note in the dirt." The bartender knew all about coyotes. Down at the end of the bar a runty rider with coyote-colored sideburns listened.

"They'll eat anything. I mean anything, watermelon, grass, wheat on the stalk, somebody's little pet doggy, grasshoppers, earthworms, skunk. It'll eat skunk, you know that?" The bartender leaned into it, his mouth snapping down on the words. "Your coyote will eat a rattlesnake. He'll eat it after the snake bit him, too. The poison don't bother him. He'll eat bark and leaves, prickly pear, spines and all, juniper berries if there's nothing else. He'll take birds, he'll take eggs, mice, rats, squirrels, prairie dogs, pronghorn fawns, elk, deer, old sandwiches, watermelons, garbage. He'll go for rabbits. He'll eat frogs and he'll eat ducks, he'll eat your big herons and your little beetles. He'll help himself to calves and lambs and if you wonder where all the pheasant or quail has gone, guess who's et it. And the old dog coyote, he'll eat on his own pups if he gets a chance. The coyote's just wrecked the hunting."

The runty rider talked out of the side of his mouth. "Yeah, I hear there wasn't any game at all back when the Indians owned it and the coyote had his way."

"Yeah, that's right," said the bartender, not listening. "You start trapping heavy into a coyote population and they'll start breeding heavy. You start trapping in the sandy washes they'll move into gumbo hardpan where you'll never see a print. Shoot 'em from aircraft they'll dig holes all over and the minute they hear a plane they'll be gone or change their hunting times to when the plane don't fly. Mister, they are a durable varmint, the killing machine of the west."

Coyote, little wolf of the plains, thought Loyal.

He saw beyond the ravenous appetite and the knowing mind to a shifting world of coyotes staking out their territories, coyotes in love, courting, raising families, playing cards, visiting each other. Coyote territories like nations. He'd listened to their yipping talk for almost thirty years, and felt he knew some of the language. He understood a coyote's night runs to the howl stations.

In new country he went with his maps and the Indian's book, charting the scent posts, noting the trails, seeing tracks in washes, in the thin scrub brush. He had pages of scribbles about summer and winter ranges of certain coyote clans he'd been trapping for years. The Indian's book was mostly coyotes now, what he saw of tracks, scratchings, droppings. He'd pick up coyote scat, see what was in it, the seedy red prickly pear, the hair-stiff turds, the dark meat droppings, the carapaces of beetles. The killing meant nothing to him; it was over in a minute.

On Jack Sagine's place he'd watched through the binoculars and seen coyotes on a big playground on the sandy flats. The young coyotes, yipping and barking, leaped over the low brush and rolled. They galloped, tongues lolling, eyes yellow and hot with excitement, skidded in sprays of sand. One pale coyote dug into the sand like a badger, and three ran in circles, suddenly reversing or shooting out and away only to roll and roll. But when he brought Jack and Starr out to see the coyotes play the coyotes didn't show and a heavy rain had smoothed their tracks. Jack looked at the sky, gauging wasted time.

"Real educational, Loyal," said Starr in her sarcastic, joking voice.

He could tolerate Starr. He could be in the kitchen with her, sit drinking coffee and talk, joke with her like she was a man. He could like her. Nothing happened. His chest did not tighten, his breath came as easily as when he leaned on the fence with Jack. Maybe it was over. Maybe that part of the problem was over. Maybe because he was so goddamn old now, and Starr was old, with white curly hair and a broad beam, but her deep-breasted pouter pigeon look and dark-fringed blue eyes were pretty and womanly. It wasn't that she was dried up or looked like a man. He could even think of lying her down in the buffalo grass and covering her, as he sat talking in the kitchen, but no heat rose in his loins and he kept on breathing. So maybe it was over. Wasn't that a sad relief.

For six seasons he trapped Jack's land, most of it not Jack's but leased by him from the Bureau of Land Management. He knew this land so well he could go blindfolded to the scent posts and scratches along the rim of the red mesa, on the crest of the ridge, at the corner post where the mesa trail started to rise, at the place where the coyotes crossed Jack's jeep trail, at the edge of the canyon, even at old sites of good kills where the carcasses of cattle or elk had decayed into stink and bones, and two years later when nothing was left but memory and white fragments.

A winter storm on Jack's place almost finished him. He

stepped out into the dry cold, the December morning ominously still. The sky was dirty. Loose snow feathered at his feet, rising up to his ankles in sly billows, lapping across the ground, the whole plain shuddering like a great sleeping animal tormented by dreams. He hesitated, watched the heaving snow. Elbows whined, rolled her sorrowful eyes longingly at the wagon. He planned to run the line, be back by three in the early winter twilight, go eat supper at the ranch house with Jack and Starr. He did that once a week to get the flavor of a different cooking. Starr sometimes made a cheese soufflé. It seemed he could not get enough of this thing.

He strapped on the snowshoes, twisted into the pack and set out. The dog trudged reluctantly at his heels, looking back often, half-turning every time he slowed or stopped. The eerie pulsing snow rose halfway up his shins. He could not see his snowshoes in the hissing swirl, yet half a mile ahead the Howling Rock stood out clear, a buff-colored shelf of stone that projected from the mesa wall like a cigarette from a smoker's mouth.

The air against his face was dead, but spinning snow rose up to his knees, a churning that dizzied him. The sky droned, the dog was drowning in snow fume. He felt it sting his legs, and all at once saw what was going to happen. He'd heard about them for years, but had never been in a bad ground blizzard before. A little frightened, he turned back. Elbows kept running up on the tails of the snowshoes, tripping him. He half-ran, eyes fixed on the wagon, a grey hump against the dissolving sky.

Less than five hundred feet from the wagon the ground blizzard boiled up over his head, obliterated everything in a scream of wind. The wind jammed his mouth and nose with crystal-filled air. He could not see. Snow caked his eyelashes, filled his nose, buffeted him from every side. The erased world tilted on edge. He shuffled forward, wondering how soon his steps would start bending off, by how far he would miss the wagon, inches or feet. He could feel the dog tread on the snowshoe heels, knew she was following blind.

Unaccountably the thought leaped into his mind that Jack was not Starr's first husband. She'd been married to a dairy farmer in Wisconsin, had grown-up children in the Land of Lakes who never came to visit. That much Loyal knew. Why think of it now? It was Jack he liked.

How long did it take to travel five hundred feet in a sixty-mile-an-hour head wind? The wagon was so small. It would be like finding a bushel basket in the ocean. The dog hung on his snowshoes. He didn't dare turn and shout at her for fear of drifting off the line. He went forward, head down, one hand over his mouth to get air. His face was numb. He pawed at his snow-plastered eyes. There was a catch in the wind as though the beast was drawing a short breath, and through the slackening snow he saw the wagon forty feet ahead and on his left. He had already curved fatally away from it.

He turned toward it, but before he had taken three strides the whiteout closed in again, hurled and shook him. Ten steps. Elbows floundered. He ought to be there but he wasn't. Another. Another. Arms out. And grazed the side of the wagon. Christ, how did the plains Indians live through these blizzards in skin cones?

Inside, the wagon rocked in the shrieking wind. He

hung the snowshoes on the back of the door and let them drip, threw a chunk in the stove. He poured water into the coffeepot and began to grind the beans, stepping over the dog. She pulled ice balls from her forelegs with her teeth and flapped her tail at him as he bent to stroke her narrow head.

"Close call, girlie. We come close to missing the damn wagon and walking all the way to Santa Fe. We didn't get that little break we'd still be out there. By now probably making a teepee out of two snowshoes and a prayer.

His pelts brought an average price of seventy dollars at the auction that spring—top money. The snowy, supple hides were prime, the hair long, fluffy and lustrous. Pierre Faure, the Hudson Bay buyer, bought Loyal a drink.

"Top dollar, Loyal. I don't know what you old-timers do but your goddamn furs are beautiful. Peyo's got some beautiful fox and bobcat too. You seen his furs? Cherry-red fox, just nice, clean furs. Beautiful. Well, eagles don't catch flies, right? I seen fur here from the young guys wasn't worth bothering the damn animal to take. Stretched all out of shape. I seen a bobcat looked like a Canada goose way the guy had its neck stretched out and the head bunched up. Waste. Them's the sons a bitches make it hard for trappers. And let me tell you, hard days for trappers is coming."

"What do you mean? Prices going down again?"

"More than that, my friend. You maybe don't hear the rumbles out there with your basket of traps and the wind, but on the dealer end we are getting it good. And it's not going away. I'm talking animal rights people, the ones against the trapping and the fur coats. Give you example. Couple weeks ago in Chicago a bunch of these bastards stood outside one a the good stores and squirted white paint on every woman come out wearing a fur coat. In New York they march up and down outside the furrier with signs saying 'Killer' and 'Only Animal Looks Good in a Fur Coat Is One that Grows It.' Then you got the others, against leg-hold traps, against all trapping. These people are getting strong."

Loyal laughed. "It's just a few people making noise. I heard the Trappers' Association put out a press release that shows them up."

"Something to think about, Loyal; if you have to prove you're right, you're probably wrong. I think there's gonna be trouble. I'd get in another line if I could."

At first he took them half a dozen different ways. Sometimes as he ran the line he'd give an injured rabbit call on a bone whistle and shoot the occasional young coyote that trotted in to see what it was all about, but his main standby was a number-three double-spring steel trap. In November everything was ready—the traps cleaned, dyed and stored in the terrain where they'd work. The treated sets of waxed gloves, the sidecutters, the kneeling tarp, the sets of boots, the lure bottles and wire and string and sticks and sifted manure and dirt and sand and grass and twigs all stored in the big outside box on the wagon.

The fourth year on the Sagines' place Starr said she'd like to ride out and watch when he made his sets. He was slow to answer.

"Well, what the hell, Loyal, see how many more of

them cheese soufflés you're gonna get." She and Jack both laughed. Loyal laughed, late and sour.

"No, no, it's just the less scent that's around the better. If I could figure a way to place my traps without gettin' near 'em, I would." Yet he let her come after she promised to stay in the truck and watch through the glasses. He didn't show she was the first woman to ride next to him in thirty-two years.

"Now, this here is going to be a scent-post set. There's a rock that sticks up at a funny angle over by the bushes—you can see it from here and see every dimple through the glasses—and every coyote for a mile around seems to piss on it when he passes by. I'm going to set two traps there."

She watched him draw on a pair of waxed gloves, slip on the prepared pack and, a hundred feet out from the truck, step out of his boots and into another pair he had taken from the bag containing a little scraped soil and sagebrush and rabbitbrush. He tied a gauze mask over his mouth.

Near the rock he cautiously set down the ash pack basket and withdrew his kneeling tarp, spreading it out with the blue, unscented side down. With a trowel he dug two holes near the base of the rock, each large enough to take a trap, carefully piling the loose soil to one side. He drove a notched wooden trap stake into the bottom of each hole, then positioned the trap over the stake and set it. The pan covers went over the set traps and he sifted a little of the soil onto the covers to hold them in place. Gently but deftly he adjusted the covers with a brittle twig, then sifted more soil over the traps, covering the springs first, then the pan covers.

When the sifted soil was level with the surrounding ground he swept gently over the places with a tuft of sagebrush. He changed his waxed gloves for another pair stored in a canvas bag that hung on the outside of the pack, took the scent bottle and dipped the brittle twig into it. He put the twig in a crevice of the jutting rock near the ground, then sprayed coyote urine on the rock above the scent twig. He changed back to the other gloves. Finally he gathered up everything, stepped to the back of the tarp, folded it up and backed away from the set. With the sagebrush tuft he smoothed out the shallow imprints from his knees where the tarp had been and carefully retreated. When he came to the place where his boots stood he removed the scentless boots and stowed them again in the bag of soil and brush.

"My god, ain't *that* a lot of trouble."

"Just basic set, but it takes coyote. That's some of what you have to do if you hope to fool them. I've had them dig out my traps, push the trap out of the hole with their nose and turn it over, then piss on it and leave it for me. But generally I make a blind set."

"What's the mask for? Looked like you was on your way to a holdup."

"Breath. Human breath stinks. Leaves scent, especially if you had bacon and onions for breakfast the way I did. Your best trappers don't eat until after the work's done." He liked telling her about it. She seemed to follow what he meant.

"There used to be a dozen ways to take them, some better than others. The dirt hole set's a damn good way and so's a blind set. Dirt hole set you use an old badger hole or dig a hole that looks like an animal dug it—bait it with fresh rabbit or rotten chunk bait. I like a blind set because for it to work you got to know your coyote. There's no bait, no lure, no scent, just a trap in a place you know the coyote is going to step. For instance, there's a little dip in one place along your fence at the foot of that mesa where all the rocks slid down and I see a little bit of hair in the low strand of barbwire. The ground there looks the littlest bit tired. That's where at least one coyote has the habit of ducking under the fence. Good place for a blind set. Bait set, especially around a carcass the coyotes are feeding on, works good, works too good. Takes the least skill. And after the way the government trappers and sheepmen been using poisoned baits like kings throwing dimes, the coyotes won't touch bait. I taken coyote with deadfalls, too, takes time to build them and the trouble is a deadfall will kill whatever walks under it, not just coyote, but anything, including a dog or a little kid. I lost a dog in a deadfall I set myself couple of years back. Little Girl. You remember Little Girl—when I first started trappin' on your place?" She nodded. "So I won't use a deadfall no more. Same thing with a snare—once the animal gets in it, it's a slow struggle."

"Hate the idea of the animal trapped there, waiting for you to come kill it. Kind of a terrible way to make a living, Loyal."

"I'm used to it. Done it most of my life. Don't even think about it. Anyway, a trapper's an angel compared to most sheep ranchers. Sons a bitchs'll shoot or trap anything that moves. I seen coyotes with their jaws wired together, their eyes put out by sheepmen then turned loose to die slow. You think it's better for the coyotes to be poisoned by the government guy? Poison is a dirty, wasteful end. That stinking 1080—the animals is no use to anyone or anything—kills other animals because it gets in the food chain, the fur's no good. It's a rotten way. Even mice shouldn't be poisoned. Get your traps out, but don't use that goddamn poison bait."

"We use traps. We had a cat once, big stripedey Buster, used to run a trapline. We'd set the traps and go to bed. Buster'd lie around, dozing, keeping one ear perked up. Hear a trap go off he'd be there. He'd pick up the trap in his mouth and come in the bedroom, jump up on Jack and meow at him in this muffled voice—he had the trap in his mouth—swish the mouse's tail over Jack's face a few times to get him woke up good." Loyal roared at the picture.

"He was just asking Jack to take the catch out of the trap and reset it."

"He do it?"

"Oh yeah. Jack's not a man to interfere with anybody's trapline, and he's a helpful feller, always give a friend a hand." She laughed a little. "Yeah, old stripedey Buster, if he'd had some little stretchers he could've made a fortune at the fur auction."

"I don't know. Last I heard the prices for mouse pelts was way down."

The Sagines were the first couple he'd ever had as friends, and Starr the first woman friend. It crossed his mind a hundred times to wonder if Starr had grandchildren. There were no photographs that he could see in their house, but he'd never been in any rooms but the kitchen and living room. Still, there was a piano and a fireplace mantel in the living room, and that was the place the pictures ought to go, he thought. He would have liked to hear about the grandchildren, could pretend to be some kind of adopted uncle when they came to visit.

"And this is Uncle Loyal, Elly, go say hello." And the little girl, scrawny, with crinkly red hair, would sidle up bashfully and whisper hello and he would give her the tiny skin doll two inches high he had bought from a Lakota trapper whose wife made them. It was a cunning little thing, made of fine rabbit skin, dressed in a white leather dress sewn with the tiniest beads. A necklace of mole claws hung around its neck. He kept it in its little leather bag in his shirt pocket and when he took it out and looked at it sometimes, it was as warm in his hand as though it lived. Old daydreams. He didn't know why the hell he carried it around.

Trapping on Frank Cloves's place was different.

Cloves inherited the Hi-Lo ranch, eighteen thousand acres of well-watered valley in the bowl of mountains. His grandfather had come into the country as a railroad worker, but the youngest son got a job as a dude wrangler on the Hiawatha Lodge Ranch and married the daughter of an eastern meat-packer. Growing up, Cloves had the best, turned out the worst. He thought of himself as a rancher. What else could he be?

The snowy Big Horns, where Cloves had additional grazing rights, floated in the sky to the west. Sweetheart Creek and Snowpools converged in the tender bottomland. On the higher ground there was timber. Cloves had a need as strong as disease to make a show of power. He married five times, and the sounds of shouting and battle from the twenty-five-room house earned the ranch the local name of "Whoop-Up." Nothing went well in his life and he attracted strange and dangerous people.

Irritated at the sight of a gravel deposit that filled a bend of the Snowpool one spring, and caused a hayfield on the opposite bank to flood, he had the idea of cutting off the oxbow so the stream would run straighter. After a morning with the bulldozer the stream velocity picked up and in one week tore a new straight route that cut off five old oxbows, dumped tons of gravel on Cloves's bottomland hayfields, undercut and washed out two big willow groves. The stream below jammed and flooded out the town of Queasy. After the state paid a call he began forced restoration work that went on for years and several hundred thousand dollars.

His cattle suffered heel flies, warble grubs, bloat, blackleg, lump-jaw, scab disease and rattlesnake bites. When he hired a ranch veterinary to exclusively tend the diseased herd, the man worked two months, then declared himself a cowboy poet and moved up to Montana to versify.

His third wife was rumored to be a transvestite.

A modest vein of coal was discovered on the property but efforts to mine it failed as oil flooded the coal and gas filled the shafts. An unlucky lightning strike started a fire which blew up the gas, burned off the oil and smoldered underground in the coal for ten years.

When the cattle failed he switched over to sheep. Because there wasn't a herder to be hired for love nor money he let the sheep take care of themselves. With the sheep he bought a ready-made hatred of coyotes and believed his land was infested with them in unprecedented numbers, that they came from as far away as the Dakotas and Montana to plague his animals.

But Loyal never thought Cloves the comic figure of his reputation.

Saw him in a bar for the first time. Cloves walked into Bite the Dust. He drank a red beer, asked for another. Loyal looked out of the side of his eye. Took in the big, oversized head, thought he looked a little like Mussolini. Brown crinkled hair moving back from a bald front. Meaty nose. The chin a stubbled pillow. Head hunching forward, muscular torso, everything thick and short as if weights sat on the man at night. He kept looking up as if his neck was permanently crimped that way.

"Anybody interested in trapping coyote I got a stock of the finest that ever lifted a leg." Snakeskin boots. The voice was low and harsh. He didn't wait for an answer but turned and went out.

"Who was that masked man," Loyal asked the jaw-wagging bartender. "Oh that's old Whoop-Up Cloves, millionaire ten times over when he started, but got it down to about two or three million now. Spreads happiness wherever he goes. He just switched to sheep and to hear him say it the biggest assortment of coyotes in the US of A is on his place."

Cloves had had the government trappers in all summer with traps, snares, shooting from planes, cyanide guns and poison baits. The carcasses, mostly young animals, had been dumped to rot in an old gravel pit near the creek. The survivors, Loyal thought, would know every trick in the book—older, smarter, bait-wise, trap-wise. What the hell, he'd give it a try. Just for the hell of it. He'd get in touch with Cloves.

"O.k.," said Cloves. "You're on. Just one thing—stay out of the northwest end there goes up into the mountains. I got a project going on up there I don't want any trapping around it." He winked at Loyal who guessed there were plots of wacky weed up there somewhere. Hell, coyotes would eat that, too.

But he had not even finished scouting the land before he knew something was going on. Pickups grinding up the steep mountain road in the night hours. Distant rifle shots. Hounds baying.

Saturday night in Bite the Dust was Saturday night. Around four in the afternoon the parking lot started filling with mufflerless pickups. Dogs in the passenger seats, in the bed. When the aqua pickup, painted with leftover swimming pool paint, pulled in, every dog in the parking lot began to bark and strain forward. He'd seen it working up and down the mountain road on Cloves's ranch.

"What the hell you carry in that rig make 'em start up like that every time you drive up," asked Bubby sitting next to the runty rider. They rode their bar stools down at the end with practiced grace. The man coming through the door was a pyramid with sparkling yellow eyes and a brown beard parted in the middle and knotted to each side with a twist of annealed wire. Necklace of badger claws dripping over his chest. Loyal smelled musk, rotten bait, green hide and something else and knew he was a trapper.

Out of season. Not coyote, not fox or bobcat.

"Meow," said the hulk.

"Lion? By god, I believe it. That'd set 'em going."

"Didn't say that was it," said the trapper and asked for whiskey and beer. When he had them he walked over to Loyal and sat down across from him. Runty rider was quiet.

"I seen you scouting around. Cloves says you're going for coyote, huh?"

"Price holds up. Prime brought seventy per, end of the season." Hell, he didn't want to sit with this outlaw.

"Get a hundred you're doing excellent. Price drops, you're in a world of shit, workin' for twenty cents an hour."

"That's right."

"Government trappers been working over that land all summer, you know."

"I know. It was sort of a challenge, see how good I can do in a troubled situation."

"Troubled is right. Know why the government guys left?"

"No. Figured they were all done."

"Hell no. Cloves drives out one day all hopped up on something and starts shooting at them. Says, 'I'll teach you to kill my sheep. I'm gonna wipe every motherfucker coyote off the face of the earth.' Thought they were the coyotes. They did look kind of mangy, but hell, I could always tell they had two legs. So you want to watch out. Got a crazy streak. Usually he ain't around in the winter, or so I hear. I only been here three months myself so I ain't seen his winter habits yet. Say he goes to Mexico to stay warm. What the hell, wish I had a nice cush of money to do that, don't you?" He winked. At the bar the runty rider was watching them in the mirror. Loyal had an absurd thought about him. The dogs barked their brains out.

"Wanna park your truck downwind so we can have a little peace and quiet in here?" The bartender was polite, but his voice bored in. The trapper went out and shifted the truck to the other side of the building. But he was irritable when he came back in and Loyal thought there would be trouble later on. He finished his whiskey and left.

At the door he glanced back and caught the runty rider's eyes just sliding away. Before he fell asleep he tried to pin down the stink on the trapper. Pine marten? Lion?

It wasn't lion.

A week later he sat at the table reading a three-day-old paper. The bar was empty. The bartender messed with a jar of pickled eggs, taking them out with stainless steel tongs, fussily arranging them in a bowl. The wind sang around and around. He rattled the pages. The bartender opened his mouth only to yawn.

"Here comes your friend," he said after an hour, hearing something Loyal didn't. He didn't catch the blatting exhaust note until the swimming pool pickup was in sight.

"He's unknown to me. Last Sat'day the only time I ever set eyes on him. I get about as much fun out of his company as I do out of a wet dog's."

"Well, he's been in and out of here since September. Claims he come over from Maine or on the *Mayflower* or something like that." The truck peeled in. The door slammed.

"Well son of a gun, look who's here. Run off on me last time and missed all the fun, didn't he? Gimmee the usual, Robert."

"There you go. Want a pickled egg?"

"I wouldn't eat one of them stinking things if you fed it to me dipped in cunt honey and rolled in sugar."

"Some like them. In fact I remember seeing you eat damn near the whole bowl the night we threw you out. So I thought you were partial to them. Maybe if you don't eat any you'll stay nice and we won't have to work the magic trick on you any more."

"Hey, what's over is over, right? I never carry a chip around." He looked at Loyal as if at a brother. He made Loyal uneasy. He put up his paper and rattled it a little, even though he had read everything except the FOR RENT classifieds. The trapper stayed at the bar and from there he didn't whiff so bad. Loyal thought he must have cleaned up.

In an hour the place was swarming with the same big-hatted rats, the runty rider on the stool at the end, getting his backward view of the world from the mirror. Another man, looked like the outlaw's partner, called him "Sylvester" and clapped him on the back. Smaller and dirtier, a soupstrainer mustache, wore an Orlon sweater under a pair of overalls that gave him a hippie freak look. Something about the sloping head and screwed-up features that was like old Roseboy in the antique chill of his grandfather's apple room. The smell of cold, fresh apples ticked up, faded. The partner wore a woodsman's tuque that didn't go well with the rolled Stetsons and high-heel boots around him. Even Robert behind the bar wore his cowboy hat. A couple of mavericks, like Loyal, had on tractor caps, NOTHING RUNS LIKE A DEERE, CATerpillar. No tuques. The partner had a southern accent. The poker tabletop leaned against the back wall. A few kids were shooting pool. Loyal ordered a steak with pickles and fried potatoes.

He was startled when the trapper sat down across the table from him, jarring it so the steak juice slopped over the rim of the plate. The son of a bitch didn't know when to be scarce.

"Hey, old-timer, I got something important I wanna talk to you about."

"Important comes in two sizes—yours and mine," said Loyal through a mouthful of tough meat.

"No, seriously, how you doing with the coyotes? Caught any yet?"

"Umhm," said Loyal.

"Yeah? How many? Three or four?" The partner came over, carrying a wooden chair. He sat down. The chair jutted into the room.

"Twelve. Any of your business."

"Well, it might be. We thought you might like to make some real money. We thought you might want to make a real killing instead of farting around with coyotes. We could use some semiexperienced help. Trapping help. The money's out of sight." He laughed, and Loyal realized he had been whispering.

"What are you taking?" said Loyal.

"Ah-ah-ah! That would be telling. You tell him, Sam."

"This is going to sound a little weird, man, but there is

a market in Japan and Korea and China for certain sub-
stances. Aphrodisiacs."

"What the hell is that?" They were all whispering.

"Stuff that the Japanese guys think will double the size
of their prick and give 'em a three-day hard-on. Sex stuff.
You heard of it. Like Spanish fly, only they don't want
Spanish fly. They want rhinoceros horn. They want powdered elk teeth. They want saber-toothed tiger fossil paste.
The want the gallbladders of black bears." Bear. That was
the smell. The partner talked while Sylvester the bear
trapper nodded.

"They will pay big big big bucks for this stuff. Plus we
got a market for the hides. We are making money like you
wouldn't believe. Been working Maine and Florida, up in
Canada. It's real hard with only two. We had another guy,
but he pulled out and retired to Hawaii. Could use somebody to work with us. Three's better. Cloves says you're a
good trapper." Loyal wanted to look up at the mirror and
see if the runt rider was taking in this huddle.

"Damn, boys, it sounds lucrative, but I've got a bad
ticker. Can't do any heavy work. Bears sounds like heavy
work to me."

"You wouldn't have to do the heavy stuff, just set out
the traps. We'd deal with the bear, man. It's not that heavy
a work, just cut them open and take out the gallbladder,
cut out the claws. Hell, most of the time we don't even
bother with the hides. We don't have the time. The hides,
the skinning. That would be your share,"

"I lifted a bear trap or two in my time. They weigh
damn near fifty pound each and that is a lot of weight.
Besides, I don't care for this country. Pulling out next

week." He hadn't known until then that he was heading back to the Sagine ranch. He'd have to go that night. These weren't the kind you turned down after they dumped their dirty secrets on you. He saw himself pulling up at the fur auction with twenty ratty, clawless bearskins. That would start a little talk.

"Obliged for you asking me. I'll just say good-by." He handed the steak plate to the bartender.

"Wonder if you'd wrap that up in a plastic bag for me. Us toothless old dogs have to chew careful." As he took the bag he looked in the mirror at the runty rider. But didn't want any part of him, either.

41. The Tropical Garden

June 3, 1977

Dear Dub, thanks for the check. The iron railing around the plot looks very good. We spent all memorial day fixing up the graves. Planted a blanket of spring bulbs over both of them. Even though we do not have her remains that lonesome mountain! Ray and I are fine. He's been in the Philippines for a month, something to do with mahogany. Any chance you and Pala can come up again this fall for the leaves? I know she likes them. Your loving sister, Mernelle

Mr. Marvin Sevins Blood
200 Biscayne Blvd.
Suite 1702
Miami, Fla.
33132

DUB, fat in white linen in the peacock chair, having breakfast beside the pool before sunrise. The chilled mimosa, the opal-fleshed melon with a twist of green-tangerine juice, then the country ham and the quail eggs flown in from Japan, blackhearted coffee that wired you for the day. He'd drink twenty cups of it until his hands shook.

His hands were steady when Mernelle called, her northern voice asking what he thought about burying Ma's wedding ring next to Da. Because that's all they had. It would ease their minds. She'd come across the ring a few weeks ago tidying boxes and drawers., She thought Ma had taken it off when Da had—

"Sure, why not?" he said.

She read him the inscription. " 'JSB Forever Thine MMB June, 1915.' At least it's something that was hers, something that ties them together," she said.

"That's right," he said.

He loved the rotten tropical smell, the heat, kept the air conditioners at lukewarm. "Turn that thing down, reminds me of 'Winter on the Farm,' famous painting by Frosty the Snowman. What the hell you think I live in Florida for?" But laughing.

A good-looking man despite the bulked chest and jowled face and the glowing bald head. Clients fell into his smiling eyes. In the mirror he saw he still had the fine mouth and, of course, he had the money. Manicured nails (on the good hand) and custom-made suits don't come without it. He had Pala, or she had him. The pirate, a little heavier, wore beige and ecru linen suits, gold chains knotted with medallions and charms hung around her neck. Smarter than anyone he knew. Secretive. He thought there might have been an abortion but could not ask. The properties were her children now.

It was all real estate knowledge, prime properties, not the crude hawking of condos and old-age death parlors to the ancients from the north, but scholarly appraisals, landmark status research, a shrewd eye for next year's extraordinary properties. They knew the importance of discreet arrangements and offerings. They could talk to sheiks, seekers of political asylum, men who had business dealings to the south. Aesthetics. Look what Pala had done with Opal Key Reef. Every major magazine in the country had run photos of the antiqued shell-stone houses and the gardens designed by Burle Marx, fantasies of curious plants.

The first needle of sun came through a hole in the canvas awning and drilled onto Dub's linen knee. Many of the properties Eden handled never came on the market when the owner wanted to sell; the sales were privately arranged by Eden, Inc. No one came close to Eden. He and Pala had an instinct for the protected properties, islands joined to the mainland by a single causeway or bridge. Peninsulas with a single approach road. They understood the clients who needed certain properties. He wished the tax people would understand him.

He tilted the coffeepot, the black fluid arced into his cup. On the other side of the pool the garden yawned with caves of shadow, early heat ricocheted off leaves, ferns arched, petals unfurled. Pala might sleep until ten. He never shook the early rising habit. He got up and walked toward the garden, carrying the white cup in his artificial hand with its perfect plastic nails.

Here was Eden. They didn't go to the Green Swamp

now. The garden's odor, heavy and perfumed as a split fruit, filled his mouth and throat. The moist air pressed against him, the moss cushioned his footsteps. The banyan tree was the center of the garden. He had bought the place for this ancient tree with its humped root knees, its branched arms and rooting thumbs, the twists of vine and florid blossom, the mottled, shreddy bark and falling, falling fragments. There was something he loved in the smell of decay.

42. What I See

Up into the pointed hills, gumbo roads slippery as snot when wet, his landscape of crooked rocks. The antelope sentinel's snoring warning to the herd in the draw, the herd bounding through a strew of flowers close to the earth like rainbow grass. The antelope step over fossil tree trunks, broken stone stumps with the rings still visible, the stone bark encrusted with orange lichens.

The worn sandstone layers hollowed and rippled by ancient water in this waterless land, this lake bottom heaved into yellow cones still booms with the hoofbeats of the horses of Red Horse, Red Cloud and Low Dog, the great and mysterious Crazy Horse, Crow King and Rain in the Face, kicking up fragments of fossil teeth. They come tearing out of ravines, rise up with killing smiles in the astounded faces of Fetterman, Crook, Custer, Benteen, Reno. He hears the slipping twinned voices canted at each other in fifths, the Stamping Dance of the Oglala, the voices whirling away and dropping, together, apart, locked in each other's trembling throats. The fast war dance, hypnotic and maddening, has irradiated the sandstone. He has only to hold a mass of stone in each hand and bring them together again and again, faster and faster, twice the speed of the beating heart.

Maddening. On the counter of a general store in Streaky Bacon, Montana, a box of discarded patient cards from an asylum in Fargo. He looks through them. Everyone looks through them. The corners are broken and greasy. Photographs: a description of the subject's mania, revivalism, melancholia, masturbation, dementia. The Indian's face balanced between his fingers. The smooth combed hair, but the jacket askew and stained. The still face, the black eyes, and the tapering fingers locked around an accountant's ledger. Although it seems to be the Indian, laconic script says "Walter Hairy Chin." Nothing of blue skies nor hundred-dollar bills.

43. The Skeleton with Its Dress Pulled Up

YEAR after year Witkin had worked on the camp, sketching plans for a sleeping porch, a double garage, adding another bathroom. There were more rooms now. He planned a stone fireplace the size of a steel mill hearth. He cut and stacked his own firewood. Built the woodshed. He thought about a sauna and a swimming pool, planned to enlarge the stone patio to a sweep of fieldstone paving. He was shrewd, called around for lumber prices. The pickup truck was new each spring, fitted with a varnished oak rack, the word Woodcroft in old English letters on the doors.

> JUNE 30 '77
>
> DEAR FRANK, THEY TELL ME
> I HAVE TO TAKE IT EASY FOR A WHILE.
> WOULD DRIVE ME NUTS TO SEE THE
> WAY YOU WORK ON THE CAMP. SO I
> WON'T BE UP NEXT WEEKEND, MAYBE
> BY FALL. MIGHT GO OUT ON
> JACK KAZIN'S BOAT, SIT ON
> THE DECK, GET SOME SUN IF ITS
> NICE. AT MOST DO A LITTLE
> FISHING.
> CALL YOU AFTER THE 4th.
>   LARRY
>
> FRANKLIN WITKIN. M·D.
> 1718 FRY PLACE
> BOSTON
>   MA

His hands and arms developed a strength they'd never had when he was young. Muscles under his old skin. Yellow callouses thickened his palms, his fingers were rough. He could have been a carpenter or worked in construction.

He told Larry it was in the back of his mind to make the camp into a retirement place, maybe a place for two if he remarried.

"You, get married again? You weren't the type to get married in the first place. You're married to work, Frank. If you knew how to relax, maybe I'd take you seriously. Who you got in mind, Mintora?" Larry brought women up sometimes, Frieda, a sculptress with thick hair the color of bison wool; Dawn, the documentary filmmaker getting ready for a trip to Antarctica; and Mintora, a breasty woman Witkin's age whose work was woodcuts, her subject, gorillas in hot-air balloons. Yes, it might have been Mintora of whom he was thinking, the unshaven slender legs, the jutting hair under her arms, the comments on his woodworking.

"Wouldn't you like to have some rice pudding?" she said once and opened a hamper packed with pots from a city deli. She brought him a brass doorknob with a beaded rim, a copper advertising plate showing, in reverse, a woman washing a corset in a sink.

The roof of the abandoned farmhouse below had fallen in. No one could guess there had been a farm there. The trailer park spread wide, dusty lanes jerked along the hillside. When the wind was from the south Witkin could hear engines and shouting. Yet on his high hundred acres the wild woods came ever closer, the trees multiplied.

Larry, grown heavy and slow, said it was harder to get around in the woods. He puffed and coughed, walked up grades in long gradual ascents that added miles to the day. They walked out with the guns but rarely fired at anything.

"Frank, I can't do this any more. I never thought I'd hear myself say that, but I can't do these climbs. Too much easy living. You don't get exercise selling pictures." They were no longer close. Yet both pretended.

Alone at the camp the oak trees scintillated at Witkin, the shrubs and young trees in color seemed to leap off the tawny ground. The sky vibrated, the taut drumhead struck. He shuffled through grass the color of bread crust, leaves of burnt sugar, charred letters, the sifting of needles, his head scratched by roots dangling in air where the soil bank had slid down, his boots slipping on the log over the water, following the miles of stone wall drifting away into the woods. He needed Larry still to guide the way. He could not sort out the trees, could not understand the wind direction or the scramble of branches. The confusion of trees pressed in on the camp. Raspberry thorn twisted under the step.

He began to put the chaos of nature in order. The sinuous woods music, once so beguiling, had taken on a discordance like a malfunctioning speaker, the same endless hum as the high-tension wires when he had stood beneath them waiting for Larry to drive the deer across, confusing him so that he had not heard the deer come, had only seen tawny motion. He had never wanted to hunt; that was only to please Larry, the unknown brother.

On Jack Kazin's boat Frieda was surprised when Larry arched his fat back in the canvas deck chair, threw his head back as if readying himself to sing an aria, then hurled over the chair arm. Full coronary block.

The week after Larry's funeral Witkin hired Alvin Vinyl and his cousin to cut and drag away the shrieking maples around the camp. Time rushed at him. He urged them on with promises of money. They cleared a great open square. Leaves shriveled in the glare, the secret moss withered. A stump puller tore roots from their two-hundred-year grip of the soil in fuming black fountains. The grader tamed the rumpled soil and Witkin sowed grass seed for his lawn in the wilderness. Other projects swarmed in his mind; he had to hurry.

The equipment for the new lawn—riding mower, aerator and dethatcher, rollers and scythes—were jumbled into the garage. He planned a toolshed, then the fireplace chimney, and the addition, two rooms and a studio. Kevin, his son, said he'd come for the summer. In his second year at university, he had no summer job. Witkin offered a season's pay for a season's work, knowing as he spoke the stiff sentences about getting to know each other better that neither of them would be suited. Kevin's mallowy hands seemed useless for anything beyond scratching and fluffing.

The first day Kevin worked with his shirt off, pretending not to hear Witkin's warnings of sunburn and cancer. He slept through the fine morning of the second day, crawling out of his sleeping bag only when the din of the chugging generator, power saw and hammer reached a devil's pitch. Slouched and spoke in monosyllables. Witkin hated him again. He did not recognize Kevin as his mortal flesh. And the other one, the twin sister, what of that timid, humorless girl in her pink blouse who unerringly made the wrong decisions, who was now in Zambia with the Peace Corps? The instinctive, binding love that loops through generations failed.

They roofed the toolhouse roof with sheets of galvanized metal. The scalding height shimmered. Kevin drank gallons of beer, hammered irregularly, pissed from high off the roof instead of coming down the ladder. Heat flared against their arms and chests. Sweat streamed. Kevin, sensing Witkin's need for martyrdom, quit on the fourth day.

"I can't hack this. I'm taking off. I'd rather shovel coal in hell than do this. What the hell are you building this big place for?" It was what they both had expected. There was no fire in their argument. Only the chewy satisfaction of mutual dislike.

After Kevin was gone the elderly stonemason, the color of stone himself, came to build the chimney. Witkin hired and hired. There was not enough time to do it alone. A crew of carpenters hammering the skeleton of the addition, filling it with wood and glass, the trucks straining slowly up the hill with loads of gravel and sand, with turf and boards, flashing, nails, insulation, hinges and latches, wire, lights, drywall, tape and spackle, paint. Hurry.

When they were done Witkin started the stone patio himself. The cast iron benches had already come, shipped from South Carolina in pine crates that smelled of resin and enamel. He would use the garden tractor to move the stones from the old wall at the edge of the forest to the sand bed.

He started on the wall very early in the day. The sky poured blue light, the backhoe popped. Stones, mottled with fine maps in lichen and moss came away growling and grinding, throwing off limbs and rotten branches. The backhoe teeth gouged the delicate verdigris patina. Ruffled edges of continents and islands tore away, the lapping moss seas bunched, showed the film of soil below. The smell of leaf mold made him sneeze. Was there no relief from that dark wildwoods stench?

The small flat stones in a pile. He would work those into the interstices once the big rocks were in place. The round and irregular shapes went into the rubble pit.

He uncovered a big stone, the black edge four inches thick, the corners neatly squared. He looped the chain around it, drew it to the patio. In its wake a crushed trail.

He turned it over to see the other side. A flower of white mold spread across the dark slate, its spidery rays like a burst galaxy. Crushed spider cocoons. He turned it again so the good side was uppermost and, with the crowbar, jimmied the stone in place.

He worked the morning scratching at the sand where one side sloped more deeply than the other, prodding and settling the stone into the best lie. If he had a dozen stones like that, he thought. He hoped for at least one more, and went again to the wall.

The stone had bridged a cavity filled with leaves and a spill of seed husks from an old mouse nest. He stooped, swept at the curled leaves with his hand. And, in startled recognition, pulled back his hand from the white curve of skull.

Larry, he thought for a moment, somehow Larry had gotten out of the Bronx cemetery and under the wall.

But it was not Larry.

Carefully he took out the leaves in small handfuls until the crooked bones lay under his stare. The flawless teeth smiled up at him, but the small bones of the hands and feet were missing. The right arm was gone. The remaining arm and leg bones, marked and grooved by the chiseled gnaw-ings of mice, were brown with leaf stain. A shoe sole, curled and twisted away from its heel, lay in the pelvis like an embryonic husk. Behind him he heard the idling garden tractor chuff.

A pioneer grave. Some early settler's wife, exhausted by childbearing, or, perhaps, scalped and slain by Indians, or killed by typhoid or pneumonia or milk fever. He had blundered into the cool privacy of her grave.

"Poor woman, I wonder who you were?" he said. In respect he undid the day's work, dragged the stone back to wall and levered it home again. He would not desecrate a grave.

44. The Runty Rider Curses Judges

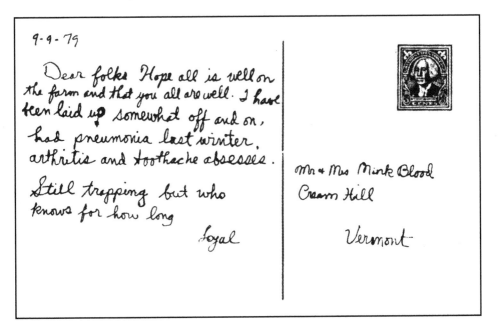

9-9-79

Dear folks Hope all is well on the farm and that you all are well. I have been laid up somewhat off and on, had pneumonia last winter, arthritis and toothache abscesses.

Still trapping but who knows for how long

Loyal

Mr & Mrs Mink Blood
Cream Hill

Vermont

SEVEN months later in northwest New Mexico he saw the runty rider in The White Pony, sitting at the end of the bar with his eyes on the mirror, wearing the same clothes, his turtle mouth hooking onto the edge of the beer can. Loyal sat down beside him, looked in the mirror.

"You ever get those guys?"

The runty rider looked like hell; his eyes were bloodshot, the dirt around his neck was deep in the leathery skin. His hands had a tremor. Well, he didn't look too good either. The runt stared at Loyal, grimaced.

"Well I'm damned. The coyote trapper, isn't it? What the hell you doing down here?"

"Desert coyote's got a different color fur—more of a red, Sort of a pretty roan color. I like to move around, do a different kind of trapping. Long as it isn't out-of-season bear."

The runty rider growled, "That damn mess."

"Have to say, curious how you made out."

"Forty people worked their asses off on that operation for almost three years. Florida, Wyoming, Maine, Montana, North Carolina, New York. We had it all—slides, videotapes, photographs, witnesses, admissions, evidence—two hundred black bear gallbladders packed for shipment, a warehouse of hides, a couple of cartons of claws, we had pictures of them with their radio collar dogs, pictures of a rotten heap of dead bear carcasses, we had statements from a Japanese end buyer and a Connecticut insurance agent middleman. We had six hundred pages of statements. We had their scent recipes—beaver oil, beaver castor, muskrat musk, oil of asafoetida and honey—you know what a black bear gallbladder is worth on the oriental market? Five K—five thousand bucks. The claws are worth another K. The Japanese got money to burn—they don't care how much it costs, got to have the stuff. You multiply two hundred gallbladders by five K each and you understand we are talking serious money. More value than cocaine. Bear gallbladders bring more money than cocaine! We are talking a million dollars. Another quarter of a million for the claws. We had all this. We had fucking confessions! The biggest wildlife enforcement investigation there's ever been. All those goddamn states working together. A miracle in itself." A muscle jumped in the runty rider's jaw.

"So what happened? They get away?"

"Get away! Hell no, they didn't get away! Well, a couple of them might of got away, but not many. We run coordinated 5 A.M. Sunday morning raids in three states and got eleven guys, the trappers and one middleman and three buyers. Those two rancid objects used to sit with you were still so drunk they weren't hung over yet. They thought we wanted to go out for more bear. They kept hollering for their flashlights and they couldn't understand about the handcuffs." He swallowed his beer in gassy gulps. "Yes, we got them." The voice was ironic, bitter.

"You don't seem happy. I'd think a successful operation would set a lawman right up."

"Yeah, you'd think so, wouldn't you. Success is defined by the end result. You know where these scum are now? Every one of them?"

"I'll bite."

"Right where they were a year ago. Doing the same thing. Illegally trapping bear, taking the claws and gallbladders, selling to the Japanese and making a fortune. You know why? You know why all that work is down the tubes? Judges. Fucking, two-bit, smug, dumb, egocentric, stuck-up, ignorant and stupid judges who cannot tell their ass from a jelly doughnut. You be interested to know those stinking humps that sat with you got fines of one hundred dollars each for 'practicing taxidermy without a license.' They peeled it off a roll as big a ham and paid up with a smile. The heaviest penalty went to a guy in North Carolina. Five-hundred-dollar fine and a thirty-day jail sentence suspended for 'hunting out of season.' " He drank in silence. He looked at Loyal in the mirror.

"The judges think it's funny. They don't take any of it serious. That's the trouble. They don't know. And. They. Don't. Care. We are going to see the end of the bears in our lifetime."

"So what are you doing down here?"

"Down here?" The runty rider laughed. "More of the same, only not bears. Don't know why I'm telling any of this to a professional trapper. I must be around the corner. I don't know, maybe I should get myself a bunch of traps and start in. There's so much money in the illegal it surprises me anybody's still on the decent side of the fence. Hell, it surprises me I am. There's been quite a few law officers switch over. They know all the tricks, all the loopholes, all the exits and do they make money. I could be rich in a couple months. I could be back home with my wife and kids, swimming pool in the backyard, drive a Mercedes, instead of working undercover on a goddamn ranch posing as a general hand."

"You got kids?"

"Yes, I got kids. Two of 'em. I don't see 'em all that much but I talk to them on the phone three, four times a week. A pain in the ass, the boy, wants to be a rock star, screaming and moaning all the time out in the garage, the girl, Aggie, sixteen and into feminist politics, women's rights, all that shit."

"You got pictures?"

"No." Wary now. Is this some kind of vicious trappers' plot to find out the names and appearances of his children? Children have been kidnapped before. Who the hell is this old coyote trapper, anyway?

45. The Lone One

October 4, 1979
This will confirm your appointment with IRS
agent Reynolds at 8 A.M. October 11, 1979,
Room 409, West Central Federal Building.
Persons being audited must bring all
financial records and documents pertaining
to the period under examination. Ref.
correspondence 8-15-79.

Mr. Marvin S. Blood
Eden, Inc.
200 Biscayne Blvd.
Miami, FL 33132

THE ranch looked different as soon as he turned off the highway and ran parallel to Jack's fence. It was the fence—half a mile of square-wire sheep fence. Since when did Jack run sheep. He looked out across the bunchgrass. None of Jack's Brahmas were in sight, but neither were any damn sheep. That's what happened when you missed a season or two. Things changed.

The front door opened before he turned off the ignition key. Starr stood on the porch. Her arms hung down, the palms of her hands turned outward. Her face contorted and he saw the wet tracks from where he sat. He knew.

As he came around the front of the truck she plunged down the steps and threw herself against him. His hands leapt to her shoulders and he pressed her away. She was so close he could smell the rank tobacco, see the yellowed texture of her eyes, enlarged pores of her cheeks. She was too close to look at and he wanted to shove her back onto the porch. But stood there, fingers clamped into her fleshy arms, concentrating on balance. There was nothing else. He could not think, his mind flew apart. She felt his shock and drew back, went to the steps and stood there.

"I'm all alone now, Loyal. Jack's gone." Snorting into the handkerchief. Salt tears in the corners of her mouth. "I would have told you but I didn't know how to get in touch. We didn't know where you were." An accusation. She lit a cigarette, threw the match down. He coughed.

"What happened? Jack." He could still feel the heat of her in the cups of his hands. But saying Jack's name restored his balance. He said it again.

"In May. The damnedest thing. He was fine, Loyal, he was just fine." The tears were drying. "Not a thing in this world wrong with him. He was always a healthy man, just a little trouble sleeping at night sometimes. Real early he went out to talk with Rudy about drift fencing and a cattle guard on the allotment, they were going to pick up the materials in Cheyenne. When he come back in the coffee was ready. He had the hiccoughs. I laughed and told him to drink some water to get rid of 'em before he had his coffee. He drank the water, Loyal, and for a few minutes they stopped, then I poured him out his coffee and he got hiccoughs again. They went on all through breakfast." An empty grain bag was wedged half under the steps. She spoke as though she had rehearsed for this. The words tumbled without inflection.

"At first we joked, but pretty quick it got so it wasn't a joke, he couldn't hardly eat. Tried all the home remedies we knew about, breathing in and out of a brown paper bag, drink water while you're bending over, eat a cube of sugar dipped in brandy, he took a glass of whiskey, drank more water, I tried to scare him by coming up behind him and clapping my hands. Finally he went out, said the ride down to Cheyenne would take his mind off the damn hiccoughs, and if they didn't quit pretty soon he'd see a doctor down there about them." How different she was, he thought. The sheen had gone off her, the lively, smart answers and the quick movement. Awkward as a cow.

"They come back around three o'clock. Truck's full of fencing and I look out and see Rudy's driving. I know we got a problem, because I can see Jack's profile bob every few seconds." She was imitating now, showing how Jack had sat in the truck, jerked by his body's mad will. "He still had the hiccoughs. He come in carrying some prescription that was supposed to quiet them down, some kind of sleeping pill, I think. Loyal he took those things, and can you believe he had the hiccoughs all night long, even while he was half knocked out from the pills. I had to get up and sleep on the couch in the living room the bed would shake so hard each time he'd spasm, but then I got real worried about him, whether he would swallow his tongue or what because he was dozing real heavy, so I'm up all night drinking coffee, pacing the floor and hearing that damn 'hic, hic, hic!' " As if she had only noticed the weeds around the porch she began to pull at them, let them drop where they fell.

"In the morning he was a wreck, he could hardly talk, his face was grey and he couldn't take anything or keep anything down. He was suffering, Loyal. I got on the phone to the doctor and he said, 'Bring him in.' I brought him in and they put him in the hospital, tried a hundred damn things, tried to sedate him out of it again, but nothing worked. Nothing worked! I couldn't believe it. The miracles of modern medicine, they can remake you with heart and lung transplants and new arms and plastic surgery and they cannot stop the hiccoughs. I was screaming at the doctors.

"I think Jack knew then nothing was going to work. He says 'Starr, the pulley's slipped off the drive shaft.' That was more or less his last words. He lasted until the next morning, and then his heart just quit. You could tell he wanted to die just so's the hiccoughs would stop."

He wanted to get back in the truck and light out, but Starr brought him into the kitchen, then troubled the cupboards and refrigerator, getting out eggs and flour, dropping the measuring spoons. Her talk veered around the compass, the thing she was making, of course he'd stay to supper, it wasn't cheese soufflé but even better, a *keesh,* and the rain that was slow to come, what she might do now. They seemed to be through talking about Jack.

"I been thinking I might go back to singing. Bet you didn't know I used to sing, Loyal."

"No, I sure didn't." His image in the steel bowl on the table, his face crushed and drawn sideways, mouth a rubber band tied behind his head, hat brim like a pie plate.

"Oh yes! Used to sing at the intermission at the rodeo in Cheyenne. Of course it was a long time ago, fifteen, eighteen years. But I got to practicing one day. Oh, it used to be a lot of fun—the crowd, good-looking men. That's how I met Jack, at the rodeo." She rocked a curve of wires through the flour and butter. "God sake, I got to do something."

He didn't know how to talk to her. She had been Jack's wife, fixed in that character. Now she was a person he had never known, the crying, talk about doing something, singing. A woman, a solitary woman—what the hell to say to her?

"What's the story on the sheep fence out by the turn?" He tried to sound like he wanted to know. Hell, he wanted to know.

"Oh that. Well, you know Jack didn't leave me too well fixed for cash. Like most ranchers, land rich and cash poor. Course he didn't expect he was going to go so sudden. I had to do something. I tried to find a buyer for the Brahmas. Nobody around here would touch them. You find out who your friends are, Loyal. All Jack's rancher pals. Finally, a feller came up from Texas and bought them. I'd written to the feller down there where Jack had bought them in the first place, and he told this guy. So they're down where they started out. Texas." She rolled the yellow dough with an empty wine bottle. A cat came out from under the table and ate a fragment that fell to the floor.

"I didn't make anything on that sale. Fact, we took something of a loss. Then Bob Emswiller asked if he could lease part of the ranch for sheep range. Summer range. Promised he'd watch they didn't graze it down too heavy. That's his fence."

"Didn't see any sheep."

"Yeah." Her neck was red, maybe the heat of the oven. The oven was set high, a smell of scorching came from it.

"He didn't pay what he said he would so I told him to take his sheep and skedaddle. No sheep this year. He said he wouldn't pay, either, that the fence was enough, I ought to be glad of it. After I told him no more sheep, there was a few shots fired at the house one night. Broke the spare-room window. A woman wants to learn what kind of neighbors she's got, let her husband die. They always thought I was an outsider here."

"So you took a loss on the cattle, got skunked on your range lease."

"That's only the beginning. I got to sell the ranch. I know Jack loved this place, and I did, too, but I don't any more. They've done that to me." She gestured with her chin, her old woman's chin, downy and soft with fat. "I want to do something with the rest of my life. If I sell the ranch I can get away from here." She poured the egg onto the cheese and bacon in the dish, slid it into the oven. She turned to him. God knows what she saw. She was playing in her own movie.

"How'd you like to hear me sing, Loyal?" The voice suddenly bright and silly.

She put a record on the turntable. The record player was still on the sideboard where it had been for years. Loyal studied the album cover; five men in musician's chairs, a swirl of yellow color coming from their hands to the top of the cover and red letters bursting, "MUSIC TO SING ALONG WITH • Volume 7 • Country Ballads."

The record rotated, double-stop fiddle harmonies of a sentimental country song filled the room. Starr stood in front of the oven, feet side by side, hands folded in a knot of fingers, held in front of her crotch. Middle-aged, in wrinkled whipcords and a sweatshirt, but something of the old vulnerable beauty persisting. Perhaps she knew it.

She counted silently, then sang "He was just passing through, I was all alone and blue." The words forced themselves up into her nose, she reached for the cheap sadness. Loyal couldn't help it, felt the barroom tears jerking out of his eyes. That song always got to him, but here he had to sit in a damn kitchen chair, couldn't even hunch over a beer. So he closed his eyes and wished Jack had lived.

The quiche was good, and they ate all of it. It was easier now, no talking, the food on the plates, the forks spearing and lifting. She put a paper napkin near his hand. Jack's chair was empty. Pickles. The coffee perked. How many times had he sat here?

"So, what do you think of my singing, Loyal?"

This was the kind of question he couldn't answer.

"It's fine. I like it fine."

Sour face. She poured coffee while his fingers pinched up crumbs in the quiche dish. All of Jack's things were scattered around as if he'd just stepped out. Well, that's what he'd done, just stepped out. The rope he knotted while they watched television on a peg by the door, a pair of boots, stiff now from disuse. Bills still on the Victorian spindle. The grey rancher's hat, the band stained with Jack's sweat, on top of the sideboard where he always slung it when he came in for dinner.

"Think you might go back to Wisconsin, see your kids? Must be all growed up now."

"Them ties was cut too long ago. With blunt scissors."

She said the milk was on the turn. He smelled it and said he'd take his coffee without.

"I know I'm not going to sing at any rodeo, Loyal. My voice is weak, I'm too old. Old ladies don't sing at rodeos. But you know, I don't feel old. I feel like I've got the liveliest part of my life still ahead. I could stay on the ranch, Loyal, but not alone. A man is needed." She couldn't say it much clearer.

The coffee. Its blackness in the familiar blue cups. He stirred in sugar. Her spoon clinked.

Then all at once the awkwardness was gone. Stories of things he had seen began to pour out, the words firing from between his loosened and gapped teeth. He told her about Cucumber drowning in a mine, midnight driving with Bullet over dangerous passes when the headlights failed, the mountain lion. He, who had talked little, talked much, swelled to a glowing huckster selling stories of his life. At two in the morning, Starr nodding off, wanting nothing but sleep and silence, he stopped. They were tired of each other, each longed for the relief of solitude. He said he would sleep on the daybed beside the stove. The kitchen stank of cigarettes.

In the morning she gave him Jack's pearl gray cowboy hat.

46. What I See

A booth in Dot's Place. The plastic Owl's head on the wall glows. He's reading the local paper, arms folded on the plywood table. There is the smell of grease dissolver. Dot squats and wipes at the encrusted stove.

The coffee is the color of river bottom dirt. Elk, big horns, whitetail, moose heads on the walls, coated with grease from Dot's cooking. French fries. Eggs over easy. Dot's old man, Harry S. Furman, shot them. In the right light anybody can see the dull crust of grease on the glass eyes.

He turns the pages of the paper, glances at a photograph of a Basque family posing with relatives from South America. Some of the men squat in the front row, their knees straining their polyester trousers, their sports coats hunched. There is the grand matriarch of the group, Celestina Falxa, from the House of Little Children, Ttipinonia, unsmiling, stout and bow-legged, the little eyes staring straight into the camera. She wears a rayon dress printed in squares, grips a handbag. Eighty-four and flies a single-engine plane over the flaring distances says the caption. Never learned to drive.

He studies the picture, the direction of their eyes. No one else looks into the camera. An elderly woman with harlequin glasses smiles tentatively and looks at Celestina. The three South American cousins have matching hair and delicate smiles. They, too, gaze at Celestina. The men in the back row stand on chairs. Their foreheads gleam white, their faces are sunblackened. Three of the men are missing front teeth. To the side stands a woman in a plaid pantsuit. The pants stand away from her legs like culvert tubes, the vest has been cut and sewn in a way that makes the plaid stagger. In the background is a television set near the ceiling, the plastic walls of the Holiday Inn, a chrome chair, a soiled nylon carpet.

"What the hell you got there, Mr. Blood, clue to the secret of the ages?" Dot titters. She grips a tub of frozen meat patties.

"You scrutinizing it so hard I thought you found your long-lost brother."

This is what it comes down to, the study of photographs of strangers.

47. The Red-Haired Coyote

Dear Pete,

what the hell is happening with fur prices. Can't make a living on those prices. Prime coyote was three X what is now a couple of years ago. If it doesn't get better, might as well hang up the traps.

L. Blood

Pete Faure
Growley Lake, B.C.
Canada

HE didn't think there would be anything under the rabbit-brush. But as he came in to pull the trap and stake he saw her, a late-season coyote with a strong red color, stronger on her face, chest and haunches. The hot spring sun reflecting off the late snow had frizzled and burned her pelt like a cheap permanent. She pulled back from him with a gape that showed her teeth, she cringed and twisted in submissive posture, the yellow eyes fixed his. She looked at him. The crimped red hair, the extraordinary expression on the animal's face, in her body language, mingling appeasement, fear, anger, threat, resignation, pain, horror, and more, the terrible and thrilling sense of her life's imminent end.

Billy.

The fur was no good. Red, yes, but singed and rubbed. The foot didn't look too bad. She hadn't been chewing on it anyway. Quickly he threw the kneeling tarp over her head, twisted it tight so she couldn't lunge at him, and pried the trap open. The foot was swollen, but still warm, there was still circulation. He got up and pulled the tarp away in almost one motion. She was gone.

PART FIVE

48. The Hat Man

In the Dead Letter Office

Oct. 1982

Dear Mr. Blood, Dr. Pinetsky would like to
speak to you about your lung X-rays. Please
call this office to schedule an appointment
at your earliest convenience.

Mr. Loyal Blood
General Delivery
Hammerlock, Colorado 89910

IN the garden Kosti and Paula threw sheets over the tomato
plants to protect them from the night frost, old sheets Paula's
mother had given her years ago, and patched in all the hues
of white, marble, ivory, milk-silver, snow, chalk, pearl,
birchbark, ghost, moonflower, cloud, ash, quartz. The teeth
of autumn gnawed at the light. They trampled back and
forth over the silvered clods, working together, the only
ones left on the mountain farm now. Leopard Lady, Inks, the
three sisters with the trunk of antique dresses, the Grass Man
and his hundreds of friends, all pulled out and gone. Some
of their funky rags still in the empty rooms, posters of Bob

Dylan gone magenta, stacks of paperback books, Brautigan, Hoffman, Kesey, Wolfe, Fariña, McLuhan, the covers curled by summer heat, the sentiments outmoded, the ideas betrayed.

The tomato plants reared in creamy columns against the black trees beyond the clearing. Their numb hands seized new sheets, snapped them open. They could feel the soil stiffening with cold. The smell of burning grass replaced the summer scent of wet grass. The air seemed banded as sharply as jasper with cold.

"Gonna be hard frost tonight. These old tomatoes ain't never gonna make it any farther than they already are with nights like this," said Kosti. "Do better to pick them green and put them in the woodshed."

"If it looks like frost again tomorrow we'll pick them. I'll make four hundred quarts of piccalilli. What the hell, I don't care. I'll fry green tomatoes until spring. 'Johnson boys ate green tomatoes, they have eat them all their life,' " she sang. There were streaks of grey hair at her temples. Kosti swatted her across the rump with a dried flower stalk from the rhubarb. As they went into the warm kitchen they heard the barred owl throw her voice, fixing hunched crows to their branches with a glue of fear.

"After supper want to go down and see the old Hat Man? We could bring him down some green tomatoes."

"Bring him down some of the gingersnaps. Last time he was around he ate damn near the whole jar full." They called him the Hat Man, old Mr. Blood, because he always wore a hat, sometimes a cowboy hat, usually a farm cap, his white hair sticking out the arched hole at the back.

He had come in his rust-scabbed truck the spring before

with an ancient dog who let no one near him without showing her teeth. He made a deal to rent a couple of acres of a fallow potato field and backed his humpbacked wagon onto the level ground.

One day there was nothing there but weeds and scrub brush, and a week later the Hat Man was anchored down, surrounded by a chicken wire fence strung on flimsy posts, meant, perhaps, to give a boundary to his life or keep the dog in. He turned over a garden with a rented tiller and as soon as the seeds were in he got some kind of a job at the sawmill. Something an old guy could do, tallying, maybe. Maybe Bricker had took pity on him, said Kosti.

In a month it looked like he had been there forever. He bought or found an old Dodge truck for parts and stowed it in the weeds, picking away at it to keep the truck he drove running.

From the first week Kosti got the habit of stopping by at the end of the day, leaning on the truck's fender and drinking beer in the long summer light while the Hat Man worked on his greasy internal mechanics and talked and talked around his persistent cough. It was like punctuation, a few words, a couple of coughs, a sentence or two, more coughing. Or they sat on the wagon steps in a human pyramid, like they were waiting for a ball game to begin. But they were only enjoying the evening. Listening. Nobody could get a word past the Hat Man. He had the talking cornered sitting on the highest step coughing and spitting into the darkness in the pauses of his wandering talk. He was a rank old man, grease and dirt and dog, hard face under the scarred forehead, hat brim tipped over the eyes. You could see he'd been good-looking though, said Paula. One of the tough old ones, said Kosti, never mind how he looked. He wished he could wander around the country like the old Hat Man.

He kept peculiar time. Sometimes weeded his potatoes at ten o'clock at night, the trouble light he used to illumine the oily guts of the engine hanging on a post in the garden, casting enormous shadows of potato leaves on the bleached soil and throwing down the shapes of gargoyles from his hunched shoulders and cowboy hat. While he worked the dog watched him like a new apprentice, snapping moths out of the air with a wet chop.

Once, in the rain, the three of them cramped inside the Hat Man's rolling house. Kosti and Paula sat on the bench. The Hat Man sat on his bunk. Everywhere objects hung and dangled, frying pans, ropes, coil of wire, a coffee can with a wire bail, filled with nails. The only clear place was on the back of the door where Mr. Blood had pasted a creased cowboy movie poster that Kosti coveted.

Carl Laemmle

Presents

Hoot Gibson

in

'Chip

of the Flying U'

It showed a peach-faced man with blue idiot eyes, gap

teeth and red, red lips in a smiling Cupid's bow.

In the corner was the Hat Man's television. Looked like the dog had been licking the screen. Cupboards and shelves and hooks, magazines, deer horns. Hats. He had some hats he never wore.

"This one," he said to Kosti, turning a wilted black brim around and around in his cracked hands like a prayer wheel, "This one might be valuable. This might be Paul Revere's hat that he wore the night he done his ride. It might be valued at a thousand dollars." Paula noticed the smell of moldering wool and fur and old sweatbands that filled the trailer like invisible gas.

"See this one?" He held up a brown cap, the rotting crown so soft it lay flat on the brim. "Belonged to Dillinger. You know I can't get insurance on this hat collection. I started out to collect them about three years ago. The widow of a friend gave me the first one, but I've worn hats most of my life on account of I got a few scars. You want to know why?" he said, voice racing between coughs. He picked up a white cowboy hat with a snakeskin band. "I bought this off somebody out in California. He had a sign nailed up on the telephone pole, 'Good cowboy hat, been in the movies, too big for me, $20.' I took one look and paid him what he was asking, didn't even try to bring his price down. You know who wore that hat? Hoot Gibson, up on that poster, that's who, Hoot Gibson in *The Bearcat* in 1922. They made Hoot Gibson into some kind of hero, but he was just a knock-around when he got started, just a guy bumming around from one rodeo to another, doing stunts, picking up small change by fooling around. Drifted to the movies. Got hired as a stuntman after somebody rented him for a day to handle some rough horseflesh. Couldn't act his way out of a paper bag. Movie stars was smaller in the old days. Their heads was bigger. That's my hobby, the old movie cowboys. Two years ago I watched most of them on TV. I was hooked up to some good electricity. Bought that TV set." He pointed to the corner. "Never paid attention to movies before then. But I'll tell you, I could go on one of those trivia shows now. J. Warren Kerrigan in *Covered Wagon,* Antonio Moreno in *The Trail of the Lonesome Pine* and *The Border Legion,* Christ, I know a lot of them. Tom Mix in anything he done. You know who used to stand all stiff and puffed up like those old boys? Mussolini. World War Two. Like the old movie cowboys. You know what else is funny about them?" They waited through a storm of coughing, waited until he had his breath back and wiped his wet eyes. "Where their waists are. They all got their waists right up there, their pants're hauled up, up to their chests, gives a short look to their bodies. These are the silents I'm talking about. You can't see them at movie houses. I see *The Bearcat* every time I get a chance. Watch the TV listings. Film festivals sometimes, so I read the papers. I have seen this *same hat* right here that I'm holding on the head of Hoot Gibson in that movie. Gives you a funny feeling to look at a hat you own up on the television. It's like he's dead, but the hat's still alive.

"The reason I can't get the insurance on my collection is because I don't stay put. A few months here, then move on. I have to keep moving along. Got my house-wagon, got my truck, got my dog, I can find work anywhere because I am not too proud. I'll run a garbage truck. I'll carpenter. I'll build you a wall or a doghouse or a observatory. I'm not in that social security system, though. Never paid a penny of it, never collected a penny of it. Made my own way through thick and thin." Paula looked half asleep, leaning back against the wall. Her knees glittered with fish scales.

"I got good hats that way, not out of the garbage, but asking people, 'You got any old hats you'd like to part with?' That's how I got this ski hat, a lady's husband was goin' down the street in Dog Boil, Manitoba where I was for the wheat harvest once. The husband was going to the hardware store to get window caulking. A geode rolled off a windowsill of the hotel room of a geologist who was doing oil exploration and the geode hit the husband on the head. This hat saved his life. You wouldn't think to look at me that I could build a observatory, would you?" But Kosti and Paula were tired. They'd split wood all day and now sleep was coming down like a numbing spell.

On Saturday night they were back again with green tomato pie. It tasted a little like apple pie, but that was because of the spices, Paula said. The same spices, cinnamon and cloves. Green tomatoes had no taste of their own. The Hat Man boiled water for coffee, Paula got out their tea flask, pineapple weed and dried strawberry leaves. A healthy drink.

"The biggest trouble with building an observatory," old Blood said, was in deciding where to put it. "There's things you wouldn't even think about. You don't want it near a big city or even a shopping mall. Light pollution, dirty air. Find some place that's dark at night. Like around here. Not many places left that's pure dark. I used to sleep out on the prairie at night, see those stars. Highway lights, streetlamps, yard lights, they all throw their light up on the bellies of airplanes. Ruin the sky." He coughed. "This would be a good place to put an observatory." Paula looked at the black window, clouded on the inside with a film of moisture.

"A dark spot's only the first thing. Any fool could think of that." He shuffled his chair closer, looked into their faces to see if they were getting this. Ticked off the points on cracked fingers.

"You can't pick a cloudy place. So, number two, the sky has to be clear most nights. Here you got your dark, all right, but you also got cloudy nights. But even if there wasn't clouds, then, see, your atmosphere has to be steady. The air is like a river, like a thousand rivers stacked on top of each other, and the way the currents of the air rivers run, smooth or rough, depends on the shape of the ground below." He could hear Ben telling him in the mountain night. "See, it's like stones in a river. Hills and canyons and valleys and mountains make the air up over us rough. Like river stones rough up the water. The more stones in the river the rougher the water gets. And you go out to your observatory that's built up in the mountains, say, like here, to look at the stars, and it's all twinkly and bleary and you can't see dog-shit on a plate. It's better to set your observatory up on the top of a lone mountain. Even better if the mountain's on an island or along the coast. Air smooths out when it crosses water. Oh, there's a lot to know," he said, looking Kosti straight in the eye. "Haven't even begun to tell you. I've seen it when it was fine. We'll get to it some other time. I got to change the bandage on the dog's back."

Paula spoke in the sad voice she used for crying babies and conversations with her bad-news sisters, the words drawn out mournfully in the vowels. "Poor old thing, what's the matter with her?"

"I believe she had a fight with what used to be my winter income. You hear that?" Outside under the wavering starlight a coyote pack called with pitched short cries like the cries of hens running for lettuce leaves. Paula leaned against Kosti. Presently an exquisite thin note rose off the hill across the road.

"That was my getaway money in yesteryear," said the Hat Man. "Oh, fur prices were good once. They'll probably come back up. Maybe this season. I might try it around here. I might trap some this winter, maybe, get enough money to move on. There used to be good money in trapping. But it's rough on you. A rough life."

Paula's face was cold. She thought of innocent animals cruelly pinned, their mouths dry with fear while this old man with the hard blue eyes crept toward them, talking, talking, but carrying a bloodstained stick.

But he was already in new stories, a prospecting story where in the dark he stepped on a rattlesnake in his bare feet, jumped in the air and landed on the snake again. She did not want him to tell the story about the wild ducks with the string through their guts, the trailing ends tied together so that they jerked against each other, the string sawing at raw tissue, or the pack rats thrown alive into the campfire.

Kosti and Paula rolled up on their futon in the yellow kerosene light, playing hand-spider. "Creep, creep, creep," whispered Kosti, thinking Paula smelled pretty ripe, burned cheese and skunk, but as soon as she grasped his hoe handle his nose went blank.

"Hope you don't turn into a talker when you get old." She buffed in his ear.

"In my family the men die young. You'll never know what stories I might of made up. Big elk hunts! Mine disasters!" They laughed, but the thought of the Hat Man's reeling, loose-mouthed age drove them to a panic of kissing, of slamming each other with their springy pelvic bones.

49. What I See

He's not sure where he is. So many roads look the same, the repetitive signs, the yellow stripe to the horizon. The same cars and trucks are repeated over and over. But in the early morning when he is not jostled by traffic he finds a way to the back roads where he sees box elder, sumac buds showing green tips.

He comes on a few landmarks, unchanged since he drove along this road a long time earlier. Through the pink rocks, through the stunted oaks the wind roars, the crane shrieks from the swamp. In the morning fight the sky comes alive with birds. He remembers the smell of cave-riddled rock. A fox moves over the matted grasses.

He takes the turnoff that runs along the foot of the cliffs. The old rig beats along. The greasy stone is bored with tiny caves the size of stick ends. Travelers have cut their names in the rock in footed capitals and florid ampersands. The dates flood past him July 4, 1838, 1862, 1932, 1876, 1901, 1869, 1937.

The cliffs darken. Words well out of the rock in burning colors, "Epiphany H.S. '67," "Bobby loves Nita," "Christ Will Come," "Fedora." "Write Belerophon." Pheasants fly over the truck trailing stringy tails. On the edge of the fields ruined farms, slatty buildings weak and ready to go. The land heaves, crawls in great, undulating rolls. Tumbleweed banks the fences. LAKE FEDORA. KNIGHT CRAWLERS. FOR A GOOD NIGHT'S REST SLEEP AT THE CUCKLEBURR MOTEL. SEND $60 FOR THE COMPLETE SET.

Now he's seeing horses, the goddamn beautiful horses he never could ride. Indian singing from the Rosebud reservation, singing like the howling of the wind. The woman announcer's voice, breathy, quick cadenced, "And this for Johnny White-Eyes, died in 1980, he would have been thirty-two today, his mother and all the rest request this, 'I'm Proud to Be an American.' "

And when he stops and gets out the silence roars.

He thinks he is going east but does not cross the Missouri. Instead, turns west-northwest on an old man's reckless hunch. What difference does it make?

Gets to Marcelito, California, stands at the Stars & Moon bar telling them about the real uranium days, about Bullet Wulff who would be a stranger to these times, while in the dark someone uncouples his trailer hitch and makes off with the old round-topped wagon. There go the traps, the Indian's book, the hat collection, the frying pan and tin dishes, the forever-smiling face of Hoot Gibson.

But he still has the truck, rust starring through the paint. Busted, broke, he drifts to the orchards and fields, into the Stream.

The Stream of migrant labor flows north and east, south again, then west, splitting and doubling back in cranked-out buses and throbbing Cadillacs to the avocados, oranges, peaches and frilly lettuces, beans like alien fingers, potatoes, beets, hairy dirty beets, apples, plums, nectarines, grapes, broccoli, kiwi, tangerines, walnuts, almonds, gooseberries, boysenberries, strawberries. Gritty strawberries, sour and rough in the mouth but as red as fresh blood. It's easier to get into the Stream than out again.

50. The One Only One

Aug 4 '84
Dear Doc. Fitts, Decided (finally!) on thesis topic—study of the One Only Ones, Sioux society of older women who had ''only one man'' in their lives. Not much written on their impt. social role. Before I get started I'm going back east. My twin brother is going through some kind of ident. crisis and I ought to see him before I start. I know what he's going through. Really excited about the thesis! Will make appt. as soon as I get back. Sincerely, Kim Witkin

Prof. Roman Fittshew
Dept. Sociol.
U. Utah
14 E. 2nd S.
Salt Lake, UT 84105

RAY took so long to die, was so unwilling to give up life,

that Mernelle thought of plastic bags, sleeping pills, thought of disconnecting his oxygen or crimping the tube until he had to let go. He twisted in death's gripping hand like a drowning cat in the scruff-clenched fingers of a farmer, yet the hand did not open. The cancer gnawed inside him, sometimes quiescent enough to let him smile, say a few sentences, his guileless eyes fixed on her, his thinness stretched under the sheets. She imagined it in him, a wet maroon mass like a cow's afterbirth, pulling his life into its own.

Ray's doctor told her to go to a special counseling group. "Coping with Death." They met in the doctors' lunchroom. A room with a thin carpet, maple chairs around a long maple table. A nurse handed her a blue plastic folder. Inside she found a photocopied poem, "The Fading Light"; a list of seven types of dying people; stapled pages of practical advice on wills, organ donation, undertakers, funeral costs, tombstone cutters, cremation parlors; lists of nursing homes and hospices; telephone numbers to call for home help; a pamphlet, "Dying At Home"; a roster of clergymen, rabbis and priests; advice on choosing a cemetery. She read through the seven types, looking for Ray. The Death-Denier, The Death Submitter, the Death-Defier, the Death-Transcender. That was Ray, The Death-Defier.

Five others at the table. Seven chairs empty. A chubby Irish nurse, black-lined doe eyes. The nurse said she was trained in dying techniques. Her voice was gentle, slow, the voice Mernelle associated with cancer. The name tag read "Moira Magoon RN." She looked rosy with vitality. The six around the table wore no name tags. They were tired and slack, their fingers repeated senseless little motions. That was usual, said Moira; sitting beside someone you loved, watching them die, was a death itself. It would take a year to get over it, a full rotation of the thirteen moons before . . . A ruined father whose only daughter would die that night bellowed "Never!" then wept in front of them with noisy gobbles and hawks.

They went through the blue folder. Moira Magoon explained, as one giving a recipe, how to help a dying person like Ray who wouldn't give up. The Death-Defiers were the most difficult. Mernelle listened, nodding. Moira Magoon made death sound sensible, a logical decision one could make. The decision was easier once the living gave permission. She was saying it was Mernelle who would not let Ray die. Just say yes.

That evening Mernelle sat by Ray's bed. He was sweaty, half unconscious with drugs and opiates. His mouth was crusted white, parched. The dry hospital room. She took the thin hand, ruined now with needle bruises and discolored fingernails, wasted to a tent of skin over stick bones.

"Ray, Ray," she said softly. "Ray, it's o.k. to let go. Ray, you can quit now. You can let go. You don't have to fight it, Ray. Just let go. It's all right." She said it many times, keeping her voice soft. He breathed. He fought. She wanted to open the window but there were moths. She could not keep up the soft cancer voice. Her own scratchy iron, low and quick.

"Ray, you quit fighting, now. Let go, Ray. I mean it! It's time to quit, Ray."

He roused. His eyes floated in the translucent face. He

looked at her, beyond her at some scalding childhood scene, the mind's machinery jerking, opening forgotten cupboard doors to the color of a candy apple, the fury of the drunk father, spurting neck of chicken, piles of lumber falling, falling, the lonely smell of coming rain. He looked through the screen door mesh at the girl, her slender back to him, her bare arms, the square of sunlight on the floor enclosing his own shadow.

"Too bad we never did," he said and died.

51. The Red-Shirt Coyote

Dear Chief Check out Kortnegger's potato farm. Mexicans work there but they don't get paid. They don't complain because they get killed & left in cottonwood grove. Ask Mr. Kortnegger how all those skulls and bones come to be in his cottonwood grove. yrs truly,

A Friend who Knows

Police Chief

Erpf, Idaho

THE cottonwoods were still, the leaves hanging as limp as if the roots had been severed. In the windbreak grove beyond the house the crows were at something, short hard stossquarren hammering the air.

"In some scran or other," said the woman, throwing out

her words like a handful of grain, scraping and scraping at the scum behind the faucet with the broken blade of the jackknife.

"How much longer are you goin' to scratch away there?"

"Scratch away? I wouldn't have to scratch away if you'd do somethin' about this rotten linoleum. It stinks and it's caked up so's I can't get it clean. I give up," she said, throwing down the knife and going onto the porch. He heard her out there, sniveling and snorting. She was asking for it. His hands throbbed.

He might have gone out and given her a clop or two but she came back in after a few minutes.

"Somebody, some old bum just come in the gate. Looking for work, I bet. Look at that truck. Some old drifter."

"Yeah, the employment said they'd send somebody over. What the hell you think I been waiting around here for all day, sight of your blue eyes? He was supposed to come an hour ago."

"You ain't goin' to take him on, are you?"

"Why not? He can be the foreman, go pick 'em up. Why the hell not? So's I don't have to keep on draggin' down there."

"He looks pretty bent up. He's an old drifter. Old and skinny."

"We'll see."

Loyal had fourteen dollars left from the oranges. Most of the orange money had gone for the clinic bill. He'd slipped coming down with a full bag and the weight swung him against the ladder and broke a rib. Tough luck.

And slow to mend. He used to mend up fast, but now he still wasn't right. Tender and painful to take a deep breath. Every time he coughed it was like spears. So an overseer job sounded all right. He needed the money. Let the Mexicans dig the potatoes. He'd done his share of potatoes and lemons and everything between. California and Idaho, then back again.

But Kortnegger looked like a bad bet, feed cap tugged low over his unseeable eyes. Potato farmers were rough. Baggy pants rolled up at the bottom, pack of cigarettes in his shirt pocket, pencil stub sticking out. Work shoes. The face just long dirty folds like a bellows of flesh. The woman wasn't much better. Grubby blouse hanging over a spread of pale green stretch shorts with ribbed front seams to simulate creases, socks around her ankles. But she was the one who asked the questions while Kortnegger hung back and glanced out from under the hat bill. They told him to wait on the porch. He could hear them. She had a voice like a fly in a Coke bottle.

"I don't think he'll work out. He's half crippled up. Listen at how he coughs. He'll be down sick most of the time. If he don't take off he'll make trouble."

"He'd have to be a double-bladed razor to get in front of me. And why the hell don't you keep your nose out of my business."

"Well, you asked me," she shouted. "Try to give you a civil answer, thanks I get!"

Kortnegger put his face to the screen door.

"O.k. You're hired. Put your stuff out in the second bunkhouse, room says FOREMAN on the door. Then come back down here I'll show you what to do. Tomorrow or the day after I want you to go pick up a bunch of workers, be coming in on the bus with Gerry. Gerry's my roundup guy. I'll give you some money, you pay him five dollars a head. Your main job, go pick the stiffs up, keep 'em on their feet. Don't get no ideas. I know how many's comin'. You might think number two means second in command, but around here it means shit."

They were the worst-looking bunch of skags Loyal had seen. Old bindle stiffs, half of them coughing their lungs out and blue with emphysema, the younger ones caved in with malnutrition and liquor and confusion. A couple of them were Mexicans, no English except 'Hello, I wan' work,' probably new to the game or they wouldn't be on Kortnegger's farm, red shirt on the one, fancy rag at his neck. Must have been following the farm work route and got mixed in with the end-of-the-road bunch. He'd bet Red Shirt had run the harvests before. He'd brought the other one. Money had changed hands. That was the coyote, the red shirt, the one who knew the ropes. Oh, they'd take the money, all right, they liked the sound of twenty dollars a day cash. And they'd get it, too, for a ten-hour day of more work than any of them had seen in years, looked like.

"That them? They look like they been dug up."

"I guess there wasn't too big of a choice. Your roundup guy said there's been a drop in the transients. And there's very few unattached Mexicans. A lot of farmers get the same guys back every year. Your man says this is all he can get to come up here. This is pretty far up. It's off the route. I don't know what the problem is but this is what you've got."

Actually, the man had said he couldn't get anybody who'd ever heard Kortnegger's name to sign on. Said he wanted to quit himself. Told Loyal to watch out.

"Bunch of pukes and patchcocks. I can smell 'em from here. If half of 'em makes it to sundown I'll be surprised."

The two Mexicans worked hard and steady. The old bindle stiffs drifted along down the rows, missing half the potatoes. Kortnegger stood for half an hour watching an unsteady pair. When they got to the end of the row he opened his mouth, then closed it without saying anything. He went back to the house, then called to Loyal, "You got to stir them up, there. Know what I mean? You got to stir them up."

Loyal was tough all afternoon, walking up and down, "Come on, come on, pick it up, pick it up," whacking the side of his shoe with a piece of lath. In the night one of the old men took off. The next night Kortnegger locked them in the bunkhouse and said nobody would smell pay until all the potatoes were in.

The weather, already dry and hot, baked the rows. The men labored on, potato forks rising and falling, the scooping hands dropping potatoes in the bags. The earth cracked the skin of the men who did not have gloves. Cotton gloves, "French-Canadian racing gloves" said one of the old pickers contemptuously, wore out in a few days. The heat built until the men stripped off their shirts in the row, until they were sunburned and parched and called to Loyal for more water.

The sky darkened, Loyal's breath drew slow fire lugging the slopping buckets. He'd get coughing and have to stop, doubled over with it. Thunderheads piled up in the west. Maybe a storm would break the heat. Too hot for fieldwork. Lightning, as delicate and rapid as cracking ice, flickered.

Kortnegger came out of the woodshed.

"It might pass to the north of us. It's dry here. Two years of drought. I remember the goddamn year when every storm went past. You could see the goddamn rain fallin' up in Gackle. Two mile north and we never got a drop. Fuckin' goddamn country. Oughta give it back to the goddamn Indians."

The rattler trees began to dither. Wind out of the northwest, corkscrewing leaves off the trees, snapping the woman's dish towels on the line. The men in the field started to straggle back toward the buildings. They looked like potato bugs.

"Where the hell do they think they're going?" bawled Kortnegger.

"Storm's comin'. They can see it as good as you can."

"You tell them sons a bitches they want to draw their pay, they keep working. A little rain won't hurt 'em."

"There's a damn good chance they'll get hit with lightning. Nobody ever stays in the field through a thunderstorm."

"These are goin' to." Kortnegger shouted into the wind. "Get back to bloody work you buggers. Any man comes in from that field don't draw no pay!"

"They can't hear you."

The windbreak trees flung up the white undersides of their leaves like foam on wave crests. The crows cawed in the branches. Strange that they hadn't gone for shelter.

Ravens now, ravens were different from crows, ravens would wheel on the storm currents, mounting the towers of rising air, flying even in the pelting rain, but there were no ravens. The old men stumbled down the field under the pulsing platinum light.

Upstairs the woman pulled down the windows, paint flaked away. The lightning stuttered through the cloud scrim. Kortnegger started the pickup, the engine muttering under the thunder. The woman ran clumsily out to the clothesline to take in the dish towels. They twisted and leapt like gutshot cats. A hard drop struck Loyal, then another. The pickup was halfway to the men. They faltered; some stopped walking.

Think he's going to give them a ride, thought Loyal. Kortnegger's voice cursed and smote them. Through the sheet of rain he saw most of the old men turn back into the field. Three or four of them paid no attention but walked forward, bent against the rain, leaving the field. He could see the sodden red shirt of the feisty Mexican. Where he was, so was the other. The two best workers.

Kortnegger's pickup truck cut a muddy arc. It stopped in front of the men for a minute while Kortnegger spoke, then some of them climbed into the back, huddling against the thunderous pour. Lightning stabbed the streaming fields. Kortnegger didn't stop at the buildings, but kept on going, onto the hardtop road where he turned left, toward town. He'd dump them on the highway, thought Loyal. Good way to get potatoes in for nothing. Fired without pay. Who they going to complain to?

A week, ten days later, another work crew, his rib toughening up, crows in the grove again, blaring caws laid upon each other like loud paint. They woke him at first light. He had to get out of this place no matter how broke. This was bad medicine. He twisted in the blankets trying to block out the staws and haws, but wondered at the crows' persistence. In the last week they had clamored on and on in the grove of trees. He'd never known crows to keep on that way unless they had a dead beef to fight over, then they'd squabble until it was gone.

He got dressed, half asleep, his grasp of things accelerating until, by the time he leaned over to tie his shoes, he was ready to kill a crow or two. The boards of the porch floor were wet. He heard the passionate barking of a distant fox. A shimmering light coated everything like translucent wax. He went to Kortnegger's pickup to get the .22 in the window rack, but was not surprised to find the truck doors locked. The sour bird was as suspicious as they came. Afraid one of the bums would sneak out and steal his truck. He picked up half a dozen stones from the driveway.

As he came near the grove, the pearly sky showed through openings in the branches, phosphorescent shapes that shifted and closed as the birds jumped about. Venus, rising, bobbed in the leaves. The lookout crow gave the alarm and the flock took off in a screaming cloud. There had to be sixty or seventy of them, he thought. The fox was silent. He walked into the cool trees. Hundreds of twigs and small branches littered the ground, snapped underfoot. A tree was down, a big cottonwood. The trunk was splintered but it had not broken through; the crown was lodged high in two or three mangled saplings.

Widow-maker. The weight would bend and press the saplings until their branches gave way and the cottonwood plummeted the final twenty feet. A limb, broken from the trunk, had landed on its branches in a way that resembled a nightmare beast on thin, scurrying legs. The torn wood was as white as a staring face.

The ground was heaved up, a welt of soil like a crooked furrow snaking through the tree roots. Lightning stroke. He kicked at the seared earth. A heavy white bone protruded from the furrow. A dinosaur bone. The biggest he'd ever seen. A strange one. After all this time to find another.

He pulled and it stirred in the loam. With a stick he dug the soil away. Something bad in the back of his mind about a stick in the leaf mold, the smell of the rotten leaves. The shape of the bone flattened, thinned out a little like a scapula, a shoulder blade, but different. He looked at it, the great bone, glimmering greenish white against the earth. He could hardly lift it, this ancient thing. What the hell was the name of that guy he used to dig bones with? Cartridge, something like that. Big sweaty guy, what the hell ever happened to him?

The strange bone had to be worth money, and if he could manage it, Kortnegger wasn't going to get anything from it. Funny, it wasn't the kind of place he'd expect to find fossils, this deep farmland. But, excited now, he dug deeper in the churned earth hoping for the other bones, but found nothing.

He walked through the grove kicking at the soil, lifting fallen branches. Because he was looking for the shapes of bones he saw the tibia quite easily, and then the skull, and knew what drew the crows to the grove, for there were still fragments of flesh on these bones. Wads of rotten cloth, the feisty Mexican's red shirt.

Forty minutes later, the truck idling in front of the post office, he wrote his postcard and dropped it in the blue humped box. He was out of town before the sun was up.

52. La Violencia

Septem. 2
Dear Mernelle, It's awful about
Ray. He was a good man. Sorry
we couldn't make the funeral.
Things down here are bad. Killings
riots, drugs, bankrupts, crime,
hurricanes. It used to be so
beautiful. Tax probs. continue.
Some retirement! Pala has
a new project. Be happy for
what you and Ray had. Letter
follows,   Love, Dub.

Mrs. Mernelle MacWay
Randall Court
Bethany, VT 05086

"LA tristeza de Miami," said Pala, commenced in the year of the Mariel exodus, with the flood of demented people into the city. An old and murderously tense mood persisted. There were too many strange people, too much strange money in too few hands.

On a hot afternoon she heard on the car radio that the four white police accused of beating Arthur McDuffie to death had been acquitted up in Tampa. In minutes the city vomited blood.

She always drove home herself. Liked driving, liked the new business, the travel bureau, the people in a hurry. Dub was tired of it all but she still had the Cuban energy, the push and drive to make things work. She had to work. Couldn't retire. Didn't want to retire. Dub and his orchids.

She steered through the heated early evening, listening to the excited announcer. The sun struck her eyes and she hesitated at the top of the ramp feeding the highway. A swarm of men flailing bats sprang down on the car, heavy little chunks of windshield glass cascaded into her skirted lap, a stone smashed the fingers of her right hand clenched on the steering wheel and through the denting and shattering the voice of the announcer went on excitedly as though he were there watching, leaning into the car to notice how much blood there was, or if, perhaps, the tongue was cut out and a red rose jammed into the seeping orifice.

But the pirate tramped on the gas and scraped onto the howling throughway, accelerating, the wind plastering glass dust across her chest. She twisted the car, throwing off the men, except one who clung to the ragged edge of the windshield opening, his body stretched along the hood.

She steered the battered car through the commuter traffic, pounding on the horn. What else could she do? But the other drivers, transfixed by the same announcer's voice, slowed in the flooding red of brake lights, cut into adjacent lanes for a few feet of progress, sped forward, and none seemed aware of her hood ornament. A black man. She could see his black fingers and the nails squeezed white. Still he hung on. In the center lane she accelerated, eyes slitted against the blast of air. When there was a clear patch behind her she stood on the brakes, saw the man vault ahead onto the roadway. She accelerated again, jolting over his legs. She stopped then, in mid-lane, turned the engine off and waited in the stalled traffic until the police came in a cacophony of horns and tape decks and the black man's hoarse crying.

She did not want to drive alone in Miami again. Did not want to be in Miami. Thousands of people did not want to be in Miami. The glossy city emptied, the money-men and investors fleeing with condos unsold, office towers unleased, undeveloped properties foreclosed. Pala picked Houston. The travel agency was a natural for Houston she told Dub.

"I would like to get out of real estate. All of it. We don't need the money. You play with the orchids. This is my hobby. The travel business is fun for me."

They left the month Christo began to fit the pink plastic around the bay islands. Pala had a bathrobe the same color of pink, thought Dub. Flamingo pink. There would be nothing like it in Houston.

53. The Fulgurite Shaped Like a Bone

A Postcard Under the Windshield Wiper

```
Welcome to CICERO. Sponsored by Cicero
Business and Professional Association.
Burrow rides free every Wed. Nite in Season.
Located in central South Dakota, Highways 18
& 42A. Community served by 32-bed hospital,
one medical doctor and a dentist. School
Museum! See 1945 Tornado Car found in Tree!
Pickel Jar Sub Shop! Free tours. •Lighted
Tennis Courts •Free Campground and dump
station •9-Hole golf Course •Two Service
Stations •Motel •5 Eating Establishments.
Come to Where It's At!
```

YOU should have called, the receptionist said. Smooth Indian face, blue-tinted lenses and streaked perm. Dr. Garch keeps his own appointment book. Who knows if he'll show up at all? He isn't on the out-of-town list, but who knows? She told him he could wait in the hall outside Garch's office. If he wanted.

Loyal sat there all morning, the dinosaur bone wrapped in newspaper and binder twine against the wall behind the wooden chair. It had been hard getting here. He'd been laid up in the truck for a week with the damn bronchitis again. His lungs were shot. Sleeping on the front seat. Still sick, confused about the time of year. Truck not in good shape, either. Timing off, engine about shot, exhaust system finished. Sounded like a bomber coming through town.

At noon the receptionist went out to lunch, her Chinese cloth shoes winking open with each step.

When Garch came, keys rattling in his hand, Loyal was asleep, his head resting on the wall, his mouth open. He woke and saw a short man in a ready-made suit, brown hair crinkled on the top and cut short on each side, a pencil mustache like a Mexican radio announcer, soft chin. Eyes gleamed watching Loyal dragging at the bone.

"Got something?" He waved at a green Formica table in his office. Underneath were stored boxes of bones, dusty concretions, ochre sandstone slabs, red lumps. Loyal coughed, the waking-up cough that left him breathless.

"Used to dig dinosaur bones, used to look for tracks, Dakotas, Colorado, Wyoming, Utah, those places. What, twenty years ago. Been all over. But I never seen one like this one." He got the thing up on the table but stood back to let Garch unwrap it. Goddamn, he could feel himself shaking and wrecked. Garch was sure-handed, a fit and healthy man. The bone lay there, a polished stony glare to it. Garch leaned over, ran his finger along its length.

"I guess," said Loyal, "I'm here for two reasons. I'd like to know what in hell the thing is from, but there's also the question of value. I mean."

Garch straightened up. Were the bright eyes a little wary? "Yes. You want to sell it."

"Well."

"It's not a bone—"

"The hell it isn't. There's nothing else it could be. It's a strange one, a strange anatomy, but there's nothing else it could be. Don't try to tell me it's a rock. It's no rock."

"No. I agree with you. It's not a rock. I think it's a fulgurite. I'm pretty sure." Smirking.

"What the hell is a fulgurite?" He didn't like Garch. Smartass didn't look like he'd ever been out in the field, ever sweated over easing fragile fossils out of the crumbling earth.

"Lightning made this. A lightning strike can hit rock or sand or earth and vaporize it. Ten thousand degrees Kelvin, you know, that's approaching the temperature of the sun's surface. This is like a hunk of fused glass. There could be rare metals. It's a big one, a very large one. I'd like to look it over for a few days. Buy it? I think the department or the Museum of Geology would certainly be interested. I don't know what they'd offer, but if you want I'll talk to them. Give me your phone number. I'll be in touch with you in a couple of weeks."

"I'd sort of want to sell it today. See, I'm on the move and I want to get on my way. I want to get going as soon as I can. I've been sick and I want to get back." There was no place to get back to.

"Look, you'll have to wait a few days. I'll have to talk to some people, they'll want to make a few tests. Et cetera. You know, I just don't carry acquisition money around in my pocket."

God, he hated this little shit. "I'll just take it somewhere else, then." He remembered Crazy Eyes and suddenly, the name Horsley, that paleontologist with the sunburned wife. The days with old what's-his-name.

"I'll take it to Horsley."

"Horsley? Fantee Horsley?" Garch squeezed out a sour

little smile. "Horsley's dead. He died in the St. Helena's eruption. On vacation. Ironic. His work was in quite a different field anyway, nothing to do with fulgurites.

"I'll just take it then."

"Look, Mr.—I don't know your name." He waited, but Loyal said nothing. "Look, this is just not the way it's done, old-timer." The forced patience. "You can't just walk into a university off the street and sell something, no matter how interesting it is scientifically. There are departments and budgets and acquisitions procedures. Channels. This is out of my field. I specialize in cranial osteology of the hadrosaurians. I'd have to find out who's interested in this kind of thing—maybe one of the petrologists. Maybe a geologist."

Loyal began to wrap the thing in newspaper again. That gink with the cowboy hat out in Utah who used to buy bones. He'd buy it. He'd buy it as soon as he saw it. Loyal remembered just where the place was, could see it clear, the way the dusty road hooked left as you came down from the mountains, then opened out into tumbled low hills and the river flats and after a while there was the bone man's bar and the back room full of boxes of these things, the fulgurite bones.

"If that's the way you feel," said Garch, "but I think you're making a mistake."

"No mistake," said Loyal and left. He hoped he had enough gas to make it to the bone man. If his place wasn't in Utah it was in Montana. He'd know the road when he saw it. That was clear, as clear as yesterday.

The receptionist looked up from her computer, a glowing screen of colors like a geometric movie.

"Find him?"

"That's where I'm going now. Find somebody who doesn't stand with his hand on his ass for a year. What town is this?"

"What town? It's still Rapid City, same as it was this morning."

54. What I See

He is on the wrong road, caught in heavy traffic. He cannot make out the route signs until he is abreast, too late to get into the right lane and maneuver the exit. Where in hell is he? There is fog. Water. Thousands of geese fly over him, cross the road obliquely on set wings. They float in ditches and lakes, skim the bending river, nasal, unchanging cries like crowds of angry petitioners marching through the water weeds. He drives slowly. CONSTRUCTION NEXT 48 MI. The road dwindles to one lane, streaked with clots of earth, metal-legged barriers force him to drive half on the shoulder. Power lines dip and climb, dip. White wire.

Ahead of him, going north, pickups hauling trailers loaded with mud-spattered ATVs, cars pulling motorboats, grinding their tires across distance. The land erupting with sores, bulldozers tearing.

The voice on the radio warns that tests show the drinking water in Fan Hill is polluted, residents should contact someone. Over a crumbling bridge, exposed cable in frayed rust flowers, past twisted mufflers and black half-moons of tires. The geese fall away into the smoking distance. Traffic crawls as arterial roadways feed in more cars and hissing trucks with lofty airfoils. In the filthy air he cannot tell in what direction he travels.

A diner hangs over the road. Traffic sucks into its entrance funnel, enticed by painted roof, promises of steaks and home-cooked breakfasts. He manages to pull in. The fog will burn off while he gets some coffee. Coffee to clear his head.

The customers lean on a golden counter. Men read sports news. A couple slumps, hands on melamine coffee cups. The men wear caps, the hair of the women is curled. Laminated scenes of hunting dogs, pack-horses in distant snowy mountains are screwed onto the wall. The wall simulates knotty pine. Loyal orders coffee. He cannot eat. But there is a little money for coffee and some gas. If he sleeps on the front seat. There will be a wait, says the woman. The cook has not shown up and they are shorthanded. He wants to ask her where he is but she turns away.

Motorcycles drone like sick bees. The riders come in chaffing their hands, snapping their arms. The woman is enormously fat. Her feet disappear into scuffed engineer boots. The others wear cowboy boots. The skinny man leads them to a table in the center of the room. He pushes back his Harley-Davidson cap and lights a cigarette.

"Shit, remember that guy? What the hell was that place? Man, I went in there, said 'Man, what the hell is old Larry doing in a place like this?' " The men speak to each other in hard voices, the women lean forward and laugh.

"Well, I figured after a while the goddamn thing is gonna get hot."

The woman brings their menus. She carries a coffeepot in her right hand. Loyal's coffee is lukewarm and low in the cup. He beckons to the woman.

"Put a little of that coffee in my pocket, will you?" Tiny fluted cups of nondairy creamer from her apron pocket. Loyal feels the heat of her body in the white stuff.

"Was you there when goddamn Tom had that there goddamn cream of wheat yesterday?"

"No, what was it, lumpy?"

"Jesus Christ. Yeah, was like gravel."

Now the worn tires pound across seamed cracks, a rock shaped like a castle stubs through the fog. The radio says a man arrested on rape charges has escaped.

He is on a back road. The traffic is thinner. But it's all wrong. He is turned around in some way. He should be moving into the dry country, but instead sees cemeteries, dots and pots of plastic flowers. Names spring at him from white stones, Heydt, Hansen, Hitzeman, Schwebke, Grundwaldt, Pick. A corncob lies on a grave. These roads are wrong. He turns onto dirt that cuts away through the black fields of Schwebke and Grundwaldt and Hitzeman.

Red-winged blackbirds flare, the shadows of clouds flow over the soft country, storefronts, corrugated metal of machinery repair shops, grain storage, farm chemicals. Tractors churn. God, it has to be Minnesota. He's going east, must have driven northeast all the way across South Dakota. Turned around. Completely turned around.

The color of the soil changes to deep, deep blue. Jets of herbicide spray from the behemoth tractor tanks. An old farmer carries a chair from his kitchen into the field. Painted stones balance on fence posts and stumps. The rows of poplars, wind harps behind the farmhouses.

And beside an empty field, on an empty road taut as stretched wire, with a final stutter of worn-out pistons the truck breaks down. Worn out, worn down, used up. That's all, folks.

55. The White Spider

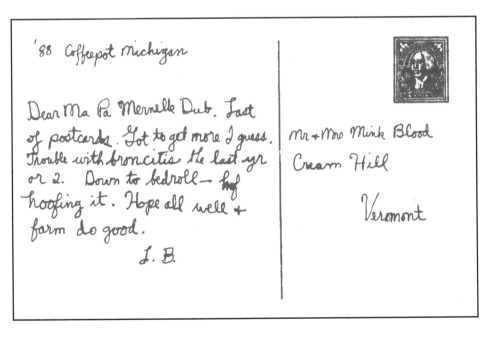

WHEN Loyal opened his eyes he was looking at a white spider crouched in the petals of a daisy. The round cream-colored abdomen reflected the buttery pollen rods. No wind. Daisies floated in the grass like doll plates. He could not remember what they reminded him of, something like wafers. Or another spider, not white.

He had slept badly; the cough wrenched through sleep now. With his tongue he felt there was a festering sore in the corner of his mouth, the kind made by a sliver of fine grass sunk so deep in the flesh that it became invisible, the kind from eating handfuls of unhulled wild strawberries raked out of the grass. It was not the season for strawberries. He braced his forefinger against his thumb and suddenly catapulted the white spider into the air. It fell, a brief, pale dot.

He walked along a narrow road bordered by arched trees, almost a lane, except for tire tracks in the dust. On his back the bedroll, a few utensils, a change of ragged clothes, wad of paper, pencil stubs, jar of instant coffee, plastic razor with a dull blade. Miles behind him the fulgurite was buried in a secret grave. Only he knew its location.

The pieces of sky that opened above were pallid. He could get no grasp of the day except a feeling of dry chill. When he saw a meadow above him through the trees he headed for it instinctively, drawn by the possibility of a high, searching view.

The air sweetened with flooding light as he labored through birch and poplar. Breathless, coughing, when he reached the meadow, he was disappointed to find it was only an opening in the woods, a clearing of lichen and red-tinged strawberry leaves, but he could not tell what he had expected. He had come around so many corners they all looked the same.

The meadow was what he imagined summer in Russia was like, frail and empty. Now he could see half the sky. Mare's tails and mackerel scales, ice-crystal streamers. It was a high sky, windswept cirrus in the stratosphere like paintbrush strokes. At the end of the strokes were gleaming scribbles like Arabic writing. The cloud spread north in sweeping waves, a vast fan tipped with plumes. He turned on his heel to look into the south where cirrocumulus packed the sky with dense pearl ripples. Fair weather and clear.

"When the bird's flight is over,
When the tired wings fold," he mumbled.

He took up a half-rotten branch from the edge of the field. "Dance, honey? 'When the bird's flight is ooooover,' " he bleated, stumbling in the moss cushions, holding the branch at the waist, pumping it to and fro, tipping it in a way that would have had a woman's hair loose and down, small jumps and whirls, an old man with bees in his sleeves. He half-fell. "Trip me, you bitch. Get out." Panting, retching with the cough. And hurled the branch, glad to see it break in a spray of red pulp. His loneliness was not innocent. Under the blows of the cough he vibrated as though his body had been struck, as a taut anchor rope struck by iron, tears crept along the channels of his contorted face, he stood in the silent meadow without even a rotted branch.

He thought: it's almost gone.

And saw the blue smear of woodsmoke coming from a hole in the trees below.

He imagined: A man and a woman sitting at a table. A

fringed cloth hangs to the floor, their feet are hidden in the folds. The woman chooses a heart-shaped strawberry, not a wild strawberry, from a bowl of fruit. Her hand, her arm, her face half erased, but the strawberry gleams brilliantly, she holds its stem between index finger and thumb, the tip of the thumb touching the puffed cap. The black seeds are like commas embedded in the red pores. The man is himself.

56. The Face in the Moss

Dear MR. GIAGO, please RUN This on obituary page.

    Joe Blue Skies passed away FRIDAY Night AFTER A LONG iLLNESS. Though blind from injuries He got in A TORNADO WHEN HE WAS A YOUNG MAN, He DEVOTED HiMSELF TO CoLLECTiNG AND UNDERSTANDiNG THE TRADiTioNAL MEDiciNE PLANTS OF His PEOPLE. He spoke To HUNDREDS OF SCHOOL CHiLDREN. THE SMITHSONiAN iN WASHiNGTON CALLED HiM A NATioNAL TREASURE. YET HE LiVED iN A MoDEST WAY. HE is SURViVED BY His WiFE WANDA CUT HAND. His soN RALPH BLUE SKiES DiED Aug. 11, 1939 AND DAUGHTER WANDALETTE DiED iN 1972.

    KEEp UP THE GooD WORK.

MR. TiM GiAGO, EdiTOR

LAKOTA TiMES

RAPiD CiTY, S. D.

ON the terrace of The Silver Salmon restaurant in Minneapolis the woman leaned forward. She was wearing a magenta cotton dress that came down to her ankles. The shoulders of the dress were padded. Her red hair, crinkled in waves like Chinese noodles, cascaded to her breasts. There was, her first husband saw, a piece of used dental floss in her hair. Maybe it was a new fashion. He listened, looking at her bare feet, at the yellow calloused pads on the toes. Those came from tight shoes. She had kicked the shoes under the wrought iron chair. She lit another cigarette.

"Do you know what he told me?" she said. "He told me, 'We'll go up there, Sweetheart. I've rented a little camp for the month in the lovely wild country. The silent sky and the purple spruce. And the little canoe and loons and a fire in the fireplace when the nights are cold. We'll throw stones into the water, Sweetheart, and see how far they skip. We'll live off the land and it'll be lovely.' " She said this to him in the flat voice—that cut like a pitched slate across the troughs of pleasure, struck only the crests of events she wanted to regret.

"So we went. Never, never, never trust a bloody, black-hearted, lying Irishman." They were alone on the terrace, the glass tables, the metal chairs around them like a wood. The terrace was at the back of the restaurant and opened on a wide alley. He had to go into the bar to get a waiter's attention. There was a faint stench of garbage and he guessed the dumpster was behind a ragged paling fence. Across the alley an empty loading dock at the back of a building. The light overhead like slack canvas. Her nails and the raised veins on the back of her hands reflected the colorless light. She drank from the wine. He drank from his own glass. Like warm water.

"The wind blowing on reeds is like the wind on prairie grass. Like home, like Saskatchewan prairie, back home where we came from. Pure, puking prairie, only a little gouged up, only a little ruined by plows and roads and wheat and machinery, just like I was only a little ruined before I got tied up with you and then the bloody black Irish."

"Oh no," he said, "you leave me out of it." Rail about the Irish all she wanted, the big fight and the way the Irish left her facedown in the muck after three days, but leave him out of it. His crime had been one of omission.

The luminous windows of the building across the alley in a black grid; the half circle of his ring caught the light like an eye beneath a lowered lid. His ex-wife slid down in her chair, stretched out her legs; shins like shapely rods of metal.

"You can't imagine what it felt like, to have your face pushed into the stinking gagging moss, right down into the stinking mud. I thought I was going to die, I couldn't breathe. The force was tremendous. He was trying to kill me. To smother me in the moss."

The loading dock was sinking in shadow. An old derelict edged along, shuffling on glassy legs, one hand gripping the platform. A crumple of paper bunched over his left foot, made a sliding sound. The lighter snapped, his ex-wife lit another cigarette, jetted double plumes from her fine nose. Drained her glass.

"The only reason he stopped was because the fire spotter plane went over. Right over us. I could feel the motor in my bones. He was that low. The pilot must have seen us because he circled and came back. And that's when the Irish ran. I could hear him going through the trees, just crashing, hear the jeep engine start up. And I was grateful to be abandoned in the wilds. Can we get more wine?" He rose, went into the lighted bar.

When he came back, stumbling against dark chair legs and slopping the wine over the rims of the glasses, she pointed at the loading dock. The old bum inching away again. A phlegmy cough that went on and on.

"He's been in the garbage," she said. "I wish the city would scrape up the drunks and bums and dump them up in the swamp. Solve the homeless problem for good. Instead of yelping about shelters." Her wineglass clinked against her teeth. "So, can you believe that when I got up his weight on me had been so intense that the shape of my face was pressed into the moss? My profile. Filling up with muddy water."

"Let's go in. Let's go order dinner. I'm going to have the Yucatán lime soup."

"I'll wait until I see the menu. I never want the same thing twice."

57. The Jet Trail in the Windshield

Dear Kevin Witkin, CONGRATULATIONS! You have won a glorious all-expense trip to HOUSTON TEXAS, ABSOLUTELY FREE! That's right, absolutely FREE, if you call Blood's Texas Travel Productions, at (990) 311-1131 within 72 hours (three days) from NOW! Don't delay, Kevin Witkin. See what Texas is all about! CALL US RIGHT NOW!

Mr. Kevin Witkin
Woodcroft
Trailer Park Rd.
Cream Hill, VT 05099

IT was not just the divorce, the divorce was only a contributing factor to the mess of his fucked-up life, everything, the phone ringing with potscrubber scam artists and bill collectors. Maybe he'd get the phone pulled out. If he had another place to go he'd go there. The stinking camp. His father had put every dollar he made into it. Couldn't invest in stocks or something, oh no. Now they were all stuck. He paced. He walked. He knocked the dirty pans onto the floor and kicked the cupboard door under the sink. Nobody would buy it. Face it, he shouted.

He took long runs. He didn't know what to do. When he quit working for Bobby he quit having money. When he quit having money he quit having coke. No money, no drugee. Everything was gone. All except the goddamn camp. Here he was. He didn't know what to do. Why had he come up here? He hated the camp. And down in the trailer park the skirl of motorcycle wheelies in dirt. Busted-muffler trucks. The fucking trailer church with its tin steeple. Morning noon and night loudspeaker serenade of carillon tapes. Noise was driving him crazy. Let's see now, let me count the ways the noise annoys me.

Start with the inside. The refrigerator noise. Like a jet taking off in the kitchen fifty times a day. The radio. The television. Music, the tapes and records. The damn VCR. The electric shaver. The roaring gurgle of the toilet. The water coming out of the faucets. The pump. The pump was bad. The freezer. The fan. The computer's sickening hum and its chirping alarm. The clock by the bed. Tick. Tick. The energy-conserving automatic switch at 5:00 P.M. The flies knocking against the ceiling. The birds that smashed into their own reflections in the windows. The wind. No, the wind was an outside noise. Mice in the walls. Sounded like a western town, Mice-in-the-Walls,

Montana. O.k., that was it for the inside.

Now the big problems. Outside. The trailer park. Cacophonous symphony of slamming doors. Shouting women, children crying and calling. Saturday afternoon target practice. Assorted trucks, cars, motorcycles, snow-mobiles, three-wheelers, ATVs. Fifty, a hundred barking dogs. Men laughing, whatever the hell they found to laugh at. The carillon. Radios. And on the road below the trailer park the mailwoman's truck, the UPS man. Log trucks, oil trucks, gas trucks, lumber trucks, milk trucks. Federal Express, the sheriff, fat Buddy Nipple going to the coon dog trials with his pickup full of howling contestants. The traffic.

Buddy Nipple leaning over the counter toward him, taking the money for the six-pack. "Yup! Yip! Haya! Yup! O.k.! You got it! You bet! You're a good man! Wanna bag? O.k.! You bet!"

The planes overhead. Thousands of them every day. Jets and fighters, new pilots wobbling their way over him, the commercial flights taking a bead on Montreal a hundred miles north. And the helicopters. State police looking for marijuana plots. Game wardens looking for deerkills. Fire spotters looking for smoke and burning. Christ! Yup! Yup! You bet!

And the birds. Do not forget the birds, he told himself. The loud, repetitive bird shrills and burrs. Twittering buzzing over and over. The crickets, cicadas, cicadas with the terrible droning. The night heron's shriek. In March the squalling of cats. The seasonal clanking of geese up and down his corridor of air. The sound of air through leaves, the falling leaves crashing his breathing like heavy wind fingers tapping deafeningly on the table . . . What's thaaaat? That riiiiight? Yup! Yup!

Beyond these maddening noises that wouldn't let him concentrate on anything, on anything at all, there was the wind. The wind up here never quit, shook the house. And the rain, the rain against the windows, on the roof Then hail and snow and thunder. At night the howling of cats and coyotes.

He was ruined. He was pretty sure he was ruined. You bet! Filth was washing up around him. Yup! He walked along a washed-out road that went nowhere, smelled filth, found a decaying pig's carcass. Crows had pecked the eyes out. The skin pecked into pebble finish. Loosened reddish hair on the ground in sheets. The crows had been at the culvert. Inside he could see the rib cage crammed tight into the ridged metal. The guts pulled away by something. Wanna get on the road! Read the bumper stickers! Yup! That's riiight! A hawk screamed.

He opened the beer, sat in front of his television set. The screen was blue. Then filled with purple-skinned powdered young men sitting in chairs. Gold crosses hung around their necks. A man, insane but calculating, sat before them on a wooden throne. He wore a leather jacket and was reading aloud an article on ants. Every few minutes he would put down the magazine, cluck his tongue and say that the ants were just like certain church people he knew; always cutting leaves. Yup! Kevin opened all of the cans of beer and lined them up before him. How long had he been here? Six weeks? Six years? He was ruined. Yup! Yip! He changed the channel to the porno station and watched simulated intercourse, watched a blonde whore with a big loose blue tongue like a steer's lap at a man. Or something like a man.

Drove to the store for beer. Buddy leaned over the counter toward him to take the money. Swollen hand sliding down the counter. Forearm the size of a thigh. Foreskin like a banana peel. Black teeth. "Yup! Yip! Haya! Yup! O.k.! You got it! You bet! You're a good man! Wanna bag? O.k.! You bet!"

On the way back he made a wrong turn and bounced through the rutholes of the trailer park. He went up and down the muddy lanes unable to find his way out. He turned and turned past burned-out trailers, past rolls of wire, a reeling man with hair like broken cement, pants soaked in piss. The trees were like pipes. The sky was an X ray. A purple plastic horse on springs in the fireweed. A needle. Crystal. Red water. The trailers were packed closer and closer together. Overhead a jet roared. Yellow-eyed dogs on chains. In the doorways women holding beer cans or cigarettes or babies. Watching him. He drove faster, the car swung in the greasy ruts. The exit loomed suddenly as if hands had raised it from the ground for him. Men leaned on fenders, the clefts of their buttocks visible above the oily pants. The jet shook their beer cans.

He drove up the hill. The jet trail filled the windshield. The noise unbearable. And at the camp ran inside for the rifle. A silvery capsule at the head of the vomiting trail. He pulled the trigger. Again. Again!

You bet! You bet!

58. What I See

Loyal, rolled up in something, seeing through closed eyelids. The stiffening lungs seize, the heart is drowning.

The Indian's book falls open. He is astonished to see the pages are the great, slanting field. At the top of the field a black scribble of trees, a wall. And through waves of darkening he sees the wind streaming down the slope of land, rolling down the grass, the red awns combing the sunlight, flashing needle stems, the close-stitched earth, the root, the rock.

Center Point Publishing
600 Brooks Road • PO Box 1
Thorndike ME 04986-0001 USA

(207) 568-3717

US & Canada:
1 800 929-9108